Dakota
and new da... ... awaits her.

Graffiti on a cemetery wall comes to life and kills one of the best-liked vampires in Atlanta's Edgeworld while his friend, Dakota, watches helplessly. Dark and deadly magick is at work on the city's walls, challenging even the power of Dakota's extraordinary tattoos. With her adopted were-daughter, Cinnamon, by her side, Dakota—the Southeast's most famous magickal tattoo artist and skindancer—must once again track down a supernatural killer who preys on his own kind.

Book Two of the award-winning Skindancer series.

PRAISE FOR BOOK ONE, FROST MOON
Winner of The EPIC Award, Best Fantasy 2011

"**Frost Moon** is a choice and fascinating pick that shouldn't be overlooked for fantasy readers."
—*Midwest Book Review*

"Dakota's take no prisoners investigation provides readers with the vivid vision of Anthony Francis' Atlanta Underground inside an exhilarating thriller."
—Harriet Klausner – Amazon.com top reviewer

"Let me warn readers that they are going to be blown away. **Frost Moon** is one of a kind and pure genius. I devoured this book in one night...Definitely worth the loss of sleep because there was no way I was going to stop reading **Frost Moon** once I started."
—*Book Lovers Inc.*

"A dark and gritty Urban Fantasy with rich characters, great hair-pin turns . . . and enough tension and danger to keep you on the edge of your seat madly flipping pages to find what happens."
—*Sidhe Vicious Reviews*

"You got me Anthony Francis, you got me! **Frost Moon** is an exciting Urban Fantasy that starts off strong and keeps up the steam throughout. Anthony Francis has created an interesting take on the usual paranormal world incorporating magic and mysticism into a dangerous world where both humans and paranormals live side by side."
—*Fiction Vixen*

"I am hard-pressed to adequately describe the latest book to be shifted in my direction for review. Thank you to the powers-that-be for the opportunity to be one of the first readers captivated by Dakota Frost and her magical tats. Addictive, sassy, sexy, funny, intense, brilliant...any and all of these adjectives describe not only the book itself but Anthony Francis' tall, bi-sexual, tattoo-specialist heroine...Mr. Francis has delivered not only a sexy and spectacular heroine but given depth, emotion and memorable personalities to the many faces found in the supporting cast that give life to this paranormal tale."
—*Bitten By Books*

SKINDANCER
THE MAGIC CONTINUES

BLOOD

ROCK

ANTHONY
FRANCIS

BELL BRIDGE BOOKS

Copyright

This is a work of fiction. Names, characters, places and incidents are either the products of the author's imagination or are used fictitiously. Any resemblance to actual persons (living or dead,) events or locations is entirely coincidental.

Bell Bridge Books
PO BOX 300921
Memphis, TN 38130
Print ISBN 978-1-61194-013-8
Epub ISBN 978-1-61194-036-7

Bell Bridge Books is an Imprint of BelleBooks, Inc.

We at BelleBooks enjoy hearing from readers.
Visit our websites – www.BelleBooks.com and www.BellBridgeBooks.com.

10 9 8 7 6 5 4 3 2

Cover design: Debra Dixon
Interior design: Hank Smith
Photo credits:
Butterfly (manipulated) © Realrocking | Dreamstime.com
Girl (manipulated) © Peter Kim | Dreamstime.com
Thorn background (manipulated) © Unholyvault | Dreamstime.com
Cinnamon Frontispiece and Butterfly / Rosevine © Anthony Francis

:Lrb:01:

DEDICATION

To the Dragonwriters, who restarted my writing
To the Write to the End group, who keep me writing
To my beta readers and editors, who keep my writing honest

CINNAMON

1.   CINNAMON AND FROST

"Dammit, dammit, dammit!" I cursed, slamming the school doors open and stomping out into the cold January Atlanta air. Once outside, facing bare trees in a bleak parking lot under a graymetal sky, I regretted my words—because the example I was setting was the problem.

I stopped, swung back, and reached one lanky arm out to stop the door from closing. Moments later, my daughter stepped out of the darkness, eyes blinking, whiskers twitching, holding her tiger's tail in her hands before her like a portable lifeline.

The two of us looked as different as can be: me, a six-foot two woman in a long leather vestcoat, wearing my hair in a purple-and-black deathhawk that lengthens into feathers of hair curling around my neck, and her, a five-foot-nothing teenager in a pleated school skirt, taming her wild orange hair with a blue granola-girl headscarf that poorly hid her catlike ears.

"It's OK," I lied gently, putting my hand on Cinnamon's shoulder; though we both knew it was very *not* OK. "We'll find a school that will take you."

She hissed. That school *had* been the top of her list—until Cinnamon cussed the principal out in the middle of the interview. And this was after she'd promised to be on her best behavior. I was starting to worry something was wrong with her, and not just her being a weretiger.

Not that there's anything wrong with being a weretiger; if anything, lycanthropy was the *least* of my worries taking an abused, illiterate streetcat into my home. This adoption was turning out to be a lot more than I bargained for—and we were little over a month into it.

I had learned, however, to put my foot down. "Cinnamon. What you said—"

"I'm sor—" she began, then snapped her head aside violently in a kind of a sneeze, pulling at the collar around her neck. "Who cares? School stinks. They *all* stinks."

I felt my collar in sympathy: I didn't like mine either. OK, so I lied again: we *didn't* look as different as can be. First, we both had silver collars around our necks, a kind of fangs-off sign provided by the Vampire Queen of Little Five Points; and second, we were both tattooed.

Cinnamon's tiger stripes were beautiful, eye-catching . . . and forced upon her by her last guardian. She'd hide them if she could, but they come all the way up to her cheeks and down to the backs of her palms, and our attempts at covering them with makeup were a disaster.

My elaborate vines are even more eye-catching, a tribal rainbow beginning at my temples and cascading over my whole body in braids of flowers and jewels and butterflies. Today I was in a turtleneck, but normally I make no effort to hide them. I want people to see them move.

Unless you know what to look for, it's subtle: out of the corner of your eye, a leaf flutters, a butterfly flaps, a gem sparkles—it's like magic. And that sparks the conversation: *Actually, they are magic, all inked here in Atlanta by yours truly—*

"Dakota Frost," I said, as my phone picked up, "Best magical tattooist in the Southeast."

"Dakota." The voice was deep, male and familiar.

"Hey, Uncle Andy," I said. When I had been a kid, Sergeant Andre Rand had been my father's partner on the Stratton police force—so close to the family I'd called him "Uncle Andy" though he was nothing of the sort. Now that I was an adult, *Detective* Andre Rand was my guardian angel in the Atlanta Police Department. "And before you ask, I *did* call Dad—"

"This isn't about that," Rand interrupted. "It's—look, where are you now?"

"Out school shopping with Cinnamon."

"Not *what* you're doing," Rand snapped. "Where, I mean geographically—"

"Downtown," I said, now worried. Rand was normally polite and uber-smooth, but now he was curt and *very* stressed—and that scared the hell out of me.

"What's goin on?" Cinnamon said suddenly, staring at me—never underestimate a werekin's hearing. "Who died?"

Immediately when she said it, I felt she was right. Something catches in a person's voice when they report a death. Pay attention, in those few awful times in your life when someone gets the call: you can tell from the grief in their voice, from the crumpling of their faces.

"Andy," I said. "What's wrong? Is someone hurt?"

"How quickly can you get over to Oakland Cemetery?"

"Ten minutes."

"Whatever you do, hurry," he said. "Just—hurry."

We hopped into the blue bomb and headed to the Cemetery. Actually, the 'bomb' was a very *nice* new Prius I'd picked up last year after besting the magician Christopher Valentine in a tattooing contest. His Foundation had yet to pay up a dime, so I didn't know if I'd be able to keep it—but it sure beat riding Cinnamon around on the back seat of my Vespa scooter.

Oakland Cemetery was a time capsule. All around us were gentrified warehouses and decaying apartments, but the Cemetery was protected from downtown's churn by low brick ramparts lining Memorial and Boulevard. Within those long red lines stood sparse trees, from which the winter chill had long since stripped the leaves, leaving branches stretched to the cloudy sky like the claws of dying things pleading to Heaven.

When we hooked around to the entrance, we found an officer guarding the driveway. As we pulled up to the striped sawhorse they'd thrown up to block the drive, I steeled myself for a runaround. My dad was on the force, Rand was a friend, heck, I was even sort of dating a Fed—but somehow being six-foot-two with tattoos-and-deathhawk just never mixed well with cops.

But the officer's eyes lit up when he saw us. He didn't even check for ID—he just pulled the sawhorse out of the way and waved us forward. This was bad—they'd closed off the whole cemetery, and it was huge. I rolled down my window and asked, "Which way—"

"You're Frost, right? Straight back," he said, eyes wild. "Straight back! And hurry!"

"This is bad," Cinnamon said, head craning back to look at the officer. "Rand's sweet on ya, but we never gets special treatments from the piggies."

"Don't call them piggies," I said, speeding down the tiny road.

"Why?" she asked, flicking an ear at me. "You knows they can't hear us."

"Really? So you knows that none of them are weres?" I asked, miming her broken diction. "You knows for sures?"

Her face fell. "No, I don't."

We bumped down a worn asphalt road through a canyon of winterbare trees, elaborate Victorian markers, and rows upon rows of Confederate graves. The road sank down, the graves grew smaller, more sad, and we rolled to a halt in a forest of headstones at the bottom of the hill between the Jewish section and Potter's field.

What seemed like a thousand flashing lights waited for us: police cars, an ambulance, even a fire truck, surrounding a crowd of uniforms, paramedics and firemen gathered at the end of the road in front of the low brick wall that ringed the cemetery. Striding out of them was a well-dressed black man, sharp as a model and sexy as a movie star: Detective Andre Rand.

I opened the door, my boots crunched on gravel, and my vestcoat swished as I stepped out of the car, *fhwapping* behind me in the wind as I slammed the door shut. The officers stared. Their eyes narrowed. My normal getup was conspicuously out of place in this land of grey tombs and black uniforms. I'd been more comfortable talking to the buttoned-down principal of the school we'd just visited; now I just wanted to go and change.

"Hi, Rand," I said, forced cheerful, putting my hand on Cinnamon's shoulder as she materialized beside me. "What you gots—ahem. What do you have for me?"

At my grammatical slip Rand glanced down at Cinnamon briefly, trying to smile. His neck was covered with in a stylish turtleneck, not unlike mine, but the rest of him was in one of his GQ suits that never seemed to get dirty no matter what he'd gone through. Today, however . . . his suit was torn. There was blood on the back of his hand. And not even Cinnamon could spark a smile in him. Rand was off his game. Rand was *never* off his game.

He glanced up, frowning. "Dakota, thanks for rushing. We really need you but . . . this is bad. Really bad. Cinnamon can wait in—"

"I can takes whatever you gots," Cinnamon said indignantly.

"And I'd rather not let her out of my sight," I said quietly.

Rand's eyes tightened. He knew *why* I never let her out of my sight: just before I took her in, a serial killer had kidnapped her to get to me. It wasn't that I never let her out of my sight . . . . but whenever things got sketchy, I'd pick bringing her over leaving her every time.

"I understand, Dakota," he said, turning back to the knot of first responders. "Let me show you what we're dealing with."

"Sure thing," I muttered. "No one thinks to ask me whether *I* can take it."

Rand just kept walking. "McGough, this is Dakota Frost."

"You didn't mention she was a civvie," said a small, wiry, wizardly man in a Columbo trench. Like Rand, his coat was torn, his hands bloodied, but where Rand was thrown off his game, McGough's movements were still crisp, his eyes sharp. A few nicks and cuts? *Bah.* Didn't even slow him down. "Bad idea, having a civilian on a crime scene—"

"She was practically raised on the force," Rand said, "and I think she can help."

"Well let's hope somebody can, we're outta options," McGough said, sizing me up. "So you're Rand's fabled Edgeworld expert. Jeez, you're tall."

My mouth quirked up. 'Edgeworld' was slang for the magical counterculture. Unlike most practitioners throughout history, who'd kept magic secret, or most normal people today, who tried to pretend it wasn't there, Edgeworlders practiced magic openly—something which did not endear us to either group.

"What gave me away?" I said. "And it's Edgeworlder, not 'Edgeworld expert'—"

"Ah, she knows the lingo. Good, but it's still a bad idea," McGough said, frowning. He glanced down at Cinnamon, and his frown deepened. "And on the note of bad ideas, you really want to bring a minor along?" Rand and I just looked at him, and Cinnamon raised a clawed hand and mimed a swat. "Fine, fine," he said. "When the Department of Family and Child Services comes calling, don't come crying to me." He waded back into the officers.

"All right, boys and girls," McGough said, voice crackling with authority, making the officers jump. He was barely taller than Cinnamon, but his presence dominated the scene. "Move aside and let's see if Rand's pet witch can figure out how to handle this."

Before I could even *try* to correct the 'pet witch' crack, the officers—all nervous, most worried, many scratched up like they'd been in a fight with a cat—parted so I could see the outer wall. My breath caught, and it took me a moment to realize what I was seeing.

The brick wall was sprayed with graffiti, a huge flock of exaggerated letters exploding out of a coiling nest of elaborately thorned vines. The graffiti "tag" was amazing work. Even *I* had to admire the roses woven into the vines—they're a specialty of mine—but the artwork was just a backdrop. Dead in the center of the tag, a person was crucified in a web of twisted and rusted barbed wire, half-standing, half-sprawling in a splash of his own blood.

The man moaned and raised his head—and with a shock I recognized him as our friend Revenance, a guard at the werehouse, Cinnamon's former home. Revenance was a vampire of the Oakdale Clan—so *what was he doing out in the day?* I looked for the sun, relaxed a little at the cloud cover—and then something clicked in my mind, and I looked back in horror.

Revenance wasn't crucified in the wires, but in the graffiti itself. Painted vines had erupted from the wall, fully dimensional, moving as if alive, curling around him, sprouting metal barbs, hooking into his flesh, drawing blood and pulling outward—pulling as we watched.

The graffiti was tearing him apart.

2. | BOILING BLOOD

"Revenance is a vampire," I said loudly, and the officers around me pricked up and listened—but made no move towards my friend, trapped in that nest of bloody wire and thorned vines. "He needs protection from the sun right now!"

"You know this guy?" one of them said uneasily. He stood his ground, but several of the other officers began backing further away. "I mean, is he really a—"

"Vampire," I confirmed, and more officers backed off. *Pathetic.* OK, I once felt the same about vamps, but Revenance was the nicest vampire I knew. True, he looked like a biker—OK, he *was* a biker—but he acted like a perfect gentleman. I even got on well with his girlfriend; she was down to earth, with none of the nonsense of a typical vampire flunky. If any vampire deserved to be saved, *he* did. "Did you hear me? Get him out of there! Protect and serve, man—"

"We, uh, *tried*," the officer began, starting forward, then halting. "But those vines are vicious! They damn near tore Lee apart when she tried to check on him."

"Oh, crap," I said, staring at the sky. The sun was beginning to break through the clouds.

"Oh jeez, *jeez*, that's *Revy!*" Cinnamon said, suddenly getting it. She took a step forward, and the vines seemed to twist, to bunch in anticipation of her approach, making Revy moan. "Wait, wait—one thing atta. If the sun pops out, just for a second, it'll kill 'im!"

"Yeah," I said, scowling. "We need something to shield against the sun."

Cinnamon's ears pricked up. "You gots tarps in the backs of your mobiles?"

"What?" McGough asked blankly.

"Tarps, covers, blankets, anything," Cinnamon said, tugging at her collar and grimacing. "And poles. We makes a tent, keeps the sun off him long enough to get him free of that crap!"

The officers remained frozen, and then McGough spoke. "Rand," he said calmly. "Could you have your boys check their cruisers for tarps, blankets—"

"I'll get on it," he said. "Dakota, deal with the vines."

"Sure," I said. Yeah, right—dump the magical problem in the lap of the magician. I know I'd gotten a reputation for fighting other magicians after taking on the serial killer that had kidnapped Cinnamon, but *"Deal with the vines?"* Fuck. How was I gonna do that?

I stepped forward, and the graffiti tag convulsed. Revenance groaned, then opened cloudy eyes in a face cracked like burnt paper. I recoiled. Scattered ultraviolet had to be killing him.

And while I was noticing all that, a tendril of barbed wire snapped out like a whip, nailing me in the temple. Only a last second flinch saved my eye, and I threw myself back into a crouch, hands raised, tails of my vestcoat whapping out around me. I was actually a bit surprised at my own reaction, I guessed a product of my recent training. Apparently karate *works*.

"Girl's got moves," said a voice, and after a glance at the vines, I looked over to see a crewcutted black officer stepping up—Gibbs, one of Rand's friends. "You OK, Dakota?"

"Yes," I said, touching my temple, fingers coming back with blood. "Where's Horscht?"

"Your kid has him running to the grounds shed," Gibbs said. His clothes and face were scratched too, worse than the others, and one eye was darn near swollen shut. *I* had been lucky. "Looking for wood to prop up a tent around your fang there."

"He's not my 'fang,'" I said, staring back at Revenance. The vamp writhed, and with shock I realized what I'd thought was stylish frosting in his hair was actually sunbleach, where the light had blasted the strands to pale brittleness. "But he is a friend."

I glared at the graffiti, at the live, hungry vines erupting from the wall and twisting through the air. They seemed to swat at me just for looking at them; but I was not deterred. It was just graffiti. Just ink on a wall. Whatever magic had animated it would slowly fade away, unless it had some source of external power, which was not likely on a dead brick wall.

Grimly I wondered whether the graffiti was powered by Revenance himself; vampires had powerful auras. But vampiric life was endothermic, sucking energy out of its surroundings. That's why their flesh was often cold; that's why necromancers considered them dead.

So, as fearsome as this thing was, it should run down—but I had no such limits. I was the tattooed, and my magic marks were powered by the life in my beating heart.

Time to draw my weapons.

"Keep this safe for me," I said, pulling off my vestcoat and handing it to Gibbs. Then, gritting my teeth against the brisk January air, I pulled off my turtleneck, exposing a torso covered in dozens of intricate tattoos.

I've thought about this outfit carefully. It's sort of my new uniform since I seriously decided to *use* my magic tattoos, and not just wear them. Tattoo magic works best when skin is exposed to the air—but I'm *not* gonna get naked in front of a bad guy. So my leather "pants" are actually chaps, unzipping down the seams quickly to leave me in cutoff jean shorts, and under my shirt is a black sports bra. Even the boots have side zips—I want to be able to run if I gotta, but still be able to peel them if I need the braided snakes on my ankles.

"Whoa," Gibbs said, holding the leather and snakeskin in his hands like he was looking at his favorite collection of porn. "Didn't expect that, girl—"

"Don't get too excited," I said, grimacing. I'm a total weather lightweight—the mercury couldn't be lower than fifty-five, but I already had goose bumps rippling down my arms. I hoped it wouldn't interfere with the magic. "I only dance for the magic."

I straightened, then let my body ripple. There was an art to tattoo magic: my old magical tattoo master had called it *skindancing*. I bailed on him early, so I didn't know half the art—but with the little I did know, I could concentrate the lifeforce within my body, the living magic, the mana, hold it within like a growing flame—then let it out to make my tattoos come alive.

Tattooed jewels glowed, snakes slithered, butterflies fluttered—and then my vines curled out from my skin into a coiling thicket around me. My finest tattoo, the Dragon, was gone—I had released it to attack the serial killer that took Cinnamon—but with the dozens of tattoos I had left I had more than enough to make a glowing shield of living ink.

"Holy—" Gibbs said, backing up, and in the corner of my eye I could see the other officers backing up further, even more afraid, faces lit green by the glow of my marks. I was getting better if you could see the glow of the vines even in the bright sun, and I smiled.

Time to show that wall-painter what real magic was.

"Spirit of fall," I murmured. "Shield my path."

There is no "spirit of fall," of course. I *do* admit there are intangible entities in the world, but I *don't* believe in actual spirits, "of fall," or of any other kind, and I could have used any words for my incantation. For tattoo magic, what really matters is the intent of the wearer—and powered by the intent behind my words, my tattooed vines unfurled into a glowing perimeter that would keep me safe as I rescued Revy.

Or so I hoped. I stared into the churning knot of barbed wire and menacing vines, coiling over each other like a nest of snakes. How the heck did it *work?* I had never heard of magically animated graffiti. In theory the mana that powered it should have been draining away slowly, but it actually seemed like it was getting stronger. But *how?*

I stared into the design, trying to grok it. For graffiti it was so . . . *complicated*, built layer upon layer upon layer. Revenance was embedded in a rosette of vines; coiling out from that were thick, stony tentacles, a grey brick octopus clutching at cartoon images of the trees and buildings around us. Colorful lettering in the exaggerated "wildstyle" font floated behind the octopus, and behind *that* was a fully painted backdrop of a grassy hill against a black sky. Almost like an afterthought, the base of the design sported two groups of curving, cracked tombstones, one on the left, one on the right, drawn to look like they erupted from the base of the wall.

I considered whether the tombstones could be the graffiti's power source . . . perhaps by necromancy? No, they were dry of blood. Earth magic from the hill image? No, I would have felt it if this was a ley-line crossing, and that also ruled out the idea that the octopus tentacles were drawing power from the nearby buildings. So *how* did it *work?*

Surely not . . . graphomancy, or something like tattoo magic? I stared past the weaving vines, into the letters, trying to see past the tag's art and through to its logic. It was difficult: the wildstyle letters were distorted, overlapping, intertwining, and I could barely pick out a single letter. But every stroke was amazing work, and there was a glittering texture to the pigments, almost like the magic inks used in tattoos. Perhaps a variant of tattoo ink, reformulated to let the magic work on rock? But the designs of tattoo magic only work because skin is a canvas infused with living magic. Where was the graffiti getting the mana?

And then Revenance moaned, the blackened tongue in the dark hole of his mouth looking like he'd been left to die in Death Valley. No one does that to my friends.

"All right," I whispered. "Your vines versus my vines. Let's go."

I stepped forward, letting my vines curl out, green and glowing. The barbed tentacles twisted towards me, and now I could see that they were a braid of wire, roses and chains. They slapped against my thicket of magic, initially just questing, then with increasing rage. I shimmied forward, then whirled and drew my glowing green blanket in. The hooked braids pounced—just as I threw my arms out and let the vines explode outward, tearing the barbs to pieces.

Colorful, bitter powder puffed through the air as the braids flew apart, a residue of the materials used in this tag. The thin layer of oil chalk was weaker than the ink woven into living flesh that made my tattoos. But there was a hell of a lot to the tag, and it kept getting stronger, two more tombstone images erupting as a dozen more tentacles hungrily pounced on me.

Instinctively I crouched back, hands raised in a guard as the braided vines whipped around me, shoving me roughly through my shield. How was I going to get Revenance out if I couldn't even reach him? Then I noticed what my crouch and guard had done. I'd fallen back into a Taido karate middle stance, and it hit me: *karate* was a kind of a dance.

I dropped into a low stance my instructor called *jodan*, legs a low coiled crouch, one fist jutting forward to guard me, the other pointing straight backwards at the sky, the karate version of thumbing your nose. Immediately my legs began to throb: I wasn't strong enough to use the stance yet, but it was *stable*, damn it, and coiled in a way I could use for my magic.

I began writhing again, making my tattoos shimmer; working with the stance; and then, just like in class, I raised my fist to protect my face, shot the back hand and leg forward together and *moved*, planting myself five feet forward in the mirror image of the same stance.

The thing flailed at me like an animated octopus; but with every step I poured more power into my marks, pushing in closer, closer; my vines pushing its vines back. I didn't feel the cold anymore: I was sweating. My bum knee began pulsing with pain, but I ignored it.

The pressure was intense; my boots ground against the gravel as I punched forward, step by step, shoving myself to the heart of the barbed wire rose. Twenty, ten, five—then the wires parted, I stretched my arm out, my fingers brushed Revy's coat—

Then the rose reared back and struck me square on the chest, hurling me thirty feet backwards onto the street. It would have knocked me on my ass, but as I saw my feet flying into the air, something inside me clicked, and I coiled my back and turned the impact into a roll that flipped me clear over, tumbled me roughly back into a crouch—then back to standing.

I mean, *holy shit*. Karate *really* works.

But the end effect was that I was back where I started, knee throbbing, arms scraped, back covered in gravel, watching Revenance screaming in pain as the tag coiled back inward. Sure, I was standing, but it *felt* like I had been knocked flat on my ass.

"If you're so damn strong," I muttered, glaring at the tag, "why haven't you killed him yet? What the hell are you waiting for?"

"Good try, Dakota," Rand said, handing off a tarp to Gibbs. Behind him other officers were running up with blankets, tarps, ropes, and poles. "We've got enough to cover him, but we need something tall to . . . what the hell?"

I turned to see Cinnamon and Horscht running up with a . . . a *portable basketball goal?* Where had they *gotten* that? Big beefy Horscht struggled to keep his grip on the backboard while little old Cinnamon easily carried the concrete-filled tire that was its base, and when *he* slipped, *she* kept going, backing towards the rosette of wires before I could speak.

The graffiti surged and pounced, but Cinnamon leapt up with werekin speed, kicking off the edge of the weighted tire so the goal flipped upright into the barbs. The graffiti caught the metal pole and shoved back against it; but the goal stayed upright, weighted by its base.

"Hah!" Cinnamon said, head snapping in her funny sneeze as the graffiti battered against it, more weakly now. "That's not alive. It's got nothing to trigger on now. Now we makes a tent—makes an X with the poles, so we can run a top pole from the goal to the wall—"

"Pretty damn smart," Rand said, waving to his men.

"That's my girl," I replied, taking the other end of the tarp from him.

We crossed two poles against the backboard, making a rough triangle in front of the tag, which had given up whacking at the goal and had curled back around Revenance. Two officers climbed the wall and fed another pole up over the top. The vines snapped at it halfheartedly, but they were near the end of their reach, and the improvised framework was holding—for now.

"Dakota, give me a hand with this," Gibbs said, trying to unroll the tarp and getting himself tangled in it. "The wind is a bitch—"

No single tarp was large enough to cover Revenance, but we patched together a piece as big as a sail by joining eyelets and tie straps, slid it up over the back of the wall, over the tag, so it draped down over the top pole to make the sides of the tent. The tag still snapped at it, but lethargically now, and we started to nail it down, three to a side, fighting the wind.

But then the sun burst forth and Revenance screamed as light reflected off cars burned him with a thousand pinpricks. "More tarps!" Cinnamon said. "We covers the front—"

But the sun wasn't our only problem. The wind actually started whistling, then *singing,* eerie cries timed with vicious surges that tore at our tent. I grabbed my end of a tarp and stood on it, looking around for a stake, a rock, anything to nail it down—and then I saw *him.*

He was far away, halfway across the cemetery, a dark figure leaning against a tombstone, hand extended towards us as if he were controlling the wind. He was small, no larger than a kid, and dressed the part down to baggy pants and a skateboard, but even from this distance I was struck by his horribly oversized cap, a cross between Cat-in-the-Hat and the Mad Hatter. It hid his eyes—but not his gleeful, vicious, *satisfied* grin.

"There's a guy creating the wind!" I shouted—and the tarp tore from my grasp. "Fuck!"

"What?" Gibbs said, trying to look, but the corner of the tarp I'd lost snapped at his eyes. "Fuck! Frost, help me!" he said, flinching, nearly losing his corner too as the wind tore at it.

I lunged for the end I'd lost, pinning it down so Horscht could stake it.

Drifts of dust surged over the hill under the wind, whipping past us in seconds like stampeding ghosts. There was no way this was natural. A terrific gust tore away a corner, letting sunlight shine on the pooled blood at Revy's feet. It steamed and began boiling away where the light touched it.

I snagged a flapping edge of the tarp, cursing, but the wind roared, dragging me and two officers aside, exposing Revy completely. His pooled blood had already boiled away to a black crust of ugly tar, but under the full light of the sun, it began to smoke—and burn.

"God *damn* it," Rand said, coming to help us. "What the hell—"

"There's a guy manipulating the wind!" I shouted, trying to point. "We gotta stop him!"

"Dakota?" Revenance said suddenly, raising his head, his eyes staring straight at me without seeing. "Dakota! Are you there? Can you hear me?"

"Yeah, Revy," I said. "Hang on, we'll find a way—"

"It's already got me," Revenance said, twisting in agony as vines drained his flesh and flames licked his feet. "Don't let it get you or Cinnamon! You gotta take out that skateboarding fuck, but to stop him, you gotta find the Streetscribe. But whatever you do—*don't awaken it!*"

Then the wind tore the tarp away, and his body burst into flames.

3.   ISOLATION PROTOCOL

"Nobody fucking touch *nothing*," McGough said, as we all stood in shock, watching firemen back away from the blackened corpse. Revy's death had taken only a moment, but it had taken an eternity to put those tenacious fires out. "This just became a crime scene."

"Wasn't 'magical assault with intent to kill' already a crime?" I said, cradling Cinnamon against me. She was crying. I hadn't realized how much she liked Revy. "I'm sorry, baby—"

"I *liked* him," Cinnamon said bitterly. "The fang was *nice* to me—"

I drew a breath. "Rand," I said. "There was someone else on the scene, a short little prick with baggy pants, a skateboard, and a huge-ass hat—"

"I-I saw him too," Cinnamon said suddenly. "When I went to get the pole. Sittin' on a wall, watchin' it all, grinning with some nasty ol' silver grill on his teeth—"

"So?" McGough said, eyes sharp. "What do you think that had to do with this?"

"I saw him right when the wind picked up," I said.

"I caught that too," Gibbs said. "Just a glimpse, but I definitely saw the guy—and as soon as I looked, the wind snapped like a bitch and near ripped the tarp out of my hands."

"Can't be a coincidence," I said. "He may have been magically enhancing the wind—"

"Oh, *hell*. Thanks, Frost. We'll search the area," McGough said, motioning to an officer. "First things first, though—this is a crime scene now. I need you to wait by your car—"

"I wasn't done," I snapped. "He was pretty far off. At first I thought he was trying to watch from a safe distance, but I surveyed the ley line crossings a few years back and one goes through the Cemetery right where he was standing. He could be a technical practitioner rather than a bloodline witch, which might affect his choice of escape routes—"

"Oh, hell, we've got one who thinks she can be *helpful*," McGough said, putting his hand to his to his brow. "Rand, get your pet witch and her pet cat out of my crime scene—"

"Now *just* a minute," I began hotly. "You can't just—"

"He can't, but *I* can," Rand said. "It's *my* crime scene now." McGough twitched and frowned, looking less like Mr. Wizard and more like an angry garden gnome, and Rand just raised an eyebrow at him. "Are you going to be a dick about this?"

McGough raised his little hands. "No, no, Homicide gets first crack at a body."

"Thank you. I've called ident, but the Black Hats obviously can have the scene when the coroner pronounces," Rand said. "Look, Dakota, seriously, McGough's not trying to be a dick, we just need to get you physically off the crime scene. If you could wait by the car—"

"*Not* until he apologizes."

"What, about the pet witch crack?" McGough said, laughing. "Look, babe, if your skin's that thin you shouldn't have scribbled all over it—"

"To Cinnamon," I said coldly.

McGough looked down at my daughter. "Hey, little lady," he said, a little of the kindly wizard creeping back into his features. "Sorry I called you a cat—"

"I *am* a cat," Cinnamon said, hissing. "but don't be calling me a *pet*."

McGough stared blankly at her a moment, then forced the twinkle back into his eyes. "Sorry, little lady," he said, "I was just kidding around—"

Cinnamon smiled, then suddenly barked, "Fucking *toad*—"

"Cinnamon!" I said.

"What?" she said, looking away. "See how *he* likes bein' called a name."

McGough straightened. "Rand," he said. "I ain't trying to tell you your job, but clear the site—and take some separate statements before they're completely cross-contaminated."

"I know, I know," Rand said, running his hand over his bald head. "I'll take care of it. You get on the warrant for me. I don't want this fucked up, not for any reason—"

"Why do you need a warrant?" I said, as Rand began herding us away from our improvised tent and the foul black smoke billowing out of it. "We all saw—"

"*That* was a public safety operation. *This* is a crime scene," Rand said. "Technically we could get by on the permission of Oakland Cemetery—"

"What aren't you tellin' us?" Cinnamon said, stopping so suddenly I ran into her.

"Cinnamon, Dakota," Rand said, motioning to a sandy-haired female officer. "I'm . . . going to need to split you two up for a minute. Just long enough to take the statements."

"Fuck that—" I began, then put my hand to my head. "Let me guess, it's—"

"Just standard procedure," Rand finished for me, staring at me and Cinnamon cautiously. Then he grinned. "You're not going to be a pain about this, are you, Kotie?"

"No, we've been around the block," I said. The female officer smiled at us, through a dozen little white tape bandages on her face, and I nodded at Cinnamon to go with her.

Rand walked over to his cruiser, sat down on the hood, and motioned for me to join him. I did, and for a few minutes we just watched the swarm of police activity. I folded my arms over my chest: I was still trembling with adrenaline and the crisp air felt good against my hot skin.

After a few moments, instead of working the case, Rand surprised me by touching a sore spot. "Look, Kotie . . . you *are* going to see your Dad, aren't you?"

"Yes," I snapped. "This Saturday, in fact." Then I softened. "Look, I know Dad and I don't get along . . . but you're right. He deserves to meet his granddaughter."

"Yeah," Rand said, and then fell silent.

Instinctively, I looked for and found Cinnamon, talking with Officer Lee next to a distant grave. But ultimately my eyes were drawn back to that horrible smoke, now just trailing wisps. Revenance was gone, burned up before our eyes, and I couldn't believe it. "We *saw* it. You really need to go through all this?" I asked sadly. "A warrant, separating the witnesses—"

"Absolutely," Rand said grimly. "A robber opened up on your Dad and me in a crowded store, but the evidence—spent casings, slugs, even the gun with prints—got thrown out because we didn't get the shopkeeper's permission to search. Another case went sour when two witnesses convinced each other a house's blinds were up when the cruiser's camera showed them down."

"And them?" I said, motioning to the officers milling about. "Aren't they witnesses too?"

Rand looked up sharply, seeing McGough yelling at an officer who had peeked under the tarp. "This is a fucking mess. You shouldn't have been here. *He* shouldn't have been here—"

"Who is the little toad?"

"Head of Magical Crimes Investigation, the Black Hats," Rand said, still staring. "Homicide normally calls them *after* whatever's gone down."

"Come to think of it, Revy wasn't—" I began, then stopped. I didn't want to say *Revy wasn't already dead* out loud; my mind hadn't wrapped around that yet. But my question remained: "So . . . why *was* Homicide here?"

"To get you," Rand said simply, and I leaned back to stare at him. "You attracted a lot of attention with your little stunt at the Masquerade a couple of months back, and I owe McGough a favor, so . . . when he couldn't handle this, he called me, and I called you."

"Thanks," I said. "Now I know how a marker feels—called in."

"I'm sorry," Rand said. "If I'd known that fang . . . that Revenance wasn't going to make it, I wouldn't have called you. This is why McGough suddenly turned into a dick. Having someone with magical training at the scene of a magical crime creates a horrible mess."

"Why?" I asked. "Seems like you'd want the knowledge—"

"If we ever *do* catch the guy," Rand said grimly, "his lawyer will argue *you* did it."

"*What?*" I said. "*Me?* How? You called me after it was already started—"

"People don't understand magic," Rand said. "*Anything* sounds plausible. If they can't pin it on you, they'll try McGough next, and he couldn't even do a card trick—"

"The largest School of Magic in North America is five miles from here," I said. "Emory University—a billion dollar endowment, my alma mater? Maybe you've heard of it? There are plenty of expert witnesses you can get who can explain magic."

"Not to a jury," Rand said. "Not so they'd understand. And defense lawyers know it. And the only thing that scares juries more than a wizard on the loose is a cop with a wand."

I sighed. I just wanted to create art, to fill the finest canvases on Earth with marks of beauty. Ours is a great world, full of magic and wonders, and yet there I sat, mourning a friend, my skin still tingling with stray mana from the spell that had killed him.

"Why," I asked, "do people have to go fuck everything up?"

And then McGough was yelling at Horscht, who was . . . holding a spray can.

"Oh, hell," Rand said, rising—and I followed. "This is why we clear first responders—"

"What do you mean, put it down?" Horscht said, jerking the can back from McGough protectively, making the little gnome even madder. "This, this is evidence—"

"But where did you *get* it?" McGough barked. "Did you take a picture? Did you make some notes? Did you bother to use a glove or a baggie before getting your stupid paws on it—"

"No, I didn't have one," Horscht said, jerking it back, but I noticed he *was* holding it with a piece of paper so his fingerprints wouldn't get on it. "And you don't either. I came to get an evidence bag. This is *important*. He *had* to use this to spray the tag—"

"It wasn't spray painted," I said, cocking my head back at the mess that was left of the tag. "Hard to tell now, after all that fire and water, but it *had* to be infused oil chalk."

McGough looked over at me sharply, then back at the tag. "You're right," he said slowly, "he couldn't have . . . or could he—"

"Horscht, put it down before McGruff the Crime Dog bursts a blood vessel," I said. "I'm sure he wants to fingerprint it, even though the killer couldn't have used it to make this mark—"

"I get the point, I shouldn't have touched it," Horscht said, staring down at the can, a plain white affair with a larger-than normal top and glittery gold oozing down one of its sides. "But I *did* take a picture, and I *do* remember where I got it—in the yard where we found the basketball goal. These crime scene guys, they think they're so sharp but they *miss* stuff—"

At that crack, McGough, who had calmed down as Horscht explained himself, suddenly glared at Rand, who scowled back at him. I remembered the 'first responders' crack. Oh, great. *I'd* just blundered onto some internal rivalry in the APD. Joy.

"—and I thought *this* was evidence," he was saying. "Why are you so sure that it isn't?"

"Fair question," I said, "but Home Depot doesn't sell spray cans filled with a thousand bucks of magical pigment, and even if they did you wouldn't want to *spray* a magical mark—"

"Why not?" Horscht said, shaking the can experimentally. "I mean—"

"NO!" yelled McGough, but it was too late. Horscht squeezed the top, and a screaming blaze of golden flame erupted as the magical ink—*magical ink, oh shit!*—reacted against the stray mana floating through the air. He flinched and screamed, dropping the can, which skittered across the pavement, propelled for a moment by an elaborate trail of fire.

Like a fat number six made of yellow and orange sparkles, the fireball folded in on itself and curled lazily up into the sky, taking the trail with it, coiling off into the clouds. Horscht was still screaming, chest and face covered in glowing wildstyle flames, but I grabbed him, flexed my hand over his face and chest, generating enough mana to pull the ink out of his skin before it could set and do damage. The sparkling stuff began attacking my skin now, a thousand pricking ants, but I just shook my hand until it dissipated into a cloud of colorful, acrid dust.

"Damnation, Horscht," Rand said, steadying him. "You'd think you'd never been on a crime scene before. What were you thinking?"

"I don't know, sir," Horscht said, scared. "I'm sorry, sir—"

"You can't play around with this shit," I said. "Magic is really dangerous."

"Cut him a break, he showed us all up," McGough said. "Sorry I went off on you, Horscht. This is the best piece of evidence yet."

We all stared at him in shock. McGough's bluster was gone, replaced with a quiet seriousness. He'd put on a rubber glove and picked up the can, turning it so I could see an air valve sticking out of its neck, like you see on bicycle tires—a rechargeable spray can.

"Hell, Frost," he said, "I sure wish you hadn't been wrong about this."

I stared at it. "Me too," I said. "I'd never *heard* of magical marks this powerful before today, and if someone has learned to spray paint them . . ."

" . . . we have a big problem," McGough finished.

---

4.   STICKY AND SWEET

Gibbs questioned me, and it didn't take long—he was polite, efficient, and to the point. "That does it," he said, putting a few finishing touches on the statement. "Anything to add?"

"No, but I do have a question," I said, shivering, hands on my scraped knees, staring down at my jeans shorts. "Can I get my clothes back, or are they evidence now too?"

"I'm having them dry cleaned," Gibbs said, deadpan.

"*What?*" I said, then blinked as he grinned. "Oh, very funny."

"Sign this, and I'll fetch your things so you can get dressed," Gibbs said, handing me his clipboard. "Just to warn you, they'll probably want you at the station later."

I sighed and looked over the form. It summed up my morning in a few short lines: school shopping with daughter (with name and address of my alibi), police summons (with time of call noted), and failure to prevent magical attack (which resulted in watching friend die.)

As awkward and painful a morning as I could imagine. I signed the statement and looked up to see Officer Lee leading Cinnamon back to me. They were smiling and laughing, but then Cinnamon cussed and tossed her head angrily, as if poked with a cattle prod. Lee took it in stride, but she looked up at me, not angry, just—eyes filled with immense pity.

"Thanks, Officer," I said, holding my arms out to Cinnamon, who leapt upon me and squeezed her arms around me in a breath-defying hug. "I appreciate it."

"Not a problem," Lee said. "Your daughter is very observant. And colorful."

Cinnamon snorted and twitched her head, but smiled back at Lee.

Gibbs brought my clothes from his squad car and I gratefully grabbed my turtleneck—I was now freezing. I pulled it on, chanting, "Brr, brr, brr—"

"Get some fur," Cinnamon sang.

"—*no* thank you," I finished, as my head popped out.

Rand was just looking at us, one hand in his pocket, suit frayed but soul unperturbed, a snapshot of a black GQ Kojak right after a fight with a horde of zombies. It was *so* good to see him back on his game, even after all that horror. "You guys sure are *sickeningly* sweet."

I forced a smile—Cinnamon could get me goofing, but Revy's death still weighed in my mind. "Just standard procedure," I said at last, slipping on my leather chaps. "Are we done?"

"For now," Rand said. "But, look, we all saw what went down—but not even McGough can explain it, and he's seen more weird shit than you and me put together. He's already asked me to pull in the DEI's experts, and I'll guess Philip will want you looking into it too."

"Fine, that's all I need, another excuse to talk to Philip," I said, slipping on my vestcoat. Philip Davidson was my contact at the DEI, the Department of Extraordinary Investigations. We were dating, whenever he could make it to Atlanta. It was an odd match—he was politically right of Attila the Hun and I was an uber-treehugger—but he still drove a Prius when he wasn't riding to my rescue in a cool black helicopter. "I'll give my favorite bod in the spook squad a ring."

"Also, there's another thing," Rand said, kneading his brow. "Dakota, I know this is going to be difficult for you but . . . could you please inform the Consulate?"

My smile faded. "The . . . *Vampire* Consulate?" I asked, though I knew exactly which consulate he meant. "Why me? I mean, shouldn't the police do that job?"

Rand's face flickered a bit—*ah, you caught me*—but he persisted, nodding at the collar about my throat. "Normally, yes . . . but since you were their representative on site . . ."

I tugged at my stainless steel collar. It was lined with neoprene to make it comfortable, but it wasn't coming off. "I'm not their 'representative,' I'm just . . . under their protection."

"Whatever," Rand said. "Dakota . . . could you break the news to Savannah? I know Revenance was a mutual friend, and she'd probably appreciate hearing it from you."

I stared at him. "You *suck*."

"That's her you're thinking of," Rand said, "and to be honest, I find it a bit creepy to think that a girl I once bounced on my knee now drinks blood. Will you tell her?"

"Yes," I said, scowling, dialing the next school on my cell. "*After* our appointment—"

"Hello, Clairmont Academy," a female voice over the phone answered.

"Hello, this is Dakota Frost," I said. "We had an appointment for noon."

"Oh, yes, well," the woman said, spluttering a little. "Things are filling up."

"I know you have a full schedule," I said, watching Cinnamon's eyes grow wide. "I'm sorry, but we were detained by the police—"

"Got caught speeding?" the woman said, suddenly conspiratorial. "You should give yourself more time to get places, you know. I heard this article in the AJC . . . "

She nattered on a bit. I didn't really know how to deal with that, and frankly I didn't want to. "Look, I'm sorry, I wasn't speeding," I said quietly. "One of our friends just got attacked—"

"Oh," she said. "I-I'm so sorry—are they OK?"

I stood there, swaying. "No, he's—" My mouth grew dry. "He didn't make it."

The line was quiet. "Oh, God, I'm *so* sorry," the woman said.

"Yes, well, yes," I said. "I hate to inconvenience you, but . . . can you fit us in?"

"I'm so sorry," she said. "I-I'm *so* sorry. We just filled our last slot an hour ago."

I was stunned. I had known they were squeezing us in, but—"Are you sure?"

"We had three slots left and filled five before the principal called me and told me to stop," the woman said. "I've been calling the rest of the appointments and canceling—"

"I see," I said quietly. "Thank you." I hung up the phone, staring at it. "*Damnit.*"

Cinnamon stared up at me, eyes welling up. "I'm goin' for a walk," she said.

"Go to her," Rand said, taking the phone from my hand and redialing. "Hello? Clairmont Academy? Yes, this is Detective Andre Rand with the APD, badge number—"

I followed Cinnamon, who kept her back to me, snuffling. "I don't wanna talk to you," she said. "You wants me to go to school, but can't even find a good one—"

"We'll find you a school," I said, putting my hands on her shoulders. "Look, I know what you want. I'll find a way for you to have a real life—"

"How?" she said bitterly, turning. "I'm a total freak. Look at me. Look at me!"

I stared down at her. At her orange hair, her yellow cat eyes, her tattooed stripes, her huge ears, her twitching tail. This time of the month, fine orange fur began encroaching upon her pale olive skin at the edges of her normal hair. You couldn't *not* know she was a werekin.

But none of that mattered to me. "What?" I asked. "All I see is my daughter."

Her eyes welled up even more, and then she grabbed me and squeezed me so hard the air once again left my lungs. "You big sap," she said, still crying. "Always gets me with the sticky-sweets. Lucky for *you* Rand snagged us an appointment at three."

I looked over at Rand, smiling, but there was a glint in his eye which seemed to say there was more to his favor than just soothing Cinnamon's broken heart . . . and I knew *precisely* what he wanted for his *quid pro quo*.

"Wonderful," I said. "*More* than enough time to break the news to my ex-girlfriend."

5.   UNDYING LOVER

We delayed the inevitable by getting breakfast-for-lunch at Ria's Bluebird Café. And not just because it was right across the street from Oakland Cemetery: I love the place, and for more than the food. It's always amusing to watch a server's expression as tiny little Cinnamon plows into beef brisket, while big old me nibbles at soysage, sweet potatoes and a tofu omelet.

While Cinnamon finished up, I sipped my sweet tea, scanned the street, and found myself noticing graffiti where I'd never seen it before: a sloppy caricature sprayed on the side of an Atlanta Journal-Constitution newspaper box; something political stenciled on a sidewalk; even colorful bubbly capitals sprayed on the brick wall of the Cemetery itself. Nothing as elaborate as the tag that killed Revy, but, still, graffiti was ever present.

But then the check came, it was only twelve-thirty, and our appointment at the school wasn't until three; and so we no longer had a good excuse not to drive the five minutes to the nearby Consulate and deliver the bad news to my childhood sweetheart.

The Vampire Consulate of Little Five Points isn't actually in Little Five Points. It's at another five-pointed intersection in the Sweet Auburn area downtown. There, hidden away in a quiet set of buildings made from a deconsecrated church, is the court of one of the most powerful vampires in Atlanta: the Lady Saffron, nee Savannah Winters . . . my very *ex*-girlfriend.

"Fucking fang," Cinnamon muttered curtly, and when I glanced at her, she glared and looked away. "I—I means, I hates this place. She always smells funny."

"She *is* a vampire," I said, pulling into the tiny lot behind the converted Victorian that served as the Consulate office. I dug out our vampire district parking tag and hung it from the rear-view mirror. "She may be almost vegetarian, but she's got to drink at least some blood—and who knows how much her girlfriend drinks. There's bound to be a smell."

"Hey, I *likes* the smell of blood, but she's always stinking of leather . . . or rubber."

"Damnit." I put my hand over my eyes and rubbed. "I really didn't need to know that."

"Share the love, I says," Cinnamon said, and I looked over to see her grinning.

"You set me up," I said.

"And knocked you over," she replied, flicking a hand out, catlike. "After all, she was your *giiirl*friend. Don't you knows what she's into?"

"Better than you," I grumbled. "Fine, fine, just for that, you're coming inside."

"No problem," Cinnamon said, and then: "I do *too* likes her. I was just messing with ya."

We stepped through wrought iron gates and passed signs for Darkrose Security Enterprises and the Junior Van Helsing Detective Agency. The former was the security force belonging to Darkrose, Saffron's new girlfriend; the latter was a Scooby-Doo grade paranormal detective agency which had tried and failed to take out Saffron shortly after she became a vampire. Now, through a sequence of events that had never been adequately explained to me, both rented space from the Consulate, even down to sharing a receptionist.

Through the glass doors of the porch we could see that today that receptionist was Nagli, a cute little Indian college student that was one of the better Van Helsings. She looked bored out of her mind, but after buzzing the two of us in she immediately perked up.

"Hey, Cinnamon," she said brightly. When Nagli was perky, she was darned cute, and I couldn't help grinning back at her. "And hey, Dakota. The Lady Saffron is in the garden."

I led Cinnamon through the middle door behind Nagli, through the shared conference room, and out into the garden. In the church's former preschool playground now stood trellis after trellis of honeysuckle, hydrangeas, and clematis. When first planted they were low hedges that burst with stunning color in summer and fall. Now they were a maze of high vines, winter green and oppressively dark, that opened up around a white gazebo.

Savannah Winters stood there in the sunshine in a ruffled Southern belle dress almost as red as her hair. Over the dress she wore a black leather corset with red lacing, that daring touch that I had so liked. Dark leather gloves protected her hands to the elbow, and she wore a huge red bonnet with black lace; but where Revenance had caught fire at the first direct touch of daylight, "the Lady Saffron" strolled through it unconcerned, with bomber goggles and a UV monitor as only concessions to the nuclear fire of the Sun.

Once I had thought Savannah had won her post as the Queen of the Little Five Points district through vampire nepotism—after all, her maker was Lord Delancaster, the head vampire of Georgia and one of the most famous vampires in America.

The truth was, "the Lady Saffron" was immensely powerful, frighteningly brilliant—and a daywalker. I think your typical vampire was scared shitless that she would crack open their coffin at high noon and ram a polished sandalwood stake straight through their heart.

"Da*k*ota," Saffron said, turning, smiling at us from beneath her umbrella—a broad, closemouthed grin which dimpled up her delicate oval features. "And Cinnamon too! What a wonderful surprise. Come, you *must* join me in the gazebo."

Her dainty little gloved hand leapt out and grabbed mine in a vicegrip of steel. Typical—you couldn't date Savannah without learning to deal with being tugged around—but now she had vampire strength I stayed extra close so she didn't accidentally pull my arm out of its socket.

Cinnamon started actually skipping alongside us, a victorious little smirk on her face as she watched me being dragged along. I reached out and snagged her wrist, and Saffron led us both up onto the gazebo in a little train. Happy happy, joy joy.

"Something to drink?" she asked, releasing me and gesturing towards a wicker table, where a frosted pitcher filled with a green liquid sat precariously close to her laptop. She picked up a heavy-bottomed glass and twirled the green leafy sprig sticking out of it. "Mint juleps?"

"Sure!" Cinnamon said brightly.

"No, and no," I said. "I'm driving, and she's underage. And really? Drinking, before one in the afternoon? Isn't that a bit early—"

"A bit late, actually," Saffron smirked, sitting down in the table's matching wicker chair and bumping the mouse on her laptop to bring it to life. "I should have already turned in hours ago, but I've been burning the mid*day* oil working on my thesis."

"That's . . . wonderful," I said. I couldn't complain: I'd been on her about her unfinished PhD for years. "But for us it's too early, in Cinnamon's case by several years. Sweet tea?"

"*Certainly*, Dakota," she said, tapping the laptop and speaking into its microphone. "Nagli, could you—" There was a curse out of the laptop's speakers and then the "intercom" went dead. "Well!" Saffron said, mock shocked. "You certainly can't get good help these days. But no matter, I'm so glad to see you! You never come around anymore. Cinnamon keeping you busy? How is the school shopping going? You *must* look into a Montessori school—"

This was ridiculous. Whatever Saffron was, she was no Scarlett O'Hara, and the weird bomber goggles made her look more Victorian steampunk than

Civil War plantation. Finally I could take it no more, and said sharply, "Kill the Southern belle act, *Savannah*."

"Now, Dakota," Savannah smirked, "I've told you never to call me that, not here—"

"You're right," I said, remembering my real reason for being here. "My Lady Saffron, I'm here on Consulate business."

Saffron froze, staring at me with those bizarre goggles; then she lifted them up and squinted at me. "But . . . I haven't *given* you any Consulate responsibilities—"

"No, but wearing the sign of the Consulate means responsibility can fall in my lap," I said, leaning forward to pat her dress. "Saffron, I have terrible news. You remember Revy?"

"Revenance, from the Oakdale Clan? Of course," she said . . . and blanched. "No!"

"Yes," I said. "He . . . he's dead."

"You're certain he's not just . . . missing?" Saffron said, leaning forward. The wicker arms of the chair creaked under her delicate gloved hands. "Are you *absolutely certain?*"

"Yes," I said. "He died right in front of me, Cinnamon and Rand—"

"Dear God," she said, crossing herself, her mouth opening in unguarded shock, exposing her cruel fangs for the first time since we'd arrived. "Wait, Rand? You mean, Revenance died in front of Uncle *Andy?* But why . . . why was he even there? What happened?"

"It was a magical attack," I said. "The police's expert couldn't handle it, so they called me in. I tried to save him, but . . . " My face fell. "But I failed. I'm so sorry."

"A magical attack?" Saffron asked suspiciously. "You mean a wizard attacked him?"

"No. Not directly," I said; vamps and wizards didn't mix. "It was enchanted graffiti."

Saffron's eyes widened. "I . . . didn't even know that was possible."

"I didn't either. Incredibly powerful magic—and fast too," I said, gesturing at my forehead. "That's how I got dinged—"

"Fast? The graffiti . . . *moved?*" Saffron said.

"Oh, come on," I said. "You've seen my tattoos move, same principle—"

"Oh, do *I* remember your tattoos moving," Saffron said, first lascivious, then embarrassed in the very next moment. Cinnamon sneezed, and Saffron raised a gloved hand to her brow. "I'm sorry, that was inappropriate, given the circumstances and company."

"Yes, please, thank you," I snapped. "If you would stop hitting on me every time I came over here I would be much more likely to come over here."

"Dakota," Saffron said. "I thought we were going to be friends again—"

"*Friends*," I underlined. "Not *girl*friends."

"Dakota," Saffron said reprovingly. "There's no need to get snippy—"

"I'm goin' for a walk," Cinnamon said, hopping up and leaping over the banister of the gazebo, tail fluidly slipping over the rail. She glared back at me. "The reason I said I hates this place is that you always fights when you comes here."

In the silence that followed, Saffron and I stared at each other uncomfortably.

"Sorry," I said, embarrassed. "I thought we'd stopped bringing up reminders of 'us.'"

"Sorry," Saffron said, equally embarrassed. "You've recently bled. It's, uh, agitating me—and can we please leave it at that? You were trying to tell me—"

"About a magical attack," I said. "A giant graffiti tag, all magical, all energized. Revenance was trapped in it. It was tearing him apart—"

"Oh *no*," Saffron said, swallowing. "Did it—"

"No," I said. "But it had him effectively trapped. The police tried to rescue him, then I tried. We all failed. He held on as long as he could—"

"But he wasn't a daywalker," she said soberly, putting her goggles back on.

"No," I said. Watching a vampire die was . . . horrible. I could still hear his screams. I cast about for anything else to talk about. "What I don't get is how it *worked*. It held him there for hours. The mana should have dissipated, but it seemed like it was getting *stronger*."

"Perhaps there was a hidden caster," Saffron said, "feeding magic to it—"

"There was a guy," I said, describing the jerk with the hat and skateboard, gloating as Revy died. "But he was hundreds of feet away, and there was no magic flowing off him, like from a classical wizard. I can feel it, with these vines. The tag, on the other hand, was just *bleeding* mana. It was definitely a power source, or maybe plugged into a power source—"

"Maybe," she said thoughtfully, "it was feeding off *Revy*."

"Can't be," I said. "Magic is derived from life force, and vampires aren't alive—"

Saffron hissed, quietly but with full fangs. "I'm shocked to hear that from you, Dakota," she said, and with her eyes behind the goggles I couldn't tell if she was really angry or just messing with me. "I had to devote a whole chapter in my thesis to debunking that myth."

"Well, send it to me," I said gladly. "Prove me wrong."

"It *is* a bit technical," she said smugly.

"*I* was a chemistry major," I replied. "I can handle anything the soft sciences put out."

"Them's fightin' words," Saffron said, turning her laptop towards her with a vicious smirk. "I'll email it to you. Maybe you can send me comments."

"Sure," I said. Then, again bringing the conversation back to Revy, "But even so . . . he may have been writhing, but he sure wasn't *dancing*."

Saffron paused her search. "Who cares whether he was dancing? Just because he's not an official skindancer doesn't mean his writhing couldn't generate magical power—"

"Except that normal movements don't obey skindancing rules," I said, "so the random surges of magic they generate usually average out to a null effect."

"Could it have been . . . a magical capacitor?" Saffron said, resuming her typing. "Powered up slowly over time by sapping Revenance's life force?"

"I . . . don't think so," I said.

"Don't think so," Saffron snapped, "or don't know? Did you think to check?"

"*Yes*, Saffron," I said. What was *wrong* with her today? The explanation about the blood wasn't cutting it—the news about Revy had really put her on edge. "I studied capacitor designs after last year's incident, and I looked for them while the tag was active. I didn't see any—"

"Well, now that it isn't, check again," she said. My face fell, and she frowned. "What?"

"They're not going to let me back onto the scene," I said. "The magical investigators, the Black Hats, seemed to think that some clever defense attorney would make hay of a magician—"

"For the love," Saffron said. "Well, hopefully they took pictures—*what?*"

"Savannah," I said softly. "This is me. I did doublecheck. But after the firemen put . . . put Revy out, the tag was a burnt ruin. There's nothing left to photograph."

"*Damn* it," Saffron said. "Sorry. I should have known you would look."

I shrugged. *Yeah*, but—"Anyway, a tag with that kind of surface area is usually a magical radiator—any mana Revenance generated would just leak away in the air. I've never seen such a large magical mark, except for maybe the Harris Mural at Emory."

Saffron looked up into the air sharply, sun reflecting off her goggles, remembering. The mural was a striking slow-moving magical pageant in Emory's Harris Hall, powered by the rays of the sun. No Harris School of Magic alum ever forgot its ever-changing abstract colors.

"You should check that out," Saffron said slowly. "It's only about twenty-five years old. The painter might still be alive. There can't be too many people who could paint a magical painting big enough to kill a person—maybe the painter of the Mural could give you some names that could kick-start your investigation."

"I'm not really investigating this," I said, taken aback. "I mean, it's a police matter, and they practically kicked me off the scene—"

"Dakota, you *have* to look into this," Saffron said urgently. "I mean, it would be stupid for them to not ask you after all you did for them last year. Who's more qualified?"

"Rand said as much," I said. "He seemed to think Philip would want my help, and he definitely wanted me to talk to you on behalf of the Vampire Consulate, so here I am."

"Well, that will make things . . . simpler," Saffron said, oddly uncomfortable. "So, if you are our representative, Dakota . . . can you deliver a message to the police for me?"

"What? Has someone else died?" I said, flashing back to Cinnamon's insight. "Savannah?"

"The Consulate has kept this quiet," Savannah began, "so we won't anger the Gentry—"

"The who?"

"Atlanta's old-school vampires," Savannah said, clearly irritated. "But now the police are involved, we need the opposite tack. We must show Sir Leopold and his crew of wingnuts we're doing something," she said, pulling off her goggles. Behind her squint, I could see that she was pleading. "We need someone who knows vampires, and magic, *and* has good relations with the police: you. We really need your help, Dakota."

I swallowed. "Help with what?" My head was buzzing with questions, but I was stuck on the idea that she needed me to be her go-between. "What do you want *me* to tell the police?"

"Revenance isn't the first vampire we've lost this week. He's the third."

6. EDUCATIONAL EXPERIENCE

"Thanks for handling this, Rand," I said, slowing the Prius for the turn into the Clairmont Academy's drive. "Savannah says to call Nagli, she'll give you all the details."

"Why can't she call me directly?" Rand's disembodied voice asked. "If vampires really are disappearing, they should have called the police right away—"

"Of course they should have," I said. "But her high-and-mightiness 'the Lady Saffron' got deliberately vague, started talking about the Gentry, about keeping an arm's length between factions. I gather vampire politics are involved."

"Jesus. Vampire politics are *always* involved," Rand said. "Thanks for passing on the message, Dakota, we'll handle it. Good luck to you guys today."

"Thanks." I hung up and glanced at Cinnamon. "Are you going to be all right?"

Cinnamon nodded, swallowed, just staring.

Clairmont Academy was a modernist structure, nestled into a hillside so cunningly Frank Lloyd Wright would have been proud. The main offices were long straight jet of glass and slate erupting from a stand of magnolias. Classrooms climbed the hill behind the offices in an arc of terraced wedges: the overall effect was of a wave curling over a surfboard. Oh so chic.

I pulled into the visitor spaces angled off the dropoff lane. "Just . . . try to be nice?"

Cinnamon nodded again, then pulled down the vanity mirror, trying to fix her hair. Then she slipped out a tiny vial of her distinctive cinnamon oil perfume, which I now knew she used to hide her tiger musk, and dabbed it behind her ears and whiskers.

"Just relax," I said. "You look fine. Better than I do, in fact, my little schoolgirl."

Cinnamon hissed and swatted. "OK, DaKOta," she said, fwapping the mirror back up. "But remember, this getup is *just* to impress the squares that runs the schools. I'm not gonna change on my days off, and don't *you* goes all Laura Ashley on me either."

"How do *you* know about Laura Ashley?" I asked. "You were, what, two years old?"

"Thrift stores are your friend," Cinnamon said. "Not that I'd buy one—"

"Hey, don't go dissing her. *I* have a Laura Ashley," I said with a grin. "A big old floral tent feeding the moths back home in Dad's house in Stratton, South Carolina."

Cinnamon grinned and unbuckled her seat belt. I did so as well, resisting the urge to check *myself* in the mirror: she was finally relaxing, and I didn't want to make her nervous again. Saffron had let me clean the blood off in her bathroom, after insisting that I clean the sink and flush the wipes. I looked as good as I was going to get, and that would have to be good enough.

We got out of the car and walked to the front door, a huge glass slab. In it I could see our distinctive outlines: tall, coated, and deathhawked, hand resting on short, skirted and cat-eared. The door slid smoothly aside on its own, replacing our reflections with a small, mousy brunette, in circa 1980s ecru wool crepe jacket and navy floral dress, who was staring at us in horror.

After a few awkward moments, I broke the ice.

"Dakota Frost," I said, extending my hand.

"Catherine Fremont," the woman replied, eyes taking me in from ankles to earrings. Then she seemed to notice my hand and took it gladly, like a lifeline—and I found her tiny hand surprisingly strong in mine. "Catherine Fremont, admissions."

"And this must be Cinnamon," I supplied, as she kept pumping my hand.

"What? Oh! Yes. I'm sorry," Fremont said, letting go of my hand awkwardly as she did a similar double-take at Cinnamon. She pulled a pair of half-rimmed glasses out of her hair and peered at Cinnamon, as if never taught it's not polite to stare. "And this must be Cinnamon."

And then her mouth quirked in a skeptical grin, and she raised the glasses to look at me. "Is her name *really* 'Cinnamon Frost'?"

"*Yes,*" Cinnamon hissed, but I squeezed her shoulder.

"And no," I said. "Her birth name is—unfortunate. We don't use it anymore."

"And so why did you pick Cinnamon?" Fremont said, frowning. "You *wanted* your daughter to be the butt of jokes?"

"Believe it or not," I said, "it was a complete accident. I didn't know I was adopting her when I suggested her name. Actually, I didn't even know I was suggesting her name—I just called attention to her perfume and it . . . stuck."

"Mmm-hmm," Fremont said. "Well . . . shall we get started?"

She gestured, then followed her own gesture back into the lobby, clearly expecting us to follow. Cinnamon and I stared at each other a moment, weighing the unspoken question: should we bail? But neither of us made that first move away, so we followed.

Catherine Fremont was tiny, no taller than Cinnamon, but she carried herself well, the navy dress flaring out widely as she turned the corner. I could now see her outfit was brand new, with retro classic touches; still, there was something familiar about it . . . and eventually I got it.

"Laura Ashley?" I asked, with a smirk.

"Bramble Brooch," she replied, with a toss of her long, straight hair. I caught a bit of a smile in her cheek as she leaned her head back at me.

"Basically Laura Ashley, remixed."

Her high-heeled Victorian boots clicked against the slate tile, drawing my attention. *Nice.* Just then Fremont pulled out a keyfob and clicked it, and what I thought was a glass wall slid aside to open on her office. Fremont's office had a huge plate window overlooking the courtyard and classrooms. It looked like it could slide open the same way the hallway glass had. Fremont sat behind a dark wood desk and mouse-woke an old-school, blueberry iMac.

"Speaking of dress," Fremont said, lowering her glasses again, "I appreciate Cinnamon's efforts to conform to our dress code, but it also extends to makeup and accessories. The henna will have to go—as will the cat ears, I'm afraid."

Cinnamon flattened her ears, mortified, and I frowned. "Cinnamon's ears and tail are not 'accessories,'" I said coldly, sitting and motioning for Cinnamon to do so as well. "They're a part of her. I thought I was clear that she was an extraordinary needs child."

Fremont looked up sharply, then seemed to jump. "Oh my goodness," she said, staring at Cinnamon's head so hard I thought her gaze would knock it off. Then she sat up a little to get a glimpse of her tail. "I'm sorry, I didn't realize she was a . . . a *compulsory* were-cat—"

"Were*tiger*," I said, even more coldly, as Cinnamon squirmed, "and I thought you said Clairmont Academy was equipped to deal with extraordinary needs children."

"I-I'm *so* sorry," Fremont said, embarrassed, putting her hand over her mouth. "I-I mean, yes, we are, but I *personally* have never seen a werekin, that is, one who couldn't change back."

"How large is your extraordinary needs program if a lifer weretiger is a surprise?"

"We don't use the term lifer, and as it turns out, we don't have a compulsory," Fremont said. "We *do* have, though, a *variety* of extraordinary individuals. For privacy reasons I can't go into specifics, but we have, um . . . werewolves, and, and . . . a dhampyr, I mean, dhampyrs—"

"Meaning one of each," I said. "For a total extraordinary enrollment of, what, two?"

I considered getting up and walking out, but Fremont seemed to gather herself. "I may be new here, Miss Frost, but I assure you that this is not new to the Academy," she said quietly. "We have a dozen individuals on staff who have experience with extraordinary needs children, of whom we have several. I'm sorry that I was insensitive towards Cinnamon's condition. It was a misunderstanding. My comment about the henna tiger stripes still stands, however."

"They're not henna, they're tattoos," I said, and Fremont raised her eyebrows. "And before you ask, I didn't do them. Tattooing minors is illegal."

"Don't lets the tats fool ya," Cinnamon said. "She's more square than you are."

"The proper way to say that would be, 'Do not let her tattoos fool you,'" Fremont corrected, mouth pursed up. "You will need to learn to express yourself properly."

"If Clairmont Academy can correct her grammar," I said, laughing, "that alone will have been worth the price of admission."

"We'll do our very best," Fremont said with a grin, starting the paperwork. But when done with name-address-and-phone-of-parent, she bit her lip. "And her real name? I do need it for the record." Cinnamon lowered her head and mumbled something, and Fremont canted her head, making her glasses into reflective half-moons. "What was that, dear?"

"Stray," Cinnamon said, quiet as a mouse. "Stray Foundling."

Fremont's head stayed frozen. "Is that another joke?"

"I'm afraid not," I said, squeezing Cinnamon's hand again. "Her former guardians aren't bad folk, but they basically warehoused her. The only reason she has a name on record at all was a trip to the hospital when she was six. We're petitioning to get it changed—"

Fremont kept staring at us, eyes hidden behind those half-moons, then she shook her head and began typing. "Is Cinnamon spelled like the spice?"

"Yes," Cinnamon said eagerly.

"I hope you get it changed soon," she said, smiling. "People really called you Stray?"

"Until DaKOta," Cinnamon replied, with a big toothy grin at me.

"Good for you," Fremont said. But she didn't look happy as she took the rest of the information we could give her. Finally she muttered, "no transcript . . . no transcript."

"Is that *really* going to be a problem?" I asked. "Because I haven't found one in my back pocket while you've been typing. I hope we haven't all been wasting our time."

"No, it's just . . . this *is* a middle school. There are certain skills she'll need coming in," Fremont said, focusing on Cinnamon. "What books have you read recently, dear?"

"I hates reading," Cinnamon shrugged, not meeting her eyes. "I likes audiobooks."

"You read audiobooks?" Fremont raised an eyebrow. "Like what?"

"I dunno," Cinnamon said sullenly. "Fuck, I didn't knows it would be a test—"

"Cinnamon!" I said.

"We do *not* tolerate such language at the Clairmont Academy," Fremont said. "And we have standards here, which you will have to meet to become a student."

"What's 'standards' means?" Cinnamon said, sharp and suddenly scared. "You don't means cuss words. What's 'standards' means?"

"Since you have no academic record, you will have to take an entrance exam."

7.   ENTRANCE EXAM

"But . . . but the letters, they swims!" Cinnamon said, eyes going wide.

"How can you ask me to take a test before you teaches me to keep them still?"

Fremont's brow furrowed when Cinnamon said the letters swam. "*Can you read?*"

"Would you ask that if I was blind?" Cinnamon said. "That's why there's audiobooks."

"You're quite right, Cinnamon," Fremont said, glancing at me. "So consider this the start of an aural test. *What have you been reading?*"

"I-I—dunno," Cinnamon said nervously.

"You don't know because you don't remember, or because you don't read?"

"I do *too* reads," Cinnamon said. She slipped out her iPod and began thumbing the wheel. "Magical Thinkin'," she said. "The Omnivore's Dilemma. Kafka's Seashore—"

"You . . . have all those on there?" Fremont asked Cinnamon—but her eyes flicked to me, sharply. "You have *all* your books on there?"

"Not *everything*," Cinnamon said. "Just recent stuff. It only holds thirty gigs."

"May I see?" Fremont asked. Reluctantly, Cinnamon handed her the iPod; equally reluctantly, Fremont took it from Cinnamon's long, clawed fingers. Once she had it, however, she clickwheeled like a natural. "*The Year of Magical Thinking? Kafka on the Shore?* Really?"

"Yeah," she said. Nervously, she grabbed an odd, numbered Rubik's cube off the desk and began twiddling it with her bony claws. "I ran out of Mom's books, but we knows this blind witch, and she gave me lots of books off her laptop. She says it was the 'audible list'?"

"Witch isn't a nice thing to call someone," Fremont said.

"Unless it is accurate," I replied. "Jinx—our friend—is a graphomancer."

"Ah," Fremont said. "How did you like Jinx's suggestions, Cinnamon?"

"*Magical* was sad, but I liked *Kafka* OK," she said, scowling at the cube. "At first I was pissed 'cuz I thought it was a bio of the guy who wrote the bug book, but it reads OK."

"Do not say 'pissed', say 'upset,'" Fremont corrected. "What bug book?"

"*Meta-more-foe-sizz*," Cinnamon pronounced uncertainly, avoiding Fremont's eyes, twisting the cube in her hands. "The guy becomes this bug and everyone freaks."

"Mm-hm," Fremont said, clicking through the iPod. "Who is Stephen Dedalus?"

"That writer dude?" Cinnamon said sullenly.

"That could be a lot of people," she said. "Do you remember which book he was in?"

"Two," Cinnamon said. "The portrait one, and the useless one."

Fremont leaned forward, intent, scowling. "Who is Leopold Bloom?"

Cinnamon brightened. "The guy that likes the kidneys," she said, half-glaring, half-smiling at me. "Sounded yummy, but the big square won't get me none though."

"I didn't say *never*," I said, surprised. "I just didn't want, uh, kidney that night."

"Good Lord," Fremont said, staring at her. After a moment she seemed to notice the iPod in her hand and gave it back to Cinnamon. She seemed like she was weighing something. "Thank you, dear. Reading will clearly not be a problem. I'd still like to assess other areas, though—"

And then the glass door slid open.

"Doctor Yonas Vladimir," a man said, smiling warmly as he limped inside. "So, you must be Cinnamon. The girl without a past."

I smiled. I bet everyone tended to overlook the rumpled, chalkstained pants and the oversized Mr. Rogers sweater. I bet everyone ignored his bald dome and the clownish spray of brown curls beneath it. You just saw those eyes, sparkling behind his round glasses, and that smile, peering out from his trim goatee, and knew: this man was intelligent, and *alive.*

"I gots a past," Cinnamon said, still fidgeting with the Rubik's Cube, but smiling now. His grin was infectious—you couldn't help it. "I just don't gots an education."

"Yonas," Fremont said, half standing. "I'm so glad you could make it. Dakota Frost, Doctor Vladimir is head of the mathematics department."

"Pleased to meet you, Miss Frost," he said, extending his hand.

"Please call me Dakota," I said, standing. He was my height, or a shade less—not as big as he looked, or perhaps that was the stoop. But what a smile he had.

"Of course," he said. "Dakota . . . that's quite an unusual first name."

"Funny," I said. "I was just thinking Vladimir's an unusual *last* name."

"I'm guessing my grandfather ran into a little confusion at Ellis Island," Vladimir said, the warm smile sparkling into a deprecating grin. "It hasn't been a common Russian surname for a thousand years. So, Katie, what did you need me for?"

Fremont smiled. "I hoped you could proctor young Miss Frost's exam while I gave her mother a tour of the school. She's got a reading disability, so it may need to be oral—"

That was great news, but Cinnamon wasn't listening. It looked like she was stifling a sneeze—or a curse. Then her eyes seemed to widen, and she stood. Decisively.

"This is stupid," she said. "A waste of time. Fuck! I can't read for shit—"

"Cinnamon!" I said, as Fremont flinched and Vladimir just . . . chuckled?

"What? You cusses, in front of God, the police, everybody," Cinnamon said.

"Cinnamon—" I warned.

"I can't read enough to take a test," she said, tossing the Rubik's Cube, tail flailing about as she stalked back and forth in the room like a caged animal. "She just wants to get rid of me. *You* wants to get rid of me. You *all* wants to get rid of me. We should go. We *gots* to go—"

"Cinnamon Frost," I said quietly, folding my arms. "*Sit. Down.*"

Cinnamon sat in the chair abruptly, eyes wide. It surprised Fremont, even Vladimir—but not me. She just sat there, hands clenched on her skirt, watching me out of the corner of her eye, frozen—except for her rapidly switching tail.

"What was our agreement when we started school shopping?" I said.

"If I wants to go to school," she said, stretching her neck, "I gots to behave myself."

"The other part."

"That if I don't behaves myself," she began—and then the words began tumbling out like a running stream. "I'm sorry, Mom, I really am, please don't takes my iPod away, but you don't understands, we *gots* to *go*."

"Quite right," Vladimir said, patting Cinnamon on the shoulder as he walked past. He sat down on the desk and smiled at us. "I think it is a bit much to expect Cinnamon to have learned all our rules before she's heard them. Have you heard of the Seven Dirty Words, Cinnamon?"

"Uh . . . no," she said.

"Well, they're words that the FCC—that's the Federal Communications Commission, which you will learn about in Civics class—won't let people say on TV," Vladimir said. "We don't use them at the Clairmont Academy, and I won't say them here, but if you're web savvy I'm sure you can look them up on Wikipedia as a guide for what *not* to say to your teachers."

"Doctor Vladimir," Fremont said. "To point a student to . . . *such* a *list*—"

"What happened to Yonas?" Vladimir asked, smiling at her. Idly he picked up the Rubik's cube and stared at it. "Our job is not to hide the truth from our students; it's to teach them how to learn the truth and use it responsibly. Huh. Two sides. Not bad."

"I had four," Cinnamon said reproachfully. Her tail was twitching something fierce now, and she had started to rock in her chair—but she still answered. "I was shooting at five, just so I could see the pattern on six."

Vladimir stared at her, then tossed her the cube. "Show me."

Cinnamon twitched as she caught it. "We gots to go," she said, grimacing, but stared at the cube for a second before turning it a few times and flipping it back to him. "Four back at you. The counts, the pairs, the lonelies, and the pretties. I still wants to see what the other ones are."

"Wholes, evens, primes," Vladimir muttered, turning it. He held a side to us—it had 6s in the corners, 28s at north, south, east and west, and 496 at the center. "Are these the pretties?"

"Not all of them," Cinnamon said.

"We call them perfect numbers," Vladimir began. "That's because if you add—"

"Fucking *clown*," Cinnamon snapped, abruptly turning away from him.

"Cinnamon!" I said, shocked beyond words. "*What did I say* earlier?"

"Who cares? I can't pass another fucking test," she said. "We *gots* to *go*—"

"Not before you apologize to Doctor Vladimir," I said sharply.

"There's no need," Vladimir chuckled, winking at me. "I can go on a bit, and I *do* have the look. But she is right, you do need to get going right away." He turned to a set of cubbyholes beside Fremont's desk and pulled out a folder and some papers. "The Academy is *not* a public school and we hold our students to a *very* high standard. Classes start Friday, *not* Monday, and we expect our students to get cracking over the very first weekend. We distribute textbooks here, but it will really help if you can get some of the supplemental books for her grade level, and after some assessments on Friday, I may have a few more suggestions—"

But I was barely hearing him. I just stared down at the folder he had placed in my hands, then held it up to show it to Cinnamon. It said, in bold gilt letters:

Welcome to Clairmont Academy:
A Guide for Students and Parents

"Yonas!" Fremont said, as Cinnamon seized the folder and her eyes started welling up. "You—you can't just let her in, just like that—"

"Sure I can," Vladimir said, shrugging. "We each get one pass. Just because you used yours doesn't mean I can't use mine."

"But . . . but her accreditation," Fremont said. "Her behavior—"

"Katie, you're new here," Vladimir said, a little less patiently. "A good ten percent of our good-reco kids will go bad and a similar percent of the bad-recos will go good. You know this. And as for her behavior, she *is* an extraordinary needs child—"

"Thankyou thankyou thankyou," Cinnamon said, hopping up, tugging at her collar. "I'll do my very best, I promises, but, like, we gots to go—"

"Sit down, Cinnamon Frost," I said. "I'm sure I have forms to sign—"

"We can't *wait* for that," Cinnamon said, whirling. "Fuck, Mom, we *gots* to go—"

"Cinnamon!" I said, astonished. "What's wrong with you?"

And then I saw it. Cinnamon wasn't acting out because she was angry. She was terrified—and her whiskers were visibly growing out.

"I—I can't stop it," Cinnamon said, eyes in tears. "I . . . I'm *changing*."

8. FUR AND RAGE

"I knew it. I just *knew* it. When does the moon come up?" Vladimir asked, whirling to look at Fremont's wall clock. It showed **3:54** pm. "How long do you have?"

"An hour," Cinnamon said, clenching her fists. "Fuck! Not even."

"Is it really the full moon *already*?" he asked. "Shouldn't you have another day?"

"I haven't changed in three months," she whispered. "I can't hold no longer—"

"That's not healthy," Vladimir said, frowning at me. "Changing is part of who she is. You shouldn't be trying to suppress her gift."

"I didn't tell her not to change," I said angrily. "She was *poisoned*."

"Silver nitrate?" he asked sharply. "What's that called, hyper-argyle-something?"

"Hyperargyria," I said, squatting so I could look Cinnamon in the eye. Her eyes were actually *glowing*, and her pupils had narrowed to vertical ovals. "It damn near killed her."

"Damnit," Vladimir said. He looked at Fremont, who was gasping like a fish, and then he came to join me, watching the fine growth of fur on Cinnamon's face. "Cinnamon, honey," he said loudly. "Cinnamon, can you hear me?"

"I don't knows," she said. "Speak up a bit."

Vladimir nodded and drew a breath as if to yell, but I poked him and shook my head. "Oh!" he said. "That wasn't nice. Cinnamon, do you need a safety cage?"

Cinnamon clenched her fists, staring at them, then nodded.

"We have one in the basement," Vladimir said.

"No, we don't," Fremont said, horrified. "Marian Joyce was complaining it was cramped so . . . I'm having it replaced."

"You're WHAT?" Vladimir said, clearly angry.

"Classes don't start until Friday," Fremont said, eyes frozen on Cinnamon. "The new one is going in this weekend. I didn't think—"

"No, you didn't," Vladimir snapped.

"How could I have known?" she cried. "The next full moon isn't for, what, a week?"

"It isn't *legal* to offer an extraordinary needs program to a werekin without a safety cage on site, full moon or no," he said. "We'll have to tell Cinnamon *and* Marion not to come in on Friday, and how will *that* go over with Miss Frost, much less the Joyces—"

"Stop fighting stop fighting *stop fighting*," Cinnamon said softly, and Vladimir and Fremont both shut up. "For the love, *keep quiet*."

We all froze. Cinnamon's little fists were trembling, and I swallowed as a tiny bit of blood beaded in the clench of her hands. But her shaking subsided, her fur faded, and her whiskers slowly drew back in.

"Mom, take me home," Cinnamon said. "We gots to go. Take me home *please*."

"Of course, Cinnamon," I said, putting my hand gently on her shoulder and handing her a wet wipe. I always carried them. Werekin blood, even a scratch, had to be cleaned up. I gave Fremont and Yonas an apologetic word and ushered Cinnamon out. In moments we were stepping through the doors onto the setting sun, and I sighed: this place *was* beautiful.

"Wait," Vladimir wheezed, running (well, limping) up behind us. "Whoo. Ah, wait, please wait," he said, holding up the folder. "I don't want to hold you up, but, please. We would love to have Cinnamon as a student at the Clairmont Academy."

"Doctor Vladimir, I'm Cinnamon's guardian," I said. Actually, we were still working through the adoption, but as far as the law was concerned I was still legally responsible for a werekin minor. "I don't want to get sued, or, God forbid, go to jail if something happens—"

"I'm sure we can make adequate arrangements before classes start."

"Oh, gimme that," I said, taking the folder and handing it to Cinnamon, who cried with delight. "Cinnamon would love to be a student at the Clairmont Academy."

"Thank you thank you thank you!" Cinnamon said. "We—*ah!*" And then she raised a hand to her cheek, felt her whiskers, and said meekly. "We gots to go."

We got in the car and drove off.

"Well, that went—are you OK?" I said. "Are you going to make it?"

"Just drive," she said, leaning back in the seat, eyes closed, holding the folder tightly in her hands. "Just get me home."

"Damnit, we still need to go by a pet store," I said. Cinnamon snarled at the word 'pet', and I winced, but we still needed to go. I had planned a real safety room in the house we were buying, but the closing was on hold until the Valentine Foundation actually started coughing up the payments they owed me. We still didn't have a cage at the apartment; we'd been planning to go get one this evening. "We've put this off too long—"

"Forget it," Cinnamon said with a growl, leaping between the seats to land in the back, tail thwacking me in the face as she went. "Take me home. Lock me in the bathroom."

"That's too small," I said.

"You *wants* me to tear up your bedsheets?" she said, a growl growing in her voice.

I glanced back: she was on all fours, eyes glowing, pupils oval and staring at something ahead of me. I turned—and slammed the brakes before I rammed the car stopped in front of me.

"Jesus!" I said, as the Prius squealed to a stop amidst a chorus of angry horns. Ahead, on Clairmont road, early evening traffic stretched off in an endless line of red taillights. I could see a distant blue flashing light, complete with a knot of rubberneckers. "Fuck! This is *not* fair—"

And then a low, gut churning growl rumbled through the Prius.

Swallowing, I carefully reached up and adjusted the rear-view mirror, and stared straight into the yellow eyes of a huge tiger. Cinnamon was snarling, nose wrinkled, eyes oval against the sun. The steel collar about her throat had become chokingly tight as her body swelled, and she tugged at it with a paw broad enough to claw my face off.

She seemed to fill the entire back seat with fur and rage. I'd never seen her like this: real tigers had nothing on the werekind. She was absolutely terrifying. But oddly, the threat of messy death was not the first thing on my mind.

That horrible paw raised again to tug at the collar, and I said sharply, "Cinnamon Frost! Stop messing with that, you'll pull out a claw."

She snarled, then roared at me, a fearsome sound that stung my ears and reverberated in my gut.

I blinked—I couldn't *not* blink at that sound—but did not flinch. She reached to claw at the collar again, and I got worried. "Are you choking?"

The tiger's eyes tightened, its nose wrinkled up, and I could see huge fangs in the rearview as she flinched back. But among all that, I saw the head twitch . . . in a clear no.

"Good," I said. My right ear hurt, and the steering wheel creaked under my grip, but it stopped my hands from shaking. "We'll get Saffron to fit you with a larger one. I don't want you choking, but I don't want some vamp tearing into you because you're not wearing her collar."

Cinnamon snarled again, striking the back of the seat with that paw so hard I felt the seat squeak. The car rocked under the blow; I understood her strength, but where was she getting the *mass* to shake a ton and a half of plastic and metal? The steering wheel grew damp under my death grip, but I didn't turn, didn't back down, didn't give her any reason to strike.

"If I can find a p—" *don't say pet,* **don't** *say pet* "—a . . . store," I said slowly, swallowing as her crackling snarl rippled through the car, "can you wait in the car until I purchase a cage?"

The tiger lowered her head, shaking it. A definite no.

"Great, wonderful," I said. But I had an idea, and pulled out of the traffic to the left into a nearby driveway so we could turn around. "Don't worry, Cinnamon," I said, reaching up to put the gearshift into reverse; when I did so, my hand was trembling. "I know what to do."

Only when my hand was calm did I flick the Prius in reverse, put my hand on its seat, and look over my shoulder to back up, coming face to face with Cinnamon's tiger form. Her head was big enough to bite mine off, her body was twisted in rage, her claws were raking the seat—but her voice was mewling in terror, and the human in her eyes was wide and pleading.

"All right," I said, backing out. "No choice. We go to the werehouse."

9. JASMINE AND STEEL

The entrance to the Oakdale Werehouse was hidden away on one of South Atlanta Road's tiny tributaries, a dumpy dirt road hooking off into the forest. Past the bend, almost hidden behind heaped jasmine vines, was a narrow gravel driveway. A NO TRESPASSING sign warned away humans; a triangle of magical runes scared off Edgeworlders.

And to stop the determined driving their Priuses, a simple chain hung over the drive.

I saw it almost too late and slammed on the brakes. The Prius noisily slid forward on the gravel, stopping just shy of dinging her nose on the chain.

Nervously, I glanced back, but Cinnamon did not stir beneath the white hospital blanket I'd thrown over her to hide her from prying eyes. Only the deep sound of her breathing betrayed any clues about exactly what made the lumps beneath its white folds.

I got out. The werewolf defenses were simple: anyone stupid enough to walk the drive would be isolated from their vehicle, easy pickings. But I had no intention of playing their game. I just stepped up to the chain, concentrated, and murmured: "Image of tooth: clear my path."

The snake tattoo on my left wrist came to life, reared, and struck the chain. It parted with a sudden bang, slipping to the ground with a quiet rattle of its own. "Thanks, my trusty serpent," I murmured, stroking the glowing phantom with my free hand as it merged back into my flesh.

Then I hopped back in, started her up, and shot us down the drive.

The sun was still up, barely, which meant we wouldn't be dealing with the werehouse's nighttime guardians, the vampires of the Oakdale Clan. This was not good news: I was on good terms with Oakdale, mostly through Revenance and his friend and maker, Calaphase.

Then it hit me. I was going to have to break the news to him once dark fell.

I was so distracted by the thought, I almost ran over one of the werehouse's daytime guardians as he stepped in front of me to bar the road. He was an older man with a wild iron-grey beard. He played a good ol' boy in a worn woodsman's jacket, but beneath his black fedora, glinting eyes screamed werekin.

He cried something I couldn't hear over the rattle of the road, thwacking his walking stick at me as if I was going to stop—then leapt nimbly aside when I didn't, mouthing a curse as the Prius skidded to a stop beside him. He shoved bushes aside with his staff and squeezed over to my window, but I'd already rolled it down and didn't give him a chance to tell us to 'git.'

"I've got a werekin turning in the back," I said, and then, when he opened his mouth to object, I amplified, "It's Cinnamon—Stray. She needs your safety cage. Where do I take her?"

The man stared briefly, then cursed again, whipping out a cell phone. "Go to the upper loading dock," he snapped, thumbing a button and jamming the phone into his ear. "Not the lower one. You can back right in. Chris? This is Fischer. We got two comin' in, one for the safety cage and her handler. Yeah, it's Stray and her bitch Frost."

And then he glared down at me. "What are you waiting for? Go!"

I put her in gear and trundled down the rest of what they called a road. The smell was awful; there had to be a sewage treatment plant or something somewhere nearby, and I couldn't imagine how the werekin stood it. I rolled up my window just as the road shot through the chain-link fence and ended in the cracked parking lot of the werehouse.

Once it had been an ironworks on the banks of the Chattahoochee, but a fire had taken half the complex, leaving graffiti-covered hulks. I rolled forward, trying to get my bearings; the last time I'd been here had been at night, on foot, approaching from the other end.

I was starting to feel lost when a youngish blond boy, little older than Cinnamon, ran out of one of the least bombed looking buildings. Even from a distance his eyes glittered green. He waved towards a roll-up entrance door, and I whipped the car around and backed it in.

The Prius slid backwards through the door into darkness, and the view through its backup monitor was not enough. Once again I threw my arm over the seat to guide myself. Through the car's wide windows I saw the huge space swallowing us up, a giant box barely lit by dying light slipping in through stained skylights. Then we were in and stopped, and the boy ran through the door, hit the button and dropped the roll-up, and only then, as the light faded in its groaning descent, did I reach back and begin to pull aside the blanket to check on Cinnamon.

She was in human form again, sleeping in a little curled ball, tail coiled around her so she looked more like a housecat than a tiger, even with her tattooed stripes. For a moment, I marveled at her marks: the Marquis did artistic, masterly work, legal or no. But then I saw her new school clothes: shredded, practically destroyed, just like the upholstery and lining of the Prius's cargo area. She had not been gentle. She would be crushed.

"Cinnamon," I whispered. "Wake up. We're here."

She just moaned and shifted in her sleep.

I got out of the car and the blond boy stepped up beside me, fidgeting. He looked to be a werewolf, though it was hard to tell: he wasn't as far gone as Cinnamon.

"Is that Str—is that Cin?" he asked, sniffing, peering into the car. "What gots to her? Is she all right?"

"Yes, it's Cinnamon, and she changed early. I'm sure she'll be all right," I said, patting his shoulder. "Don't worry—and you get points for not calling her Stray."

I opened the trunk, thoughtlessly exposing Cinnamon's curled form, and the boy's green eyes widened, drinking her naked body in the way only a teenaged boy's eyes can. "Whoa."

"You just lost those points," I snapped, pulling Mom's death-blanket over her. Really, I was more angry with myself; what kind of mom was I to have exposed Cinnamon like that? Adopting a teen had left me missing a whole lifetime of mom reflexes I was just now learning.

"Tully!" a sharp voice said. "You preps the room. I'll tend to the stray."

Tully's eyes widened again, fearful, and he darted off. I tucked Cinnamon into the blanket, picked her up, and turned to find myself facing a sharp-featured man with severe glasses and even more severely cut red hair. His clothes looked almost normal: a navy turtleneck and brown jacket, almost like a businessman. But his eyes were wrong, the pupils . . . off. Too wide, almost horizontal slits. He could pass for human. But just barely.

"Here," the werekin said, reaching as if to take Cinnamon from me and scowling as I made no move. Instead I just straightened, looking down at him, and the werestag reassessed. "Krishna Gettyson, day captain for the werehouse."

"Dakota Frost, Cinnamon's mother," I said, picking a hand out of the blanket and extending it to him awkwardly. "Thanks for taking us in. This was a real emergency."

"You aren't the stray's mother," Gettyson snapped. His eyes flicked sideways to the car. "And you gots no idea how to take care of a were."

"Well, I'll have to learn," I said, meeting his eerie gaze. "And she goes by Cinnamon."

He just frowned at me, then cried, "Tully! Where's the wheelchair?"

"I can carry her," I said. "She's light as a feather."

"You're an outsider," Gettyson said flatly. "You shouldn't even be here, and I sure as hell don't intends to let you into the dens."

"I'll carry her there myself and watch over her, or we'll go elsewhere," I said.

"I won't let you," Gettyson said.

"You think you can stop me? Mother. Cub. Do the math," I said, and Gettyson tensed.

"Dakota," purred a warm, masculine voice, smooth as silk. "How good to see you."

A stern pale man stepped out of the darkness. A long-tailed coat clung to his trim form, and a glittering chain dangled from the pocket of his vest, but the overall effect was high style, not old fashioned. His once-frosted locks were now wavy and styled, but against his ivory-pale skin, his blond hair looked almost brown, and his blue eyes almost seemed to glow.

Or perhaps they did glow. He was Calaphase the vampire, head of the Oakdale Clan, my second-best ally in the werehouse . . . and Revenance's best friend.

"Gettyson," Calaphase said, smiling icily. Clearly the status of the Oakdale Clan had risen with the werekin. Last time I'd been here, Calaphase had been walking on thin ice, but now there was an edge in his voice as he warned the werestag off. "I'm sure we can bend the rules for Dakota—"

"That's a bad idea," Gettyson said. "Every time we brings in an outsider—"

"You said the same about me," Calaphase said. "But haven't we proven our worth?"

As he talked, I realized this is how things started first time I met him. Calaphase had shielded me from his fellow vampire Transomnia, ultimately kicking him out of the clan. For his shame, Transomnia had beaten me and nearly murdered Cinnamon. Not again.

"No," I said. "Wait, Cally. I screwed up. Gettyson, I came here for help and then turned into an ass." Oddly, Gettyson's nostrils flared at 'ass.' How had that offended him? "I'm sorry. I just get protective about Cinnamon. Not too long ago, someone tried to kill her."

Gettyson just stood there, jaw clenched, and then I realized what pile I might have just stepped in: perhaps he wasn't a werestag. So I decided to risk one step further. "And if you're a were-donkey or something, sorry about the 'ass' comment. I didn't know."

"Werehorse," Gettyson said curtly. "There's no such things as were-donkeys."

My mouth opened to correct him: from what I'd learned in school, you could make a werekin out of anything with a genome. Then I shut my mouth—there was no point in getting into an argument with him about his beliefs.

"My apologies," I managed finally. "I've never met a . . . a werehorse."

Gettyson's nostrils flared, but he nodded as Tully pushed up a wheelchair, stopping just out of reach of Gettyson's arm. "Apology accepted," Gettyson said, in a tone that clearly indicated that it wasn't accepted. "But no exceptions, and no outsiders in the dens."

I didn't even have to think through it: I knew what waking up here alone would do to Cinnamon. "Then we go somewhere else," I said. "Cinnamon has abandonment issues. I have to be there when she wakes up, or she'll think I'm trying to get rid of her—"

"Bull," Gettyson said. "She knows you wants her in your entourage."

"She is wanted, but she's not in my 'entourage'," I said.

Gettyson reached in and grabbed Cinnamon's hand, showing me the butterfly that I'd transferred to her skin the very first time I met her. "So why did you mark her?"

"Maybe the Marquis 'marked' her when he took her in because all he wanted a canvas," I said, "but I don't do things that way. First, it was a free gift, no strings attached, and second, I'd have never transferred it if I'd known she was so young. Tattooing minors is illegal."

"Illegal?" Gettyson laughed, looking at me incredulously. He turned away, shaking his head. "Illegal. Of all the crazy—all right, all right. Set her down."

"I can carry her," I repeated quietly. "She's light as a feather."

Calaphase smiled again. "Give it up, Gettyson," he said gently. "She's the only person I know more obstinate than you, you old were-mule."

Gettyson just stared at me with those eerie eyes, as if he expected me to crack. His gaze drifted up and down, at Cinnamon, then my face, then my feet, then my face again.

"She's not getting any heavier from you looking at her," I said.

Gettyson snorted. "You can take her in, stay till she wakes. But that's it," he said firmly. "The moon will be damn near full before it sets. You gots to be gone before it gets too close."

I sighed. He wasn't just determined to be an ass, he had a point. "Fair enough."

Gettyson nodded and led us towards the back of the werehouse, into the stack of offices and labs that had been converted into living space. There was no need of worry, they were just rooms and hallways, dirty, poorly lit—and covered with graffiti.

I paused, staring at the dark, spray painted marks. Some of the lettering looked familiar, but they had little of the artistry and none of the movement of the tag that had killed Revenance. I shook my head, and descended the stairs into the depths of the werehouse dens.

Beneath a dim bulb in a damp hallway was a wall of bars with a steel mesh door, locked with a deadbolt. Immediately I could see that it would keep in an animal with just paws, but a human could put his hand through the bars and let himself out. Gettyson opened the lock with a snap and took us in to a small cell with a cot and chair. It was surprisingly cozy.

I laid Cinnamon down on the bed gently and arranged the blanket over her.

"If you have any clothes for her—"

"I'll get some," Gettyson said. "You needs to get a room like this."

"We're having it built," I said, patting Cinnamon's head. "In the new house."

"Fine," Gettyson said. "When . . . Cinnamon wakes, it would help me if you'd vacate. She knows how to let herself out, but the other residents won't take too well if they finds you in here."

"I'm all right, Mom," Cinnamon said weakly, and I looked down to see her reach up and squeeze my hand. "It just had been so long. I'll be all right. Someday, when I'm old enough to wrestle the beast myself, I won't need these stupid rooms anyways."

"You had me worried back there," I said, tousling her hair.

"Afraid I was going to slit your throat?"

"No, afraid you'd step on your iPod," I said, holding it out to her. "Safe and sound."

Cinnamon took it from me, holding it to her chest like a teddy bear. "Safe and sound."

It killed me to ask, but . . . "Are you sure you'll be safe with it if you turn?"

"It's 'change'," Cinnamon said, pointing with one long finger at a cubbyhole beside the bed, "and there's a change safe. Easy to drop in, hard to paw out."

"All right," I said. Clearly they'd thought this through better than I had. But still, it was terrible to think of my baby all alone here. "You know what? Fuck this. I'm going to stay—"

"No, Mom," Cinnamon said. "Gettyson's right. The others—they won't like it."

I smiled. "So scratch me, we'll fix that right up."

"Mommm!" Cinnamon said, sitting up in the bed. Immediately she winced and lay back down slowly, gingerly, like she was an old woman. "Don't even joke—ow. Ow. Owsies. Don't even joke about it. Lycanthropy sucks, I can tell you that."

"Muscle spasms?" I guessed, helping her sink back into the bed and pulling the covers back up. "Want me to see if Gettyson has any aspirin?"

She cocked her head, ears flicking. "Ibuprofen's better. He's gettin' it."

I leaned back slowly. "Never underestimate a werekin's hearing," I murmured.

"Mom, 's OK," Cinnamon said, very softly. She was fading fast. "This was my room, this time of the month. Sometimes I just hangs here. You go. You do what you gots to. For Revy."

I had been trying to forget my next unpleasant task. "I will," I said, squeezing her hand. "You be safe, sweet—" But she was already snoring.

And she was right. I was putting it off. It was time to break the news to Calaphase.

Time to tell a vampire I'd failed to save his best friend.

10.   CALAPHASE

I looked up to see Calaphase standing by the door, smiling closemouthed. "Gettyson's right," he said. "Cinnamon knows how to let herself out, but the other weres won't want you back in the den unsupervised, and neither I nor Gettyson can hang here all night with you."

I stared at the trim, rakish vampire, far upgraded from the goth-punk I'd first met. I avoided his eyes, and not just because he was a vampire: he reminded me of my failure.

"Right," I said. I frowned. Calaphase had turned out quite decent for a vampire, but I didn't know how he was going to take this. "Calaphase, can we take a little walk? There's something I need to talk to you about—about

Revenance."

Calaphase's eyes widened and his nostrils flared, but he kept his voice quiet. "Not here. Outside," he whispered. Then he shook his head and hissed, exposing his fangs. "*Damnit.*"

I squeezed Cinnamon's hand one more time and left.

Tully met us as we were leaving the cages. "Sir?" Tully said nervously.

"What is it?" Calaphase said, not pausing as he tromped up the stairs. "I'm busy."

"They hit us *again*," Tully said, backing up as Calaphase advanced. The young werewolf looked scared and *really* unhappy. "Right under my nose. I wants to tell Gettyson but—"

"I'll tell him," Calaphase said crisply. "Go clean it up."

"Don't you wants to see it?" Tully asked. "They hit us really good, I mean, *pieced* us—"

"No, I don't want to see it," Calaphase snarled, and Tully flinched. "I'm done with that. Buff it over. I'll tell Gettyson you're doing it. Maybe it will save you a beating."

"Yes, sir," Tully said, deflated.

"What was that about?" I asked, a bit nervously. I was dreading this conversation, and wanted to talk about anything else. "What does 'pieced'—"

"Vandalism," Calaphase said sharply. "You'd think no werekin would be fool enough to do it, and no human skilled enough. But they've hit us again and again."

"You're worried about vandalism?" I asked. "*Here?*"

Calaphase glared back at me, a blue glint in his eyes that was more than just anger: it was his vampire aura, bleeding out into the air. "You think this place should look *more* shitty?"

"No," I said, ashamed. I was *definitely* dreading this conversation now.

We emerged into the barren cavern of the werehouse. The last time I was here, it had been filled to the rafters with drums and fires and sweaty werekin and presided over by the monstrous lord of the werehouse, the Bear King. Lord Buckhead, the ageless fae sprit behind the wild revelry of Atlanta's eponymous party district, had stood as my guardian when, before the hungry eyes of the crowd, I dueled another tattooist for the right to ink a werewolf. And a young stray werecat girl followed me home . . . and had rarely left my side since.

Now, robbed of its heat and light, it just looked . . . decrepit. In the perverse gloom of the few shafts of twilight leaking in, even the huge metal throne of the Bear King lost its charm and looked like a pile of old Cadillac parts. Only the upper decks of the living quarters seemed the same: as before, they were filled with cold, inhuman eyes . . . staring, and waiting. I swallowed. Cinnamon could easily have been among those hungry eyes. Gettyson was checking a clipboard when he saw me, then jerked his hand, *out!* Not wanting to look back at those hungry eyes, I hurried to keep up with Calaphase. The vampire checked his pocket watch, then kicked the door open savagely, flinging it open onto the twilight with a tortured squeal of rusty hinges.

As I followed, Gettyson called after me. "Frost, I—go on, get it done, cub," he said, idly cuffing Tully behind the ear as the boy walked past with a can of house paint. "I wants the whole thing wiped. Anyways, Frost, you did good bringing her here. We'll take good care of her."

"I'm sure you will," I said, exchanging a sympathetic glance with Tully before following Calaphase out. Like the other werekin, his eyes were still hungry, but when not shrouded by fear and darkness, that glance looked less like hunger for flesh and more like longing for a normal life. I'd seen that look before. "But I'll be back to be certain."

The door screamed shut in a sudden gust of wind, and I was alone with a vampire underneath the darkening sky. Calaphase didn't seem to notice the sudden cold; he just kept walking, heels cracking against the pavement as he led us away from the werehouse, out onto a tongue of concrete that jutted out over the lower level of the parking lot like a pier. I followed the vampire uncomfortably, not sure whether I was really scared of being alone with him at night, or just filled with willies over having once again to be bearer of the bad news.

"Tell me," Calaphase said, staring into the distance, silhouetted against orange twilight.

I told him about Revy's death—as many details as I thought he could bear.

"That's . . . horrible," Calaphase said at last, still staring into the distance.

"Yes, it was," I said.

"Revy was my first, you know," Calaphase said. "The first vampire I ever made. This is like . . . like losing a child. No, this is worse; a child can't do for you what Revy did for me."

"I'm sorry," I said flatly. I sympathized, though I didn't approve—

"I've never killed anyone, you know that?" Calaphase said, turning back to me, grim. "Never. Not even my master. Revy did that. *He* freed me. He made it possible for me, for the whole Oakdale Clan, to be something different. Even this shit job, guarding this dump . . . Revenance made it possible. Werekin normally *hate* vamps, but at least here, Revenance changed that. He really cared about them, especially the cubs. I owed him *everything*."

He snarled and kicked a tire brake lying on the end of the dock; the rotted rubber triangle flew out over the parking lot and disappeared into the darkness.

I stared at him in shock. I never expected to scratch a vampire lord and find so many layers underneath. I'd never asked about the relationship Revenance had with Calaphase, and now I found it was most important relationship in his life.

And Revenance himself? I'd thought of him as just a second banana in a vampire gang—but to hear Calaphase tell it, Revenance had been a man of insight, protector of the werehouse's feral children, perhaps even a protector of Cinnamon.

I was taking people for granted a lot lately. When did I become such an insensitive bitch?

I stepped up beside him, cautiously, deliberately grinding my boots against the pavement so my touch would not be a surprise. "Hey," I said, rubbing the arm of his jacket. Unlike Saffron, his flesh was cold. "That's OK. There's nothing you could have done—"

And then an awful scream rent the air.

"Oh hell," Calaphase said, whirling. "Not again."

We leapt down from the concrete pier, my knee immediately throbbing with pain. Calaphase ran like the wind, me, somewhat less so; but I managed to keep him in sight as he curled round the lower side of the werehouse's main building and then stopped.

"Help, help, it *gots me*," someone screamed—familiar—the boy *Tully?*

I wheezed and skidded round the corner and stopped next to Calaphase in shock.

Paint cans—whitewash—were spilled about; half of it had already gone to cover a huge graffiti tag on the wall. But beneath the white paint something thick squirmed and bubbled—and where the paint ended, coiling tentacles twisted into the air, pulling hard at Tully, who was pinned on the wall by a massive band of graffiti about his chest.

"Don't worry, we'll get you out," Calaphase was saying, picking up a long handled paint roller and holding it out to Tully like a lifeline. The boy grabbed for it, but a coiling tentacle reached out and snapped the handle in two—*and then reached for Calaphase.*

I jerked him back just as a dozen tentacles whipped out and snatched through the space where he'd been standing. Unbalanced, Calaphase tumbled backward into the mud with a curse, eyes glowing. "Fuck!" he said. "What the fuck is wrong with you, Dakota—"

But I'd already turned my back on him. "You know what's wrong," I said, eyes running over the curving lines, the tombstones, the grassy hillside, the familiar wildstyle letters. *They 'pieced' us*—a 'piece'—oh, I am *such* an *idiot.* "You know exactly what is wrong."

Behind me, Calaphase scrambled to his feet, but I held out my hand sharply to bar his path. He cursed, but didn't try to pass me. "We've got to get him out of there."

"If we can," I said. "That tag is just like the one that killed Revenance."

11.   A THANKLESS JOB

"No vampires," I said, shoving yet another of Calaphase's guards back behind the line I'd drawn in the pavement. "It seems to like you guys. Talk to me, Calaphase. You said again."

"We heard a scream last night," Calaphase said, staring at Tully, pinned within the tag. "Sounded like Josephine, a panther who ran with one of our transients. I sent Revy into the Underground to check on her—"

"The Underground?" I asked. It was a series of ancient tunnels honeycombing the central part of Atlanta, but I had no idea it stretched almost all the way out here, nearly to the Perimeter. "There are entrances to the Underground in *Oakdale?*"

"Oh, yes," Calaphase said. "Don't try to find the ones out here, the werekin use them as escape routes and they're . . . protective of that territory.

Revy went into the Underground, but never came back. I thought he was waiting for dark, until you showed up with the news."

I tried to remember whether there was an entrance to the Underground near Oakland Cemetery. Then I noticed the sharp, questioning glance of a vampire guard, a striking man with a thundercloud of dark curly hair rising over his bushy eyebrows, and I explained, "Revenance died in a tag just like this one on the other side of town."

"Something like *that* killed Revenance?" the guard said, in a reedy, deliberate European accent which was hard to place. He returned his piercing gaze to the squealing tag and the crowd of werekin who were splashing paint on it—no longer just whitewashing it, but covering it with as many colors as they could find. "Really, *killed* by that *scrawl*—"

"Yes, *really*," I snapped, "and I won't have any more of you dead on my watch!"

Calaphase stood, scowling behind the line, as more of his crew firmed up around him. "Some guardians we are," he said bitterly, hands jammed in his pockets. "Can't even protect our clients from a can of *paint*. Think we could get a pole, lever him out of there?"

I glared at the serrated band of graffiti on Tully's chest. "It might cut him in two."

"*Jesus!*" Fischer shouted, leaping back as part of the tag ripped out from beneath the paint and snatched at him. His hat came off as he danced back out of reach, and the barbed tentacle sliced it in half. Fischer kept going, stumbling back over the line without ever fully losing his balance. An ugly scar was torn in his woodsman's jacket, top to bottom, and he stared at it, then me, his wide eyes even more shocking against his worn, seasoned face.

"This isn't working," Gettyson said, hands on his hips, watching another tentacle ripping out of a splash of paint just thrown by a were. "You hears me, Frost? This isn't working."

"It was worth a try," I replied, thinking furiously. I'd warned him how dangerous the last tag was, and after a quick conference we'd decided to whitewash the rest of this one. But the graffiti tentacles were squirming out of the wet paint. "At least it's slowing it down."

"Slowing it down?" Gettyson said. His creepy wide pupils seemed *made* to deliver scorn. "This thing's cutting him to pieces! *You're* the magician—gimme a damn plan!"

"I'm working on it," I snapped. *What could I do?* The splashed paint had cut the exposed area of the tag by half, but it wasn't enough: the tag was struggling out of its Jackson Pollock coating, and the free parts were alive and vicious. My tattoos weren't strong enough to hold this thing off. I glared at the tag, its geometry, at the pavement beneath it. Once again, I wished I'd finished my degree, rather than dropping out after I'd learned enough magic . . . to tattoo . . .

"Rock salt," I said.

"What?" Gettyson said, blank.

"You got a kitchen?" I asked. "A real, human, fully-stocked kitchen? I need rock salt. And cane sugar, ginger, cinnamon-the-spice, basil. As much of all of that as you got. Any of your kids like crafts? I need chalk and glitter—and *play sand*, if you've got it—"

"What the hell are you planning?" Gettyson said.

"'Give me a place to stand, and I can move the world,'" I said. "I'm going to build a magic circle, and use the tag's own magic against it. Now move!"

As the remaining weres and vamps scattered across the grounds, I surveyed the ground in front of Tully carefully. The pavement was cracked, weedgrown, but basically whole, and there was just enough area for what I planned to do. I cocked my head: yes. Yes. I *could* do this. Then Tully cried out in pain, and I looked up at him. Then I was certain: I *would* do this.

Gettyson returned with bowls, cinnamon, and a big box of Kosher salt. "Will this do?"

"It's a start," I said, tasting the Kosher salt, then dumping it and the cinnamon into the bowl. "More cinnamon. This will work as a conductor, but the circle will need a magical capacitor. I'll need basil and cane sugar if we don't have sand—"

"I found sand," the curly-haired vamp guard said, seeming to have popped out of nowhere with a sack over his shoulder and an oddly pleased grin on his oddly worn face. "*Liberated* it from a nearby factory. I'm sure they won't mind."

"What kind is it, play sand?" I asked, tearing at the package. "Quartz granules? Good."

In minutes the plan was taking shape, both in my head and reality. I sent Gettyson to get more bowls and started two mixes, one with Kosher salt, cinnamon and sand for the circle, and a second with the basil flakes and sugar. But we still were short ingredients, still had no chalk—and had long since run out of paint, while the graffiti was just getting stronger and stronger.

Tully screamed, pulled tight against the wall, barbed tentacles coiled diagonally around his chest, half metal octopus, half sadistic rosevine. If the whole thing had been exposed, it would have spreadeagled him and started tearing him apart; as it was the tentacles slid evilly, cutting across his chest, into his flesh, oozing blood.

I closed my eyes, then opened them again, trying to see past the anger and really look at the tag. I had thought it the same, but really, it was similar without being identical: same general logic, same layout, but different motifs. There was a central coiling mandala, but it was barbed wire octopus rather than a rose. The octopus's feelers were woven with masonry, but this time stone columns rather than brick. There was a semicircle behind it, but this time a planet rather than a hillside. And the cityscape was replaced by a forest. Even the brushstrokes were different. The more I looked, the more certain I became: this tag was from the same series as the one that killed Revenance, but it wasn't by the same hand.

The graffiti hadn't been inked by one artist. The bastards had a whole crew.

Tully screamed again. The vines had started sawing into his flesh, dripping a diagonal curtain of blood. It was killing him slowly, almost sadistically; but it was still killing him. This was no time to dither; we had to get him out of that thing now.

I gritted my teeth, stripped off my vestcoat, and handed it without thinking to Calaphase's curly-haired guard. When I pulled off my turtleneck, I could see he was glaring at me.

"What *good* do you expect a *striptease* will do?" he said, his deliberate emphasis now sounding like menace, his strange eyes slitted at the vest and shirt I'd dumped in his hands.

"I'm a skindancer," I said, unzipping my chaps, and now, rather than being embarrassed, I relished the sudden raise of his bushy eyebrows. "I expect it will do a great deal of good."

Just then there was a rushing of air and suddenly Calaphase and another guard popped out of the darkness, with four bags worth of groceries from Kroger.

"Honey, I'm home," Calaphase said, smiling as he saw me undressing— and then his smile faded when he saw Tully. "Hell, it's killing him—"

"I know, but *damn*, that was fast," I said. "I didn't think vampires could really fly."

"We can run," Calaphase said. "And I *think* we found almost everything you needed."

"Great," I said, pawing through the bags. Chalk, cinnamon, rock salt, more Kosher salt—and *fresh basil*—in *January*. I pulled out a twig and twirled it: *perfect*. "Let's get cooking."

"*I* often cooked with cinnamon, basil, and salt, back when I was alive," the curly-headed vamp said, watching me mix. "And those ingredients never did anything special but *stew*."

"You're as alive as I am," I retorted, not looking up, "and iron filings won't do anything special but rust—until you add a magnetic field. Then they line up like soldiers."

"You expect me to believe *basil* is *magnetic*?" Curly asked.

"No," I said, "but I expect to show it's magically active—if you know how to unlock it."

I finished the basil mix, said a small prayer over the bowl, picked it up, and then stepped up to the right side of the tag, where it was completely coated with paint. Against the dirty back wall of the werehouse, beneath the many splashes of color, thick cables writhed and bubbled. One had nearly torn itself free, but it did not strike; and so I got almost close enough to touch.

"I cannot wait to see," the vamp guard said, "the magic of *Julia Child*."

"Showing your age, Curly," I said, scooping a fistful of coated basil sprigs. "Me, I prefer Alton Brown, but for this job, you need a little Emeril—*BAM!*"

And I tossed the sprigs out through the air, where their coatings absorbed stray mana, discharging it into the leaves until they glittered like feathers of blue flame. They cascaded down the wall, some sticking, some falling, and collected on the pavement in an odd hexagonal pattern that clearly didn't look random. Magical energy flickered across the pattern each time the tag stirred beneath the paint, and it began to get more sluggish. Even the tentacle that was tearing itself free started to go limp . . . and then sank back into the paint.

"You did it!" the vampire said, leaping forward to grab Tully.

"No!" I shouted, shooting my free hand forth in a sinuous motion. Mana rippled through my skin and one of my vines leapt off my skin like a green glowing whip, faster than even I'd expected. It caught the vampire on the chest and flung him back just as three barbed tentacles tore free from the wall and struck where he would have landed. The momentum rippled back along my glowing vine and near tore my arm out of its socket, knocking me forward, down to the pavement on my already throbbing knee. I cried out in pain—and looked up to see the three tentacles, right above my face, turning slowly towards me.

I hurled the rest of the bowl at them and scrambled back. The tentacles cracked to the pavement where I had lain, batting the remaining bowl aside with a KHWANGG, scattering basil everywhere. The herbs lit up like blue flame, as before, but without the protective barrier of paint diffusing the flow of mana between them and the tag, the basil sprigs turned to real flames.

In seconds, my magic mix disintegrated in a cloud of sparks.

---

12.   THIS WILL BE A BIT TRICKY

"Damnit," I cried. I retrieved the overturned bowls. I'd lost almost all of the mix, save a few scraps left in the bottom of the bowl the tag had struck. All the rest was sprayed out over the dirt and in the grassy cracks through the pavement, ruined. I glared up at the vamp, who lay half sprawled in Calaphase and Fischer's arms. "*Asshole!*"

The vamp's hazel eyes glowed. "I tried to *save* him, and you *insult* me?" he said, trying to regain his footing. "In Lithuania I stood in the Gentry! No mortal speaks to me that way!"

I crouched, hooked my right foot behind my left, and stood back upright, twisting like a corkscrew as I did so. Mana built up in my skin and brought it to life, bursting my vines outward and making every gem on my body sparkle and every flower unfurl. The shimmering light burst onto the clearing in a rainbow of colors, washing all natural color from the vamps and weres and leaving their faces pale circles of shock.

"I don't care what country club you were in. This *ain't* Lithuania," I growled. "Now stay back, or this thing will kill you too dead to hear this mortal tell you what an *idiot* you are."

I twisted round, expanding my vines, recreating my glowing shield. "I'm coming for you, Tully," I said, stepping straight towards him slowly. "But this will be a bit tricky."

The tag's free tentacles snapped and bit at me, uselessly, then folded back on Tully, clenching on him. He screamed—but his eyes were on me and he nodded. Behind him the planet motif shimmered, eerily real; through some trick of perspective it almost looked like the tag's tentacles were pulling him into the wall, towards it. There was a cracking sound, and I looked over to see ugly lumps begin to form at the base of the wall, beneath the splashes of paint. Tombstones, no doubt—the only element in Revenance's tag that had been missing from this design. The basil and paint had suppressed the tag a little, but there was no doubt: it had the same logic as the one that killed Revenance, and was getting stronger.

I knelt and drew the first arc of a magic circle, just beyond the safety line I'd drawn earlier. The chalk broke against a crack in the pavement and I dinged my knuckle, wincing, but I didn't stop, feeling the tag writhe before me in malevolence and hearing Tully moan. Soon I had the inner rings, the layer of runes, and the outer circle that would hold what little magic powder I had left. I studied the bowl, then began picking out pinches of dust, laying them around the design, trying to stretch each little bit out so that I'd have enough left for my final trick.

Somehow, I managed to complete the circle, scraping enough out of the bowl to complete the final arc—almost, leaving one gap in front of Tully. The circle of powder looked dangerously sketchy, but it would have to do. So I poured all the dusty remains in the bowl at the edge of the gap, creating a pitiful little heap of fine powder on one end. *Too much!* The lines of the circle began glowing, like a flickering neon, as the mana it absorbed from the tag began sparking over the gap. I scooted the heap aside, and the sparking stopped. If the circle closed before we were inside, it would shove Tully and me into the tag rather than protect us from it.

Then Tully moaned again. I flung the bowl aside. There was nothing left to be done. I had to do it now. I crouched down, concentrating.

"Spirit of Earth," I murmured. *"Shield our lives."*

Then I lunged forward and threw both my arms around Tully's chest.

Tully screamed as the vines tried to saw him in half—then the *tag* squealed in rage as I wrapped Tully in a protective cocoon of mana. Tentacles flailed at me as my vines whipped around him, barbs wearing at my defenses as my trusty wrist snakes snapped at the tentacles on his chest. More tentacles curled around me, pulling me forward, *into* the wall, into the *tag*, like there was a whole world behind the paint. I felt an immense magical pressure weigh on me, like water weighs on your ears at the bottom of a pool—but I jammed my boot against the wall and shoved, hurling myself backward into the circle with Tully in my arms.

The tentacles refused to give up, wrapping around us, hot, burning, pouring mana out around us in elaborate arcs of living flame. I couldn't see anything through the blazing light. I'd like to say I used skindancing to fight it off, but I didn't. I just ground in my feet and held on to Tully for dear life, forcing the tag to expend as much mana as possible. The tentacles squeezed tighter; we both screamed in pain—

And then finally the excess mana the tag was pouring into the air closed the circle's magical circuit, like a spark leaping a gap, and Tully and I collapsed gratefully to the ground. The tentacles leapt back, wounded, and I quickly shoved the tiny pile of mix back over the gap with my boot, making sure the circuit stayed closed.

But almost immediately the protective bubble began to flicker and sparkle as the tag, squealing, renewed its attack. The clouds on the image of the planet began whirling furiously. I could see the images of tombstones cracking up through the join of the wall and the pavement, struggling to break free of their layer of paint. A horrible scream rent the air, and a dozen new tentacles whipped down on us, screaming with rage as if the tag was a living monster. It was *still* getting *stronger*—but Tully was out of the circuit!

"So much for Saffron's theory," I said.

The bubble began to crack. My mix was thin and poorly refined, and the pavement beneath us was an uneven mess; there was no way it would hold. *Fine*—I was *counting* on it. I took a deep breath, sinuously stretching within the bubble until all my vine tattoos came to life again and wrapped around Tully and me, a green glowing shield. Then I grabbed him tight.

"Hang on, Tully," I said—and leapt backwards out of the circle.

The tentacles closed on the magic bubble right as it collapsed with a bright flash. All the built up mana discharged with a bang, rippling back through the graffiti like blue lightning. As Tully and I landed, the whole tag sparked and shorted out, a brief two-dimensional fireworks display, leaving nothing but black crinkled smudges dotted with glowing red embers.

For a moment, Tully and I just lay there in the dust, staring at the intricate concentric rings that were all that was left of the design. Then we looked at each other.

"Congratulations, Tully," I said. "You get to live to run another day."

"Thank you thank you *thank you*," Tully said, trying to give me a hug, then grimacing as the gesture squeezed a new river of blood from his chest. "Aaah—I'm so sorry—"

"Thank you, Dakota," a voice said, and I looked up to see Calaphase staring down at me. The vamps and werekin were all standing over us, all looking down gratefully—except Gettyson, who just stood there, jaw clenched, before turning on his heel and stalking off.

Tully kept sobbing. "I'm so sorry, I'm so sorry, I had no idea this would happen."

"There's no way you could have known," I said.

"I means, it was just magical graffiti—"

"Wait," I said. "You *already* knew it was magical?"

"You can't miss it," Calaphase said quietly. "These tags, they're always moving—"

"Wait *wait*," I said, alarmed. "They? This has happened before?"

"An attack, no, but the tags—yes," Calaphase said, even more quietly. "We've seen tags like this for weeks, nothing this elaborate, usually just little ones, though they seem like they get bigger over time—or else the prick keeps coming back to flesh them out. Revy said he saw a huge one yesterday, though he never got to show me where. For all I know, this was it—"

"No," I said. "This thing loves vamps. If he'd gotten close to it, it would have caught him—and then how would he have ended up in the cemetery?" I asked. Then I recalled the odd sensation I'd felt in the graffiti's grip . . . like it was pulling me inside. The conclusion sounded outlandish, but was just too damn obvious to ignore. "Unless . . . that's where this one . . . led?"

But before I could go any further, Tully began convulsing in my arms.

"I gots—I gots to *change*," he said, holding his bloody hands up, staring at them, at the gash in his chest. The graffiti had dug down to the bone, exposing white flashes of ribs, and I felt my stomach churn. "I can't *heal* like this."

"Come on, cub," Fischer said, squatting down beside us, taking Tully from my arms and picking him up. "I'll carry you out to the clearing, to the light of the moon."

I got to my feet, groaning, covered in grime, dirt, blood and basil. More and more weres and vamps were gathering; the ones who had watched stood in awe, but the newcomers stared at me with cold, hungry eyes. Wonderful—I was covered in Tully-flavored barbecue sauce. Fortunately the curly-headed vamp guard was on crowd control, keeping both the weres and the vamps away from the tag.

"She's Lady Saffron's troubleshooter," he said to a new arrival, following with a glowing account of my recent duel with the graffiti. I half smiled. I wasn't Saffron's 'troubleshooter,' and it hadn't been that easy. I turned to correct him—and got a bucket of water in the face.

"Wash up, *wash up*," Gettyson said, splashing the rest of me with cold, stinging liquid, then attacking me with a towel. "You gots to get Tully's blood off you, get it *off* you."

I took the towel and began scrubbing gratefully. The fluid stank of ammonia and disinfectant and other things besides, and felt harsh against my hands. My eyes were watering from the initial splash, and my lips were actually tingling . . . surely he hadn't just splashed *wolfsbane extract* in my *face!* But then, a thin purple haze began lifting off my top, chest and shorts—not smoke, but mana, from Tully's moon-charged werekin blood—and the grateful magician in me won out over the worried chemist.

Gettyson handed me a dry towel for my face and looked me over roughly, checking my chest, my hands, under my arms. He daubed a more concentrated form of the stinging substance on a cloth and began wiping scrapes on my legs, arms, finally my forehead.

"That was from earlier," I said.

"But still," he said, frowning, wiping it clean. "You feels like you're cut anywhere?"

"No, no," I said, feeling myself up and down. "I'm good."

Gettyson seized my hand and inspected the knuckle. "That's not from earlier," he said, holding my hand firmly in the cloth and pouring the stinging fluid straight on the wound. "Keep watch on this. I don't wants you turning wolf unless *you* wants to."

"Ow. Thanks," I said, taking the bottle and cloth gratefully. He nodded, barely looking at me, his odd, slit-pupiled eyes angry and tight; not at me, but at a memory. I had a feeling *he* hadn't 'turned horse' because he wanted to.

A sudden howl rent the air, and Gettyson looked off. "Tully's changed," he said. "If he has, the other young ones will too. It's like a trigger. You gets yourself out of here."

"We don't have time for all this werekin bullshit," I said. "A tag like that killed Revenance. This one nearly killed Tully, started to drag us both *inside*. I think the different graffiti is connected somehow. I need to see the others—"

"In daylight," Gettyson said. "*After* the full moon. The last thing we needs is you here covered with the scent of blood right when we gots a crowd of wolves changing."

And then a crackling growl rippled across the pavement. I looked up to see a monstrous bear lumbering past, larger than a horse, eyeing me sideways as he planted himself at the edge of the darkness: the Bear King, leader of the werehouse, in full animal form. A young, slender wolf came up and fawned before him, but the Bear King batted at it. The wolf whined, rolling on its back, exposing its white chest marred with a ragged stripe of bloody fur; and then it looked at me with Tully's eyes. He was safe. The werehouse was a rough place, but they cared for the least of their own. And that meant, somewhere behind me in the werehouse, Cinnamon was safe too—at least while she struggled through her change.

But a thousand glowing eyes still stared at me hungrily from the darkness.

"On behalf of the werehouse, thank you," the Bear King rumbled. "Now leave us."

13. SWEET AND STICKY

Less than a quarter hour later, but seemingly a million miles away, Calaphase scowled, eyes closed, brow furrowing in pain as he took the straw of the Frappuccino from his lips. I winced in sympathy. "Is even liquid food too hard on you?"

"Yes—no," he said, kneading his brow. "Drank too fast—brain freeze."

I laughed.

The Starbucks in Vinings was in a quaint little converted house tucked into a cluster of similar shops off of Paces Ferry Road. Vinings was a full mile inside Atlanta's northeast Perimeter, but the steep hills and dense forest made it feel like a cozy mountain outpost. The café's outdoor patio was cradled in clusters of trees and bushes, and in that cradle we lounged beneath the warm light of a heating lamp—and while the vampire was trying his best to suck down the moral equivalent of a coffee Frostee in the beginning of January, I was drinking a hot chai latte and feeling it down to my toes, thank you very much.

"Why did we come all the way up here?" I asked, grinning as he put the delicious sludge down. "There's a Starbucks up South Atlanta Road, not a mile from the werehouse."

"Do you know where *all* the Starbucksen are in Atlanta?"

"Not *all* of them," I replied. "And you ducked my question. Why here?"

"One," Calaphase ticked off with his finger, "the cats here know me and blend the way I like, rather than just handing me a cup of crushed ice with coffee poured over it. And two . . . Vinings is inside the Perimeter. Safer for you."

"I wondered why you ran us down all those back roads," I said. To mundanes, the Perimeter was Interstate 285, twin ribbons of asphalt that ringed Atlanta like a black eye. To Edgeworlders, it was a mammoth magic circle, protecting the residents within from the full chaos of the magical Edgeworld. Fae battles and demon possessions didn't happen here.

At least, they didn't happen . . . much. The vampires saw to that. I tugged at my steel collar. It was the sign of Saffron's protection, but it didn't mean too much OTP—"Outside the Perimeter"—where the delicate truce established by civilized vampires broke down.

Most humans never noticed, of course, but an Edgeworlder traveling outside the safe zones had to watch her back. There were rules, as old and ancient as those governing trolls under a bridge. First and foremost, you didn't expose Edgeworlders without their permission.

That, of course, hadn't flown with Rand when I'd called in to report this new graffiti attack. He blew up at me when I refused to divulge our location, cussed me out, in language more suited to me than him. And then he hung up, on me! And rather than support me . . .

"You *can't* tell Rand where the werehouse is," Calaphase said, with quiet authority. Calaphase and I had met most often at weekly meetings at Manuel's Tavern, with Saffron and our mutual friend Jinx. My memory from Manuel's was just gleaming blue eyes flashing across the table, but close up his hair was wiry gold, his skin like polished ivory. "You know the rules."

"I know, I know," I said, still avoiding his eyes. "I won't out an Edgeworlder. But that's going to make things difficult. Someone's got to analyze the crime scene, take pictures of the tag. Secrecy will make it harder to find the bastards that killed Revenance—"

"Bastard*s*?" Calaphase asked. "Plural?"

"The tag had the same motifs as the one that killed Revenance," I said, "but not the same style. They were inked by two different people. This isn't one tagger. It's a crew."

Calaphase stared off into the distance, thinking. "This is bad," he said. "Revenance dead. Two more vamps missing, plus Josephine. And now this attack. Look, talk to your pet cop—"

"Andre Rand is not a pet," I said. "He's like an uncle. I can't believe he hung up on me."

"I can't either, Dakota, but *call him back*," Calaphase said, again with quiet authority. "We've got to investigate this, but we can't lead cops to the werehouse. Rand will have to work through you. Get him on board and ask him what evidence you need to collect."

"I'm not a crime scene investigator, Cally—"

"Then learn what you need to do," Calaphase repeated. "Get a copy of *Criminology for Dummies* if you have to. When you come for Cinnamon on Thursday, you can take pictures—"

"Wait, what about Thursday," I said. "I'm coming back tomorrow."

"No, Dakota," Calaphase said, staring off into the distance with the same quiet finality. I glared at him, about to speak, but he abruptly looked over, his blue clear eyes meeting mine. I quickly looked away at the table, and he sighed. "I'm not going to put the whammy on you. You can look at me. Please. Look at my face, if not my eyes."

Reluctantly I looked up, not quite directly meeting his gaze. It was a pity that he was a vampire, that his eyes could project his aura and work on my will. Otherwise I would have enjoyed gazing into them, two gems of blue sky embedded in a statue of dark cruelty.

"The werehouse is a private haven for a private affliction," he said gravely. "No police, no outsiders—and *especially* no fresh meat on the full moon." His eyes sparkled. "Unless you're planning on providing a one-time catering service for Wednesday night's hunt."

I couldn't help but smile. "When you put it *that* way—what time on Thursday?"

"Right at six—the moon will just be coming up, but the sun will just have gone down, so I can protect you," Calaphase said, taking a sip of his Frappuccino. He got the same pained expression, and this time I was certain it wasn't a brain freeze.

"What gave you the idea to eat human food?"

"Not a what," Calaphase said, eyes still closed, now just as clearly savoring the taste. "A who. You, Dakota." His eyes opened, catching the shock in my glance before I looked away, and he laughed. "This is the Saffron diet. You told her to try human food."

"I did?" I asked . . . and then I remembered. "I did. When she was thinking about becoming a vampire, she told me she'd have to give up human food—"

"And you said, 'Why? Aren't you going to even fucking *try* it?'" Calaphase responded, miming my diction uncannily. "And so she did. *Every* vampire tries eating rare steak and pukes it up. Saffron analyzed vampire digestion, started off with sugar water, and built up from there."

"So . . . if it's so bad, why torture yourself? Are you going vegetarian—"

"Hell, no," Calaphase said. "I love the taste of blood. But . . . Saffron's a daywalker, Dakota. She can stand in the sun and not catch fire. And she thinks a diet of human food—ahem, a diet of food humans eat—has a lot to do with that."

"Did Revenance follow the Sav—uh, 'Saffron' diet?" I asked, pleased and horrified: pleased that vampires were cutting back on blood, and horrified that it might loose these predatory superhumans onto the daylit world. "He lasted a long time under a cloudy sky."

"So it *did* work," Calaphase said. "Revy always was bolder than me. Since I started the diet, I've felt less oppressed by the daystar, but I've not been brave enough to face it."

"Don't be in too much of a hurry," I said quietly. "He survived the clouds . . . but direct sunlight killed him." That unpleasant reminder hung there between us, and Calaphase took a sip of his beverage, again staring off into the distance. Eventually I filled the gap. "So . . . where are you on the Saffron diet?"

"I could show you. Canoe is my current favorite restaurant in the area," Calaphase said. "You'd like it. I should take you there."

I blinked. "Did . . . you just ask me out?"

Calaphase blinked as well. "No, I was just thanking you for—" he began . . . and then stopped. Then he looked me straight in the eyes, blue gems gleaming in that handsome statue, and said, with quiet confidence, "Yes, I did. Would you like to go to Canoe, Dakota?"

My heart leapt into my throat and I felt my face flush. *Oh. My. God.* I had just attracted the attention of a vampire, one who probably chased his steaks with O Positive. *Very* bad news. I don't like vampires. I certainly don't *date* vampires. And why was I thinking of dating, when I was dating Philip Davidson . . . Philip, who was off in Virginia, and who was never here?

"I don't give blood," I blurted.

"Never on a first date," Calaphase said with a smile. Then the smile faded. "I'm serious. Never on a first date. It means as much to me as sex."

"Then how do you *live*?" I said, brow furrowing. I don't trust vampires because I was trained as a chemist. Vampires were powerful and fast—so *something* had to be powering those hyperactive metabolisms. If blood was no richer in calories than a good Frappuccino it would take something like a gallon a *day* to feed them—and a human can't safely donate more than a pint of blood every few *months*. "I mean, the amount of human blood—"

"Cow's blood, actually," Calaphase said, a bit embarrassed. "Kosher butchers have been selling it to vampires, both above and below the table, for hundreds of years."

I blinked.

"I can show you where I buy it," he said, sipping his Frappuccino.

"I think I'd prefer Canoe for our first, uh, date," I replied, with a nervous little laugh.

"Call it a dinner in thanks for your service if it makes you more comfortable. Besides, the Lady Saffron doesn't share well with other clans," Calaphase said. "Still . . . is that a yes?"

We were just staring at each other now. I was afraid to breathe. Did Calaphase breathe? Saffron would say, if he eats, he breathes, but I wasn't sure; come to think of it, vampires were magic. Could his metabolism involve magic? Would our date?

"Are you free tomorrow night?" I said suddenly.

"Yes," he said. "No—damnit, yes. I will have to return to the werehouse, but I can take a break around dinnertime. I'll meet you at the restaurant. You'll feel safer."

"I'll feel safer or *you'll* feel safer?" I asked, tugging the ring on my collar. "I know I'm safe around a vampire, unless you want a 'Lady Saffron' garlic enema. Don't trust yourself?"

"Oh, I trust myself completely," Calaphase said, staring straight at me. "No matter how good the dish looks, I know the stew tastes better if you let it simmer."

Calaphase's phone rang, more werehouse business, and while he spoke I excused myself with a nervous wave, hopped in the blue bomb and fled out into the dark. My brain was buzzing: finish the paperwork for the Clairmont Academy, buy Cinnamon's books, get the Prius fixed up, find a good lawyer to handle the adoption and the Valentine Foundation's missing payments, and, *oh, yeah*, track down a graffiti killer. There were a thousand things to do.

But mostly my brain was buzzing with the obvious: I was having dinner with a vampire. Oh, man. How did that happen? And why was I so jazzed about it? My palms were almost as damp on the wheel as they had been when Cinnamon had been ready to rip my head off.

I tried to force myself to relax.

So I was having dinner with a vampire. What's the worst that could happen?

14.	MAGICAL FALLOUT

"You want me to *what?*" I said, bringing the Prius to a screeching stop.

"Stop what you're doing and *stay out of this*," Rand ordered through my Bluetooth headset. I'd called him back, just as Calaphase had asked . . . but bringing him back on board was proving to be difficult. Rand wasn't going down without a fight. "This investigation is getting hairy. Having a loose cannon is going to complicate things."

"But I've already started," I said, and I had. I'd not yet found anything on magical graffiti, but I had found a little on magical pigments and a lot about regular graffiti. Now that I was primed for it, I was seeing graffiti everywhere—on walls, on street signs, even on the street itself. It was hard not to get lost in the raw folk beauty of graffiti, but already I was starting to notice patterns, possibly crews, and even the occasional magic mark, and was convinced we could catch this guy. "In fact, it's hard to see how I could stop—"

"Try this. Just *stop*," he said. "The Atlanta Police Department does *not* want a registered freelance magician nosing around this case. Especially not if you're going to help by stirring up a hornet's nest in the local werehouse and then not even telling us where you were—"

"I tried to tell you before," I said sharply, "I was *not* there to stir up a hornet's nest."

"Then what *were* you doing?"

"Trying to get help for Cinnamon," I said, and the line stayed silent. "She hadn't changed since she was poisoned . . . and apparently that shit builds up. She turned early, and I didn't know where else to take her. I don't have a radar for evil graffiti. Being there to help was blind luck."

Rand was silent, so I pressed my case. "Cinnamon's safe because I took her there, and our werekin friend is alive because I was at the right place at the right time. If you don't like blind luck, call it dumb luck. Did you really want me to let that boy die, Uncle Andy?"

"No," Rand said. "No, I'm sorry. The attack's clearly related to the one on Revenance, so I assumed it was a reaction to you poking around. I didn't realize it was a coincidence—which actually makes our problem worse. I shouldn't have hung up on you—"

"No, you shouldn't have," I said, starting up the car as the light turned green. I was silent for a moment, just driving, then said, "Not before you got the whole story."

"Look, the DA freaked when she found out you'd been at the crime scene. We can't have you connected to the investigation *in any way*, or we can kiss a conviction goodbye."

"No way," I said.

"No way, no how—no investigating," Rand said. "You've got to promise me that you'll stay out of this—or you might end up attached to the investigation as a suspect."

"Uncle Andy," I said. "Are you . . . threatening me?"

"No, I'm trying to make you see how serious this is," Rand said. His voice was so stern and important I could almost see his expression. "You have to promise me, Kotie—"

"Oh, please," I said. I automatically crossed my fingers, then glared at them. I was not going to play this game. "Cross my heart and hope to die? Detective Andre Rand, don't you think we're both a bit old for this? This thing murdered a friend, attacked another and almost killed me. I want to help you get this guy. These guys. Whoever it is."

Rand was silent for a minute. "Fine," he said. "I love you like a daughter, but I promise you that if you stick your nose back into this I will have you up on obstruction charges."

"Andre—"

"I mean it, Dakota," Rand said. "Butt. The Hell. Out."

And he hung up, leaving me and the blue bomb sailing into Midtown in near silence. Once Midtown Atlanta had been a graveyard of half-filled mid-height office buildings and closed hotels, but now it was having a comeback, with new buildings in brick and stone with nary a bit of graffiti on a one of them, except for a mural, clearly commissioned.

It was new, fresh, vibrant—yet sterile: even though the cars on West Peachtree's wide one-way expanse held enough people to make a crowd, I felt alone. Sometimes I missed riding my Vespa. No matter how comfy my Prius was, it left me disconnected from my environment.

Then the phone rang, and I blooped it through without thinking. "Dakota Frost," I groused. "Best magical tattooist in the Southeast—"

"You won't get many customers with *that* tone," the caller said.

"Philip!" I said, smiling with pleasure. "It's so good to hear your voice."

"Good to hear yours too, Dakota," Special Agent Philip Davidson said. You could still hear the warmth, even through the Bluetooth. I wanted to see his face: his wavy brown hair, his cute little goatee, the blue-gray eyes he always hid behind dark glasses. I was glad he couldn't see me, cheeks red with guilt. I waited a second too long to keep the conversation going, and Philip caught that. "Is everything all right?"

"Yes," I said, abruptly, turning onto West Peachtree. "Damnit, no, things aren't all right. One of my friends, Revenance, was just killed."

"Rand told me—I'm so sorry. He *also* mentioned you witnessed a second attack," Philip said, slipping into his smooth-but-not-accusatory tone of disapproval that made me feel as big as a bug. "But that you refused to divulge its location because it was 'Edgeworld' business."

"That I did," I said. Philip Davidson and the Department of Extraordinary Investigations had definite ideas on how to treat Edgeworlders, and respecting Edgeworld privacy was about the last thing on their list. "Like I told Rand, it isn't my place to divulge their secrets."

"Dakota," Philip said, voice softening. "I'm not calling to bust your nuts.

Rand *also* told me you were there to help Cinnamon. She hadn't changed in a few months, had she? Jesus. And that was your first time dealing with it too. That must have been very difficult for you both."

"You have no idea," I said, glancing back at my torn rear seats. As my head turned back, the car in front of me pulled away, the car behind honked, and I cursed, "All right, *all right*, I'm going!" and hooked onto 5th Street into Georgia Tech's new campus village.

"What are you doing, Dakota?" Philip asked.

"I'm on the last of my rounds of 'would you deliver the bad news for me, Dakota' that Rand and her Highness the 'Lady Saffron' dumped in my fucking lap," I snapped. "I'm going to go break the news about Revenance to yet another friend, and while they're getting over that, I planned to start interrogating them about some weird fucking shit I saw while I was pulling Cinnamon's childhood sweetheart out of a magic graffiti tag that was eating him alive."

"*Cinnamon* had a childhood sweetheart? From how you've described the werehouse—"

"Oh, maybe I'm romanticizing it, but I could tell they had *some* relationship—and don't change the subject," I said. "I'm being serious here. One dead, three missing. Do you really want me to stop? If so, where do you want me to draw the fucking line, Philip? After I saved a kid's life, but before I find out what we need to stop this shit from killing anyone else?"

"What's wrong, Dakota?" Philip asked. "I mean, what's *really* wrong?"

I'm having dinner with a vampire when I'm supposed to be dating you.

"You're never here, Philip," I said. "I haven't seen you since November."

"December 4th," Philip said. "It was a Monday."

"It was fifteen minutes for breakfast at the Flying Biscuit before you rode off to the airport. Which puts our last real date, what, a month ago today?"

"I've been busy," Philip said. "I can't fly down to Atlanta every week."

"But you won't *let* me come up and see you in Virginia," I responded, which was true. "Philip, I haven't even heard from you since . . . since before Christmas."

"You've found someone, haven't you," Philip said.

"Damnit!" I said, screeching to a stop as the light in front of me turned red. "No, Philip, someone found me. Someone just asked me out to dinner, and it's making me feel guilty. Happy now? Why, why, why do I always have to be the *guy* in the relationship?"

Crickets chirped. It was that silent on Phillip's end. After a long pause he finally answered. "Oh. I should have seen this one coming, huh? A girl. And you."

I laughed. I could see how he jumped to the wrong conclusion,. "Sorry, Philip," I said. "You don't get off that easy. You can't blame this one on the other team. I do still like boys. I just like ones that are here, at least once in a while."

There was a second silence over the line, as cars streamed down the broad lanes of Spring Street before me, narrowly missing Tech students bolting through the traffic as they darted from the restaurants and bookstore and back again. Finally Philip spoke.

"All right, Dakota," he said. "You have your date, if that's what you want."

He sounded crushed. "Hey, Philip," I said softly. "That's not what I meant—"

"No, you're right," he said. "I'm never there, and that's not fair to you. Take your friend to dinner, and that's OK, but if you're still . . . interested, I'm willing to give us another shot next time I make it down there. If things are as bad as Rand said . . . well, it won't be long."

"I'm sorry, Philip," I said.

"I am too," he said. "And sorry about the 'investigating this on your own' crack. We really appreciated you helping us track the tattoo killer last year, but please, please, *please* wait until we bring the problems to you instead of making trouble on your own. I worry about you, Dakota. You're a . . . a valuable resource, and I'd hate to lose you. Take care."

"I'd hate to lose you too, Philip," I said, but my headset *blooped* and my brain put the words "valuable resource" on an endless loop.

He was already gone. He'd called his girlfriend a valuable resource and hung up.

Damnit! Damnit! Damnit! This was *not* what I wanted. A dalliance with a vampire had just cut me off from a man who was both my boyfriend and my spook contact, and said dalliance hadn't even happened yet. And protecting the werehouse's privacy had alienated Uncle Andy.

Maybe Philip was right; things were already blowing up in my face.

Was I getting sucked in too deep?

But then I saw Revy's face, burned up like paper. No one did that to my friends. And no matter how much I liked Philip, he was first and foremost a monster fighter, not one of their guardians. And no matter how much I trusted Uncle Andy, he had to work within the law. Not on the Edge, where I lived. *Someone* had to protect these people—someone who *understood* them.

The light turned green, the car behind me honked, and I gunned the blue bomb over the 5th Street Bridge into Georgia Tech proper.

"*Fine,*" I said. "My *own* damn investigation it is."

---

15.   NUCLEAR WIZARDRY

A great chasm of asphalt cuts across the heart of Atlanta—river-wide, canyon-deep, and filled with a current of cars faster than any rapids: the Downtown Connector. The Connector had contained Georgia Tech's growth for decades, until finally a spray of new buildings had burst over the recently completed 5th Street Bridge.

As I crossed the bridge, I saw Tech shift from shiny glass towers to aging red brick. Winding through the campus was like traveling back in architectural time, from the 90s to the 80s to the 70s . . . next stop, the 1950s, and one of the oldest buildings on the campus: the Georgia Tech Nuclear Research

Center.

The NRC was two cubical buildings guarding a squat ribbed tower, ugly and alien, that once housed the reactor. Now decommissioned, the NRC held something different, and perhaps more dangerous: the very first laboratory in the country studying the Physics of Magic.

In a pebble-floored, low-chaired lobby, I signed in an ancient log book that looked like it really did date from the 1950s. As I put the pen back into its tiny, conical holder, Annette, the lab secretary, asked, "Is everything all right, Kotie? You look flushed."

I frowned, trying not to take it out on her: Annette was all pink hair and bubblegum, so sickeningly sweet you wanted to punch her in the nose—but she really was the nice sort, even though she dressed in poufy florals that even Catherine Fremont would have punked up a bit.

"I just had an argument," I said. "Nothing important."

"Sorry to hear it," she said, picking up the phone. "Don't worry, you'll find someone."

"How did you . . . " I began. "Am I really that transparent?"

"Yes, she's here," Annette said, hitting the buzzer. "Doug and Jinx are in the tower."

"I remember the way," I said, opening the heavy metal door. "And thanks."

"Remember, there are lots of fish in the sea," she chimed sweetly.

"Thanks," I said, as the door clanged shut behind me.

The chilled, dark metal corridor felt cramped as a submarine, but soon opened into a cavernous vault big enough to hold a house. I wondered the chamber had held in its heyday, when these idiots had thought to contain nuclear death smack dab in the middle of a crowded college campus at the center of the Southeast's largest city. But now the vault was almost hollow, a birdcage of cranes and catwalks over a huge single-cut slab of polished marble inscribed with the largest magic circle in the country.

A darkhaired, cleancut man in a Georgia Tech sweatshirt was adjusting some equipment in the center of the circle. At a console outside the ring, a young, gothy, bonneted woman in an exaggerated Victorian outfit read numbers out loud to the thin air. Doug and Jinx.

Doug saw me and smiled, a wicked twinkle belying his clean cut look—which didn't fool me anyway: the first time I'd met him, he'd been wearing leather puppy gear. Jinx, on the other hand, never changed her style to suit the circumstances. I don't think I'd seen her wear anything less elaborate since . . . before she went blind. Today, however, she had a new accessory.

"Dakota?" she asked of the air, even as she turned towards me, eyes hidden behind her dark glasses. Her hand shot out, delicate black lace glove now adorned with a new sparkle—a gleaming diamond ring. "Guess what? We're getting married!"

Oh, how wonderful for them. "That's great," I said, with forced cheeriness, reaching to take her hand. It wasn't a large rock, since they were both graduate students, but still—how wonderful for them. Really.

"Dakota?" Jinx said—and pulled down her glasses slightly. I looked up, expecting her spooky geode eyes—and saw instead spooky black snowflakes gleaming within her formerly clouded marbles. "Oh, Dakota, what's wrong?"

Damnit. I had forgotten she could partially see now, some positive fallout from a magical injury last year. I forced a smile. "Nothing, just a bad day," I said, casting about for something else to talk about. "Look, I'm sorry I haven't coughed up your fee from the tattooing contest . . . "

"When the Valentine Foundation pays you, you can pay me, but, *really,* Dakota," she said reprovingly. "That's the worst attempt to change the subject ever. All I can see is a blurry spot, but even I can tell that smile is fake. It's not just a bad day. What's wrong?"

"It's nothing," I said. And then I remembered what I had come for, and forgot all about Philip. "Actually, you're right," I said gently. "It is something. Jinx, I have some bad news."

Doug and Jinx sat in shock at the break table as I told them about Revy, about the attack on Tully, and about the other vampire disappearances that were almost certainly connected. Jinx, the best graphomancer I knew, agreed to tackle the graffiti without a second thought.

"I know the literature on decorative marks quite well," she said primly. "But I'll need more than a description to build a model of how it's working. I need good digital photographs, and hopefully video, thirty seconds or a full sequence if your camera will last that long."

"I know," I said, speaking up to compensate for the sudden whine of the air conditioning. "I'm supposed to take pictures tomorrow at the werehouse when I go pick up Cinnamon."

"Why is Cinnamon at the werehouse?" Jinx asked, brow furrowing. She didn't bother to speak up at all. "I thought you were trying to rescue her out of there."

"It's a long story," I said. And potentially embarrassing. My daughter might not want her mother telling people she had trouble controlling her changes. "I'll let her tell it, if she wants to. But I have a question for you, Doug. The first tag was powerful, but didn't do anything I haven't seen a tattoo or any normal spell do. The second one, however, did something unusual—"

A crack like thunder rang through the dome, and I flinched back from a flash like controlled lightning. "Jeez!" I said, raising an arm, seeing goose bumps ripple up as stray mana flooded out through the room. "What the hell are you guys *doing?*"

"Testing a theory of magical capacitance," Doug said. "Lenora, give us some warning next time!"

"Why? Nothing is going to happen," said a brown-haired woman, stepping out of a control booth—and then blithely stepping over the glowing outer ring of the magic circle as if the sea of energies it contained couldn't turn her into a pumpkin. She used tongs to extract a metal disc from the equipment at the center of the circle, stomped back over to us, and tossed the disc on the desk. "Yet another failure."

Inside the metal ring was a pinkish membrane with a gridlike test pattern at its center. I stared at it with growing horror. "Don't tell me that's real *human skin.*"

"Of course it's *real,*" Lenora said, "you can see it with your own two eyes—"

"Down, Lenora," Doug said, holding the membrane up to the light. "Yes, Dakota, it's human skin, but not *from* a human. It's grown on a synthetic matrix in the Biotech building—they're hoping to use it on burn patients. Dang—it looks exactly like it did before."

"My point exactly," Lenora replied. "I don't care what mana flux you use, you're not going to get any accumulation in a single layer. There's no such thing as 'tattoo magic.'"

I raised an eyebrow. "So what is it that *I* do for a living then, chop liver?"

"Oh, so *you're* the Dakota Frost that got him on this wild goose chase," Lenora said. "It was bad enough when he started dating the witch and eating granola—"

"Lenora!" Jinx said, putting her gloved fingers to her breast in mock shock. "After all the wonderful spells I've shown you . . . "

"Which are supposed to do what, exactly?" Lenora asked, smirking.

"I don't know in particular, *Scully*," I said, cracking my neck, "but if you can't get them to work, don't blame Jinx. Start closer to home, like with *yourself*."

"Down, Dakota. I need a Scully to keep me honest," Doug said, handing the disc back to her. "Please photograph it and run another control. So, Dakota," Doug said, pulling out a tan gridded notebook and writing a few lines, "what did the graffiti do that was so unusual?"

I stared at him: as his smile faded he was left calm, like that little discussion hadn't just happened, and he was actually taking notes. He hadn't taken it personally, like I had. Doug was going to be a good scientist someday. Maybe he'd be open enough to listen.

"Tully was trapped against it, and while I was pulling him out it got a really good grip on us," I said. "It's really weird, but it felt like . . . it was sucking us *inside*. Not just pulling us against the wall, but *into* it, like the graffiti had made a doorway into a space beyond."

Lenora, walking past with a fresh disc rolled her eyes. "Oh, for the love of—"

"This time I agree with her," Doug said. "That sounds impossible."

"If you're that susceptible to new age mysticism," Lenora said, "maybe I should loan you some back issues of the *Skeptical Inquirer*—"

"Whoa!" I said, holding up my tattooed hands. "I am simply reporting an experience and asking you to help me interpret it. I'm the *last* person to go in for cosmic woo-hooery."

"You supposedly have magic tattoos," Lenora said. "What are we supposed to think?"

I glared at her. "*Fine*," I said, and flexed my hand.

I have large tattoos—vines, snakes, tribal patterns—but small ones too: flowers and jewels and butterflies. The littlest ones are easy to tattoo. I can do them in one sitting—so I'm not above using them to make a point.

My skin glowed. Lenora's eyes widened. And then a pretty little honeybee I'd tattooed on one of my vines came to life, buzzing up into the air. Lenora cried out in delight, and Doug laughed. Only Jinx seemed nonplussed. With a gentle wave of my hand, I guided the sparkling bee over the test membrane, and it gently settled down and became two dimensional again.

"You can pretend that's a yellow jacket," I said—the Tech mascot—and folded my arms. "Look closely at the connections that make up the design, particularly the Euler circuits. Skin only holds essentially one layer of ink, so it's the *design* that holds the magic. Using a grid pattern in your tester, you were almost guaranteed to fail, except maybe at the edges."

"I *tried* to tell them that," Jinx said, nudging Doug with her shoulder, "but my little scientist here kept going on about his need for proper controls."

"Holy cow," Lenora said, rubbing at the membrane. The bee stubbornly remained where it was and did not smudge off. "Holy cow. I can see why Doug had a bee in *his* bonnet."

"I'll take that as a compliment," I said. "And for the record, I've subscribed to the *Skeptical Inquirer* for the last ten years."

"Oh!" Lenora said. "That's . . . uh . . . can I put this in the tester?"

"Knock yourself out," I said, and Lenora took the membrane into the test chamber like she was carrying a baby made of gold. I looked at Doug. "How can she not see the evidence right before her eyes? I mean, isn't that the point of science?"

"She's come a long way," Jinx said defensively. "You shouldn't pick on her . . . "

"But it's so fun," Doug said, ducking when she whapped him with her cane.

Lenora moved behind a sheet of glass, touched some controls, and then a rising whine started at the top of the tower. I'd heard it earlier—I'd thought it was an air conditioner—but now I could see it came from a big device far above the magic circle, like an upside-down glass jar wrapped in hundreds of sheets of metal: a massive magical capacitor. As it charged up, I could see a dance of light sparkling off a silver spear, pointing down out of the glass.

"So, now that we've established that I don't make wild claims without *something* to back them up," I said, "can you answer my question about how the graffiti bent space?"

"Sure. It didn't. It had to be an illusion—you didn't go anywhere, after all. There's no way graffiti could affect the metric enough to change its topology." At my baffled look, Doug tried again. "Look, it isn't likely that *any* magic could bend space. It's a matter of gravity."

The rising whine reached its peak, and with another crack of thunder, a beam flashed down from the point of the spear. The test membrane flared with blue-white light, and the bee buzzed back to life. Doug looked back at it, amazed, as Lenora frantically took pictures of the moving tattoo. Then he shrugged and used what we'd just seen as his argument.

"That's the largest magical capacitor on the East Coast," Doug said. "Two hundred layers of infused papyrus and cold iron. When it fires, it puts out more mana than any magician in history—and *it* doesn't affect gravity. If it can't, then your graffiti can't. It just can't."

"But it didn't feel like the graffiti was affecting gravity," I said. "Like you said, our feet were on the ground. The tag was . . . I don't know what else to call it but bending space . . . "

"But bent space *is* gravity," Doug said. "Gravity is just . . . a kink in time that makes matter want to move together. It's like setting two bowling balls down on a trampoline—first they'll dent its surface. Then, slowly, the dents will come together."

I squinted. "I'm . . . I'm not quite seeing it."

"Don't worry," Doug said. "There are PhDs in physics that never get it. But the point is, bending space is so hard it takes the entire mass of the Earth just to keep our feet on the ground. And that's just attraction, a dent in the trampoline. To make a tunnel from place to place—"

"You . . . couldn't do that," I said, starting to get it. "That's not just bending space, it's punching a hole—changing the topology, like you said. You can't *stretch* a surface to make a hole—the trampoline would burst and the springs would snap back, going everywhere."

"I'm not sure what that would mean in terms of my little example," Doug said. "But either way, the amount of mass needed would be . . . astronomical."

"But the tags aren't using mass," I said. "They're using magic, and magic breaks all the rules. We don't know how it works, or what its limits are."

"And that's why I hope you're wrong," Doug said. "Magic gravity would be completely new—and the last time that happened in physics was when we realized matter was energy. No one ever thought we'd be able to use that, but a few years later, we had atomic bombs."

I felt my eyes widen.

"So that's why we're stuffed in this building," Doug said. "We're afraid magic can make nuclear weapons look like firecrackers. And if the graffiti can affect *gravity*—"

"If a tag on a wall," I said, "can bend space harder than an entire planet—"

"—then graffiti magic," Doug said, "is powerful enough to *crack open* the planet."

16. VAMPIRE FOR DINNER

There was nothing left to do. I'd finished the paperwork and gotten Cinnamon's books. I'd made an appointment to inspect the school's safety cage and picked up a cage of our own. I'd worked out a schedule at the Rogue Unicorn that let me juggle my tattooing, karate workouts, and shuttling Cinnamon to and from the Academy. I'd even found an auto repair shop that had given me a loaner while they repaired the seats; with any luck, I'd be back in the blue bomb when I picked up Cinnamon at the werehouse tomorrow.

There was nothing left to do but dress, drive, and meet the vampire for dinner.

Canoe was only a short jaunt up I-75, a river of black asphalt swimming through hills green with trees. Red taillights blinked northbound, and scattered headlights winked on to my left as the sun went down. I rarely went to Vinings, but somehow I remembered Exit 255 and soon found myself going into deep green hills along the winding path of Paces Ferry Road.

I'll admit I was apprehensive. I had no idea what kind of restaurant a vampire would have as a current favorite. Based on its name, I was pretty certain Canoe wasn't an ancient Victorian nestled deep in the woods, with creaking iron gates or mysterious valets to take my car, trapping me there to dine by candlelight under the watchful eyes of my predatory companion, served by black-garbed waiters trained not to notice when the vampire started noshing on me instead.

And I had a moment's fright as I came to the Paces Ferry bridge and snatched a glimpse of graffiti. But it turned out to be what I was now calling wanker graffiti: white lines, hastily drawn, not magically active. And then I was over the bridge into Vinings, staring down into a cluster of quaint, cozy, houselike shops.

I gave the loaner Accord to the valet without a second thought, and stood before a warm wooden canopy topped by a glowing sign that spelled C A N O E, watching uber-chic yuppies from the Buckhead party district and upper-crust natives of Vinings itself flowing in and out of the restaurant with warm, friendly, *satisfied* smiles.

OK, this is the *last* place I'd expect a vampire to have as a favorite.

Even more heads than usual turned towards me as I ascended the steps, but I tried not to mind. I knew I was doubly out of place. In addition to my deathhawk and tattoos, I now wore a tight, patterned corset bustier, my most stylish leather pants and my best matching leather vestcoat. The outfit went so well together there was no doubting that this was eveningwear, but there was no escaping that it wasn't *normal* eveningwear either.

Inside was warm, cozy, brick, with huge glass windows looking out onto garden paths. I was early; even with traffic it was still only six-ten, so I decided to wait by the bar. The sun had set only minutes ago; it was highly unlikely that the vampire would be . . . early?

Calaphase glanced up from the bar and smiled at me. He was wearing another long-tailed coat, narrowly pinstriped, expertly tailored, that gave the impression of impossible elegance from a bygone age. He saluted me with a glass of what looked like liquid gold, finished the last swigs with a flourish and grimace, and then pushed the squat empty glass back to the bartender with a wink and a twenty. I just stared, as the man I'd once known as a biker walked up to me, as sharply dressed as a Victorian James Bond—and twice as appealing.

"Dakota," Calaphase said, with a smile and a gracious bow. "I'm glad you made it."

"Afraid I'd jilt you?" I responded.

"Never," Calaphase said, his eyes drifting over my tattooed midriff, my corset, my breasts. Then he caught himself and looked up. "Sorry. That is quite the outfit."

"Thank you," I said, smiling. "Yours is easy on the eyes as well. Shall we dine?"

"We have fifteen minutes," Calaphase said, extending an elbow. "Care for a stroll?"

I looked outside. "Are you sure you want to go out there? The sun just went down."

"I like twilight," Calaphase said, pulling out sunglasses. "A benefit of the

Saffron diet."

Canoe's garden was as inviting as its interior and as friendly as its clientele. Another glowing sign hung over the patio, lending electric color to the warmth of the torches; under their luminous glow we strolled through green, inviting gardens, watching the Chattahoochee ripple past. Somehow the river looked cleaner here, even though I knew it was the same water that flowed past the werehouse only a few miles to the south.

"So . . . " I said. "How much *does* a vampire on the Saffron diet eat?"

"Not much," Calaphase admitted. "I rarely have more than the squash bisque and a glass of wine. If I indulge in too much solid food, I have a thermos of cow's blood at the werehouse."

"Appetizing," I said. "It looked like the drink was killing you."

"It's difficult," Calaphase admitted, stopping to stare out into the black flowing water, barely lit by flickering torches. "But the Lady Saffron is right. It's worth it. I hunger less, and stay awake longer, every day. I've seen the aftermath of sunset, and withstood the onset of sunrise. I can't yet face the sun, but the day is coming."

Staring out over the water, he looked noble, even heroic, like a sea captain of old contemplating time passing in the night, the essence of his profile, pale skin and blond hair captured by the torchlight, abstracted and made eternal, like a statue of brass.

"And I have the Lady Saffron's bravery, and your challenge of vampire assumptions, to thank." He glanced back, weighing something, then smiled. "I bet you usually go Dutch," he said, again extending an elbow, "but may I buy you dinner in thanks, Dakota Frost?"

"You know, Calaphase," I said, taking his arm, "perhaps I can make an exception."

"Here's to promising exceptions," he said, patting my hand with his free one.

I smiled, looking down bashfully. Calaphase was charming. Well, yes, handsome, sexy, and in all reality terrifyingly dangerous, but—absolutely charming. I felt no pressure from him, nothing to fear. We would have a nice dinner, and that would be it.

Then Calaphase froze in his tracks. "Speak of the devil . . . "

And I looked up just in time to meet the eyes of the Lady Saffron and the Lady Darkrose as they stopped dead not five feet from us on the path.

Saffron wore a stunning red dress of flaring silk with matching red gloves that left her shoulders bare beneath her flaming hair. Her South African vampire consort, the Lady Darkrose, wore a white-trimmed robe open over a black leather catsuit that went well against her dark skin. A typical evening out for them. I could see echoes of smiles and laughter on their faces, and Saffron even had her arm in the Lady Darkrose's, just as mine was in Calaphase's; but as they registered my arm in Calaphase's, the Lady Darkrose's face went carefully blank . . . as Saffron's face turned beet red. I hadn't even known vampires could blush.

At first, I just thought innocently, *Oh, this is awkward.*

Then the shouting started.

"*Dakota?*" Saffron said—*not* in her indoor voice. "Why are you *here* with *him?"*

"Sav—" I began, then bit it off as she glared. "Uh, my Lady Saffron—"

"I thought you disapproved of vampires," she said, voice rising, "but you just disapproved of *me?"*

My jaw dropped. When had I ever loved this petulant *bitch?* Her voice rose further.

"What, did you get *tired* of your man in black and decided to move on to the next cock?"

"Saffron!" Calaphase said, shocked as I was. "That was *completely* out of line—"

"*You* shut your mouth," Saffron snapped. "And it's *Lady* Saffron to you."

"I thought we were friends now, but if you really want the respect due a vampire queen, you have to *be* a vampire queen," Calaphase said, tilting his head. Diners on the nearby patio had recoiled in shock at her outburst, and Darkrose had intercepted an angry waiter and was speaking in quiet tones. "Is this the example the leader of a great house sets, much less the Queen of Little Five Points?"

Saffron flinched. She opened her mouth, then immediately closed it. Then she nodded to Calaphase, not meeting my eyes, and turned to Darkrose, who was still calming the waiter.

"No, Lady Darkrose, please do not cover for me, that was my fault," she said, spreading her hands graciously. "Ladies and gentlemen, forgive my rudeness, I was just startled. Please accept my apologies . . . and a complimentary dessert, courtesy of the House of Saffron."

With a nod to Darkrose to arrange it, Saffron stalked off. "Walk with me."

We followed her to a secluded part of the path, and she turned to us.

"Thank you, Lord Calaphase," she said coldly. "I had that coming. I was out of line. Becoming a vampire hasn't turned out as liberating as I expected."

"I know that feeling," Calaphase said—lightly, but it backfired.

"*Don't* think I'm distracted," Saffron said, "from this . . . this *insult.*"

"Saffron!" I said. "Look, I'm sorry, but *you're* the one who turned on *me*—"

"That excuse worked when you stuck to humans," she said coldly, "but not when you're parading around with a rival vampire lord while wearing the sign of my house."

"I'm so sorry to have offended you," Calaphase said. "I made my offer to dine with the Lady Frost as gracious thanks to someone who helped a friend."

"She's still wearing the *sign of my house*," Saffron said, glaring at the collar around my neck. "You're a vampire—and a clan leader. You should have cleared it with me."

Calaphase stiffened. "Yes, yes of course, my Lady Saffron."

"What? No, no of course *not*, 'my Lady Saffron,'" I said. "Calaphase said you didn't share well with other clans, but this is *ridiculous*."

"You're being naïve," Saffron snapped. "If I had the reputation of 'sharing,' the Gentry would eat me alive—or, more likely, eat *you* alive, first chance the Lady Scara got—"

"But this is Calaphase," I said. "He's a friend—*our* friend. And we're here for dinner-as-food, not dining-on-companions. He's on the Saffron diet, maybe you've heard of it?"

"*You're* wearing *my* token," Saffron said. "Calaphase still needed *my* permission."

"Look, Saffron," I said testily. "I'm a full grown adult, not a teenager on curfew."

"If the sign of my house means nothing to you, we can dispose of it," Saffron said, voice unexpectedly level. "Lady Darkrose, bring me the key please."

My hand went to my throat. The steel collar I wore was my shield against the world of vampires, my guarantee they would treat me decently. I'd only worn it for a few months, but it had been fitted just for me, so I had gotten used to it—and forgotten that only Darkrose had the keys that could take it off. As possessive as Saffron was, I never thought that would happen.

In moments, Darkrose rejoined us, her dark face a mixture of shock and embarrassment. Without a word, she slipped a leather-gloved hand inside her robe, briefly exposing the hard ribbing of her corset, boots that seemed to come to her hips, the handle of a whip. But she was Saffron's dominatrix only *inside* their bedroom. Outside, Saffron called the shots. And when Darkrose's hand returned, it held a single silver key on a golden chain.

Saffron took it and stepped up to me. "Turn 'round."

I just stared at her in shock. "Saffron . . . "

"I said, *turn 'round*," Saffron snapped, reaching out, then jerking her hand back.

I felt my hands *tingling*, and looked down to see the religious symbols tattooed on the back of my knuckles glowing slightly as they reacted to the hostility in her aura. That *never* happened—Saffron normally kept her aggression under such a lid that she could safely live in a deconsecrated church, complete with exposed crosses. She was more steamed than I thought.

"Don't touch me," I said quietly, meeting her cold red gaze. Scratch that—she was *much* more steamed. "Vampire queen or no, *do not touch me* without asking."

"As you wish," Saffron said. "But you have something of mine and I want it back."

"*Fine*, then," I said, turning, sweeping the long tail of my deathhawk out of the way.

I felt Saffron step up behind me, felt her hands fumble at the lock, felt the coolness of the keychain against my neck. Then there was a pop, and the lock opened—freeing my neck from the collar for the first time in two and a half months.

Saffron pulled it off, scraping my neck, and angrily I turned to face her. We glared at each other a moment, her holding the collar—and then Saffron flung it into the darkness over the Chattahoochee, where it vanished with a distant *plop*.

"But . . . you had it *made* for her," Darkrose said, staring after it.

"That was a long time ago. A different life—when I believed we could still be together. Or at least close," Saffron said. I felt my throat. I'd never liked it, but now I was sorry that it was not just off, but . . . *gone*. "I should have abandoned that hope long ago, and the collar with it."

"That ... was ... *foolish*," Calaphase said, fangs clenched, pale face livid. Saffron glared at him, but he just straightened his jacket with a sharp jerk. "Dakota—the *Lady* Frost—has performed *invaluable* services to my clan and our clients."

"Then *you* give her protection," Saffron said.

"Perhaps we will, but she has provided even greater services to *you*," Calaphase said. "You do *not* know how much her dispatching that magician last year helped your reputation with the clans. It's bad enough you'd withdraw her protection, but it is worse that you'd do so as such a public stunt in front of the humans. Not even old school vampires would—Oh, *damnit*."

Suddenly Calaphase cursed and pulled out his phone, which I now could hear faintly buzzing. *Never underestimate vampire hearing.* His brow furrowed, his thumb hovered over the button to kill it, but after a long pause he said, "Sorry, I have to take this."

"What? Am I not here? Is this not important? Don't you have voicemail?" Saffron said, looking legitimately astounded. "Am I really *nothing* to you two?"

"Yeah Gettyson, now isn't the best—" Calaphase began, waving her off. "What? *What?* What the f—speak up, I can't—Holy *crap!*"

It was hard to believe, but that pale stone face became paler, drained of all color. "Do we need help? Should I tell—" and he looked up at Saffron, then at me. "I've got them both right here. Yes, yes, no promises. Yes, I'll hurry—I'm on my way."

Calaphase closed the phone, and I asked, "What's wrong?"

"We have to go," he said. "The werehouse is on fire."

---

17.   THE TAGGER'S REVENGE

We screeched round the corner down the old ironworks drive, debris rattling up a storm beneath the green loaner as it slid through loose gravel at every curve. Calaphase gripped the dash in fury, hunched forward, eyes intent, hands curled like the claws of a predator.

"Hurry," was all he said.

But I was already stepping on it. Vines and bushes tore greedily at the Accord's exterior. Then we were through, darting through chainlink and rumbling over concrete, speeding towards a vast pillar of glowing smoke looming over ruined buildings lit by yellow flame.

"And God moved over the desert in a pillar of flame, destroying everything in his wrath," I said, eyes wide. "My *daughter* is in there! In a *cage!*"

"Get as close as you can," Calaphase ordered. "Then we do what we can. *Everyone* gets out. *Stop here!* I don't want your car to catch on fire, we may need it to evacuate the wounded."

I hit the brakes and we scrambled out. The rollup doors to the werehouse were open and Fischer burst out of the smoke, beard grimed with soot and eyes glowing with power. A young boy was in his arms, and an endless stream of animals swarmed out around him: mostly wolves, but also mountain lions, deer, even a horse—but no Cinnamon.

"Those are all the cages," he shouted at Gettyson. "I checked the whole level!"

Gettyson nodded—he was in the throng, gesticulating, using the vampire guards and the unchanged elders to sort predators from prey. He caught sight of us and waved. "You two, take the side wing," he shouted. "Get anyone out of there before the flames cuts them off!"

We ran round the right side of the building, opposite the wall where I'd saved Tully from the graffiti. Here was a long, low blockhouse, half buried in the ground, that had perhaps once been a storage area. It abutted the main building of the werehouse, where smoke was already billowing out an open door and jetting through cracks in the dark, sooty windowpanes.

"I'll take the upper level doors, you the lower," Calaphase said, vaulting up over the railing onto the next level and touching the first door with his hand. He cursed and jerked his hand back, then ran to the next door.

Stairs led to the lower level doors. They were all in a long low trench, sealed off by a chain link fence like a cage. The stairs stopped at a chain link grate with a simple padlock. I tried to bolt forward down the stairs, hoping to snap the padlock with one of my snakes, but was pushed back by a new wave of smoke from the door closest to the stairs.

"Help us!" a voice screamed, and I caught a glimpse of cat eyes and furred hands reaching through the links for help. Not Cinnamon, but for the grace of God—"*Help us!*"

But the fire wouldn't let me: wind goaded it on. Ugly, roiling yellow smoke boiled out of the door, breathing in and out like a living thing, surging every time I tried to get past. I tried crouching and slipping past, but the heat was so intense it staggered me, and when I tried to catch my breath the hot stale air and the tightness of my corset left me dizzied and coughing.

Well, *fine*. There's more than one way to save a cat.

"*Spirit of fall,*" I murmured. "*Extend my reach.*"

A long vine uncoiled from my wrist and curled past the smoke, down the stairs, and I prepared myself, stretching my body, as best I could in the corset, to bring the snake to life. It began to crawl down the vine, and I willed it to slink down and snap the link on the chain—

And then the door screamed with rage and vomited forth a great blast of flame. The roiling fireball knocked me back, the flash of heat singing my skin even from dozens of feet away. And for a brief moment, the fire enveloped the snake on the curving vine.

Pain hit me like a live wire.

I screamed. The vine recoiled, trailing sparks through the air—sparks of flame, not mana, as heat destroyed the delicate pigments. The vine snapped back onto my skin and I jerked back uselessly, curling up into a little ball as white-hot pain burned into my flesh.

"Dakota!" Calaphase said, coming to my side. I tried to answer, but the corset was still crushing my diaphragm and I just gasped for breath. "Dakota!" he said. "Are you all right?"

I held up my hand. The snake itself was completely gone, the vine tattoo's color had faded to a dull brown, and the skin around it was red and beginning to blister. *The fire had burned me*, burned me through the magic, even though my skin never touched the flame.

I caught my breath and looked at Calaphase helplessly. "I can't help with this."

"You know what? I can't wade through fire either. So *screw* magic," Calaphase said, punching my shoulder. "Get up, let's help these people."

He sprinted, no, *shot* down to the end of the low building with vampire speed. By the time I caught up with him, gasping, limping, my knee throbbing, he had torn the chain link fence away, and all I had to do was help lift the poor trapped werekids out of the dark hole.

"Where's Cinnamon!" I asked the werecat. "Cin! *Stray!* Where is she?"

"Down by the weight room," she said, coughing. "Lucky bitch was going on a hunt—"

"Show me," I said.

We ran back around the werehouse, past the main entrance, jumping down onto the lower level, again curving around towards the same area where I'd fought the graffiti yesterday. When we got there, I paused, gasping again, looking up at the fire, at the tongues of flame now licking through the smoke—curling, artistic, like brushstrokes.

"Oh, hell," I said. It wasn't just fire.

"Come on, Dakota," Calaphase said, beckoning from the corner. A great orange glow came from behind him, and I ran around him, bracing myself for the horror of the flames.

Rippling tongues of flame coiled up the wall that had held the tag, starting about ten feet off the ground. Above was all concrete, all concrete and yet it still burned; below, where the tag had been, was a huge expanse of cracked, sooty darkness that had once been white.

"Where would Cinnamon be?" I said, holding my side.

"Damnedest thing," Gettyson said, staring up at the flames creeping up the cinder blocks. The fire reflected eerily off his odd eyes, like two slits of flame. "The damnedest thing."

"Gettyson! Where would—what the hell," I said, staring at the remaining wall. They'd gone back over it since the night of the assault on Tully. "You whitewashed it? *All* of it?"

"Of course," Gettyson said, glaring. "It damn near killed Tully—"

"You *fool!*" I shouted. "*This is a magic fire!* How are we gonna fight it now, if we can't see or even *touch* the magic mark that's generating the flames?"

Gettyson stared at the wall, and then he saw it too. "Oh, *shit—*"

"Get *anyone* not needed to fight the fire and comb the woods," I said, glaring across the parking lot at the dark green Oakdale forest. "Somewhere out there, the prick that killed Revy is fanning these flames, and we gotta stop him. Short skater dude, white or maybe Latino, baggy clothes, big-ass hat—and if he's wearing the same shit-ass grin, kick his teeth in for me."

Gettyson grabbed a half-changed wolfling that passed. "You heard her," he said. "Go!"

"And if he's got any spray cans *don't touch them!*" I screamed after him. "They're filled with magic pigment, and can blow up in your face, literally!"

"What does we do about the fire?" Gettyson said. "What does we do?"

"We get everyone out," I said, holding up my burned arm. "We get everyone out, and then let it take the damn building. And we start with Cinnamon. *Where is she?*"

He pointed at a low side building jutting out of the back of the werehouse. Its roof was in flames, and as we watched the whole front awning collapsed so that there was no way inside.

"Oh, hell no," I said, staring, looking at a small barred window that was the only remaining exit. I half expected Cinnamon's hand to reach out, to slap the glass—but more of the roof collapsed around it, barring even that entrance. "Tell me there's another way in there."

"Through the living quarters," Calaphase said.

"Fischer already tried that," Gettyson said. "The smoke will kill you—"

"Then we go this way," Saffron said, stalking past us towards the flame.

My eyes followed her, but I could barely overcome my shock. "Saffron!"

"Where the hell did *she* pop up from?" Calaphase said.

"We were *right there* when you said there was a fire, and right behind you most of the drive in," Saffron said, staring up at the building. "With all my power, did you really think I'd just sit by and let innocent people die, much less a child under a vampire queen's protection?"

"Well," Calaphase began—and then shut his mouth at her quick sidelong glance.

"My Lady Saffron," Darkrose said, running up after her, white-lined cloak flying open, gleaming black catsuit reflecting flickering red as she flinched back from a sudden surge of flame. "*Saffry!* Please, it is fire! Not even you—"

"Then stay back!" Saffron said, red dress whipping past her in the sudden wind. She looked around, scowled, then said, "Dakota, we're getting weather effects like you reported at the Revenance kill—send the werekin out looking for the rogue magician."

"I already have," I said.

"Good. Calaphase, Darkrose, go make sure the other entrance is clear," Saffron said, turning her back on us. "I don't like the looks of this roof."

Then with one hand she lifted the huge iron beam that had been part of the awning, tore it aside in a groaning shower of sparks, stepped forward with a savage blow that burst the metal door inward off its cinderblock frame. Then she disappeared inside.

"Oh, hell, she's as powerful as they say she is," Calaphase said.

"Why *is* she so strong?" I said, bewildered.

"She's almost completely vegetarian," Darkrose said. "Her vampire and human flesh exist in near perfect symbiosis. But it doesn't make her fireproof."

Then the flames picked up, started punching through the roof of the low outbuilding. Moments later, the whole structure collapsed, leaving half of one wall holding up smoking embers and the glowing bones of the roof.

I stared at the others. "You heard her," I said. "Let's go clear the path."

But flames licked at the big roll-up door that had been the entrance to the werehouse, thwarting our attempts to get inside. Before we came up with another plan, Saffron strode out of the flames like the Terminator, holding Cinnamon half-changed in her arms. Saffron's flaring red dress caught fire as she stepped through the threshold, but she ignored it and stomped straight up to me, holding Cinnamon. Gratefully, I took Cinnamon in my arms and held her tight.

Saffron patted her dress out idly, as I kissed Cinnamon's half-feline face and tried not to wince at the embers that were burning my skin. My little girl was half-conscious, but breathing normally. She was safe. "Thank you," I said.

"Do *not* mention it," Saffron snapped. Her mouth pursed. "As for her collar—"

"Please," I said, eyes jerking down to Cinnamon's throat, to her silver collar. I couldn't imagine a clearer demonstration of the value of Saffron's protection. My eyes returned to Saffron, pleading. "She's no part of whatever I have done to—"

"Don't mention it," Saffron repeated, more softly, then turned back towards the flames.

"No," Darkrose said, seizing Saffron's bare arm firmly in her glove. "You'll die."

"Please, dear Rose," Saffron said, extracting her arm. "There are more to save."

"Saffry, *no*," Darkrose said, shaking her head. "There aren't. It's too late."

And then we were all pushed back as a new surge of fire blossomed out of the werehouse. The flames grew more intense, burning white, streaming out of every orifice, screaming under the pressure like steam escaping a teakettle—or tortured creatures screaming in pain.

Then the main roof collapsed inward on itself and a huge backwash sprayed out of the door like a river of fire—then was abruptly sucked back with a rattling gasp, snuffing out all the flames at once. In its wake, a roiling black cloud erupted through the ruined roof.

"I'm no fireman," I said, "but *that wasn't natural.*"

"Agreed," Calaphase said. There was little left of the fire but embers. A few tongues of flame were springing up again, but intermittently, almost like the fire's heart was no longer in it. "The rush of fresh air should have made it worse, but it's like—"

"It's like she said," Gettyson said heavily. "It was a magic fire."

We pulled back to my loaner car, an impromptu island in the parking lot for a group of survivors. According to Gettyson, there were a few still missing, but . . .

"We were lucky," Gettyson said. "Damn lucky. Full moon proper was at eight this morning. Half the kin are gone, and most of the rest were out on an early hunt."

"Not *that* lucky—we lost the werehouse," I said. "Damnit, Gettyson, you knew covering it with paint didn't work, you *knew* I needed to take pictures, and you went and painted it anyway! Not that I know we could have stopped it if we could have seen it—"

"I thought if the paint dried, maybe . . . " Gettyson said. "He sure showed me."

Saffron, Darkrose and Calaphase made one last sweep for survivors and returned empty handed. "Do you have any further need of me?" Saffron asked, as Gettyson and I tended to Cinnamon on the hood of my loaner car.

"No, my Lady Saffron," Gettyson said. "On behalf of the Bear King, our thanks."

Saffron nodded, then glanced at Cinnamon. She sighed, seemed about to say something, then looked up at me and Calaphase and stomped off. Darkrose bowed slightly, eyes lingering on me in apology, then followed her mistress back to their Mercedes, which quickly squealed off.

"Mom?" Cinnamon said weakly, coughing. "Mom, why are you here?" Then her eyes widened. "Oh my God! What—what happened?"

"A fire, little Cinnamon," Gettyson said, tousling her hair. "Don't worry. Your little wolf cub is safe. I gots Tully out looking for the punk that set this, and when we finds him . . . "

"You'll bring that little punk back *alive*," I said, patting down Cinnamon's brow with a wet-wipe. "You'll bring him back alive. He is *not* working alone, and I want to question him."

Gettyson started to retort, then looked at my eyes. Remembered what ignoring me had already cost us. He looked away, then back at Cinnamon as I cradled her. "All right," he said, relaxing a little. "We does it your way. You earned it. We knows where your loyalties lie."

Then the blinding white light of a spotlight pinned us all where we were, and we looked up to see a knot of smoke pushed away by a black helicopter, descending in silence.

"This is the D-E-I!" a loudspeaker screeched. "Everyone stay where you are!"

18. ATTACK ON THE WEREHOUSE

Werekin scattered like cockroaches. Two more helicopters appeared— sleek as fish, black as night, quieter than vacuum cleaners: Shadowhawks, the stealth helicopters favored by the DEI. And then the loudspeaker blared again: "This is the D-E-I! Stay where you are!"

"Oh thank God," I said, staring up into the light. I knew the voice. "That's Philip!"

"Hell," Calaphase said. "We need to get out of here."

"Why?" I said. "We need the help, and we've done nothing wrong—"

"*You* maybe," Gettyson spat, tearing off his jacket. "But the werekin here just got outed!"

"But . . . " I said. "But I never gave away the werehouse's location."

"You idiot! You *let them track you!*" Gettyson shouted, throwing his jacket at me.

The moment he said it, I knew he was right. Stunned, I watched him tear off into the distance as DEI agents slid down from two of the helicopters on wires. Several followed him, and a team of four converged upon us as the Shadowhawks swung round and settled towards the ground. They had their guns out. *They had their guns out.* I had to stop this.

"Let me handle this," Calaphase said, starting forward. "I—"

"No," I said sharply. "Stay here. Cop doesn't mix well with vamp. You too, honey, you just lie here," I said, patting Cinnamon's head. "Let me deal with the police."

"Mom?" she asked, then sat up sharply. "*Mom!*"

"Hey, hey," I cried, waving my arms at the flak-jacketed agents. "Thank God you're here, but what's with the ordinance? We need fire fighters, not a fire fight."

"On the ground!" the lead agent shouted, a big, tough black man with close-trimmed hair and a no-nonsense demeanor—but his eyes were a bit wild. "On the ground now!"

I was appalled, but I didn't let him stop me. He was a cop, and, fundamentally, we were on the same side. All I had to do was keep everyone talking until we were *all* calmed down.

"Whoa, gentlemen. I'm the official representative of the Little—of the Oakdale vampire clan," I said, spreading my hands. "We provide security on this site under the umbrella of the Vampire Consulates of Atlanta, and as you can see we've got a situation here—"

"Shut it!" the agent shouted—enraged, buzz cut, *jaaaar head.* "On the ground."

"Where the hell do you think you are, federal land?" I said. "Maybe you didn't notice zip-lining down from Shamu the Flying Leafblower there, but it's posted—you're *trespassing.* If you ain't here to help, I sure as *hell* hope you have a no-knock warrant—"

"What the hell's this?" a second DEI agent said, training his shotgun on me. It was a Benelli, the kind Philip used. "A street lawyer?"

"More importantly, what the hell's *that?*" a third agent said, pointing behind me. "It's like she's half tiger or something."

"Oh, shit," the second one said. "We've got a lyke changing here."

Oh, hell no. "What you've *got* is more than you can handle," I said, raising my hands towards them and sliding one foot back, "unless you cough up a warrant—"

"Shut it!" the first agent said, as the others tried to flank me. "All right, street lawyer, back to law school. Myers, cuff her. Johann, Briggs, secure the lyke before she changes."

"*Spirit of justice, shield my stand,*" I said—and shot both hands out wide.

My vines unfolded, and in shock the agent fired. The blast scattered off my growing shield, stung my skin—*what were they using? silver? salt? a mixture?*—and knocked me back. I was shocked by the noise and impact and my face flushed in terror—but there was no way the agents could see that through the green glow of my vines shining on their astonished faces.

I settled into a solid karate stance, extending my vines out into a thicket to bar their path to my child and friends. As I settled and my vines thickened, they glowed brighter, their green overpowering the red light of the flames— and the officers backed up. Apparently skindancing was rare enough they simply weren't prepared, and just looked dumbfounded.

"Settle down, gentlemen," I said, trying not to let my shaking show. *Jesus Christ. I just got shot in the chest.* But these men had been coming after my child, and if I'd learned anything from Taido, it was this: don't *initiate* violence, but once your guard's up, never let it down. "Until I see a warrant, you aren't badges, you're just trespassers on private property."

"Down, Dakota," said Special Agent Philip Davidson, striding briskly forward from the now-landed copter, shotgun over his shoulders. He wore a flak jacket over one of his thousand-dollar suits, his brown hair looked black in the dying light of the flames, and his goatee made him look like a villain—but he was smiling. Part of me was glad to see him; the rest wanted to punch him for letting his officers get this far out of hand. "And stand down, gentlemen."

"This ain't your op, Davidson," the first officer cracked. "And Namura said—"

"*I'm* the ranking officer," Philip said, "and *I'll* deal with the Director. Stand down."

"Philip," I said, easing down, furling my vines—slowly. "I'm so glad to see you."

"Dakota, you should know better than to interfere with Federal agents. I should arrest you on general principles." But he stopped next to the agent who'd fired, radiating the calm disapproval he was so good at. "I *said* there would be civilians on scene. Did you just discharge your weapon point-blank onto my *unarmed girlfriend* while her hands were empty?"

"But there's a lyke—and she was—" the agent began. "Uh, no, well, uh, sir—"

"Make that 'uh, *yes* sir'—he *did* shoot little old unarmed me," I said, not giving Philip 'girlfriend' after the 'valuable resource' crack—but folding my arms so he wouldn't see my hands tremble. "And yes, my hands were indeed up—"

"But she was resisting," the agent said, as Philip just stared at him.

"Standing with my hands out pleading for calm?" I said, glaring. "Look, maybe I was being hardnosed; but that's my daughter back there. You didn't leave me any choice."

"Only you, Dakota, could take a shotgun blast to the chest and then apologize for being hardnosed," Philip said, amazed, stepping right up to me, hands touching a hole in my vest.

"Holy shit," I murmured; my vines had protected me, but not my clothes. I deflated a little. "I didn't expect that."

"Lucky woman is the phrase I'd use," Philip said. "After your 'emotional experience' you had toned your bravado down; I take it the volume's back up?"

"I wish you hadn't brought *that* up," I said. 'Emotional experience' was a bit of Fed jargon for getting the shit kicked out of you—in my case, by the vampire Transomnia. It didn't take much for me to see his cold red eyes, to feel my fingers in those garden clippers, to remember that I could tattoo now only because he'd let me go. "I was trying to forget."

"I was trying to *make* you remember," Philip said, finger picking at a hole in my corset. "You've *got* to think things through. No agent will take chances arresting a werekin—at the first sign of resistance they'll shoot first and sort it out later. What if you'd been a half second slower with your shield? You'd be dead and probably would everyone else on your side."

"What was I supposed to do?" I said. "Lie down and hope?"

"That's the law," Philip said firmly. "Anything else is resisting arrest—"

"The phrase I'd use is *defending my daughter*," I said hotly. "Philip, I was raised on the force and I reject the idea cops can't listen to reason. Why didn't you prep the agents?"

"I tried, but I can't be everywhere watching over every agent's shoulder—and what if I hadn't been here at all?" He reached out and briefly squeezed my shaking hand. "You *can't* count on me to always ride to your rescue, no matter how much I'd like to."

"I know," I said. I was still steamed, but I still tingled at the brief brush of his fingers. Then Calaphase shifted behind me uncomfortably—and Philip caught it.

"That your new beau?" he asked, leaning slightly so he could stare around my shoulder. Philip was shorter than most, though it didn't show, given how he carried himself. "The *fang?*"

"If you mean the blond vampire," I said, frowning, "we've had one *half-date*, and if you feel jealous, you should have seen the look on Saffron's face when she ran into us."

Philip looked up sharply, saw the missing collar. "Oh, I'm sorry," he said. "Though I could see how she would see it as a breach of trust."

"Breach of trust?" I said. "*You* had me tailed—"

"I'd never have *you* tailed," Philip said, glancing over his shoulder, "and you *have* to know sending an assault unit into a werehouse filled with children was not my idea."

I followed his gaze to see a trim young Japanese man striding towards us in a neat, pinstriped suit. He surveyed the officers, the huddle of survivors around my car, and then me and Philip, and then stepped up and said, "So, Agent Davidson, I take it you have secured the scene."

"Yes, Assistant Director Namura," Philip said. "There's the issue of—"

"Not quite," I said, folding my arms again. "There's the small matter of the warrant, not to mention the illegal surveillance you had to be doing to follow me here."

"And you must be Dakota Frost," Namura said, black eyes inspecting me with amused displeasure. "Are you aware it is illegal to practice magic in Georgia without a license?"

"I'm a licensed magical tattooist," I said. "Licensed to 'ink magical marks and perform related tattooing magic.' Just because people don't understand what tattoo magic can do . . . "

But Namura closed his eyes suddenly, and you could see them working back and forth rapidly beneath his lids, like he was scanning something. "Yes, yes of course," he said, voice almost bored as he withdrew something from his coat pocket. "That will do."

"What, aren't you going to claim to be offended?" I asked, staring at what I guessed was a warrant in his hand. "To make a case that I'm skirting the law—"

"The point of the law is that you have training to use magic and know how to handle magical materials safely," he said, unfolding the papers. "Clearly you have training, and if your skin is the spellcasting material, there's no danger of it falling into the wrong hands."

"Don't be too sure of that," Philip and I said simultaneously.

The man raised an eyebrow, then held the letter out. "Our warrant, Miss Frost."

I took it. I'd never seen a Federal warrant before; I had no idea what they looked like. I hadn't even known they were issued by the U.S. District Court. For all I knew they'd made this up at Kinko's—but it looked official, and I took careful note of the most important details:

Takashi Namura and any Authorized Officer of the United States, . . . *having trumped up the necessary evidence and waved around the scary word 'werewolf', are hereby authorized to roust the nearby werehouse for* . . . **concealed on the person or property Un-Licensed Lycan-thropic** *(sic)* **Housing Facility**.

"You see this *is* a no-knock warrant," Namura said. "This conversation is a courtesy."

"As long as everyone's talking, no-one's shooting or biting," I said quietly.

"My apologies," he said, more quietly. "I saw you take a shotgun blast and *not* strike back. Most impressive. On behalf of my men, thank you for trying to defuse the situation."

"Maybe I did that a little for them," I said, "but mostly it was for my daughter."

He glanced at her, then closed his eyes again, letting them flicker behind his lids. Then he opened them, nodded, and turned to his men. "Where are the sirens? Where is our police backup, the ambulances, the fire trucks? There are injured people there. Why are you not helping them?"

The agents jerked at the sound of his voice, like he'd cracked a whip; yet he had barely raised his voice, and you could tell nothing from his face. Even Philip twitched, but Namura said, "Stay with this group. I don't want to lose them, even if they aren't the fish we hoped to catch."

"All this wasn't a response to the fire," I said, understanding growing in my mind. "It couldn't have been. You were going to roust the werehouse anyway."

"This," Namura said, "is the inevitable fallout of the attack you *partially* reported earlier. You called in *attempted murder by magic*, but didn't give us enough information to perform a proper investigation. We had to follow up. You should know that."

"Of course," I said. "No good deed goes unpunished."

"Maybe," Namura said, turning to survey the fire, the swarming agents. "But, now that we are here, know that 'rousting' the werehouse is going to take a back seat to responding to the fire. In the end, the safety of these . . . well, these *people* is our first duty."

"All right," I said heavily. "On that note . . . we couldn't get everyone out."

"There's always a further complication," Namura said, striding off towards his men, motioning to one of them. "We'll send rescue crews in everywhere we can—"

"Have them watch out," I said. "I have strong reason to believe this was a magic fire."

Namura scowled. "We'll want to question you," he said. "Don't go anywhere."

We all stood there in uncomfortable silence, not wanting to look at each other. Philip remained damnably quiet. I expected my big bad vampire beau to bust out with some creepy bullshit to knock his human rival off guard, but Calaphase looked actually embarrassed. Every time he looked like he wanted to say something, he just bit it off and kept quiet.

I certainly wasn't going to say anything

In minutes there were sirens in the distance, followed by police cars, ambulances, and three or four fire trucks. The firemen made short work of what was left of the blaze and stopped a fire that was left in the woods. Only the tag itself kept "burning," but it was no longer real fire: it was just colored streamers of magic that only looked like flame, slowly weakening.

Namura summoned me back to the tag to explain to the firemen how to set up a magic circle. They nodded, but I don't think they were really listening. They just kept their eyes on the tag hoping that the magic would fade on its own without them having to deal with it.

"Oh, hell, it's you," cursed a familiar voice, and I turned to see a dwarf Columbo wannabe stomping up to me—McGough from the Black Hats magical crime squad.

"It is indeed me," I said, smiling back at him, surprised to realize I liked the guy. Something about having been through this before put us on the same team. He radiated calm, thought on his feet and the look he gave Namura's team spoke volumes. I was betting he didn't like Namura's tactics any more than I did. "And how the hell are you?"

"I was fine until I saw you, you tattooed witch," he said, trying to suppress a smile: apparently he liked me too. He leaned back and stared at the slow rainbow fire leaking out of the top of the whitewash. "What kind of mess have you gotten yourself into this time?"

"I didn't get myself into anything, you little toad," I said, holding up my hands. "This was Cinnamon's home. She was having a bad change, and we came here for help. *Then* all hell broke loose."

"Yeah, yeah, likely story," McGough said, still staring, his wrinkled little face lit up by the strobing light like he was standing on a dance floor. "Before anyone from the D.A.'s office shows up and tells me to lock you in the clink, any ideas?"

"Oh, I've got ideas," I said, reaching out and touching the whitewash. A bit of it came off on my finger, and I held it up to him. "Under this shit is the mural that attacked T . . . the werekin I reported. The other werekin painted it over before I could take pictures, but it was definitely by the same tagger, or more likely, crew of taggers that killed Revenance."

"Oh, shit, don't tell me it's a crew," he said, raising a hand to scratch the back of his neck. "Don't you tell me that. How are we going to track them now?"

"Different hands, but the same style," I said. "Also, we noticed some wind effects, like when we tried to save Revenance. I think at least one tagger was within eyesight, helping fan the flames. I wouldn't be surprised if they set the fire as revenge for whitewashing the tag."

"I'd believe it, the jerks," McGough said, nodding. Then he smiled. "Alright, go back and wait with the civvies before someone notices you're over here. Last thing I need is some idiot D.A. trying to force your foot into a 'misuse of magic' slipper."

"Namura *asked* me to come over here," I said. "You don't really think—"

"—people look for their keys under the lamplight because it's where they can see without having to think to hard?" McGough said bitterly. "Yeah I do, just like I think a DA tired of chasing her tail might decide you're guilty because you're always around. Now *get out of my crime scene* before someone decides to pick you up and see if you're the key to a promotion and new Lexus. Shoo! I might need you later."

I went. But, OK, I had to admit it: I really was starting to like the little toad.

But when I got back to my car, the pit fell out of my stomach. The Mercedes had returned, bringing Saffron and Darkrose. A tanned, ripped Native American man was there too, the human form of Lord Buckhead, the fae Master of the Hunt and patron of the werehouse. Saffron, Buckhead and Calaphase were arguing with Namura, who looked unhappy. But none of them moved to stop the officers arresting Gettyson, Fischer and half a dozen other elder werekin.

"These people are under my protection," Saffron snarled.

"And mine as well," Lord Buckhead said, glaring down at Namura.

"*And* mine," Calaphase said.

"That's fine in the Edgeworld," Namura responded, "but they still must follow the law."

"What the hell is going on?" I asked.

All of their eyes turned on me. When Saffron's eyes met mine, Namura abruptly cursed, and something white and gleaming dropped out of his hand. Calaphase and Darkrose flinched as a cross fell to the ground and bounced before Saffron's feet, white hot.

Saffron winced, but she stood her ground, still glaring at me. Finally, she bent down, picked up the cross, grimacing in pain, and then stood, holding it in the palm of her hand as white magical fire rose off of it, fueled by feedback between her power and her hostility.

Her eyes locked with mine, red and glowing. "I forgive you," she said. But the cross was still burning. She meant me harm. She *still* meant me harm—her flash of rage at Canoe hadn't evaporated; it had crystallized into a grudge. And, worse, she saw *me* as the guilty party.

Eventually I realized she expected me to respond. I was flabbergasted: I could barely believe she was letting our spat at Canoe get in the way of dealing with the very real problem of Namura arresting the weres. Calaphase was right: she wasn't acting like a vampire queen.

"Apology accepted," I replied, *you spoiled brat.*

Her expression flickered—she caught that *I* wasn't going to take the blame. Her face fell, her eyes softened. She drew in a breath, let it out slowly, and the flame in her hand went out. She flicked the cross to Namura, who cursed and dropped it, holding his hand like he'd been burnt.

"This isn't over," she said, not looking at Namura. "The Consulate will be in touch."

"Of course," he said, pulling a handkerchief out of his pocket. "Of course it will."

He picked up the still-hot cross and looked around at all of us, worried and afraid. His eyes fell on Philip, who was sitting next to Calaphase, talking in a low voice.

"A daywalker ruling the vampires? Vampires working with werekin? An entire werekin compound? And *skindancers* out in the open? I'm disappointed, Agent Davidson," he said. "To let this kind of power build up—"

"It was in all my reports," Philip said, standing. "You just didn't listen."

"Frost!" a voice shouted, and I saw an officer putting Gettyson in a squad car. Gettyson threw him off and glared at me. Apparently running an "unlicensed werekin housing facility" merited more than a slap on the wrist. "I told you this would happen!"

I started to say a dozen things, but stopped as I realized it didn't matter. At the end of the day, I was walking away—and Gettyson was being arrested.

As one officer, then two, then three wrestled futilely with him, Gettyson just glared at me with pure contempt burning out of his wide-pupiled eyes. I swallowed. No matter how this came out, regardless of who was to blame, I had made a true enemy.

"I was wrong earlier," Gettyson snarled. "*Now* we knows where your loyalties lie."

19.   NOT IN MY BACKYARD

The DEI held us at the werehouse as long as they *possibly* could, asking questions, telling us to wait, and asking us questions again. Apparently, having a magical fire and homicide on the site of a DEI operation had created a jurisdictional mess. Finally Namura relented when I tracked him down gabbing on his cell phone and told him to arrest us or let us go.

Now the werehouse was far behind us, and Cinnamon was beside me in the seat of the loaner—but rather than overjoyed at our reunion, she just looked sick. Her skin was covered with fine downy fur, her eyes were closed, and she kept swallowing. "Mom, hurry, please, hurry."

"Can you hold it?" I asked.

"Yeah," she said, very quietly. "God, I feels sick."

"Are you going to hur—going to throw up?" She didn't answer, and, feeling like a cad, I said, "Just let me know if you need me to stop. I don't own this one. We can't mess it up."

"I'm sorry," she said, anguished. "I'm so sorry! I didn't mean to ruin it."

"It's all right," I said, patting her leg. "You're more important than a car."

"But . . . " she said, and then shut up, swallowing again. I kept my eyes on the road, but out of the corner of my eye I could swear she was getting furrier every time I looked. "God, feels like Six Flags. Dumbasses put me on a rollercoaster, thought it was funny. Up and down, up and down, Mindbender, fuck! I was puking the whole night." She swallowed again. "Now I gots it again, except *I'm* the rollercoaster. I changes, I changes back, I changes, I changes back . . . "

"Well, don't worry," I said, pulling the car to a stop. "We're here."

My flat was on the second floor of a home in Candler Park, itself tucked behind a larger home that the owner, Donna Olsen, had subdivided into apartments after her husband died. Now she lived beneath me, in a small little ground floor flat that was "all she needed."

Given the hours I normally kept, this was not a problem; but her lights were on, and the last thing we needed was an hour and a half of Mrs. Olsen pinning us down on the stairs with Cinnamon one sneeze away from turning furry.

I pulled up into the narrow concrete drive and squeezed out. It was barely wide enough to open the door—on either side, which I'd never noticed before. The Accord was a notch bigger than the Prius, and before the Prius, I'd parked my Vespa beneath the stairs. But I got Cinnamon out and up the stairs before Mrs. Olsen could come out and trap us into conversation.

In the center of the room was the biggest dog cage I could find at PetSmart. I opened it and started looking for something to use as bedding; Cinnamon immediately began pulling off her clothes—raggedy old top, Capri shorts, the kind of castoffs she wore before I took her in, but I knew her: even if they were rags she cared enough about them not to tear them to pieces. In moments she was down to her undies, her tiger-stripe tattoos—and her silver collar.

"We should get Darkrose to take this off," Cinnamon growled, tugging at the collar—then she looked sharply over at my neck. "Where's yours?"

"Long story," I said, returning with a blanket and stuffing it onto the floor of the cage.

"The bitch found out about you and Calaphase," Cinnamon said, staring at me, changing by the moment, striped with fur now rather than tattoos, tail slashing the air, eyes glowing yellow, pupils tightening to ovals. "Someone should teach her a lesson."

"Cinnamon!" I said sharply. "In the cage!"

She hesitated, but only a second. Then she pulled off her underwear, fell onto her hands and knees and prowled forward. There were pops and shudders as her body changed, but unlike our old friend Wulf, who had been born a human and whose changes were protracted and painful, Cinnamon had been born a werekin. So by the time she passed into the cage she was fully changed, a hulking tiger who glared at me sidelong with one angular eye.

I closed the door of the cage and swallowed. That huge eye reminded me of my own cats, except for the pupil: not sharply slitted like a cat's, but oval, almost human. Then fear reminded me that a tiger's eyes *aren't* slitted: that slight oval cant wasn't a sign of 'humanity,' but instead that she was fully changed. Something *else* reminded me that a tiger's eyes only became oval when constricted in bright light—her eyes had just become six times more sensitive.

I snapped off the overhead, leaving me in the gloom with the predator.

When I felt I could control my face, I looked at her. Cinnamon was in tiger form, true, but somehow . . . recognizably Cinnamon. She shifted in the cage, snarling. Even hunched up, she was far too big for it, and its sides bowed and bent as she tried to get comfortable—but she didn't try to break out. Finally, she curled up on the blanket and began chewing at it.

"I'm sorry this is so small," I said, reaching towards her. She struck at the wire with an odd, fluttering snarl and I jerked my hand back; but when she left the paw on the wire, flexing it, I reached in and stroked the back of her paw—then swallowed. Her claws had to be over four inches long. *Jesus.* They felt hard and cruel under my fingers; but the monster paw seemed to relax under my touch. "It was the largest they had, and you're . . . bigger than I remembered."

Cinnamon blinked at me slowly, then yawned and withdrew her paw.

Trembling, I stood and stepped back from the cage. "Get some sleep if you can," I said. "We've got a lot of work to do to get ready for school on Friday."

Cinnamon just stared at me, and after a minute I turned and walked away.

What the hell had I gotten myself into?

I made busy work for myself around the apartment—turning on lights in other rooms, putting Cinnamon's rags in the washer, taking off my own worn clothes, putting my vestcoat in the hamper for the drycleaners. When I unlaced the corset, I saw the hole Philip had poked at. It went clean through the front, though I had no wound in my belly.

Half of me felt lucky to be alive; the other half just felt pissed. I had no idea how the expensive handmade garment could be repaired, and I didn't have the coin to drop on a new one, not between Cinnamon's tuition and the payments on the blue bomb. The Valentine Foundation welshing was really messing me up. I should never have bought that car before seeing the first cent of my winnings. Now, *everything* was harder.

I dumped the corset in the hamper and went to the kitchen. I laid down canned food for the cats, wondering where they were; probably somewhere in the apartment, tucked up into frozen little balls, more scared of Cinnamon than I was.

I had no idea what to feed *her* in this state. Perhaps I should run to the store and get . . . what? Raw meat? *Hell.* I threw away the pet food can reflexively and glared into my separated bins. There weren't enough recyclables to warrant the drive. Stupid City of Atlanta, all they picked up was trash. At least that was full; taking it out gave me some semblance of normalcy.

I stomped down the stairs towards the trash can and stopped halfway down. "Hello, Mrs. Olsen," I said, feeling rather than hearing her presence beside me.

"Hello, Dakota," Mrs. Olsen said. Her long hair only *looked* grey against the soft folds of her long purple sweater. She had cultivated a spinsterly appearance after her husband had been killed in Iraq, but she had a son not much older than Cinnamon on his first tour over there. She smiled, her cherubic face dimpling as she lifted a wastebasket filled with papers, aluminum cans, and an old phone book. I strongly suspected she'd left it by her own back door and waited to take it out so she'd have an excuse to talk to me. "You know you can call me Donna."

I watched her dump enough recyclables to finish off my own separated loads and shook my head. "All right, Donna," I said, marching down the stairs. "I've just always felt odd calling you anything other than Mrs. Olsen. I guess it was the way I was raised.."

"Now, Dakota," Donna preened, as I dumped off my own trash. "You've been here too many years for last names—and to think you'll be gone soon. I will miss you."

"I did want to talk to you about that. Did you get my message—"

"I've got the nicest young couple ready to move into your flat," she said, leaning forward and letting her voice drop to a whisper. "Lesbians, if you can believe that."

"Imagine that," I said, smiling.

"I'm really glad to help them," she said, gesturing with the garbage basket. "They even offered to paint my flat rather than pay a security deposit."

"But I'm willing to bet you'll just let them skip it," I said. Donna had done the same for me, a few years ago, when I'd been hard up and needed to find a place after splitting with Saffron. "Did you get my message? Can they push their move date back—"

A piercing screech erupted from the top of the stairs, followed by a loud crash. Donna's head jerked up suddenly at the horrible yowling alarm that wailed out of my flat and the weird, freakish chirping that followed. "Oh my God, I think something's killing your cats . . . "

And before I could stop her, she dropped the wastebasket and bolted up the stairs.

"No, wait," I said, following her. I reached for her sweater, but my fingers closed on the air as Donna really put on speed, bursting the door open and turning on the light. She froze in there, then jerked back so I almost ran over her.

Cinnamon remained in her bowed-out cage, but awake, alert, snarling, as two of my cats yowled back at her. Little black-and-white Xanadu stood not three feet away, spotted back arched so high it looked like someone was pulling up on her belly with an invisible coat hanger; big old raccoonish Rafael was crouched down by the kitchen door, curled up as tight as he could get, with food bowls and recycling hampers tumbled every which way around him. Cinnamon snarled again, then saw me and, eyes wide, struck the cage with her paw in a sudden plea, emitting the freakish chirp we'd heard below—like a monster bird crying for its mother.

I relaxed a little. The cats had just padded in to get their food, then everyone freaked. No one had hurt anyone; it was just another period of adjustment. Something else to get used to.

But not, apparently, just for us.

"Oh my God," Donna cried. "You have a tiger—"

"She's not a tiger—" I said, but Donna kept babbling.

"—brought it into my *house*," Donna said. "A pet *tiger!*"

At the word *pet* Cinnamon's head jerked up and she growled, making Donna press back against me. I raised my hand. "Down, Cinnamon," I said sharply. "You're not helping."

"Cinnamon . . . " Donna said, turning to me, eyes wide in horror.

"She *is* a tiger, but she's *not* a pet," I said. "This is my *daughter*, and she's a—"

"A were-*tiger*," Donna said, shrinking back against the wall. "I've heard of such things, but . . . werewolves are bad enough, but were-*tigers* . . . "

"There's nothing to fear," I said, turning off the overhead. "You've met Cinnamon."

"Yes, yes, yes, I *have*," Donna said, fear becoming *anger*. "And you had her standing not three feet from me showing her off like she was a normal human being."

"She *is* a normal human being," I said, realizing as I said it how ridiculous it sounded with Animal Planet near bursting out of a cage before us. "With a condition. She gets furry—"

"This may be all very funny to you," Donna said, straightening up, adjusting her sweater, but still plastered against the wall as far from Cinnamon as she could manage. "But it's not funny to me! Not funny at all! Lycanthropy is a *disease*. It's *contagious!* I want you out of here—"

"But we're not ready. In fact, we need to extend our lease," I said, rubbing my brow. I knew where this was going. "I told you in voicemail, our closing date was pushed back."

"I don't *care* what happened to you," Donna said. "You bring this *thing* here into my home, this thing that could *infect* me, and expect me to shelter you? I want you out!"

I exhaled sharply. "*Fine*," I said. "We'll be out Monday, like we agreed."

"No," Donna said, drawing herself up. "I want you out now, now, now!"

"Donna," I said. "We have a lease—"

"I don't care!" she said, voice growing more shrill. "I won't have this diseased thing in a home that I own for one more instant! You get her out of here or I call the police!"

"Donna—"

"Get out! Get out! *Get out!*" she screamed. "I'll not have a *monster* under my roof!"

20. A FROSTY FAMILY DINNER

"Mom," Cinnamon said softly in the passenger seat. "Why did you fold?"

The last few days had been a blur. Finding a hotel. Smuggling Cinnamon inside. Turning the tiger back into the schoolgirl; losing the schoolgirl within the school walls, if only for the day. And dealing with the awful, awful mess left by the werehouse fire.

And then it was a sunny Saturday and we were back in the blue bomb, shooting up I-85 towards Stratton, South Carolina. I got a tingle when we passed through the Perimeter—the more tattoos I had, the more aware I was of the giant magic circle buried beneath Atlanta's encircling highways—but no dragons swooped out of the sky to scoop us up, dang it, and soon, we were driving beneath happy puffy clouds dotting a bright blue sky over a rolling forested Interstate.

Unfortunately, these happy clouds did not extend to the interior of the car.

"I means," Cinnamon said, "it was our place. She had no *right*—"

"No, no she didn't," I said, "but you were changed, and snarling, and I was afraid she'd call the cops and they'd haul you off, cage and all, to the Atlanta City Jail. Or the Zoo."

"Mom!" Cinnamon said, half outraged, half giggling. Then her giggle faded. "The Academy sucks. They're putting me in the stupid class."

"What?" I asked. "Why would they do that? They know you're behind. They should have held you back a grade, not stuffed you in a *remedial* class."

"Not remedial," she said, and I was impressed that she didn't ask what that meant. "Tutoring, for math. Three days a week, after school."

"Okay," I said, pulling off at the Commerce exit. "Okay. That's not so bad."

"Why are we stopping?" Cinnamon said. "Isn't Stratton eighty-four more miles?"

"Hey, she can subtract. Sure you need tutoring?" I said, and she swatted at me. "But Commerce *is* our stop. It's as far south as Dad will go, and as far north as *I* will go—"

"Your demilitarized zone," Cinnamon said, with a sudden smile.

"Yeah," I said, grinning. "Our DMZ. I like that."

In moments we were pulling into Denny's parking lot, a bright houselike building outside the Tanger Outlet center. Once this was a dark, boxy Shoney's, Dad's favorite stop for food on family road trips; now, years later, we still met here out of inertia. I parked, slammed the door, and put my hand on Cinnamon's shoulder, steeling myself for the inevitable.

Dad stood peering at an AJC newspaper dispenser, trying to "see what they're up to down here these days." He was a big, beefy, kindly man, ex-linebacker, balding, with a light fringe of blond-grey hair trimmed close, graying a little only around his ears. His brown sweater and white shirt were old-school but high-quality, the colors rich, the whites pure and luminous.

He saw me, straightened, and threw on a smile which quickly faded.

"H-hey, Kotie," Dad said, face to face for the first time in three years. His eyes flickered over me, almost wincing at my deathhawk and tattoos; then they flickered to Cinnamon, wary. He swallowed, started forward, extending his hand. "I-it's great to see you again."

"Hey, Dad," I said quietly, trying to hide my disappointment. I already knew what was about to happen; we wouldn't even get to shake hands first. "It's good to see you too—"

And then it happened: the grey-haired, drawn-faced, beige-jacketed man who had been trailing Dad stepped between us, forcing his face into a smile.

"Dakota Frost," he said, taking one hand off his floppy Bible and extending it towards us. "I'm Doctor Price Isaacson. I'm pleased to meet you."

"Pleased to meet you too, Doctor Isaacson," I said, taking his hand and letting him pump mine. Vacant-eyed, pushy, and on a mission: just how Dad liked his pastors. "And what congregation do you preach for, Doctor?"

"Stratton Independent Baptist," he said, eyes brightening. "I'm glad to see you show interest in the preaching of the Word, but who do we have here?"

Isaacson half-squatted, looking at Cinnamon and extending his hand with a bright foolish smile like he was talking to a five-year-old. She did not extend her hand, but twitched and pressed back against me, letting out a sharp exhale of breath before she finally spoke.

"My name is Cinnamon Frost," she said, staring down at his hand.

Doctor Isaacson stood and leaned back with something like approval. "Don't trust strangers," he said. "But Richard didn't tell me you had a child."

"Cinnamon is adopted," I said. "Just recently, in fact."

"Well, well, that's great," Dad said, stepping forward nervously. "I didn't know you'd, you'd be bringing her with you. Hey, ah, let's eat."

I really don't remember what food I liked at Shoney's as a child, and I don't remember what I ate at Denny's that day either. As always, there was so much else to talk about. As a child, Mom, Dad and I had always really opened up at Shoney's, and now, after all this time, I was desperate to tell Dad how glad I was to see him, to ask about what was going on in Stratton, to find out about his consulting work, to hear about Mom's side of the family—or to tell Dad about Cinnamon. But it seemed like we never really got into that. Instead, almost immediately—

"So, Kotie," Dad said. "When are you going to stop tattooing and get a real job?"

"I make fifty thousand dollars a year tattooing, Dad," I said, "and my hours are my own."

"Kotie, tattooing is the Devil's work," Dad began. "The Bible says—"

"You eat non-Kosher meat, Dad," I said. "You shave your beard. You wear mixed-weave fabrics. All prohibited by the part of the O.T. you're quoting—Leviticus 19. Go down that path, you'll have to close your bank accounts and quit coaching Stratton Police softball on Sundays."

"He *said* you were a Bible Bowl champion," Isaacson said. "But even if we aren't going that far, there are a lot of reasons to give up tattooing. A lot of people regret them later."

"I don't do jinxes," I said. "No personal names, obscene images or religious symbols."

Isaacson raised an eyebrow, glancing at my hands: a row of religious icons was on each knuckle: a Christian cross, a Star of David, an Islamic crescent, even a yin-yang.

"I take responsibility for inking myself," I said, flashing the larger yin-yang on my palm, "but I won't put a permanent slogan on a living person who may later have a change of heart."

"That's wise—even if you change your mind, you can't easily take ink back," Isaacson said. "Did you know it can take up to a dozen laser treatments to remove a tattoo?"

"Or you can use magical ink, and peel them off with one wave of mana,"

I said.

Isaacson's eyes tightened a little bit at the word 'magical,' but he forged ahead. "But most people leave them in, and if you do, the ink can cause cancers—"

"*Not* often, and not with modern ink," I said, folding my arms. "And as you may have guessed from the Prius, I'm a tree-hugger. Everything I use is hypo-allergenic, and I subscribe to two different dermatology journals. As soon as a pigment proves bad—"

"But how," Isaacson said, "can you really *know* it isn't bad?"

"Fucking jerk," Cinnamon said, sneezing. Then she seemed to notice us all staring at her and set her chin, sullen. "Mom's the biggest—*fuck!*—the biggest square of them all, and you acts like she's doin' somethin' wrong making people look beautiful! I means, fuck—"

"Cinnamon!" I said. "We talked about your language, and the insults."

"Reaping what you've sown," Dad said. "You set a bad example. I've *told* you—"

"Richard," Isaacson said, staring at Cinnamon intently, "that's not helping."

"You tells it. Fuck, I just met her," Cinnamon said, "and I always talked like this!"

"She didn't," Dad said sharply, "and she's *my daughter.*"

"Dad," I warned, pointing a finger at him.

"*She's my Mom!*" Cinnamon said, face twisting in anger. "Fuck, leave her alone—"

"Cinnamon!" I said, pointing at her—then stopped; my hands were crossed in front of myself pointing at each of them. I put my hands on the table and sighed.

"All right, both of you, settle down," I said. "Cinnamon, you watch your language. My Dad is from the old school, but he's a good man."

"Well," Dad spluttered, "well, thank you Kotie—"

"And Dad, grow up," I said. "I have no excuse for my mouth. You gave me every advantage. Cinnamon, on the other hand, has every excuse; she was on the streets two months ago. She had no advantages, and we're all going to have to cut her a little slack."

"Well said," Doctor Isaacson said, still staring at Cinnamon intently, leaning his head on his closed fist like he was miming 'The Thinker.' "You know, Jesus once said—"

"Please, Doctor, don't start," I said wearily. "Now, everyone, please be nice to each other. I am going to the bathroom, and I don't want anyone to be dead when I get back."

But before I'd gotten halfway to the door, Isaacson had hopped up from the table and intercepted me, his weathered, wiry hand falling on my own with firmness. "Miss Frost," he said, "I hate to butt in on your raising of your daughter, but there's something you need to know . . . "

"Look, you," I said, then softened. "Doc, thanks for taking Cinnamon's side, but I really didn't need the first meeting I've had with my Dad in three years spoilt by a sermon."

"I should never have let Richard talk me into this. I'm sorry," Isaacson said, and looking in his eyes, I saw he was sincere. "But I need to talk to you about your daughter's problem."

He had that soft, sad pitying look, and I got my dander back up, ready to hear him give a whole lecture about how I needed to get her into a Christian school.

"You may have noticed Cinnamon going through a lot of changes now that she's in her teens," Isaacson began. "I've seen this before. It can be *so hard* on kids with her problem."

"There's nothing wrong with being a werekin—"

"That's not the 'problem' I mean," he said gently. "And I admit this is a snap judgment, so you should definitely get a second opinion, but . . . please, please, take this seriously. I *have* dealt with this problem before, and I'd never suggest that someone had it as a joke."

"What is it?" I said. "Just what do you think is Cinnamon's problem?"

"I'm *so* sorry, Miss Frost," Isaacson said. "I think your daughter has Tourette's."

21.   VACATIONING IN COVENTRY

Late that night, we pulled into the parking lot of Manuel's Tavern, the cavernous restaurant where we met with our Edgeworld friends every week. I was a bit nervous after Saffron blew her top, but I was more worried about Cinnamon.

I had tried to take her clothes shopping, hoping a tour of the outlet malls would wash away the taste of our disastrous meeting with Dad and make her forget about Doctor Isaacson's little bombshell. But my little thrift store queen had turned sullen. Clearly, with werekin hearing, she'd overheard everything he'd said, but wasn't ready to broach the subject.

So she sat and stewed. A lot.

In the end we just went back and rescued stuff from my apartment. She *kept* stewing. By ten we were pooped, so I decided we should drop in on the weekly get-together of our friends—even if one was gone forever, and one was being a royal vampire-queen bitch.

So it was ten-fifteen, rumbling over the speed bumps, when Cinnamon finally nerved up the courage to ask, "What's it means to 'have turrets?' I thought turrets went on castles."

I stared straight ahead, eyeing a couple leaving the Tavern and, hopefully, heading towards a parking space. "Normally you don't ask until you already know," I said. "Couldn't find it on Google?"

"No," she said, disgusted. "I didn't have time. Plus I can't spell it."

"You should try it," I said. The couple went around to the other side, and I booked it forward before someone else horned in. "They can sometimes guess the spelling—"

"Mom!"

"All right," I said, pulling us to a stop. "It's a . . . disease that makes you cuss."

"Oh, fuck," Cinnamon said—then, angrily, struck the car door repeatedly with her balled-up fist. "Fuck! Fuck! Fuck!"

I stared over at her, trying to put Doctor Isaacson's words from my mind. She was cussing, sure, but it didn't sound like an uncontrolled outburst; it just sounded natural. Her life had been pretty shitty and she didn't need anything else on her. "I'm not sure you've got it."

"But you're not sure I doesn't?" Cinnamon said, mouth closing oddly, like she was biting off more than she could chew. "I does, doesn't I?"

I started to say no, and then her head snapped aside in that weird sneeze—and now I could clearly see it *wasn't* a sneeze, but a *tic*: a quick snap and a mouth motion, miming the biting gesture she'd just done seconds ago, but grossly exaggerated. What had sounded like a sneeze was a clearing of her throat, followed by a choked-off exhalation.

Oh, *hell*. This was *exactly* what Isaacson had said he'd seen in his special needs ministries. *Not necessarily cussing*, he'd said, *but facial or verbal tics, often manifesting in puberty and worsening progressively through the teens, difficult to willfully control—*

The car in front of us beeped, and I slammed my brakes. I'd let us roll forward, and damn near hit them as they started to back out. I waved and backed us up, then pulled forward and took their space once they were gone. As I put the car into park, I looked back over at her.

"You don't gots to say it," she said, staring at her hands. "Your face said everything."

I started to respond, but she unbuckled her belt and got out of the car. Before I could smooth her feathers, a motorcycle rumbled past, nearly running us over. The biker shook his fist at us as he passed, and I started to flip him off, then laughed. It was Calaphase.

He looped around once more, then wedged his bike into a half-space at the end of the lot and came to join us. "Now *that's* how I remember you," I said, grinning, as he walked up in a long-tailed leather biker's jacket over a slightly punky take on a business suit.

"Should have known it was you grabbing the last damn space," he said, taking off a pair of gloves and stuffing them into his pocket. "Hey, Dakota."

And without thinking we leaned forward and gave each other a hug. It felt natural, and good; and he was *so strong*. Embarrassed, I leaned back and looked him over, trying to brush off the familiarity of his touch, and said, "I like it. The suit is a nice touch."

He winced. "Revy's . . . service," he said. "It was today."

"You should have told us, Cally," I said. "We wanted to—"

But Calaphase shook his head. "Sorry, persona non grata, Kotie."

Cinnamon snorted, tugging at her collar. "Kotie and Cally sittin' in a tree—"

"Hey you," I said, tousling her hair. "Shall we go in and face the music, Calaphase?"

"Why of course, Lady Frost," he said, slipping a small laminated card out of his jacket. I took it curiously: it was an Oakdale Clan Affiliate Card, with an older picture of me someone had scarfed from the Rogue Unicorn web site. "Just in case."

"Thanks," I said, still staring at it. "You don't think I'll need it in *there*?"

"You never know," he said. "Our little Vampire Queen looked pretty steamed."

"Can't hurt," I said, slipping it into my back pocket and starting across the alley towards the low brick structure that was Manuel's Tavern. "More comfy than a steel collar, anyway."

"For you," Cinnamon said, again tugging at her own. "Why am I stuck with this and you gets a card? You don't even changes—and you never actually said why you lost it."

"She did not lose it," said a smooth voice, in a lovely but clipped South African accent. "My Lady Saffron took it from her in a rage."

All three of us froze in the middle of the street. Darkrose stood there, leaning against Manuel's Tavern, form expertly blended into the black curved shape of a giant Coca-Cola bottle advertisement painted on the yellow wall. A second ago I could have sworn she wasn't there.

The black vampire stepped forward, dark cloak falling open around her to reveal another full-length leather catsuit, of which she apparently had a full wardrobe. Her tall, always striking form was enhanced by knee-high boots, with heels almost high enough to make her my height, and she stalked forward in them expertly, stepping right before us, barring our path.

"So it *was* the bitch throwin' a fit," Cinnamon hissed. "Thought so."

"You two have created quite the mess," Darkrose said, staring at me and Calaphase with dark black eyes that seemed to bore into us. Her hair was pulled back in tight cornrows which made her exotic South African features harder, more severe. "She is in a mood."

"This mess and her mood is her fault," I said tightly. "*She* chose to interpret her ex having an innocent dinner with a friend as some kind of marital betrayal."

"True," Darkrose admitted, glancing at Calaphase. "But I do not think she would appreciate seeing you tonight. Either of you."

"What?" Calaphase said. "I know she was angry, but this is *ridiculous*."

"I agree," I said. "*I* started these meetings. And it's a public restaurant."

"But she still blames you, and is too hot under the collar to think clearly." She stepped aside. "*I* will not bar your path. But I came to warn you—*it is not safe to go inside.*"

"Not *safe*? What the *fuck*? What is she, *two*?" I said. "I mean, God *damnit*—"

"Not safe—really?" Calaphase said. "You heard us coming. Can *she* hear us?"

"If she was paying attention," Darkrose said, smiling. "She's very, *very* powerful, but inexperienced. If you entered she would know, but you are safe, for the moment."

"Well, *screw* her," I said, a shade short of livid. "Come on, let's go to the Vortex."

"However," Darkrose said carefully, "I'd like to take Cinnamon inside."

"What?" I asked, putting my hands protectively on her shoulders. "Why?"

"To shame my Lady Saffron into admitting that the protection on Cinnamon still stands," Darkrose said. "Perhaps I can get her to re-extend it to you . . ."

"Now *I'm* a little too hot to go under the collar again," I said, still feeling the flush in my face. "You know, I didn't think I cared, but . . . she had that made for me, and she threw it away. Kind of like she did with our relationship when she became a damn vampire."

Calaphase twitched and Darkrose put her gloved hand to her mouth.

"I'm so sorry," I said, now feeling embarrassment. "That just popped out."

"You sure *you* don't has Tourette's?" Cinnamon asked, looking up at me.

"No, your mother is right," Darkrose said. "It is a . . . hard thing when your lover becomes a vampire, when the one you love becomes a *thing* that feeds on human life. It is very hard, for you know in your heart the first life they want to feed on is your own."

My lips parted. This wasn't a vampire talking anymore; this was a human. And it was not abstract; this was very real, and very personal. It had happened to her.

"I'm so sorry," I said. She looked sad and very old now. "I didn't know."

"It was a century ago," Darkrose said. "Another life. Another time." She straightened, smiled. "I do not blame you. Selfishly, I am glad, because I want her."

She said that simply, openly, staring me straight in the eye. But I couldn't blame her for staking her claim clearly. Some tiny part of me would always be connected to Savannah and remember what we'd been like together, when I didn't want to wring her neck. "I'm glad you have her, my Lady Darkrose."

She inclined her head gratefully. "Thank you, my Lady Frost." She extended her hand to Cinnamon. "I promise I will treat your daughter well. As if she were my own."

"You didn't turn your daughter into a vampire, did you?"

Darkrose looked up in shock. "No!" she said. "That would be unthinkable—"

"I was messing with you. Sorry," I said, squeezing Cinnamon's shoulders. "So, Cin, feel like hanging with the gang while your Mom and her fang go neck in a back alley?"

"Don't come back with no bite marks," Cinnamon said, "just k-i-s-s-i-n-g."

"When did you become the mom?" I said, hands on my hips.

"When you started dating fangs," she said, head snapping in her sneezy tic.

"All right," I said, glancing at Calaphase, who seemed amused by the 'fang' comment. "Try not to get us into more trouble with her highness."

So Calaphase and I were left there, on the corner of North Highland and Linwood, barred from our favorite restaurant. We stared at each other uncomfortably. "Sorry about the damn vampire comment," I said. "And when she called you a fang—"

"You mean Cinnamon? Oh, she mouths off like that," Calaphase said lightly—but my heart fell at the implication. "I'd love to say I don't take things like that personally, but I'd also love to say that we vampires don't deserve it, and that isn't true. There're reasons humans fear us, and werekin hate us—oh, screw it, let's get some drinks. What about Vino's?"

"Believe it or not, I was just there," I said, "but Virginia Highland *is* one of the best walking neighborhoods in the city."

"And it *is* a nice night," Calaphase said, eyes resting on me calmly, slipping his hands into his pockets. "Stroll up to San Francisco Coffee? It's right near to Beaver's Books."

"Does everyone but me love bookstores?" I said, sighing as my phone blooped at me. I pulled it out, saw a text message from a number I didn't know, and set the phone to vibrate. "I think we've been to every one in the city looking for used audiobooks for Cinnamon."

"So what will one more hurt?" Calaphase said. He poked his elbow out at me. "Come on, we can windowshop restaurants for our next date."

I took his arm. "I thought this was our next date."

"Technically our first, if the last one was an innocent dinner," Calaphase said.

"Ouch," I said. "I'm even more sorry about that than the vamp comment."

"Then I'll call this our second," Calaphase said, "and hope there is another."

"Hope springs eternal," I said. "You know, you're a very unusual vampire."

"It's like Saffron said the other night—I once thought becoming a vampire would be liberating," Calaphase said. "Dark lords of the night, free of all restraint, on an endless orgy of sex, blood and violence. But vampirism turned out to be more addiction than superpower, and vampire culture is all prancing poseurs, petty politics and turf wars. So I never changed."

"You sure about that?" I said, feeling his arm. He was lean, but his movements still had that immense strength of a vampire. If I let my hand flow with the sway of his elbow, he felt gentle; but when I got out of sync it felt like tugging on a building, or trying to stop a car. "Remember when we first met? You called me *morsel.*"

"I can put that mask on if you like," he said, smiling, but not looking at me, "but I'm not on duty, impressing my employer by terrorizing trespassers. I'd rather just be myself."

"I'd rather that too," I said, and I wasn't sure whether I was talking about him or me.

We strolled into San Francisco Coffee and in minutes were sitting down across from each other at a tiny striped wooden table—a vampire and a skindancer, wedged in with granola girls from the Little Five Points alternative district and trendy yuppies from the Virginia Highland walking district, without a one of them being the wiser. Well, that wasn't entirely true; with my coat, deathhawk and tattoos *I* stand out more than a vampire. But you can't tell a skindancer from their canvases unless you look closely.

I stared down at the beautiful leaf pattern the barista had woven into the surface of my mocha, then looked up at Calaphase, sipping a frosted slushy with a grimace. "Just like old times," I said, raising my mug and taking a sip.

"Just like old times," he responded, rubbing his forehead with two fingers. "Ow. Brain freeze."

I don't remember what we talked about; it didn't matter later anyway. All I know is that halfway through our drinks, Calaphase got a buzz on his phone, frowned, and then stood to take it. I sipped my coffee, sighing, looking at a cute girl with a woven knit cap who was scoping my tattoos; maybe I had another customer.

Then *my* phone buzzed, and I looked up to see Calaphase staring at me. With a sudden flash of fear, I whipped out my phone and saw another text message, same number: **<<check your email, "skindancer">>**

And then a picture of a graffiti tag began slowly loading on my phone's screen.

"We gotta go," Calaphase said, closing his phone with a click and picking up his coffee without sitting down. "Saffron has ordered us back to Manuel's Tavern."

"Oh, *shit,*" I said, reluctantly closing my phone, swallowing the dregs of my cup, and standing. "Don't tell me she's taken away Cinnamon's protection—"

"Nothing of the sort," he said, swigging the rest of his with a grimace and motioning for us to go. "Emergency war council. We've got serious problems. Demophage, our new Lithuanian vampire, you met him the other night—"

"Curly," I said, following Calaphase outside. "He got the sand. I liked him."

"Yeah, well, he's gone," Calaphase said. "Demophage is training a new recruit, and when the putz didn't show up at Revy's service. Demophage decided to track him down, against my orders. Now he's missed his shift and is not answering his phone."

"Maybe he's just . . . " I began, then stopped. *Maybe* nothing; he was dead. "*Damnit!*"

Calaphase wanted to run, but I couldn't. My knee was throbbing from too much recent activity. So, by the time we burst into Manuel Tavern's dark wooden cave, both our phones were buzzing, and by the time we navigated the huge round tables until we found the one where Saffron held court, we found both Darkrose and Jinx with their cellphones out—while Saffron fumed. The table looked strangely empty without Revenance and his girlfriend.

"I'm sorry, we came as quickly as I could," I said. Saffron and I glanced at each other, then we both looked away. "My knee's been acting up since Transomnia's attack."

"Still?" Darkrose said, staring at me sharply. "I forget how fragile humans are."

"Lady Saffron, what's wrong?" Calaphase said, leaning over the table. "When I reported Demophage's disappearance, you said you had more bad news."

Saffron stared down at the table. When she spoke, she sounded shocked. "The Lady Scara, the Gentry's enforcer, tells me two more vampires are missing. When I called Lord Delancaster to inform him, I got no response.

Not from him, his servant, or even his chauffeur. Vickman just called from his house and confirmed—my master has disappeared. Whatever's happening to vampires, it's taken the Master of Georgia."

Finally Saffron looked up at me, actually afraid. "We're on our own now."

22.   CAVE MAGIC

The Harris Mural is a majestic piece of art dominating the atrium of Emory University's Harris School of Magic. Three stories tall, its rippled surface is infused with magical pigment, breaking the surface into intricate polygonal shapes like a vast stained glass window. The mural's supposed subject is Edmund Harris, the magician after whom the School of Magic and Harris Hall are named. His stylized figure stands to the left of the mural, holding a wand over a hat to his right. But it is the magic bursting forth from the wand that takes center stage.

From the wand, an explosion of light and color ripples across the mural, a thousand intricate overlapping patterns that change constantly from a starburst to snowflakes to spreading leaves to striking lightning. Every day, as the sun moves across the huge glass windows of the atrium, as students crisscross the three levels of catwalks in front of it, shifting light and shadow changes the pattern of mana building up in its network of magical capacitors, making the starburst flow like a slow-motion version of my tattoos.

I stared up at it, hands jammed in my pockets. *Someone* knew how the mural was made. At Saffron's impromptu war council, we decided that I would investigate this thing, at least finding out how the graffiti worked, police approval or no. And the Harris Mural was our best lead on how magic writ upon a wall could work for as long as it had taken to kill Revenance.

My attempts to research it online Sunday hadn't gotten me far, but it was only nine, Cinnamon was safely at school, and I had three full hours before I was expected at the Rogue Unicorn—not that my fellow tattooists cared. Winning the Valentine Challenge had brought more tattooing work into the parlor than we could handle, and it was actually easier for the rest of them to take advantage of that business when the famous Dakota Frost wasn't there to hog all the inking. So . . . I had all the time in the world, and the whole library of the Harris School of Magic at my disposal. Time to crack this thing.

"Hey, Emorrhoid," a familiar voice called down to me.

I looked up and saw Michael Bell grinning at me from the second-story catwalk. In high school he'd helped me through English, in college I'd helped him through Calculus. Now we were *both* dropouts, after a fashion. But where I'd bailed before I got my degree, Michael had gotten as far as law school before skipping the bar, buying a used UNIX workstation and diving into the world of computers. Five hardworking years later, prematurely grey but with a still-dark goatee and sparkling blue eyes, he was Director of Computing at the Harris School of Magic.

"Emorrhoid? Not anymore," I said. "You can get those cured, you know."

"You can take the Emorrhoid out of Emory but you can't . . . " he said, and grinned more broadly. "Glad I caught you. I've got some leads. The café? I skipped breakfast."

"Does no-one just *talk* anymore?" I muttered—I never skip breakfast, not if I can help it.

We found a small table beneath the rear windows of the Harris School, kicked back beneath a panorama of pine trees swaying beyond the glass, and caught up. Michael had gotten a bit of a paunch since college, but he carried it well: his sparkling eyes were sharp, his smiling mouth firm, and he was never afraid to call bullshit where he saw it.

"Look, these Valentine Foundation guys have got to be pissing you off," he said. I'd dumped a load of woe about the house I was supposed to be in by now, and he'd whipped out his lawyerly training. "But try to avoid an actual lawsuit. It hurts to say this and probably to hear it, but you're much better off settling, rather than risking a countersuit and having the Valentine Foundation come shopping in your house to recoup their court costs."

"If they don't pay up," I said, sipping some water, "I won't have a house to shop in."

"Get a lawyer," Michael said, extending a business card. "Warren Moore. He was a few years ahead of me in law school, and he's now with Ellis and Lee. He doesn't do this kind of work, but he'll find you someone on staff that's specialized in cases like this."

I stared at the business card. It was finely embossed and looked more expensive than my cell phone, with an address in Buckhead, the high-rent district in north central Atlanta named after our very own fae lord. "Can I even *afford* Ellis and Lee?"

"No, *but,* they'll work on spec," he said. "It will cost you, but only if you win."

"Thanks," I said, slipping the card into my vest. "They don't do adoptions, do they?"

"Sure, but—adoptions?" Michael said. "*You?* Seriously thinking about it?"

"Seriously doing it," I said. "You saw Cinnamon this Christmas, remember?"

"I think so," he said, staring far away, then smiling. "Yeah, yeah. The little girl with the tiger stripes that could turn her invisible. That was awesome. I never asked you about her."

I explained, twenty-five words or less, and finished with, "So her guardians don't object, I've basically already adopted her. I just have to make it official."

"Well, DEE-FAX isn't involved, thank God," he said, eyes still scanning the air, "so it sounds like you'll need to do a third-party adoption. You *will* need a lawyer."

"Oh, yes," I said, rubbing my forehead. "That I *could* find out online, unlike anything else I've looked into recently."

"Speaking of which," Michael said, with that same smirk he had back in the day when we pored over textbooks together, "I *did* find out who did the

Harris Mural—one of Williamson's students, now a prof in Canada. But it uses pretty simple photoreactive magic, and I doubt learning how to imbue gel plaster will help you take a layer of graffiti off your house."

"It's not on my house," I said. "And removing it once we find it isn't the problem. I'm trying to figure out how it keeps killing people, so we can make it stop."

"Killing people? You're shitting me. Was someone actually *killed* by *graffiti?*"

"Yeah," I said, and told him a short version of the whole story.

"Holy *crap*," he said, staring off into the distance. You could almost see vampires and werewolves dancing behind his eyes. Then his mouth quirked up and he pulled out a smartphone with a tiny little keyboard. "Fortunately, Google knows everything."

"This I've got to see," I said, finishing my water.

"It wasn't me," he said, typing furiously with two thumbs. "I mentioned graffiti magic, and Williamson dug up these two guys, and we've been talking. Let me dig up their schedule and—hey, hey, *hey!* We're in luck, they're opening today. I thought it was next week."

"Who's opening what?" I asked, befuddled.

"Let me show you," Michael said. "Up for a little walk across the campus?"

We crossed the Quad to the Michael C. Carlos Museum, a white, blocky structure with high grids of windows and a keeplike main entrance flanked by two angled staircases that broke up the lines of the castle-shaped structure and made it look vaguely pyramidal.

"Quit being so mysterious, who are we here to see?" I asked, as I bought my ticket and followed Michael inside. "An expert on the magic of cave art?"

"Experts on cave magic," Michael said, grinning. "They'd like that. Here we are."

"Oh. My. God," I said.

Standing in the hall before me was a giant mural of moving graffiti.

23.   KEIF AND DRIVE

Freestanding in the exhibit hall, underneath a huge banner proclaiming MYSTIC MARKS OF THE URBAN JUNGLE, was an irregular chunk of brick wall, ten feet high and thirty long, *covered* with moving graffiti, a panorama of toy soldiers fighting a slow-motion war complete with cartoony explosions that actually said KABOOM as they dissipated.

"An exhibit of magic graffiti," I said. "What a helpful coincidence."

Of course, I didn't believe this was any kind of coincidence. I'd never *heard* of magic graffiti before, and now, when it was spreading through the city, a whole exhibit popped up before me. For a moment I thought I'd found a lead; unfortunately, my elation faded as I scanned the artwork. I didn't see anything familiar, not the colors, linework, or even the logic of the magic. This was magic graffiti, all right—but it almost certainly wasn't done by the killer.

"Not our guys," I murmured, then aloud, "Wow, Michael, I'm impressed!"

"I'm not done," Michael said, motioning to me from around the wall. "Let me introduce you to my friends Keif and Drive."

I guessed Keif was the short, hefty, Latino man in army fatigues posing for a photographer. His feet were planted wide, he held a pair of paintbrushes in folded arms, and beneath his Indian-headdress spray of dreadlocks he had a mischievous smile. Beside him stood Drive, a tall, gaunt African-American man in blue and black racing leathers, blond-dyed head turned away from the camera with a snooty, bored look. After the flash, both seemed to relax: Keif pulled his feet together and let the paintbrushes clatter together in one hand, and Drive thanked the photographer with an easy, friendly grin.

"Dakota Frost," Keif said, nudging Drive. "Look, it's Dakota Frost—"

"What?" Drive said. "Speak of the devil."

"Keif, Drive, I'd like you to meet one of my oldest buddies from high school," Michael said, beaming. "I think you know who she is."

"Do we," Keif said, pumping my hand. "You're all over YouTube, Frost."

"I go by Dakota," I said, smiling, "and . . . YouTube?" I shook my head.

"Keif, told you that floating clock bit was faked," Drive said, shaking his head. "I'm sure they jazzed it up for the cameras . . . "

His voice trailed off as I stretched a long, tattooed arm between the two of them, rippling it up and down. My tattoos glowed to life, and my (remaining) trusty asp lifted off my skin in a shower of sparks, tongue flickering in the air.

"Holy shit," Drive said.

"Oh, man," the photographer said. "I gotta get a picture of that."

"Oh, for the love," I said, coiling up my arms, then stretching them out again, releasing my vines into the air with enough mana that they would show up. My skin stung, and the vines had a bit of asymmetry, but with concentration, I compensated. "If we have to . . . "

So Keif and Drive posed again, with me standing between them, arms thrown wide to cast a net of glowing tattoo magic around them. Keif muttered, "You're not going to get in trouble over this, are you? There's not a secret tattoo magic rule—"

"I don't answer to anyone," I said, "except God and my clients."

Afterwards, the four of us walked the exhibit together. Drive actually didn't do much graffiti: he was a "defense contractor for the middle school industrial complex," creating ironic assemblages like a Big Wheels with handlebar-mounted toy assault rifles or a red wagon filled with toy soldiers pouring out into a sandbox like it was the beaches of Normandy. These had inspired Keif, who used the images repeatedly in his graffiti. Once he'd tagged all over the city, but now he made installable pieces in the comfort of his warehouse studio in the West End.

We paused before one of the larger tags—"no, not a tag, a top-to-bottom *piece*," Keif corrected—life-size takeoffs of a GI-Joe and a Ken Doll kissing in a stylized closet. While I tried to suppress my smirk at their cartoony passion,

Keif explained how the figures moved.

"It's just graphomancy, geometric magic," he said, pointing out the lines, the connections in the slow-moving figure. "Graffiti magic isn't any different from tattoo magic, but since we're largely self-taught the designs are usually primitive. That's why I wanted to talk to you after seeing that YouTube clip. A fully functioning watch—*amazing*."

"I'll put you in touch with my graphomancer," I said. "Designing magical marks and inking them are both sufficiently specialized skills that it usually takes two people."

"I'm willing to learn," Drive said.

"All right," I said. "But I still don't understand where they get the power. My tattoos are powered by the mana generated by my living body."

"Well, most of them are just photomagic," Keif said slowly.

"Photomagic doesn't explain a tag under a tarp damn near tearing a vampire apart," I said. "It doesn't explain a tag at night nearly cutting a werewolf in half."

"That is . . . difficult to explain," Keif said, even more slowly.

"Look, Frost," Drive said impatiently, "what Keif is not saying is there are a few tricks that can really jazz up graffiti magic that he thinks are his own trade secret." Keif fumed, but said nothing. "Do you understand the yin and yang of magic?"

"I've heard the term," I said, eyeing the cartoons of Ken and Joe move towards each other, then away. In the two circles of their heads you could imagine the yin and yang symbols intertwining. "Refresh my memory."

"There's the Vaiian thread, and the Niivan thread," he said. "Day and night, light and dark, werewolves and vampires. The Vaiian thread is powered by life. That's your basic tattoo magic, werekin transforms, almost all practical magic really. The Niivan thread is powered by decay. That's your basic necromantic magic and the power behind vampires and zombies."

"Uh-huh," I said, keeping my face bland. I'd heard the Vaiian-Niivan theory of magic, but as far as I knew it was just New-Age nonsense. I really wanted to call bullshit, but I was asking for help from him and that wouldn't be nice, so I just kept my mouth shut.

"But that shit's like a circle, man, the circle of life, you know? Decay *is* life—the life process of worms and bacteria and fungi," he said. I smiled skeptically, and he interpreted it as agreement. "You see. So that's what we do—we use life, just not human life—"

"He's trying to say, we tag walls that have mold," Keif said, embarrassed. "You can cultivate it, but it takes forever to prep something that big." He thumbed back at the brick wall dominating the center of the exhibit. "So back when I was still tagging walls in public—"

"Back when? You flaming liar," Drive said, shaking his head. "Mister Art Crime here thinks *there ain't nuthin' like the thrill of live taggin'*—"

"Shut *up*, man," Keif muttered. "So anyway, *back when* I didn't care about being arrested, I'd find pre-painted surfaces with mold busting out. If you grind in the right crystals with your chalk, the tags move as much under a streetlight as they do in broad daylight."

"No shit," I said. "You think that if you cultivated it you could use enough power to—"

But Keif was shaking his head. "No," he said. "No way—at least *I* couldn't. This goes back to why I wanted to talk to you. I think to do more than we do we'd need to start using more sophisticated pigments—like the kind skindancers use."

"You want my mixes," I said, and Keif kind of got an *'aw shit, she's going to turn me down'* look. "Sure, but you'll want more than just pre-made mixes that are specialized for human skin. You need to pick the brains of an actual stonegrinder, the people who make our pigments."

Keif's face broke out with a smile as I was talking. "Yeah, yeah," he said. "*Exactly.* Someone who's been doin' this shit for years and knows what works and what don't."

"All right," I said, nodding. Between Michael, Keif and Drive, I had learned enough at Emory today to know what I needed to do—*without* having to go back to the library. I had to go back to school—but not college, this time. "I'll ask my old master. No promises."

Keif's eyes widened. "So you *do* have an old master," he breathed. "I knew it, I knew it. There was no way you picked all this up starting from ground zero. What's he like?"

"He's no Obi-Wan Kenobi," I said, "but he is an old-school master, back when 'master' meant skindancing, stonegrinding *and* graphomancy. He inks, he comes up with most of his own designs, and grinds his own pigments from mushrooms and bark he gathers from the woods."

"Oh, yeah," Keif said, punching Drive in the arm. "That's what I'm talking about."

"He goes by Arcturus," I said. "Not his real name. He's real private and *real* prickly. He prefers personal referrals—so let me put a toe in the water before I introduce you."

"Fair enough," Drive said. "So, Keif, if she delivers, you gonna quid pro quo and let her see your blackbook, you damn mooch?"

Keif's expression froze. "Yeah," he said, uncertainly. "Sure."

"Show it to my graphomancer," I said. "She's mostly blind, but she'll get a real kick out of scans of your book. Half the designs I wear are hers—I'm sure she could do a lot for you."

We talked further, confirming that graffiti magic was even less well documented than tattoo magic, at least in the public literature. I'd need someone like Keif and Drive to help crack this thing—and they needed someone like me, or at least like Arcturus, who could help them develop better pigments. So we exchanged numbers, pressed flesh, parted.

I returned to the Rogue Unicorn like a conquering hero, climbing the rickety steps of the Little Five Points tattoo shop to find three customers waiting for me. Two of them had looked me up on the strength of the YouTube clip leaked from Valentine's show—and two got tattoos on the spot, which is a better than average batting average for magical tattooing. Some days, even the 'best magical tattooist in the Southeast' doesn't convince anyone to get a tattoo.

Then I tried to repair the asp that had been burned when I tried to save the werecat from the fire. Now that the swelling was down, the damage to the skin itself didn't look so bad, but a lot of magical pigment was denatured. I cleaned most of it using a skindancing trick—activating a vine and sweeping it over the damaged tattoo to cull out bad pigment. Each time I raised the vine out of the skin, a few more tiny flakes of soot disappeared into the air; each time I sank the vine back it moved through the skin more smoothly. Eventually I cleared enough space to ink a new asp, but it was coiled around a small, Italy-shaped lump of dark pigment I couldn't lift or move.

I frowned at it. There were a few ways around this, the most straightforward being laser treatments to break up the ink. But that offended my skindancer's soul. Another tack was to ink a temporary pattern over the burnt ink, allowing it to heal, then lifting it off magically. But if there was enough magic ink left in the burn, I could end up with an even larger curdled mark and no way to remove it. I fumed. I didn't have enough experience with burns to know what to do.

So I broke down and called my old master, Arcturus. After what felt like a hundred rings, I gave up and called Zinaga, the apprentice next in line after me at his studio. *She* picked up right away, but rather than putting me through to Arcturus, she called me a deserter and started to rant about how he was better off without me. After a bit, I cut her off and told her why I'd called.

First I described our problems with the graffiti, about its magic, about Keif and Drive and their quid-pro-quo requests. As I talked, she was quiet for a while, until, embarrassed, I told her about my burn. Then *she* cut *me* off and went to talk to him; after a few minutes, she returned.

"He says come out here this week," Zinaga said. "He says 'I *mean* it. Do *not* wait.'"

"Gotta love him," I groused. The *least* he could have done is come to the phone. He had to be really pissed. Then it occurred to me that the first time I'd come to Blood Rock looking for the famed Arcturus, I'd been picked up, warned off, and dumped on the side of the highway in Conyers ten miles from my Vespa. "His pet sheriff isn't going to give me shit, is he?"

"No," Zinaga said, disgusted. "You really think we'd treat family that way? Now get out here before he changes his mind—or before those burns ruin your ink."

After she hung up, I checked my email again for any new pictures from my mysterious text-message benefactor. Over the past few days, someone in the APD, probably McGough, had used an out-of-state number to send me pictures of tags from all over the city. Pieces like the one that hit Revy were everywhere, but the ones that hit Tully were focused in Oakdale. And there was a third, cruder set, in Oakdale and Cabbagetown.

The pictures told me a lot about the taggers—I guessed three: a master, a journeyman, and an apprentice or copycat—but not about their magic. I needed to see a master tag *moving* to figure out how it worked. Still, I emailed Jinx the images and printed copies for Arcturus, who couldn't tell an email address from a fax machine. One of us would figure *something* out.

I pulled up into the dropoff lane of the Clairmont Academy to pick up Cinnamon—and hit my brakes so hard the car behind me almost slammed into me. There was a Fulton County Sheriff's car pulled up on the curb, lights flashing. *Oh, God no.*

I jerked the Prius over into a visitor's space and hopped out, running up on Catherine Fremont, who was arguing loudly with a blond police officer and a darkhaired, ponytailed woman. "I'm sorry," she said angrily, "I'm not authorized to do that—"

"Ma'am," the officer said, leaning back his head, "I don't think you understand—"

"I do understand and don't you ma'am me," she snapped—and then her eyes caught me and her face relaxed in relief. "Oh, thank God. Miss Frost, we have a situation."

"Miss Frost?" the darkhaired woman said, checking her clipboard, shrugging a couple times to adjust a faux-fur-lined jeans jacket. "Dakota Frost?"

"Yes," I said, and the woman smiled. She had a pleasant face, open and expressive, with pencil-thin eyebrows that made her look far younger than she was. "What's going on?"

"I'm Margaret Burnham of DEE-FAX, the Department of Family and Children Services," she said, eyes flickering over the tattoos on my temples before returning to her clipboard. "Are you currently in custody of a child named 'Stray Foundling?'"

"Yes, she is in my custody," I said, "but she goes by Cinnamon Frost."

"Whatever," Burnham said. "We're here to take Stray into emergency custody."

24. DEE-FAX

"You're *what?*" I exploded.

"Ma'am," the officer said, stepping forward, his hand raised. "Please calm down."

"What the hell is this, Officer—" and I broke off for a second, eyes scanning him till I found his badge "—Galacci?"

"*Deputy* Galacci," he corrected, body held firm and forbidding, blue eyes distant and stony. "Ma'am, this is a court-ordered action."

"On what basis?" I asked. The expression on his stony, hard-muscled face didn't change, and I transferred my glare to Burnham. "For what possible reason?"

"Housing her in unsafe conditions," Burnham said, checking her clipboard.

"*What?*" I said. "Since when is an apartment in Candler Park unsafe?"

"According to this," Burnham said, glaring, "Stray's living in Oakdale."

"She goes by Cinnamon," I said, "and Oakdale is where I *adopted* her from."

"The address is a condemned factory," Burnham said.

"It was a werehouse," I said.

"It burned down."

"That was arson!"

"I have no info on that," Burnham said, "but according to the police report, the *second* police report she appeared in in as many days, I might add, Stray was living there as recently as two weeks ago, on the day the police went to shut it down as an unlicensed werekin housing facility—and it burned down around them."

It took me a few moments to gather my composure. "Cinnamon was *not* living in the werehouse," I said at last. "That's simply where they interviewed her *after* the *arson*."

"But why was she even there?" Burnham said. "In a condemned factory. In *Oakdale!*"

"She's a *werekin*," I said. "She was having a bad change. I took her back to the people who I adopted her from because I thought they could help!"

"Why?" Burnham said, eyes flashing with disapproval. "Didn't you have a safety cage?"

"I'm having one built in our *new* house," I said angrily, "but it wasn't ready yet."

"Well you should have had it built in your *old* one before you tried to adopt a werekin," Burnham said, oddly smug. "If you had followed the rules—"

"Hey!" I said, feeling my nostrils flare. "You have *no idea* who you're talking to about following the rules—"

"Ma'am, look, you're not helping," Deputy Galacci said firmly. "Please calm down. Getting angry at us is not going to change anything."

"That's right," Burnham said. "This police report is a clear indication of neglect."

"Oh, yeah, *this* is neglect," Deputy Galacci said, cocking his thumb back at the Academy. "Paying for her upscale private school. Look, Miss Frost, it's clear you do care for Stray—"

"She *goes*," Catherine Fremont said icily, "by Cinnamon."

"Cute," Galacci said. "The point is, I'm sure that the court will recognize what you're trying to do here and straighten this all out, but I can't ignore a court order."

I closed my eyes and rubbed between my eyebrows with one hand. All I kept seeing was that DEI agent that had practically wanted to shoot Cinnamon on sight. It wasn't helping.

"Look, Deputy Galacci," I said, "I know you're just doing your job, but I'm too damn paranoid to let you just waltz up and take her. Cinnamon was *kidnapped* last year, poisoned, almost killed, and I don't know you from Adam Twelve."

"I'm sorry to hear that," Galacci said—and then the corner of his mouth quirked up. "But Adam would mean a two-man patrol. And it's LAPD jargon. We don't use it in Georgia."

I glared at him. "Regardless, if I don't see some paperwork I'm going to call the police and let the APD sort this out. Am I making myself clear?"

"Yes, ma'am, and I encourage you to contact the police, or at least

DFACS," Galacci said. "But in the meantime we still have to take her."

I folded my arms. "Over my dead body."

Galacci looked at me, hard, jaw set. He put his hand on his pistol. "Ma'am—"

"Don't do it," I said. I concentrated my intent and let my shield blossom, concentrated mana, a millimeter beneath the surface of my skin, and let out my breath to activate it. "*Phooo.* My dad's a cop, my uncle's a cop, I've dated a cop, so I *don't want to hurt you*, but until I see paperwork for this alleged court order, you're just a man with a gun threatening my daughter."

His eyes tightened at me and he twitched a little, but he didn't move. He was angry, but behind the anger he was actually curious, eyes looking me over, trying to see what angle I had that made me so unafraid of his badge, his gun.

"I know, I know, you think I'm a street lawyer and want to take me to jail on general principles just to 'show me' and my big mouth," I said. "I'm sorry to bust your nuts like this. But I did this dance with the DEI last week, and all they needed to do to make me play nice is show me a warrant. You did have a warrant or order or *some* kind of paperwork in hand before you decided to waltz up and take a werekin from her mother, right?"

"Right," Galacci said. "Burnham, show her your papers so we can get on with it."

Burnham jerked, then came forward with a clipboard. I took it. "Thank you," I said, glancing it over. Depressingly official 'authorization to accept child for short-term emergency care,' and it all looked in order. *Crap.* "All seems in order. Now how hard was that?"

"Not hard at all," Galacci said, relaxing. "I'm sorry to put on such a hard nose, Miss Frost. If the order exists, it has to be carried out, whether the paper's on me or not. But even when we do, many of the parents I have to deal with are *not* reasonable in your situation."

"How could they be?" I said. "Either they're asses, or their kids are being taken unjustly."

"Not *unjustly*," Burnham said. "but I'll give you overcautiously. Miss Fremont, please."

As Catherine left, Galacci spoke to me in a low voice. "Was she really kidnapped?"

"Oh, yes," I said, swallowing. Fremont leaving to go get Cinnamon was tearing me up, but I tried not to let it show. "And poisoned, to get to me. She almost died."

"I'm sorry to hear it," he said, even more quietly, "but you shouldn't talk to cops about putting them down. Technically that's assault on a police officer. Less technically, it could get you shot, which could kill you even if you are a werekin."

"I know, and sorry," I said. "For the record, I'm not a werekin—but I *did* take a shotgun blast in the chest the other day, and it didn't faze me. I'm a magical tattoo artist. I can shield."

"No shit," Galacci said, curious and amazed. "You *wanted* me to shoot you?"

"No!" I said. "It would be a dick move to provoke you to shoot me in front of my daughter's school just to test my shield. She's going to have to come back here."

"Oh, come on," he said. "If you really could take a bullet—"

"Have," I said. "Have taken a bullet. Twice. Both times to protect Cinnamon."

Galacci swallowed. "Well, if you could take a bullet, the coolest thing in the world for a little kid would be to see your dad, or, uh, mom, pull a Superman in front of the school."

"It didn't impress her," I said. "She's a weretiger. Claims to soak up bullets, and given how rough she had it on the streets I take it she knows that from experience. But when I got shot in the chest, all it did was make her worry."

"Well, ah, let's . . . not make that worry worse," he said, more quietly. "This is never an easy thing. You should be the one to explain to her what's happening."

Somehow the thought of explaining things to her filled me with a sudden, urgent fear—and I realized Galacci needed to be filled in too. "Deputy, she has a mouth on her," I said. "Try not to be offended. We think it might be Tourette's. Seriously."

"Really? Oh, I'm sorry," he said. "Thanks for the heads up, I'll—here she is. You're up."

The glass door slid open on Cinnamon and Fremont. "Mom," Cinnamon said uncertainly, darting forward, then stopping to stare at Burnham and Galacci. "Mom, what's going on?"

"Cinnamon," I said, squatting down to look at her.

"Yeah," she said, eyes wide, staring over my shoulder at the deputy.

"Cinnamon," I said, and choked it off. Then I started to tear up. "Cinnamon, oh, damnit, Cinnamon, they're taking you from me. I'm so sorry. They say it's only temporary—"

"And you *believes* them?" she said, tugging at her collar, head snapping in her tic.

"Yes. No. I don't know," I said, "but, regardless—I'm going to fight to get you back."

"I—I—believes you, Mom," Cinnamon said, tearing up too. "Fuck! I *believe* you."

"Oh, Cinnamon," I said, hugging her. She grabbed me so fiercely my back cracked, but I didn't care. I just hugged her back and cried. "I will get you back."

"I knows—I know, Mom," Cinnamon said, glancing back over her shoulder at Fremont, then looking at me. The tic twisted her face, but she kept it under control. "I *know*."

She looked up, and I felt movement behind me. "It's time," Galacci said.

"This is Deputy Galacci," I said.

"I gots that," Cinnamon said, eyes flickering over him.

"And that's Margaret Burnham. They're with DFACS. They're going to take care of you, until I can come back for you. OK?"

"OK," Cinnamon said.

"Don't kill them," I said, "or you're grounded."

"Mom!" Cinnamon said, mouth quirking up at Burnham's horrified reaction and Galacci's suppressed smile. "I'll—*fuck!*—I'll be good."

"Come on, now," Galacci said, patting my shoulder. "You're just making it harder."

And so I stood, and handed Cinnamon over to Galacci, who wiped his face clean and took her with a flat, stony stare. I glared at Burnham, but she didn't give me a second glance, just handed a card to me, told me to call her office, and bustled off to her own car.

And then Cinnamon was in the back of the squad car, staring at me. Abruptly Galacci looked back and said something, and Cinnamon looked forward at him. After a moment, she smiled—and then *laughed*, and waved at me. She put her hand against the window, huge clawed fingers spread out in a five-pointed star; and then with her other hand she made a thumbs-up towards me. "It's going to be OK, Mom," she mouthed.

And then the police car started up and took her away.

25. PUNCHING BAG

I kicked and kicked and kicked the bag as hard as I could, and *screamed*.

The first few kicks had started out all right—the Taido *ma-washy-getty* kick was close enough to an old Tae Kwon Do roundhouse that I'd picked it up pretty quickly. But Taido had all these stupid rules about how to throw kicks that I didn't really get yet, and it was hard to remember to come back to the same position. I tried, really, but the more I kicked, the madder I got, and by the final three I'd lost all form and was just kicking, kicking, kicking.

"Jeez, Dakota," Darren Briggs said, dropping what he was doing. He was the black belt in charge of Emory University's Taido club. Today he'd traded out his normal blue instructor's jacket for a uniform so old and worn the belt and clothes were both shades of grey, rather than the stiff white karate gi's worn by the rest of the class. But the man in the uniform wasn't old. He was young, clean-cut, with a spray of spiky hair he was constantly dying different colors; this week, it was purple and platinum white. "Are you drinking?"

"I have a water bottle," I said, waving him off. "I'm hydrating."

"No, I meant, *have* you been drinking?" he asked. "Like, alcohol. Your face . . ."

I straightened and looked in the mirror. My face was flushed red, almost mottled, and I knew it was from more than from just working out. "No," I said, disgusted, *whacking* the bag one more time and cursing as it caused a throbbing pain in my knee. "They took Cinnamon."

"What?" he said. "Your daughter? Hey, wasn't she supposed to come tonight?"

"Yeah," I said, trying to fall back to the long low stance Darren called *choo-dan*—but it just made my knee throb and I cursed. "Yes, damnit, damnit, *damnit!* YAAAA!"

And I kicked the bag again, this time so hard it popped off the chain and fell to the floor. No big feat—it was attached with a big carabineer up top and was always popping off. But as it fell, pain exploded, and I knelt on my other knee, cradling the wounded one. "Damnit."

"Dakota," Darren said, hunching down beside me. "You all right?"

"No," I said. "And I know what you mean. No, my knee hurts."

"Same one? Damnit, Dakota," Darren said. "All right, take a break. You weren't supposed to start back until you healed, but I cut you a break because you were doing so well. Clearly you've been overdoing it. So chill out tonight, and go see a doctor tomorrow."

I hissed, and Darren pressed. "I *mean* it. Nobody's been seriously injured in the whole history of the club and I don't want to start with—"

"All right, *all right*," I said, struggling back to my feet. "Ow."

"Just . . . try to go easy," Darren said. "Keep icing it after every practice. And on your own time—don't laugh—do *sem-ay-no-hokay*, the new exercise I showed you tonight. You did really good for your first time. It's pretty advanced stuff."

"It felt natural," I said, "but, man, it wore me out."

"*Sem-ay* can give you a real workout, but it's low impact," he said. "Probably OK for your knee, but if it bugs you, focus on the breathing. Focus on the breathing if nothing else."

"Does that really help?" I said.

"Sure does," Darren said expansively. "Breathing isn't just the source of your power—it's the bridge between your conscious and your subconscious."

I looked at him skeptically, but just then, Rary, the number two in the class and Darren's off-again, on-again girlfriend, appeared with an icepack.

"No, seriously," she said, putting the ice on my knee. "The diaphragm is the only muscle under joint control of the deliberative and autonomic nervous system. Controlling your breathing lets your conscious self signal your subconscious self in its own language."

Both Darren and I were staring at her. "What?" she said. "I *am* in med school."

"Soooo . . . " Darren said. "You going to join us at Manuel's?"

"No," I said. "I have to bail. I gotta get the last of my junk out of my apartment tonight."

"You need help?" Rary said.

I shook my head. "I'm almost done," I said. "And, look, Olsen is being a real pisser about Cinnamon. She almost called the cops on me, not just that night but when I went back for the first load. I really don't want to involve you guys. I'd hate for her to call the cops on *you*."

What I didn't say is that I was scared my crazy life would bite these people. Maybe it was uncharitable, but I thought of them as mundanes: they couldn't roll minds, lift cars or block bullets, and if their guts got ripped out they wouldn't come crawling back to them.

So that's how it was that I found myself alone in the apartment at ten-thirty that night, with about fifty thousand times more crap to box up than I remembered. I desperately hoped Mrs. Olsen wouldn't hold me to the midnight deadline, but I started tossing things into boxes at random in the hope that I'd somehow get it all done.

My cell rang. "Dakota Frost," I said, taping up a box with the phone in the crook of my shoulder. "Best magical tattooist in the Southeast—"

"You should have that on your answering machine," Calaphase said over the line.

"I do," I said, "you just catch me awake whenever you call."

"My shift at the werehouse must be when you sleep," Calaphase said.

"Your shift?" I said, laying down one more line of tape and tearing it off with the dispenser's serrated edge. "You lead the Oakdale Clan. Don't you have flunkies for that?"

"I lead by example," Calaphase replied. "What *are* you doing?"

"Moving out," I said. And I explained about Mrs. Bitch downstairs and her ultimatum.

"Charming," Calaphase said. "Speaking of bitches, I have news from the Lady Saffron, delivered by the way of the Lady Darkrose."

"A four-link chain," I said, emptying a junk drawer wholesale into one of the smaller boxes. "Nicely insulated so that neither of us has to talk directly to someone who has talked to the other. Sounds good. Maybe this will keep things on an even keel."

"Don't count on it," Calaphase said. "Her high-and-mightyness the Lady Scara—"

"Who?" I asked. "I can only keep track of so many 'Lady S-something' vampires."

"She's one of the Gentry," Calaphase said. "Old, moneyed vampires who used to run the cities before the rise of the Consulates. There a few of them, the Lady Onyxa and the Lord Ian something and supposedly an ancient vamp too deformed by age to be seen in public."

"Sounds charming," I said. "And this Scara?"

"Their enforcer," Calaphase said. "Scara's informed the Lady Saffron that the Gentry officially considers the Consulate's handling of this plague a failure—because they've found out one more of their vampires has been killed by graffiti, just like Revenance."

"Oh no," I said, my heart falling. "A new wave of killings . . . "

"Maybe," Calaphase said. "Scara had been hunting the vampire's human servant, thinking he was responsible, but when she found him he was hiding out, scared shitless. He and his mistress were partying on New Year's Eve when she was caught and killed by graffiti."

"That's even before Revenance," I said. "Maybe the first vamp taken."

"And just before Josephine," Calaphase said. "And get this, same night—"

"A homeless man was set on fire," I said. "I've been reading the crime blotter too."

"Sounded awfully suspicious," Calaphase said. "We should compare notes."

"Sure," I said. "Hey, what happened to the human servant? Sounds like Scara treated him like a suspect, but since he's not involved, I'll want to hear that he was released unharmed."

"Would you now?" Calaphase laughed, a bit nervously. "I'll, uh, pass that along if I ever see the Lady Scara, not that I ever hope to."

"Speaking of hope," I said. "What about Demophage . . . "

Calaphase fell silent. "Dakota . . . the vamp he was looking for . . . the weres found his body, not two days ago. Burned to death, just like Revenance, about four miles from the werehouse—near some very familiar looking graffiti."

"Please don't tell me—"

"They'd painted it over before they even talked to me," Calaphase said, and my heart sank. "The weres that weren't caught are really pissed, and Krishna *still* hasn't made bail. But . . . they did listen to me, and took pictures. Just got them today."

"Great!" I said. Pictures wouldn't be as good as a live tag, but if they were good enough maybe we had a shot of tying the design to the behavior. "I mean, not that I'm happy he died or anything, but, maybe, *finally*, maybe we'll be able to make some progress—"

"*And*," Calaphase said, "if that sounds good, I've got an entirely new batch of pictures of suspected master tags taken by the Van Helsings, Darkrose Enterprises, and even some from Tully, all printed out in a folder ready for you to take a look at."

I was speechless for a moment. "Oh, I *love* you."

"Easiest way down a tattooist's pants is to show her some flash," Calaphase laughed.

"I'm not that easy," I said.

"I didn't say you were. Still, Darkrose wanted a report to give to Saffron," Calaphase said. "Can I bring these by and get your official opinion? Darkrose isn't a daywalker, so I need to tell her tonight. Otherwise I have to pass the message to Saffron herself, and she'll—"

"I know, I know," I said, looking around me and tossing the rest of the pile around me into a box. "But can it wait a few hours? I'm not done moving out, and I promised Mrs. Bitch downstairs that I'd be out of here by midnight tonight."

"Need a hand?" Calaphase said.

"I—thanks, but no thanks. I just don't think it's a good idea," I said. "Mrs. B—Mrs. Olsen is on a hair trigger. She wanted to call the police on me over Cinnamon."

"I'm *just*," Calaphase said, "a cleancut young man come by to help a friend move."

"Oh, damnit," I said finally. *What could it hurt?* "Sure."

---

26. A FRIEND HELPS YOU MOVE

Twenty minutes to midnight. No time, no help—and no more boxes. I had only one left, which was rapidly filling as I found bric-a-brac and knick-knacks and odds-and-ends in every nook and cranny of the apartment. I swear, the things were breeding.

And then there was a knock at the door, and I looked up to see Calaphase, holding a box of Krispy Kreme donuts which he opened with a flourish, row upon row of glazed delight.

"Oh, I *love* you," I said, hopping off the floor and snatching up an original style. It was hot and soft in my hands and seemed to dissolve in my mouth with a grand flash behind my eyes. "Oh. Oh. These are better than sex. Not really, but they're better than sex."

"I'll take your word for it," he said, laughing.

"Mmm. Mmmmm. Wht?" I said, munching, scanning the box. There were already four missing out of the dozen. "Didn't you have some?"

"No, I gave three to Mrs. Olsen," he said. At my shocked look, he laughed again, a warm sound that left me as tingly as the donuts. "Call it a peace offering. I explained that I was supposed to help you, but was late. You'll have all the time you need."

"Thank you, Calaphase," I said, taking another donut. "You're a lifesaver."

"Finish up," he said, handing me the box. "I'll take loads to your car. Can you beep it?"

With a vampire carting boxes and me cleaning up, we finished up quick. I filled the last box, taped it up, and then helped carry down the final load. So many boxes. Even with the seats folded down in the back, they barely fit in the Prius, and I couldn't see out my rearview mirror. Thank God for the backup monitor—and thank God I didn't need to make a second trip.

After the car was packed, I took one last trip up the stairs to the place I'd called home for . . . hell, at least five years. As I climbed the steps, I saw Mrs. Olsen's light was now on, no doubt from Calaphase's visit, but I tried to ignore it. This was hard enough already.

At the door, I sighed. My mat, my curtains, the little stand beside the door were all gone; it already felt like a completely different place. I went in, finding empty rooms, feeling the place even more empty than when I'd moved in. Then, it held promise: now, it held nothing.

The storage unit closed at seven, so we dropped off the load at my hotel. Hands full, I slipped the little card in the slot, saw green, and kicked the door open, dumping the boxes next to the air conditioner. Calaphase, with three boxes in his arms, stopped at the door.

At first I thought he was staring with amusement at my Vespa, parked in front of the hotel window at the management's request to free up a space in their tiny lot. Then he seemed to gather himself, cleared his throat, and looked straight at me. "May I come in?"

I hesitated—just a second—wondering if that pause was a vampire thing or simple courtesy. "Sure," I said, moving a chair out of the way to make more room.

He waltzed around me silently, murmuring, "Wouldn't want to wake— oh." He stood there, holding the column, staring at the two, tiny, *made* beds. "Where's Cinnamon? Out running with the werekin, or dare I hope, a sleepover with new friends from school?"

"She's *not here*," I said sharply, heading back to the car.

We got the rest of it unloaded, and then I came in and sat down on the bed. My hands were shaking. I could feel my face, hot, could see Calaphase standing by the door, feel the concern in his gaze, even though I couldn't see his eyes.

After a moment, I explained the situation to him, as briefly as I could without pissing myself off again. Of course, that didn't work so well. Just as I was getting really wound up, Calaphase made a motion, and I looked up to see him gesturing to the door.

"Come on," he said. "Let's go get a drink."

"Why?"

"You need one, and . . . I'm a vampire," Calaphase said. "I don't want to be alone with you, especially not for drinks. Let me take you to a nice place, frequented by many humans."

I glared at him, face still hot. "Don't you know I trust you?"

"Yes," he said. "That's not the problem."

"Then what? Don't you trust *yourself?*"

He shrugged. "Don't trust the situation."

I was still glaring, but I felt it soften. "Fine," I said. "No, really, fine."

Calaphase directed me down North Avenue to Peachtree Road, then towards Buckhead. Long before we got there, we approached R Thomas, a New-Agey 24 hour joint that made the only vegetarian burgers that Cinnamon could stomach. I was about to suggest it when Calaphase pointed to a car coming out of a parking space, right in front of a set of small shops on the opposite side of the street. "There," he said. "Someone's smiling on us tonight."

So we parked the Prius and hopped out into a row of shops that felt like a snippet of a walking neighborhood, like a micro-Virginia Highland on the other side of the road from R Thomas. We passed a Chinese restaurant and an art gallery before walking up onto a chic crowd of Buckheadites, milling around the front of Café Intermezzo.

"How late is this place open?" I asked.

"Two," he said, taking me through heavy wood doors into a dark, loud, crowded empire of wood and glass. Classic posters and slogans extolling the glories of coffee adorned the walls, a slide show of what looked like ancient Greece was projected up into a high cranny, and *everywhere* people were crammed at tiny tables, consuming an astonishing variety of drinks.

"What?" Calaphase said, after the screech of the espresso machine ceased.

"A little loud, isn't it?" I repeated.

"Two," he said, handing a twenty to the maître d', who winked and nodded. "I wouldn't do that normally," he said, a little embarrassed when he saw my eyebrow, "but Cheryl knows me. She'll get us a table in the front window. It's a little quieter, but it takes a few minutes."

We stood by a rack of newspapers on dowels, like you might see in a library. "Right across the street from my favorite veggie burgers," I said. "Why have I never been here?"

Then he handed me the menu—a thick, narrow booklet that was as comprehensive as a dictionary—and I knew. "Jeez!" I said, and Calaphase winced. "OK, the *normal* coffees aren't much worse than Starbucks, but some of the liqueurs are like, fifty dollars."

"Only if you get one that's older than *I* am," Calaphase said.

"I have dresses older than you are," I said, flipping and flipping and flipping, trying to get to the back. "All right, I can see why poor dropout me has never been here, but how can you afford it on what the werehouse crew have been paying you?"

"Vampires have many sources of income," Calaphase said, slightly uncomfortable.

"Such as what—oh my God." In a reflection I saw what I was standing next to, and turned around to see two huge glass cases of elaborate cakes in front of the espresso machine. "You had to stuff me full of donuts before I came here, didn't you?"

"Now you know how I suffer when *you* eat," he said. "Come on, she's got us a table."

The front window wasn't much quieter, but at least there we could hunch over the table and talk. I told him the long version of what had happened to Cinnamon, and Calaphase patted my hand. "Don't worry," he said, face clearly worried. "You'll get her back. I'm sure of it."

"Try not to sound so convinced," I said, slurping my mocha just to see him squirm. Unexpectedly they had delivered it with a small glass of hazelnut liqueur, which I sniffed before offering it to him. "I don't drink and drive. Not even a little."

"Aren't we here to drink?" he said, sipping, with pain, a tall blended drink. "*I'll* drive."

"Doesn't that milkshake thing have like, a shot of vodka in it?"

"Something like it," he said. "Look, you ordered it, and it *is* good. Please—"

"*Fine*," I said, taking the hazelnut and taking a small sip. "Not bad. I'm still not drinking the whole thing, no matter what you say. Just my luck, they'll pull me over and breathalyze me."

"You're sounding a little more like Dakota. Ready to get back in the saddle?"

I stared at him blankly—and then he pulled a manila folder out of his jacket. "You have pictures of the tags," I said, leaning forward. "Gimme, gimme!"

These pictures were better than any I'd seen yet. The finest masterpiece, a complicated whirlpool design almost certainly made by the first tagger, was marred by whorls of black soot emanating from its center. The soot hadn't destroyed it, but it obscured too much of the design to see it clearly, and I scowled . . . until I remembered that Calaphase had said the victim had burned. Then the soot began to look uncomfortably like a body, and I looked away.

"Both this guy and Revenance caught fire," I said thoughtfully, "and I assumed it was the sun . . . but the werehouse burned too. Could burning be part of the life cycle of the tag?"

"I hope not," Calaphase said. "That would be a disaster. There are a lot of tags."

"I'd tell Rand, but I think he'd have me arrested," I said. "Calaphase . . . can you arrange to send an anonymous tip to the police for me? I mean, we can warn the Edgeworld, but the police are looking into this too and I'd hate for some poor officer to get crisped."

Calaphase frowned. "If I can't arrange it, Saffron certainly can."

There were also pictures showing the art of the second tagger, mostly around the werehouse. Apparently Tully had been chronicling the graffiti for some time. There were a few candid pictures with tags in the background featuring werehouse regulars like Vic, a few werekin boys, and even Cinnamon, who had been caught swatting her claws at the camera.

"These are very good," I said, studying that last picture closely. I loved my girl, and already missed her terribly. "What are you up to, Calaphase?"

"What do you mean?" he said, taken aback.

"You didn't need to do all this just to get an early report to Saffron. She's not going to come stake you in your sleep because you're slow getting back to her."

"Touché," he said, raising his glass. "You caught me. I planned to ask you out again."

I leaned back in my chair. *Damnit.* "I smelled something fishy with your late-night call."

"I take it that's a no, then?" Calaphase said, smiling.

"What are we doing right now?" I asked. "Having coffee that costs as much as a meal? If the kitchen was still open, you'd be selling me on their food, just to watch me eat."

"That I would. I *love* watching you eat," Calaphase said warmly, and I glanced away, embarrassed. He laughed, then got serious. "Care to try again? A real date, no drama?"

"Someplace inexpensive?" I said. "Not four thousand dollar drinks forty miles down the backwoods of Atlanta? Someplace we can go Dutch, like real twenty-first century humans?"

Calaphase laughed. "That sounds good to me."

"OK," I said. "It will have to be after the hearing, though. I'll let you know."

"I understand—you've got a *lot* going on," he said. "Whenever you're ready—but until then, throw me a bone on the pictures, something I can pass to Saffron."

"There are three separate taggers," I said, and Calaphase leaned back in his chair. "Call them two and a half Siths: a master, a journeyman, and an apprentice. My mystery benefactor in the police force has said as much, and these pictures confirm it. The master tagger is active in downtown Atlanta, and his tags are the most dangerous. No vampire should go near them. The other two look to be wankers, copycats. Only the one that nearly killed Tully was associated with an attack, and I think that's only because he tried to whitewash it alone."

"That's not a bone," he said. "That's a labeled skeleton with a copy of Gray's Anatomy."

I shrugged and took one more sip, finding I'd finished the tiny little glass of the liqueur. "I do my best. Mind if I send these to my mysterious benefactor?"

"Please, go ahead. One more thing—if you do squeeze out some time, give me a little advance notice? One of my flunkies can take my shift and we can have the whole night together." His face fell as soon as he said it. "I didn't mean to imply—"

"I'm not made of glass, Calaphase," I said, smiling.

But Calaphase *didn't* smile. "Vampires are known for taking advantage of human . . . prey," he said with distaste. "I do *not* want you to think I'm just out for your blood."

"You know what I think, Calaphase?" I said, finishing the last swig of mocha.

Calaphase cocked his head at me. "No. What *do* you think, Dakota?"

"It's going to take more than the threat of a bite to scare me away from you, vampire."

27. LAND OF THE SKINDANCERS

Blood Rock, Georgia is a tiny little hamlet between Stone Mountain and Conyers. *Everyone* knows Stone Mountain: a mammoth single stone of granite, literally the size of a mountain, upon which some racist *idiot* carved a bunch of Confederate yahoos on horses, simultaneously the world's largest rock carving and the largest instance of vandalism. And *almost* everyone knows Conyers, a charming little town desperately trying to forget that the Virgin Mary appeared in a cornfield there sometime in the 1980s.

No-one knows Blood Rock, and Blood Rockers are happy to keep it that way. The stadium-sized knot of granite that dominates the town is dwarfed by Stone Mountain itself, dwarfed even by nearby Rock Chapel Mountain; but it is the treelined half-hill slumped over the boulder that really obscures it—and gave the Rock its name: with each rain, red Georgia clay bleeds out of the hillside, dripping down the rock in rivulets like red blood.

But it was more than just metaphorical blood. I got a tingle as I passed the ENTERING BLOOD ROCK sign. Blood Rock was protected by a magic circle, but there was no literal circle like that buried under Atlanta's perimeter. Blood Rock's barrier was projective, the magic of a sanctuary stone powered by ley lines and resonating off the Rock itself.

Rubbed into the Sanctuary Stone was a drop of blood from every magician that practiced in Blood Rock, even me. That blood magic enabled a powerful protective spell, protecting us from enemy magicians and alerting the Stonegrinder Clan, the keepers of the Stone, if any of us came to harm.

Arcturus didn't need that protection, of course; he was a fearsome magician. He chose Blood Rock for a more prosaic reason, the same reason I chose Atlanta: magic circles made it harder for stray spirits to invade magic tattoos while they were being inked.

Unfortunately, or fortunately, depending on your point of view, Blood Rock's sanctuary stone also kept out the future. In five years, it had barely changed: no new subdivisions, no big box stores, not even a Starbucks. The two lone fast food joints, a McDonalds and a Captain D's, hadn't been updated in decades. Only deep, winterbare forests, narrow, winding roads, and ancient, decaying homes infested with carpenter bees. Tilting sheds and folk art livened the roads . . . but wooden fences, high hedges, and NO TRESPASSING signs were just as common.

But as I drew into the tiny town center, I started noticing slight—and subtly ominous—differences. Red Christmas lights still hung from the trees on Old Main like rows of fireflies, but the normal foot traffic was absent. Typically, even in January, you'd see a few Blood Rockers milling about in shortsleeves or wifebeaters, showing off an astounding range of tattoos, but today even the gas station attendant was bundled up behind new bulletproof glass.

Something had happened here, and I didn't like it. One of the usually stationary police cars was actually patrolling, Blood Rock's New Age Gifte Shoppe was closed for renovations, and atop the Rock itself at last I saw a gash in the hillside and the roofs of new homes.

The police car slid by, smooth as a shark, and I caught the friendly eye of Sheriff Steyn through its window, nodding at me in greeting. I wasn't fooled. Steyn was dangerous precisely because he wasn't a big-hat, big-belly parody of a small town sheriff complete with Cool Hand Luke mirrorshades. Steyn was handsome, charming, and completely unpredictable. With Steyn, you never saw it coming until it hit you—a fact I knew from experience.

I nodded back and he smiled and drove on. Apparently, today I'd passed. Whatever had happened was not serious enough for him to run me out of town as he had on my first visit, too many years ago. So I pulled into the gravel lot of the Grist Mill Motel, an ancient brown wooden structure at the base of the hill, distinguished by its still-working water wheel and Blood Rock's best and only coffee shop. The radio kept me company on my drive down memory lane.

"—and I-20 is *finally* clearing up, but High Pass Road is still blocked by that broken tractor. And that's it for traffic this Tuesday evening. Coming up in two minutes at seven PM: Radio Flea Market with Jan Smits, helping you get your stuff to someone who wants it. Then at eight, a replay of Fresh Air. You're listening to Blood Rock Radio, WBRK 850AM."

The Prius crunched to a stop, and I sighed, staring up at the deck and the wide glowing glass of the café. Somewhere up there sat Arcturus, my old skindancing master, waiting to chew me out. Why did I feel like I was walking into another meeting with my dad?

"He ain't in there," Zinaga said, rising from her seat on the steps as I got out of the car. Half Jamaican, half Korean, with a layered Jennifer Anniston shag that went well with her dark olive skin, she had been Arcturus' 'new' apprentice for years now. Zinaga had beautiful tattoos, but today she was uncharacteristically bundled up. She'd wrapped her muscular arms in white longjohns and slipped on denim coveralls whose straps wanted to snap trying to hold in her bust—cute as ever, and she wasn't even trying. "You kept him waiting over an hour," she said, folding her arms. "He told me, fuck you."

"He told you to fuck me? How sweet of him," I said. There was little love lost between us. Zinaga had become Arcturus' 'new' apprentice right around the time I'd started to realize I wasn't learning how to ink magic tattoos just so

I could live the rest of my life in Blood Rock, tattooing backwoods mechanics trapped in the 1950s. The transition had been . . . awkward. "But it's a little late—I'm dating boys now. An official *was*bian."

"You know what I meant, Kotie," Zinaga said, uncomfortable and embarrassed. I suddenly realized she *was* a lesbian, or at least curious—and we'd worked together for six months and I'd never noticed. Some agent of change I was. "He says you're 'in Coventry,' and when I asked what that means, he said to not even bother to call him. He's really upset."

"So am I," I said. "I got kicked out of my apartment, DFACS took my daughter, and I spent the whole afternoon talking to lawyers I can't afford."

"Couldn't happen to a nicer lady," Zinaga said brightly, cocking her head, her hand on her hip. "You know, you should stick to one excuse. It sounds more believable."

"That's why I left out all the murders," I said evenly, "or maybe they *just* weren't material to my being late, whereas my legal woes are."

"Oh, the murders weren't *material*," Zinaga jeered. "You're spinning and spinning further. Are your highly-educated lawyers rubbing off on you?"

It was the same-old, same-old. I don't know exactly what I'd done to made Zinaga get off about my education: after all, she *had* a degree in communications and *I* was a dropout. But this wasn't funny anymore. And I was actually feeling a bit bad about my defective gaydar.

So I just stared at her. Her smile cracked a little bit.

"I'm sorry I'm late," I said. "And I shouldn't have brought up my friends who died. It was just last week and I'm still pretty raw about it. Now, I spent the last two and half hours in traffic trying to get here, but since Arcturus doesn't answer his phone, I couldn't call him and tell him that. And since you wouldn't answer the phone either—"

"Sorry about that," Zinaga said, embarrassed. "And sorry about your friend. What—"

"Two and a half hours," I repeated.

She cocked her head. "You gotta go pee."

"Oh, yeah," I said, leaning against the car and crossing my legs for effect. "And in the Grist Mill Café, you have to buy something or Dennis—"

"No dumpink vithout eatink," she said, exaggerating the café owner's German accent. "Yeah, yeah. I'll tell Arcturus you're paying the bathroom tax."

"Thanks," I said, looking at her coveralls. "Did they pass a law banning tattoos?"

Zinaga looked at me in alarm. "No, why? Shit, have you heard something?"

"No, it's just everyone's covered up, even you," I said. Zinaga specialized in light marks, so she could tattoo amazing marks on her dark skin that stood out like white glowing lines when she filled them with mana—but today you could just see a little silver scrollwork crawling up her neck. "I was hoping to see your masterwork—I never saw it finished."

"You've been gone from Blood Rock too long, Dakota. It gets *cold* after dark," she said, pulling her sleeve down. True enough, but in this context it felt like a lie. It wasn't cold enough to cover up, so why was she doing it? Surely . . . she hadn't ruined a tattoo so badly she felt she had to hide it? "I'm surprised you're still here in that stupid vest—hey, what happened to *your* masterwork? Where's the Dragon?"

My eyes narrowed. Interesting the way she deflected my question about her tattoos back onto me and my masterwork. She had been experimental; maybe she *had* ruined her tattoos, trying out some new design that had a bad interaction.

Finally I realized she was waiting for an answer and said, "I had to use it."

"Use it?" she said. "You mean you *detached* it? *Why?*"

I used it to defeat a serial killer who, blah, blah, blah. "It's a *long* story," I said.

She shook her head. "I'll go tell Arcturus you're here. You can tell him about the Dragon—I don't want to get an earful about the sanctity of your mastermark when I haven't even done anything. He still goes off on you from time to time whenever some random thing bothers him, and I have to sit there and listen to an hour-long rant."

"After all these years," I said.

"Yeah, welcome 'home,'" she said, walking back towards the studio; Blood Rock was *that* small. "I expect he's going to go off on you, so bring earplugs, or a sixpack so we have something to pass the time with."

"I can't stay the night," I said. "I have a court appearance in the morning."

"Well, you know how he is—don't keep him waiting too long, or blow him off again," she said, waving as she went. "Piss him off again, you could get the cold shoulder for months."

I sighed, watching her go. It was *so* good to be 'home' again.

Then I turned to go inside—and a fist exploded in my face in a flashbulb of pain. The blow knocked me back against my car and almost off my feet. Everything blurred, then my vision resolved to see a wide, greasy bearded guy grinning at me.

"You should never have come to Blood Rock, skindancer," he said, cracking his knuckles and throwing another punch before I could even scream.

My arms moved automatically, one curving in a block and the other popping out to clock the guy on the chin. The punch wasn't Taido, it was older, a college Tae Kwon Do reflex. The blow knocked his head back, but he laughed it off and moved in—straight into my follow up.

This punch *was* Taido, with skindancing mixed in: thrown from the hip, twisting over in the last half inch, absorbing mana in my skin and discharging it with a bang on his nose. Blood sprayed, he staggered back, and I moved in with a savage, full-power kick to the ribs.

It was like kicking a telephone pole. He cried out but didn't fall, and actually caught my leg before I could withdraw. I started punching him, single punch, double punch, triple punch, tagging him one-two-three in the skull, chest, and gut, but he shrugged them all off.

"Damn," he said, shoving back on my leg as a van squealed behind us on the gravel. He ducked under one blow, then cried out as my followup landed on his collarbone, but still held on as feet ran up on us. "You've got a hell of a fight in you—for a girl."

A fist solid as a brick connected with my temple, and suddenly I was swarmed by black-suited figures. I struggled uselessly, flashing on the one and only time I'd played football and ended up on the bottom of a pileup—groped, crushed and unable to breathe.

I was picked up bodily despite my thrashing—and then I saw the hood of a police car slide past the end of the van. I yelled as loud as I could, and as the window of the police car hove into view I saw Sheriff Steyn—who just nodded, smiled, and drove on.

Oh, God—he was *in* on it, whatever *it* was.

Everything went dark as I was hurled into the back of the van. I tried to scream again, but a leather-gloved hand pressed over my mouth. I *mmphed* and squirmed, but could not stop the probing fingers running over my body, picking at my pockets.

"Here are the keys. Get the car. Get the car!" a voice shouted. I kicked out, and someone howled—then a fist was planted in my gut, and the air in my lungs squeaked out my nose in a spray of blood and snot. "For God's sake, put her out before she uses her marks!"

Then my first attacker leaned over me, blood running down his beard. "Don't worry," he said, grinning. "We know how to deal with skindancers."

A stinking cloth was shoved over my face, and then—*blackness*.

28.   A TASTE FOR VAMPIRES

Choking pain gripped my neck, and my eyes opened in terror.

I saw a black-gloved hand, clamped in a steel ring, a few feet above a floor of irregular slate flagstones. The hand flexed, and I realized it was *my* hand. I tried to jerk away, but my hand just twitched uselessly in the ring. I tried to flex but my black-sleeved arm just writhed against the metal armrest of a chair. I became aware of something clammy and sticky covering my whole body, even my head. I twisted and tried to stand, but just felt an immense pain in my collarbones as they pushed against something rigid clamped tightly around my neck. Panicked, I screamed—but all that came out around the huge ball shoved in my mouth was a whimper.

*Oh shit, oh shit, oh **shit**.*

Minutes of frantic struggle yielded *nothing*. I was wrapped from head to toe in layers of black rubber and clamped into a rigid steel chair. I couldn't see much, but from my attempts to rock, it seemed like the chair was *bolted* to the floor. I was going nowhere.

A single spotlight, faint and gray, shone down on me and the chair, illuminating a small patch of slate flagstones. Beyond that was murk. I twisted as much as I could and only saw velvety blackness. No one had heard my faint whimpers—or no one had responded.

My discomfort kept building. The chair was built for someone smaller than me, and held me slumped back and scrunched sideways. I was cramped and choking, but still, I tried writhing to power my marks. But I had no tattoos on exposed skin, so what little mana I could generate burned back into my body in a surge of pain, and I sagged back against the clamps.

Then the lights came on.

Dark curtains lined the walls; metal railings hemmed in the flagstones. Before me, steps rose towards a throne sitting in front of a huge disc of stone inscribed with an elaborate ring of bloodstained roses—the *Sanctuary Stone.* It should have been in the Stonegrinder's Grove, warning them that someone threatened a magician of Blood Rock. But who had it—and me?

Footsteps sounded on the dais, beyond the stone, and level with my eyes I saw a pair of fine leather boots walking confidently towards me. They were medieval yet elegant, styled to match the tailored leggings above them, Renaissance Faire as done by Giorgio Armani.

A dark velvet coat flared like a priest's cassock as the figure stepped round the Stone, but above the straight line of the sheathed sword in the figure's hand, the coat's cut tightened, with subdued, elegant brocade. The figure came to a stop, and I craned my neck to look into red eyes set in a cruel young face, beneath a wiry shock of hair like a blaze of white flame.

It was the vampire Transomnia.

I *screamed.* A high-pitched squeal escaped around the gag, and laughter erupted behind me. My hands flailed, and Transomnia smiled, tightlipped, not bothering to expose his fangs. He turned slightly, lowering the sword behind him, and raised his other hand for silence.

"So, skindancer," he said, voice as smooth as the velvet of his cloak, "not the welcome you expected to Blood Rock? We have tired of you people swaggering through our town. Try using your marks now. Try breathing a word of power. Not so confident, are we?"

He straightened and glared down at me, voice ringing out. "We made the rules very clear. Blood Rock is *our* domain now. No skindancers are welcome without our token; none may come here unannounced." He waved a hand at the Stone. "*You* have done both, trying to sneak past—"

"Whath th fkkk, Tranth?" I choked out around the gag. After I'd saved him from Valentine, we had agreed to leave each other alone. "Whh hdd ah dhhl!"

A hand struck the back of my head, hard—but Transomnia paused. "Don't," he said, raising his hand to stay the one that had struck me, but without looking at his underling. His eyes stayed on me. His red, glowing eyes seemed to sparkle, and I felt a flush of heat against the skin of my face. Then, slowly, he descended the stairs, sword held back casually, but in what I could see was one quick move away from a decapitating strike.

I twisted uselessly in the clamps, then cringed back as he stepped right before me and leaned down. "Did you have something to say, skindancer?" he asked softly, leaning down into my face. Then his eyes widened in recognition—then further in pure, unadulterated terror.

His head jerked back—just a little—then his eyes tightened and he straightened, much more slowly than he needed to, as if to prove to himself he was not afraid. I saw his hand tighten on the sword, but as he became fully erect he said, "Then let's hear it."

"Whffk—" I choked, then sagged forward in the chair. "Fhkk yh."

He smiled, turned away and climbed two steps of the stairs. "Get it off her."

"But, my Lord," a voice said, female—and scared. "She's a skindancer, *his* protégé. We *all* know how dangerous their magic is. You warned us about her, *specifically*. You *showed* us her killing *your own master*. If we let her speak a word of power—"

"You *knew* she was his protégé and didn't think it significant enough to tell me?" Transomnia said. "No wonder the Stone did not react to her presence."

"Oh, but it *did*," the female voice said. "The blood marks resonated when she passed the barrier. That confirmed the tip we received."

"So, technically, she has the *right* to be here—and *again* you didn't tell me? Oh, get that thing off her," he said, cracking his neck. Then he turned back, and his eyes were filled with calm menace as he stared over my shoulder. "And let her out of that chair."

There was the briefest of pauses, then hands fumbled at the back of my head, and others fumbled at the arms and legs of the chair. As the gag peeled off and I coughed, I caught a glimpse of a goateed, handsome male guard and a pale, beautiful, violet-haired female vampire.

The collar came off. I spat and *bleahed* and wiped my hand with my free arm, which was stinging and stinking, pins and needles mixed with pungent rubber. My other hand came free and I hunched forward, massaging my right nervously with my left through the sticky gloves. My legs were freed, I put my hands on the armrests, I gritted my teeth, and I stood.

I swayed forward, dizzy, and saw a black velvet coat, saw a white hand reach out and steady my shoulder. Oh, God, he was *touching* me. I twitched, feeling magic trapped beneath the suit burn against my skin. Then I leaned back out of it and looked right in his face.

Transomnia stood before me, the man who'd taken two of my back teeth, my confidence and nearly my life. He was precisely positioned on the steps to give him an ever so slight advantage over my height. And, within arm's reach, holding a sword, was his hand. *The* hand. That awful hand, that had held those awful clippers, with which he'd nearly taken my tattooing fingers.

He could kill me in a second. He'd nearly maimed me for life. And I was defenseless. But I held my ground before him, damnit. I straightened defiantly—and so did he.

"Well, well, well, Dakota Frost," he said, voice careful and controlled. "I did not recognize you with that hood wrapping your head. What did you want to say?"

"I said, what the *fuck*, Trans? We had a deal!"

"*Did* we?" Transomnia said—and seized my right hand. My eyes bugged, but I stayed frozen: he could kill me in an instant with that sword, or, hell, just with one backhand. "Ah yes, I remember. Our first deal, more of a covenant, really: never cross me again, or I'll leave you with bloody stumps. Do you remember that, Dakota Frost?"

My knees began trembling, and I nodded.

"To think," he said, raising my hand to inspect it, "one little squeeze a few months ago could have destroyed this fine, precision instrument, and you would never have tattooed again." My rubber-gloved fingers now began trembling in his grip, and I felt my teeth grinding against each other, with a sharp cracking pain on the right side where Transomnia had kicked out two of my molars. "That would have been a loss to the world, don't you think?"

"Y-yes," I said, absolutely terrified.

He raised my hand to his lips and kissed my two fingers. "Once again," he said, raising his voice to address the hall, "see forbearance brings more than small favors. I spared Dakota Frost's hand, and she, in turn, helped me free myself from my master."

He released my hand and turned away, ascending the steps to his throne, behind which the Sanctuary Stone that was supposed to be protecting me was hanging like a useless gong.

"Following that, I recall, we made a new deal," he said, throwing himself down abruptly on the throne, one leg over the side, hand resting on the sword like a cane. I appreciated the increased distance between us, but somehow that deliberately casual pose made me feel even *less* safe. "That we would leave each other the hell alone. Why are you here, Dakota Frost?"

"Why am *I* here?" I said, stunned. "*You* kidnapped me and brought me here."

"Do not dissemble," Transomnia hissed, shifting forward abruptly, steepling both hands over the hilt of his sword, hair rising up above him like a frozen bonfire. "Why have you pursued me to Blood Rock, Dakota Frost?"

"Why have *I* pursued *you?*" I said—then laughed. He actually thought I had tracked him here for some reason? "Not everything is about you, Trans."

Something immensely strong struck my cheek with a loud slap, and I staggered sideways. Transomnia had not moved, and I looked to my left, straight into the blazing green eyes of the cruelly delicious female vampire. Eyes watering, I flinched away, coming face to face with the other, goateed vamp. But I didn't have time to think through the horror of standing defenseless between two hostile vampires, because the female vamp reached out and seized my neck.

"Do not speak to my master with such familiarity," she hissed. She jerked me close, and I could hear the strands of her hair brush against the suit, could feel her breath against my ear, echoing hollowly against the slick, icky rubber. "His name is Lord Transomnia—"

"Nyissa," Transomnia said. "Don't. And do *not* make me say it a third time."

Both the vampire at my throat and I jerked at the voice. It was quiet, even, and filled with deadly menace. Nyissa let me go, and I straightened, looking up at Transomnia, calm face tilted towards me, eyes following Nyissa away. Gone was the pasty wannabe spouting threats, gone was the sick whiny serial-killer taunts. All the masks were gone: *this* was a vampire lord.

"How old are you?" I whispered.

Transomnia's glowing red eyes settled on me again, and I looked away. "Not as old as you think," he said, and I could hear the smile in his voice. "But that is the advantage of turning early. I can look as young as I want." Then the humor vanished. "Why are you here, Dakota?"

"To see Arcturus, my skindancing master," I said. "To ask how to fight magic graffiti."

"Magic graffiti?" he laughed, leaning back onto his throne before the Stone in that oh-so comfortable, almost mocking slouch. "Oh, how the mighty have fallen, Dakota."

"It's incredibly strong. It killed Revenance and tried to kill Tully."

"Revenance was a vampire," Transomnia said, smiling down at me. "And you hate vampires. Why would you come all the way out here to avenge one of us?"

"He was nice to me and Cinnamon," I said defensively. "Besides, Calaphase—"

Transomnia raised a hand. "Do not say that name."

Calaphase had kicked Transomnia out of the Oakdale Clan—and forced him back into the arms of the serial killer who had controlled him. I swallowed. "Well . . . he . . . and Sav—the Lady Saffron . . . wanted me to investigate Revenance's death."

"My my my, so many vampires in your life, and you're doing so much for them," Transomnia said. "Surely you're not developing a taste for vampires? I'm sure any of the vampires here would love to get a taste of you and that hot skindancer blood."

"Yes, indeed," Nyissa purred.

"My leads had run dry," I said, swallowing. "My master is the next logical person I could turn to. I didn't know you'd moved into town!"

"*I* was here first," Nyissa said, oddly petulant. "Before that Chilean *jerk* took over."

"But all of the House Beyond Sleep stand with you now, and Blood Rock is yours again," Transomnia said. Strange that he'd said the city was hers, not his. "Odd that Arcturus didn't warn you the balance of power had changed, Dakota."

My brow furrowed. That was odd. I could see Zinaga not warning me; she hated my guts. But why had Arcturus not bothered to tell me a new crop of vampires had rolled into Blood Rock—or that Nyissa was here all along? Why hadn't I seen her? Was I *that* oblivious?

Then I remembered what Arcturus was *really* like, and grimaced.

"You're giving him a wide berth, aren't you?" I asked. Transomnia scowled, and I smiled grimly. "He can be a scary piece of work, but as long as you leave him be, he leaves you be. You could throw my bleeding body onto his doorstep and he'd just yell at me for being late."

"Why, that sounds like a capital idea," Nyissa purred.

I glanced at her: goth pale, *painfully* pretty, green eyes blazing beneath a mop of violet hair, a flaring coat/dress that exposed what looked like riding pants and incongruous suede boots, and a long, narrow stick in her hands, which at first I took to be a riding crop—and then realized was a metal poker used to stir a fire. Something about that last accessory made me swallow.

"D-don't you think it might be a bit obvious to off me the day I roll into town?"

"Off you?" Nyissa said, strutting around me, a cold runway model twirling her poker. "Why, there is no need to be so . . . indiscriminate. Bleeding and drained, yes, but not dead: a suitable warning. And what danger would you be? You don't even know where you are."

"Oh, come on," I said. "You picked me up as soon as I rolled into town. Blood Rock is pretty damn small—and you've got the Stone. You can't hide your location by driving me around for a few hours. I assure you I'll be able to find it later on Google Maps."

"Maybe we should blind her," the goateed vamp guard said.

Oh, Jesus, oh, Jesus! I thought losing my fingers was the worst that could happen to me. "I—I know a blind witch," I said, blood rising in fear even as I said it. On the surface Jinx had adapted to losing her sight, but a part of her was *still* crushed. "We'll still find you—"

"Are you sure?" Nyissa said, staring at the end of her poker. She looked past it at me, eyes glowing like emeralds beneath that mop of violet hair. "Why don't we see—"

"Enough of that talk," Transomnia said. "*No-one* is going to hurt the Lady Frost."

"You give her a *title?*" Nyissa said. "Even the Maid of Little Five Points rescinded—"

"Silence," Transomnia said firmly. "Lady Frost, this city is now *my* domain. We tolerate Arcturus and his current apprentices, but new skindancers are *not* welcome without my leave and their ink may *not* be shown. *You*, in particular, are not welcome anywhere I choose to walk."

His mouth quirked up in a smile. "Nyissa . . . *banish* her."

Nyissa perked up suddenly, flashing me a vicious grin. Then she ascended the steps to the throne, then stepped behind it, leaning against the Sanctuary Stone lasciviously. She waved a hand over it, eyes closed—then found what she was looking for, and touched the Stone.

At first, there was nothing, as she drew her fingers in a circle around one of the stained roses etched into the Stone. Somehow, I knew, that was the rose where my blood was pressed into the rock. As she moved her hand, slowly, a high-pitched tone began to build, the annoying hum of a finger playing a wineglass. It built up until my ears were ringing—but no one else seemed to notice. The noise didn't stop even when Nyissa took her hand away.

"So, Dakota Frost, I repeat the question," Transomnia said, swimming in my vision as my head began to ache, "Will you come back to Blood Rock?"

"No way, no how," I said, swaying on my feet.

"Then go home, Dakota Frost," Transomnia said. "Go home with your tail between your legs, and do not let me catch you back in Blood Rock again."

"I will know," Nyissa said, smiling back at the Stone, "the moment you do."

Transomnia smiled as well. "That suit looks good on you. You can keep it," he said, and flicked his hand in dismissal.

Hands grabbed at me, another dark cloth was shoved in my face, then nothingness.

29.   A GOOD FIRST IMPRESSION

I awoke in the trunk of the Prius, drooling on the newly laid carpeting, still wearing that stinking rubber suit. I groaned, and then heard something whoosh by. Moments later, I heard it again, then again, followed by a hiss. I tried to sit up and klonked my head. After struggling with the vanity cover, I kicked it out of the way, forced myself up into the car, and sat up in time to see an eighteen-wheeler scream by in the first light of dawn, eighteen inches from the Prius, leaving scraps of torn clothing scattering down I-20 in its wake.

After a few seconds I realized that it was *my* clothing scattering down I-20. I looked at myself: I looked like a total freak in the full-body rubber suit. More cars swept by, *whoosh, whoosh*, hissing every time they hit a wet patch on the road, scattering my clothes further. After the third one I swallowed my pride, crawled out of the car, and retrieved what I could from the highway, mortified with embarrassment every time a car honked at me as it passed.

All of it was ruined: my jeans, my shirt, even my vest. All I could rescue was my wallet, squashed almost beyond recognition where some car had run over it; but, oddly, they hadn't taken my money, and my driver's license was still recognizable.

The keys were still in the blue bomb, *thankfully*. At least I didn't have to go hunting all over the hillside in the freak suit hoping the vampires had thrown them there and not in the trash back in Blood Rock. I started her up, trying to figure out what the hell I was going to do, and let the voice of NPR's Renée Montagne soothe my wounded pride.

"This is Morning Edition. The time is eight fifty."

I sat bolt upright. *Eight-fifty Wednesday morning!* My meeting with DFACS about Cinnamon was at ten. I couldn't show up like this! Where the hell was I, and where was I going to get some clothes? I twisted round, scanning the highway for any sign—

Conyers 8. Atlanta 39.

"Oh, shit." *Forty miles—in rush hour traffic.* And still with nothing to wear.

My eyes refocused down the road, where I saw a sign for a store.

"Oh, hell," I said, starting the Prius. "At least it's not a Laura Ashley."

So it was almost ten thirty when I reached the massive complex downtown that held the Fulton County Courthouse, and ten *fifty* by the time I parked, wound through the metal detectors, found the right floor, and *finally* found the heavy wooden door of the hearing room—closed.

The deputy standing outside held up a hand. "They've already started."

"I'm supposed to be *in* there," I said. "Please."

He sighed. "All right, but I warn you she's in a mood . . . "

Judge Maria Guiterrez was a young brunette with a long sweep of bangs that came down over one eye. She couldn't even have been my age, but a crackling energy flashed in her face when she saw me enter. "Bailiff—" she began, then stopped. "Miss Frost, I take it."

"Yes," I said. One table held Margaret Burnham; the other held Helen

Yao, my attorney with Ellis and Lee. Helen glanced in surprise at my outfit—cream turtleneck sweater, tailored jeans jacket, and long flowing black skirt—but quickly motioned for me to come sit down.

"I said *tone it down,* not *turn it off,*" she hissed. "Your hair *doesn't go* with—"

"Miss Frost," Judge Guiterrez said sharply. "We were scheduled to start at ten."

"I'm very sorry," I said, coming to join Yao. "I was unavoidably detained—"

"That will not be good enough, Miss Frost," the judge began. "In my courtroom—"

"I had *no choice.* I was kidnapped," I said. And sat down at the table, shaking.

The judge's mouth just hung open. "Did—did you report this, Miss Frost?"

"No," I said. "I came straight here, because I was supposed to be *here.*"

Her brow furrowed. "Did you escape?"

"No, I did not *escape,*" I said. "People don't escape when they're kidnapped. That only happens in the movies. They're let go or they *die.* I was kidnapped, terrorized, and left to kick my way out of the trunk of my car on the side of the highway. In *Conyers.*"

A glass of water was suddenly in front of me, and I took it in my shaking hands. "They tore up my clothes. My clothes! Even my vest. I had to shop at a fucking Mervyn's—"

"Do you have a receipt, Miss Frost?" Judge Guiterrez asked coolly.

I looked up sharply at her. She was leaning her head on one hand, finger climbing to her temple. She would have been great at poker, I couldn't tell whether her expression held sympathy or disapproval. Scowling, I dug out my wallet and started rifling through it.

"What happened to your wallet, Miss Frost?" the judge said.

"A truck ran over it when they threw my pants onto I-20," I said, tossing a receipt on the table. "Eighty-nine fifty-seven, counting the manager discount because they took *pity* on me."

Judge Guiterrez beckoned, and the bailiff took the receipt to her. "This morning. Nine-fifteen," she said, rubbing her forehead. "In Conyers. And you came straight here—"

"Driving like a bat out of hell," I said.

"Well," Guiterrez said, and then a slight smile quirked her face, which she quickly tried to suppress. "Well. This isn't a traffic court, so I'll ignore that. Miss Frost, you've clearly had an, an experience, and if it's left you shaken, we can reschedule this hearing—"

"No," I said. "No, please, I came all the way here to get Cinnamon back. I don't want to wait. All that matters is that I get Cinnamon back as soon as possible."

"That won't happen today," the judge said. "But I will hear your case—*after* you have a chance to calm down and report your story to the police."

"But—" I began.

"No buts, Miss Frost," Guiterrez said, with quiet finality. "Bailiff, bring Miss Frost and counsel to my chambers and call an officer down here to take her statement. Next case . . . "

So they dragged me off—not literally—to the judge's chambers, where a sympathetic female APD officer took down the whole story. After she left, Helen came in and plopped her briefcase down on the table with a weary, wary look. "Damn, Dakota," she said. "I'm so sorry, but I hope this wasn't a stunt—"

"Helen!" I said, then stopped. Then I extended my hand. "Smell that?"

She stared at my hand like it was a snake, then cautiously leaned forward. "That smells like . . . rubber gloves? Baby powder? Mildew?" Her eyes furrowed. "What—"

"The sick fucks tore up my clothes and put me in a rubber suit because they were scared of my magic tattoos," I said. "No, I'm not making this up."

"Well, your tattoos are pretty fearsome," Helen laughed, a bit forced. "And I believe you, I guess, but this makes things more difficult. We missed our slot. Even with a good explanation, their first impression is that you were late and they had to reschedule. It doesn't look good."

"But—" I said. "But that's not *fair*."

"Dakota, let me tell you something I've learned," Helen said. "I'm a defense attorney, so I'm biased, but a child custody hearing isn't a criminal trial or a civil suit. It has its own twisted logic, and anything and *everything* can be used against you. If your child is retarded, then they've been neglected. If they're gifted, then they've been coached. If they're acting up, then you haven't been setting boundaries. If they're polite, you've been repressing them."

"Then how does anyone keep their child?" I said.

"Basically, the judge and the prosecution will decide who they think should have the child and twist everything to fit their prejudgment," Helen said bitterly. "That may not be the law, but it is what I've observed from doing this for the last seven years. That's why it is absolutely, positively critical that you present the best possible picture to the judge."

"All right," I said. "All right. What do we do?"

"First," Helen said, "we've rescheduled to Monday. Try not to get kidnapped, ill, or even disheveled between now and then. Make sure you arrive on time, dressed nicely, and that you've gone over all the materials we went over yesterday. Hopefully, this will blow over quickly once we get a chance to present our case. If not . . . well, then we can talk about that then."

"Don't keep me in suspense," I said. "What's the worst case scenario?"

"Oh, hell, I can't tell you what the judge is going to ask," she said, rubbing her forehead. "Who knows what they will want you to address? It may be as simple as documenting a fixed abode, or settling with the Valentine Foundation to show you have a good source of income."

"I have a good source of income," I said. "Fifty thousand dollars a year tattooing."

"Well . . . " she said, tilting her head, "that may not be good enough for the court."

I just stared back at her. "What are you saying?" I said. "You can't mean—"

"Magical tattooing is an unconventional profession," Helen said, "and you're not Cinnamon's biological mother. If you want to keep her . . . you may have to give that up."

30.	HEADING FOR TROUBLE

I drove back to the Rogue Unicorn early for my shift and talked things over with Kring/L, my defacto boss. The court let Cinnamon keep going to the Clairmont Academy, but it would be days, if not weeks, until I could take Cinnamon home. So I renegotiated my shifts, picking up extra hours in exchange for being able to bail more frequently to deal with the custody case . . . and the vampires, and the graffiti, and whatever else life was going to throw at me.

As night fell and I finished my last tattoo for the evening, Kring/L came to talk to me. He'd talked to the rest of the staff, and everyone was on my side. By then I had a better handle on my schedule from Helen, and we went over it together.

"We're going to have to get you a revolving door," Kring/L said with a grin. Big, beefy, bald, and completely untattooed, Kring/L was our best tattoo artist, conventional or otherwise (no, really, it hurts to say that, but he was) and the unofficial leader of our little partnership.

"As long as I could come back here," I said. "I'd hate to lose this."

"Dakota, you're half our draw," Kring/L said, following me back to my office. I glanced back at him, and his grin quickly faded. "Dakota, seriously. The rest of us know what you've been through. Hell, the publicity has made business better. Why would you even . . . "

I told him what Helen had told me, and his face turned red with rage, actually mottled.

"You do what you have to," he said, "but you are always welcome here. Got that?"

"Yeah," I said, sitting in my office chair. "Thanks."

My office phone rang. I glanced at the number, then savagely tore the earpiece off the cradle and snarled, "What the *hell* do you want, Zinaga?"

"To be the bearer of bad news," she said, and I could just hear that *smirk* in her voice. "Arcturus just gave me an earful. Like I told you not to, you didn't show, and he's really pissed. You're persona non grata now, Kotie, sent straight to Coventry, whatever that means . . . "

As she nattered on and on about how Arcturus had said he never wanted to talk to me again, two and two came together in my mind. Arcturus had bawled her out *today*—so she hadn't gone to the shop to meet me last night. She'd known I wouldn't show.

"Fuck you," I said, and Kring/L backed out of my office, eyes wide. "Fuck you!"

"Hey, don't blame me," she said smugly. "You're the one who bailed—"

"You threw me to the vampires!" I screamed into the phone. "To

Transomnia!"

There was silence. "Oh, *shit*," she said, and then the line went dead.

I slammed the handpiece back into the cradle repeatedly. "Damnit, damnit, damnit!" The phone rang again, and I picked it up. "Haven't you done enough damage!"

Again the line was silent. "What did I do?" Calaphase asked, all kicked puppy.

I laughed, an odd broken cry. "Oh. Oh, Calaphase. I'm so sorry. I've had a bad day, and I thought you were someone else."

"I'd hate to be them," he said. "Do you have any news on the graffiti?"

"Oh, hell," I laughed. "Do I have news, yes. About the graffiti, no."

I told him everything. At first, when he heard what Transomnia's goons had done to me, Calaphase looked ready to leap up and go tearing after him— but as I started to explain I didn't want to pursue Trans, Calaphase *got* it, just like that, and smoothly changed the subject.

And then . . . we talked. Really *talked.*

Not about graffiti or vampires, but instead about Cinnamon and school supplies, about coffee and restaurants, about moving and meanies, about how you always get pulled over for running a red light after you've caught yourself getting sloppy about yellows but before you've learned to put your foot on the brake earlier.

Calaphase wasn't a vampire to me anymore. He was a person who happened to be a vampire. I wanted to more than just talk to him. I wanted to *see* him, to go to another stupid coffee house and watch him grimace his way through a mocha.

But why did I need an excuse? We had talked about seeing each other. In fact, we had planned on it, sometime after the hearing was done, but never set a time.

"You free Thursday night, vampire?" I said. "Ready to go out on a *real* date?"

$$\wp \!\!-\!\! \bullet \!\!-\!\! \wp$$

Thursday night, I sat on a stool before a full-length mirror, naked to the waist at the center of a magic circle. The tail locks of my hair curled round my neck and dusted my back, resting between two tattooed wings of rainbow feathers that one day would be joined together. My arm curled around me, holding the tattooing gun, slowly inking the outline of a claw.

Once my skin had held a Dragon, a huge tattoo covering me from shoulder to toe, inked by my own hand. I'd released it to save my life, but I couldn't just let it go. It was my icon, on my business cards and stitched on my jackets. It would be a lot of work to re-tattoo the Dragon: this was my fifth session, and there would be at least twelve more, plus touchups.

Now, seventeen sessions is no little thing. I may be a bit of a masochist, but tattooing *hurts*, and it strangely seems to hurt *more* when you're doing it to yourself. Skindancers have to tattoo themselves, out of fear that a rival would leave them with a subtle—and permanent—hex. Non-magical tattooists, on the other hand, rarely tattoo themselves because it's painful, unnecessary—and darn near impossible to get a good inking angle on your own body.

And inking your own back is quite the challenge, even for someone as long-limbed and limber as I am. The outline was barely finished, and already my neck hurt, my shoulder hurt, my back hurt, and I was getting a cramp in my lower leg. But I didn't care: I could feel the buzzing of the tattooing gun, the insistent scratching that shimmered into a sensual, almost sexual warmth, and the vibration that fed back into my hand, giving me a feeling of power.

The main tattooing room had a wide plate glass window that was usually covered by a screen, but I had it down so potential customers could watch—and there was quite the crowd now. I was turned three-quarters away, my breasts hidden by a long dentist's bib, alternately inking the line carefully in the mirror and then wiping the blood away with my free hand.

Kring/L opened the door and stared at me, then closed at it behind him. "Annesthesia said you were on the prowl," he said. "I guess she was right."

"This is how I *always* do this," I said.

"Not yourself," he said. "Not your back, sitting there half naked, blinds down."

"But . . . " I began, then stopped. I did tattoo myself in here, with the blinds open, but always small marks on the arms, never my own back. That I had done back in Blood Rock, with no-one watching. Arcturus insisted that a skindancer ink their masterwork alone.

"You're right," I admitted, wiping away some blood. "Maybe I *am* prowling a bit."

"For whom?" he asked. "I thought you were dating that Virginian."

"We split," I said, eyes and hand tracing a line carefully.

"He was nice," Kring/L said. "You gotta learn to hang on to somebody sometime, or you'll end up alone as I am."

I pulled the needle away from my flesh, then looked up sharply. He was grinning, but for the first time I could see lines of pain in the friendly wrinkles around his eyes. He shrugged.

"I'm so sorr—"

"Don't," he said, eyes on my waist. He picked up a wet wipe from the dispenser on the counter and stepped forward, before I could stop him. "You should wipe—"

"Don't—" I said, but it was too late. He stepped forward across the line of the magic circle, and there was a tingling pop as the circle of protection was broken. The slight shift in the light halted him, and I jerked the needle away from my skin. "Idiot! This is a magic mark!"

Kring/L stood halted, looking around like he'd actually felt the magic for once. "Dakota, you worry too much. Nothing will get you if you break a circle—we're inside the Perimeter."

"Less likely does not mean impossible," I said, wiping myself down. "Look, Kring, no offense, but sometimes you're thick as a brick. You're the most skilled tattooist I've ever worked with—and I really mean that—but you only think breaking a circle is safe because you ink basic magic marks, too simple to hold a stray intent. I hope you're not inking any of *Jinx's* flash on clients without drawing a circle, or you risk a nasty magical infection, or worse."

"What's worse than a magical infection?" he laughed.

"A magical possession," I said.

"Come on," he said, grinning, but twisting the wet wipe in his hands. "We do moving butterflies and watches."

"And controlling charms that took a good friend's mind, whenever someone wanted," I said. "The expression of magic is dictated by its intent. Never think it can't go the other way."

I stared at the mark in the mirror: I had done enough for the day. I reached for the bandages I'd prepared, and Kring/L stepped forward again. "No, don't help me, I'm recreating my masterwork. I need to do this myself."

"All right, skindancer," Kring/L laughed, dropping the wipe into the biohazard bucket. "Mission accomplished, though. You caught a big fish in your net."

I looked over at the big window and smiled.

Calaphase stood at the window, trim and proper in a dark suit with a long-tailed overcoat, an even more dazzling turn on his vintage look. The frame of the window and the darker waiting room beyond made him look like a magazine model: his blond hair was perfectly styled, his pale face stern, and his blue eyes were staring at me with glittering fascination.

"Calaphase," I said. "So good to see you. I'll be with you in a moment."

Then I got up and walked behind the screen, quickly wiping down, pulling on my sportsbra and a 'vamp-hither' top—a tight, midriff-exposing corset with shimmering rows of chains that looked vaguely like bat wings. It just *popped* against the slightly purple folds of my best ankle-length faux-snakeskin vest, and riffed off my tight leather jeans quite nicely. I checked my hair in the mirror, then fluffed my deathhawk a little and sprayed it out.

"On the prowl," Kring/L muttered, leaning against the jamb. "Girl, you're on the *hunt*."

I smiled at him. "He's quite a catch," I said, "even if he *is* a vampire."

If that bothered Kring/L, he didn't let it show, and we walked out into the waiting room together. Calaphase waited there, lounging in the chair, one leg propped up. He had on black leather boots, a surprise beneath the suit that made him look more dashing and dangerous.

"You guys stay out of trouble," Kring/L said, grinning, his eyes even more sad than before. "I'll pass on your information to your audience."

Only then did I see that there were three men and two women who had all been watching me. Apparently I just hadn't seen them. I only had eyes for Calaphase. My mouth opened and I started to introduce myself, but Calaphase rose smoothly and took my arm.

"Now, Dakota," he said, steering me to the door, "Kring/L will look after your clients, but I am here to look after *you* and you need a night on the town."

I squeezed his hand with my free one. "Thanks," I said, as we stepped out the door. "I would have been there all night. It's hard to put the needle down. Your car or mine?"

"I was dropped off," he said.

"You never do have a car," I said.

"I have a driver when I need one," he said, "but my bike is more fuel efficient."

"I love it when you talk green to me," I said.

"Speaking of which," he said, "I propose I watch you eat a veggie burger, at a place I know I can get a decent glass of wine. R Thomas?"

"The best veggie burgers ever, served twenty four hours a day?" I said. "Let's roll!"

R Thomas was across the street from Café Intermezzo—and it's odd how until recently I would have thought of it the other way round. It's a folk-art mess right at the border of Atlanta's Midtown neighborhood and its Buckhead party district, attracting clientele from both. So, even dressed up, we fit in quite well on R Thomas's patio, staking out a middle ground between the couples in black evening wear and the flannelpunk lesbians who kept turning my head.

Calaphase's eyes, however, were only on me.

"By the way," he said, with a slight smile, "you should know, and should tell Kring/L, that vampires have excellent hearing."

I reddened. "What did you hear?"

"On the prowl?" he said, opening his mouth ever so slightly to show a hint of his fangs. "I thought *I* was supposed to be the predator."

"You are the most non-predator predator I've ever met," I said. "I felt more hunger from *Darkrose* than you. Interest, yes, but hunger—no."

"Oh, I hunger," he said, eyes glittering on me. Then he glanced slightly aside, not directly meeting my eyes. "But for more than just blood. May I have a bite?"

I stared at my plate: there wasn't an ounce of meat, blood, or even egg in it; it was purely vegan. "Are you sure?" I said, breaking off a bit of the veggie burger. "It only tastes like—"

"No guts, no glory," he said, opening his mouth slightly. His hand started to reach out, but impulsively I stretched my long arm across the table and put the bite in his mouth. His lips pressed my fingers briefly, then closed along with his eyes as he began chewing in bliss.

"That worked better than expected," I said. "Maybe I should watch you eat."

He smiled, then frowned, beetling his brow. "It's difficult to swallow."

"Spit it out, then," I said, leaning forward.

"No, I mean, that's *it*," he said, a lump appearing in his throat. "It's *just* difficult to swallow. When I first became a vampire, I tried to eat normal food once. Vegetables tasted like woodchips. Even meat tasted nasty. But after a few months of the Saffron diet—I can taste food again. That's what food used to taste like. What it's supposed to taste like."

"That's wonderful, Calaphase," I said. "I'm so happy for you—"

He coughed abruptly, catching a bit of something in his napkin—but it was just a tiny bit, far less than he'd eaten. "If I could just swallow it, we'd be in business."

"Maybe the problem is solid food," I said, staring directly at him.

"I do like soup," he said, putting down the napkin and meeting my gaze. "But I feel like I've plateaued. Maybe it's time to go further. Maybe it's time to live dangerously."

"Maybe we should have a picnic under the moon," I said, keeping my eyes fixed straight on him, and he exhaled softly. "With wine and soup and brie and soft bakery bread. I'll chew seedcake, and feed you from my mouth."

At the last sentence, surprise spread over his face. "Sounds . . . well, I want to say 'dirty' or 'sexy' but actually that's somewhat disturbing. What's seedcake?"

"I don't know," I admitted. "It's a line from an audio book my daughter was reading. I swear, she likes the strangest things. I can't understand half of what she reads . . . "

And then I trailed off. I stared at the table, at my hands, my tattooed knuckles. A pale white hand reached out and pressed against the top of mine, cold, yet firm and reassuring.

"But I would like to learn," I said finally, raising my head with a sniff. "I would very much like the chance to learn what she likes."

"It will be all right," Calaphase said, squeezing my hand. "You'll get her back."

Then he squeezed a little harder, and my knuckles popped. "Ow," I said, withdrawing my hand. "Silly vampires, you don't know your own strength."

"Vampires?" Calaphase looked to his left, then to his right. "Are you seeing double?"

"No," I said. "Sav—uh, Saffron nearly twisted off my wrist—"

"The Lady Saffron?" he said innocently. "Is she here?"

"No," I said. "It was earlier."

"Then do we need her at the table?" he asked.

I stared. "I do believe you're *jealous*," I said, and he smiled. But the lump in my stomach hadn't gone away, and I realized he was trying to distract me. "Good try. No cigar, but good try."

We talked about Cinnamon; about my loss, my fight, my lawyers. "No, I'm serious," Calaphase insisted. "The clientele of the werehouse knows a lot of good lawyers—in fact I think there *are* a lot of good lawyers at the werehouse, though they'll never tell—"

"I thought I was persona non grata after the DEI tailed me there?"

"Yes, right up until DFACS took Cinnamon from you," Calaphase said. "Really, some of them are still pissed, and for obvious reasons. But as for the rest—all they need to know is you're trying to protect her. I even had an offer to help come bust her out of wherever they had her."

"No, please," I said, shaking my head. "That's the last thing I need for my case."

"Which reminds me, I have something for you," Calaphase said, reaching into his pocket. As his hand reached in, he grimaced, then drew out his cell phone, buzzing.

"Oh, you shouldn't have," I said.

Calaphase frowned at his phone, then got up with a curse and walked across the patio. He muttered harshly, but it apparently did no good. Finally he hung up, returning to the table.

"Trouble?" I asked.

"Only for me," he said, disgusted. "My driver bailed. I have no ride."

"No problem," I said, slowly smiling. "*I* planned to take you home."

31. THE VAMPIRE'S LAIR

Calaphase stared down at me, mouth falling open far enough to see his fangs. A stunned vampire. It was a good feeling, to know I'd caused that. "After all," I said, smiling more broadly, "I assumed I would drop you off when you appeared without a car."

Calaphase hissed. "*Not* very funny," he said, frowning, embarrassed, though no blush showed in the paleness of his face. "And still not a good idea."

I kept up the faux innocent smile. "Why not? Oakdale isn't that far a drive."

"I don't live in Oakdale, I live in—" But he abruptly stopped, looking off with a hiss. After mulling things a moment, he picked up the check and pretended to review it, avoiding my eyes, "Look, I appreciate the offer, Dakota, but given the circumstances—"

"Circumstances? What circumstances? Calaphase, what's happened?"

"Nothing," Calaphase said, tossing the bill down. "I didn't mean to worry you. They *say* they had an emergency protection request for a werekin—for one of our lawyers, actually. I *suspect* it's just a ham-handed attempt to force you to give me a ride."

"Well, that's sweet of them," I said, double checking the bill as well. We had gone Dutch, we were both covered, but Calaphase had put a hell of a tip on his half. "But it isn't a problem. Like I said, I had assumed I'd drop you off."

"No offense, Dakota, but I would prefer to take a cab," Calaphase said.

"Afraid I'll learn the location of your secret lair?" I asked, slipping on my vestcoat.

"Afraid I'll lure you in," he said, still not looking directly at me.

"I'm not easily lured where I don't want to go," I said.

But Calaphase didn't respond, and avoided my eyes as we threaded out through the line of people waiting to get in at R Thomas. When he still didn't look back once we were free of the crowd, I realized he was quite serious. I stopped him in front of the bird cages the owner had set up outside the restaurant and made him face me.

"Calaphase," I said. "It's all right. It really is. I'm not afraid of you—well, I am afraid of you, you're a vampire. But I'm not afraid of what you might do."

"I do not want to be accused of . . . *influencing* you," he said, still not meeting my eyes, angry at something that must have been in his own memories. "I don't want another victim, or thrall, or flunky, or groupie. I want you as a . . . friend. Nothing more."

"You want me. As a friend," I said softly. "For nothing more?"

He smiled, still not meeting my eyes. "I think we both know the answer to that."

"I would like to hear it, though."

Calaphase looked up at me. In the dim, warm light his hair wasn't blond, but brass, and his skin did not look pale, it just looked normal. Only his eyes gave him away: gleaming and blue, not filled with hostile power, but sparkling like a movie star's, clear and direct.

A bird screeched, a parakeet or some other damn thing. We both jumped, then laughed and turned back to walk the steep hill down to my car. "Cute, those bird cages," he said.

"I always hated them," I said. "Don't get me wrong—I love birds. But it's depressing to see something that's meant to fly living its life trapped in a cage."

"That *is* depressing," Calaphase said. "And something you can't easily unhear."

"Huh," I said, smiling as the Prius powered up on my approach and unlocked itself as my hand touched the handle—that trick just never got old. "I expected you to say—"

"Something like 'Humans eat birds.'" Calaphase folded his arms over the top of the car and stared at me. "'So how is being in a cage any worse?'"

"And so?" I said, practically falling into the car: the parking lot behind R Thomas tilted at a perilous angle. "Why didn't you say it?"

"Too much respect for you," Calaphase said, climbing in on the other side. "That's a line I'd feed a vampire groupie, followed by—" and his voice went deep and Barry White "—when a *vampire* feeds, its meal goes home to its golden cage *happy* . . . my pretty little bird.'"

I stared at him, then put the car in gear.

"Not bad," I said. I preferred my sensitive vamp, but . . . "Did it work for you?"

Calaphase was staring off into the distance. "More often than I care to admit."

I took him home—not to the forests and factories of Oakdale, but to the streets and suburbs of DeKalb northwest of downtown. We wove through the forested valleys of Briarcliff Road, passing churches, condos and even a library, all signs of civilization I did not expect near the home of a vampire. Finally we turned off onto Bruce, and climbed a flat-topped hill to stop before a long, low, grey ranch house overlooking the canyon of I-85.

"Surprisingly . . . sedate," I said, as we pulled into a carport identical to the one in my parents' house, which Dad had bricked off and turned into a rec-room when I was twelve. "I expected a mansion, or a fortress."

"There is a full-sized lower level," he admitted. "I had it bricked off."

"To make a rec-room?" I asked.

"No, to keep out the sun," he said.

"Can I see?"

Calaphase shifted uncomfortably. "I don't think that's a good idea, Dakota," he said, unbuckling his seat belt. My throat constricted as his hand brushed his waist; even his smallest, most innocent gestures were turning me on, and I wanted to see him undo the next buckle, the one on his pants belt. "This is dangerous. I'm a vampire. I prey on mortal women . . . "

I reached out and touched his hair. It was soft and smooth beneath my hands, and as my hand dropped I could feel the coolness of his skin, immense strength in his neck, the swiftness with which his head turned, the sudden stiffness as my lips met his. He resisted, only a moment, then relaxed as my hand massaged his shoulders, my tongue brushed his teeth.

"And sometimes they prey on you," I said softly, leaning back, still caressing that pretty hair, that strong neck. My other hand fell on his crotch, feeling the hardness within, confirming he wanted me as much as I him. Then we were together, a soft explosion of kissing.

We exited on his side of the car, practically on top of each other, smooching, groping, as he fumbled at the lock and got it open. His hands caressed my face, my shoulders, my back. I felt his hands curve over me with his immense strength, sweeping me off my feet.

I laughed. Very few men were large enough to make me feel small, but what Calaphase lacked in height he possessed in strength. Being weightless in his arms surprised me, delighted me, irresistibly turned me on, and I kissed him passionately. He carried me down a wide staircase descending straight from the living room to the lower level, kicking open the heavy wooden door and carrying me into darkness.

My clothes fell away as he walked, and I pushed at his coat, opened his shirt, caressed his chest. At the end of the hall we turned, I swayed in his arms, and he set me down on a soft bed of fur. Normally *I'm* the active one in my sex life, but this time I just lay there, stretching out luxuriously, predatorily, my tattoos glowing to a rainbow of life—and then with a sharp flare of light Calaphase struck a match and lit a candle.

He stared at me, eyes blue points of light in a face made warm and proud by the flame. He lit a second candle. His coat came off. A third candle came alight. He peeled off his shirt. The fourth candle lit, and he stood at the end of the bed, whipped off his belt, his pants, and stood there, bronzed in the flickering light.

I closed my eyes, and he fell upon me.

He was *so* tender, and *so* strong. His hands swept over my skin as smooth as silk, tracing the lines of my tattoos, my skin, my hips—then they seized my hands and pinned them like bands of steel. His tongue touched my lips, my breasts, my sex, until I cried out. Then he moved forward and *took* me, with the strength of a linebacker, a horse, a mountain.

It had been *years* since I had a man, almost a decade. Don't think for a moment that I could be 'turned straight' by a man: men and women are just different, and I like them both for what they are. But after so many years the differences were exciting, the tender softness and intimate knowledge replaced by an almost unstoppable force, a freight train of passion.

"Oh, Dakota," he said, breath hot against my ear. "I love you."

Then his teeth sank into my neck.

32.   UNAVOIDABLE CONSEQUENCES

Light exploded behind my eyes, a sharp pain followed by immense pleasure. Hot warmth flooded out of me and back into me, tingling out to every inch of my body. With his every thrust a new surge of blood came out of my neck and down his throat. He began to lick the wound, and I melted. Moments ago my arms were wrapped tight around him, legs folded up around his back; but now I just dissolved away, eyes closed in bliss.

Calaphase ground against me, tongue pressed to my neck like a remora, a live wire electric circuit conducting through my body. Then he rolled off abruptly, leaving me gasping and sore, legs falling back to the bed, one hand caressing my breasts, the other my throat.

"Wow," I whispered, eyes closed, in a daze. "That was *wooonderful.*"

Calaphase muttered something, breathed in my ear, caressed me, shook me. Interesting. A normal man would be asleep right now, and I'd be rolled over, watching his naked body, brain buzzing with ideas as I imagined all the tattoos I could ink on his canvas. But now I was just in bliss, as his hands brushed over me, his breath wafted against my neck, as his distant, urgent voice echoed through my brain. After *that*, I would have done *anything* he wanted.

Freezing water blasted against my face and breasts.

I screamed, flinching back, jerking away from the water. My feet slid out from underneath me—I was *standing?*—and Calaphase's immensely strong arms caught me and lifted me back up into the icy blast. "Dakota? Dakota! Can you hear me? Snap out of it!"

He slapped my face, and my eyes briefly opened to an opulent bathroom in glass and grey marble, with the bright lights of heating lamps searing my vision. I squeezed my eyes tight, arms wrapping around him for support, reaching out blindly to find the spigot.

"What—" I gasped, hand twisting the knob as far as it would go. "What the—"

"Fight it, Dakota!" Calaphase said, shaking me. "Snap out of it!"

I gasped under the still-icy stream and glared down at him—and saw that Calaphase was absolutely terrified. "What the *fuck*, Cally?" I said. "I mean, what were you thinking—"

The water abruptly started to get super hot, and I dialed the big knob back, flinching again as the now-steaming water nearly burnt me. Calaphase didn't seem to notice, he just held me up, held me in the stream, as I cussed and twisted the water from hot to cold to hot to cold until finally I hit on a lukewarm setting mild enough I could focus on what was happening.

Calaphase stepped back. "Are you all right?" I didn't answer, and he grabbed me and shook me. "Dakota, answer me. Are you all right? Can you hear me?"

All right? Buzzkill! My bliss, my fireworks, my dizzy soreness were all gone . . . and as they faded to memory . . . I noticed my neck was tingling. I clapped my hand to my neck, and a wave of pins and needles flooded down my shoulder. "What the hell happened?"

"My aura overwhelmed you," Calaphase said. "You were completely under—"

I couldn't help but laugh. "I was out of it because you fucked my brains out."

"An hour ago," Calaphase said. "You don't remember anything after that, do you?"

My mouth fell open. The pins and needles were growing worse. "No," I said.

"Damnit," Calaphase said. He didn't look like a vampire anymore. He was just a man, a man conflicted with fear and shame. "I've been trying to rouse you and—I'm sorry. I never meant to—I'm sorry. Can you stand on your own?"

"Always," I said, reaching out and grabbing the soap dish just in case.

"Good," he said, stepping out of the shower. "Sober up, I'll be back."

He stormed back towards the bedroom. I started to follow, then jerked back from the coldness outside. I closed the shower and turned up the heat as much as I could stand, letting the water drum against my head. *What had just happened?*

I remembered taking him home, coming on to him, having sex . . . and after that, a blur. A pleasant, blissy blur. Almost a buzz, like I'd been drunk. But I hadn't been drinking; I never drink and drive. And my hand came back to my shoulder, feeling the tingle around the bite.

What had come over me? I'd never expected to take Calaphase home, much less for things to move this far this quickly. Not that I regretted . . . well, perhaps I regretted the bite but . . . the way it made me feel . . . oh, hell, I had no *idea* what I was feeling.

The water grew too hot, so I killed it and grabbed both towels from the rack with one long arm. In the sudden dripping chill I began to worry. We hadn't used protection. What if I'd been ovulating? What were the signs? I pressed my breasts to see if they were sensitive, but I was too buzzed and tingly and shivery to tell any real difference.

Hell, the way I'd been acting, maybe I *was* ovulating. Could a vampire get me pregnant? Despite having dated one briefly after Savannah turned, I couldn't remember what was real and what was myth—pregnancy had never come up, dating a woman. Quickly I finished drying off. When I was wrapped, body and head, I followed Calaphase back to the bedroom.

Calaphase sat on the edge of the huge four poster bed, naked to the waist, in suit pants but barefoot, talking heatedly into a cell phone. His eyes shifted over to me, then looked away as he said. "Yes, she's coming out of it now. Thank you. I've never tried to *break* a link . . . "

I stood there and watched, feeling my neck. The tingling was subsiding, but I could feel two small puncture wounds, swollen and irritated, like deep zits. He bit me. Oh my God, he *bit* me—exactly what I feared would come of hanging out with vampires. I was dizzy, almost drunk—no, that wasn't it; I felt *hung over.* I looked at the clock: it was eleven forty-five.

"No, no, I don't feel a connection," he said. He furrowed his brow at me, making his eyes glow, but it didn't feel hypnotic, and I quickly got a headache and had to look away. But beneath it all, I felt the pull: a subtle, seductive draw, murmuring out from him on the waves of his aura. "Some residual, but I don't think the link had time to set. She's safe."

I swallowed. Now I knew why Calaphase was so resistant, what he meant when he said he didn't need another thrall or groupie. It would be hard to resist his influence without his help. Fear gripped me: how could I *date* this man if he could sway me any time he wanted to?

But Calaphase wasn't done rocking my world. "Well, that's a fair question, my Lady Saffron," he said—and I would have given good money to see the look on my own face when he spoke *her* name. I reached for him, but he held up his hand—and I felt the odd tingle come back. "The lady in question is Dakota Frost."

"Calaphase!" I said, reaching for the phone. "What in God's name are you doing—"

But there was an exclamation on the line, and he got up swiftly and turned away. "Yes, that's her. Yes, *yes*, she's all right, the cold shower worked." He paused for a moment, and then nodded. "Of course—that *is* the real reason I'm calling. I didn't just bite her. We had sex."

I sat down on the floor next to the edge of the bed and looked up at him, pacing the room like a caged animal. I couldn't believe he was doing this. I couldn't see why he was doing this. I couldn't imagine how he thought this might help.

There was a screech, and Calaphase winced. "I'm sorry," he said. I scowled at him. He was *apologizing* for *sleeping with me!* But he ignored me and continued, "I didn't mean to. I tried to avoid it, it's just she was very—" he struggled for a word "—bold."

There was no screech on the other end of the line this time. There was only a long pause. Then I heard a quiet voice, almost a murmur, and Calaphase looked down at me in surprise. "Do . . . do you really think so?" he asked, eyes fixed on me. "I see."

"What did she say?" I asked.

"I called for two reasons," Calaphase said into the phone. "To apologize, and to ensure that there will be no repercussions—you know what we've been negotiating. I wanted you to know sooner, rather than—I see. I see. That's magnanimous of—I see. Thank you, my Lad—"

He took the phone away from his ear and stared at it, then sat down on the bed.

"Well," he said, hanging up the phone and scowling. "That's done, and done."

I struggled to remember what had happened. I remembered his wonderful voice telling me what to do. I recalled him leading me somewhere, light drumming against my eyelids, a flash of the bathroom, a flash of wonder. What had he planned for me now? A warm bath, a slow massage? I had actually giggled in the shower, when I swayed to one side and cold tile had touched my breast. Then he'd turned the water on.

But before that, nothing. Nothing before the blast of icy water but scattered images and a feeling of great contentment and affection for Calaphase, stretching back . . . until he had bit me.

"Oh, God," I said, feeling my neck gingerly. "Calaphase. You *hypnotized* me—"

"Not precisely," Calaphase said, still scowling. "Certainly not intentionally—but, yes I did." He sighed. "Forming a link is like a reflex. It's hard to stop once started."

"You *bit* me," I said fearfully, the implications finally starting to hit home. "*You bit me!* Do I need to use holy water—"

"There's a garlic derivative," Calaphase said. "The Lady Saffron is checking for me—"

"Fuck her! She didn't need to know about this!" I said. "*Why did you call her?*"

"Dakota, I *had* to," Calaphase said firmly. "You were *completely* under. The sex and the bite were establishing a link—in lay terms, you were becoming my human servant. You were minutes away from imprinting *completely* on me and *I couldn't stop it.*"

I started shivering. His voice now sounded different, yet strangely familiar—deeper, reverberating, echoing through my head, calling up intoxicating memories from my stupor. Even the wound on my neck tingling in time with his words. He was right. He'd had me under his thrall, my aura merging with his, and he couldn't stop it. And I hadn't wanted him to.

"This the real reason they used to kill vampires on sight. *Not* because we drink blood—but because we can enslave minds," he said. "I never wanted to do that to you—but I had no one to turn to. My master is dead, Revenance is gone, Demophage is gone—but one of the best vampirologists in the world was one phone call away. Who else could have helped me?"

"No, no, you're right," I said, still rubbing my neck. "You did the right thing."

"Thank you, Dakota," he said, sitting down heavily on an ottoman on the side of the room. The hiss of an air conditioner starting up sounded in the distance, and Calaphase glanced up briefly before looking back at me. "Believe me, I *am* sorry. I had no intention—"

"I know, I know," I said. "Unless you're the world's master at reverse psychology."

"Most of my—" and Calaphase frowned "—my *prey* are shrinking violets, desperate for me to take the initiative. I didn't expect you to be so, ah, *forward.*"

I laughed, but the laugh quickly died. As disturbing as all this was, there was another question I had, based on a curious little choice of words Calaphase had used when talking to Saffron. I struggled for a moment, figuring out how to ask it, and then just gave up.

"What are you negotiating for me, Calaphase?" I asked simply.

Calaphase looked away. "For the Lady Saffron to take you back under her protection."

"Fuck her," I said. "She threw my collar away, just like she did our relationship."

"You need her," Calaphase said, cocking his head, then focusing on me. "Dakota, the Oakdale Clan—we're punks. We're a bunch of punks with a security service that's little more than a protection racket. The Lady Saffron is the de facto mistress of the city."

"You are *not* a punk," I said. "And I thought Lord Delancaster was in charge of the city."

"Only in his mind," Calaphase said. "And on TV. No-one cares about him, holed away in his mansion. He has no more significance than the Queen of England. *Saffron's* the one who attends the Atlanta City Council meetings, meets with the Mayor, brokers deals. Delancaster gave her power, and she's used it. I do *not* want to be on her bad side. Neither should you."

The hiss sounded again, closer. Now I could tell it was not an air conditioner. It was more like a snake; it was even followed by a sinister rattling. "Did you hear that?"

Calaphase sat up straighter. "Yes. What is that? I've heard it for the last few minutes."

The rattle sounded again, followed by another sharp hiss, and I recognized it. "Oh my God," I said. "It's a spray can."

I leapt out of bed, out of the room, and snagged my leather jeans, slipping them on like I'd been born in them. I hit the light for the hall and ran forward, grabbing my sportsbra, painfully wrenching it on, scooping up my top, and running towards my coat. At the end of the hall I looked back and saw Calaphase appear at the bedroom doorway.

"Calaphase!" I shouted, slipping on my top and vest so fast they seemed to flap around me. "The fuckers burned down the whole werehouse! We gotta go!"

Calaphase scooped up some clothing and sprinted down the hall towards me, long legs closing the distance seemingly instantly. Something tumbled over in the carport, and I flinched. Calaphase slipped on his shirt, then he held out his hand for me to stay back.

"*Fuck* that," I whispered. "They're experts in anti-vampire magic. We do this together."

Calaphase nodded, holding up his hand for silence. Then, slowly, we crept up the stairs side by side, rising until we could see the kitchen door.

Something stood between the door and my car.

At first I couldn't understand what I was seeing. Then the figure resolved to a huge, floppy hat, almost an upside-down pyramid of felt—the same dumpy Seussical hat I'd seen on the grinning spectator to Revenance's death. Beneath it was a wide, olive face, shrouded in darkness—except for two glowing white eyes and a broad, evil grin that split the face open ear to ear with a jagged zipper of pebbly white teeth. A giant zipper tab hung from one ear, completing the effect.

"What the hell is that?" Calaphase said.

It was the tagger from Oakland Cemetery, but—"He's *not human*," I said.

"No matter," Calaphase said, slipping his jacket back on. "I'm a vampire—"

"He's not human, and he's not moving," I said, desperate to communicate something, but not sure what it was. "And he has to know you're a vampire."

"I don't care," he snarled, crouching, preparing to spring. "I'll tear his throat—"

"He *knows* you're a *vampire*," I said, "and he's *sprayed the door.*"

At that Calaphase finally froze, seeing the slight lines of paint sprayed on the glass—lines that looked like spray paint, but slowly shifted and moved, sinuous, hungry.

"Oh, fuck," Calaphase said, and Zippermouth reached up and *pulled the zipper tab across its face*, the metal tabs I had thought were teeth splitting wide open in zigzag, hissing grin, a long snakelike tongue sliding out of his mouth.

"Oh, *fuck me!* What *is* that?"

"Tell me you didn't brick up the back door," I whispered.

Calaphase began backing down the stairs, and I mirrored him. We turned to face each other, only for a second, then ran. Calaphase flew past the red flickering light flooding out of the bedroom and cut to the left, hurling himself at the outer door and splintering it off its hinges before I could even *begin* to say 'wait, let's see what we're getting into'.

No need to wait, though. Fast on his heels, I found out immediately.

Technicolor tentacles of graffiti wire whipped out around us, catching us like a net and jerking us aside like horizontal bungees. We screamed, both of us, the big bad vampire and his skindancer squeeze, as thorns erupted and dug into our flesh as we swung through the air.

For the briefest moment, I saw the whole side of Calaphase's house, a long low rectangle of red brick and white trim covered with a massive, elaborate graffiti tag, a tortured whirlpool of vines and chains and tentacles swirling towards a point just left of center.

Then the tentacles pulled us into the maelstrom—and we fell inside the tag.

---

33.   COLUMN OF HATE

Our screams swept away on the whirlwind. Blinding waves of color assaulted my eyes. Burning torrents of magic twisted me up like a towel. An orange and black horizon flipped around us. Then a vast octopus of graffiti exploded outwards and swallowed us up.

It spit us out into empty space. A black glittering sheet rushed forward and hit us like a wall of concrete. Pain exploded in my cheek, my shoulder, my hip, my knee, and I registered a delayed *whack-whack* as Calaphase fell to the pavement beside me.

Don't pass out. Don't give up. **Don't** *let them win.*

I opened my eyes. We were in absolutely the *worst* section of Atlanta I had ever seen, a cityscape so decrepit it bordered on the surreal. We stood in the twisted remnants of a concrete playground, hemmed in by tottering chainlink fences. Beyond the fences, hulks of building staggered up, forming a canyon of ruins. Deeper within the canyon, the pavement stepped down, a ravine of garbage piled up between a decayed tenement and a crumbling parking deck. The sea of garbage and rusted cars rippled out away from us across the broken pavement, seeming to crash in waves against a *giant* wall, a huge slab of cinderblocks that towered over us like a cliff at the dead end of the canyon.

Briefly I wondered whether this playground was a real place, whether we'd fallen into some tag-induced hallucination. But surely that was impossible; no-one could ink a whole world . . . could they? And the grit against my cheek didn't feel like phantom dirt: *it* was real.

Then my eyes registered what was written on the cinderblock wall.

I staggered to my feet, staring up at the cliff in absolute horror. Spray painted at the upper edge of the huge wall of cinderblocks was a block letter logo: THOUGHT CRIME LORD. And beneath the logo, bleeding out over every surface, *infinite* layers of graffiti.

Every graffiti artist and style I'd seen across Atlanta were represented: bare white lines, repeated stencils, finely shaded oilchalk. How had they *done* this, cover a wall six stories high? Climbing on scaffolds? Hanging from ropes? On *jetpacks?* Both toys and masters sprayed here, leaving simple tags and extensive pieces, stretched-taffy letters and elegantly shaded portraits. Even Keif and Drive were represented by a few tall, narrow tags depicting cartoon rabbits in army fatigues. But the tags, pieces and masterpieces of all the artists—save one—looked slightly old, worn by weather and time, as if all the artists—save one—had given up on this playground and yielded it to its new overlord: the graffiti killer.

The designs of the journeyman and the apprentice were absent; this place was the exclusive canvas of the master. All of the familiar signs were here: the vines, the chains, the barbed wire; but he had not stopped there, experimenting with new motifs that I hadn't seen elsewhere: ships crewed by hostile hip-hop frogs; herds of blood-dripped sheep with sparkling eyes; a vast writhing worm wrapped around the arc of a swinging pendulum—figures tortured and amazing. But across the cliff I recognized a familiar design: the skyline of Atlanta, a grassy dome of a hill, and a coiling rose hovering between two sets of tombstones.

The same type of tag that had killed Revenance.

The vast tag seemed to shiver, a wave of wind rippling over the grassy dome, and I seized Calaphase by the arm, pulling him to his feet. "We have to go. We have to get shelter. We have to get *you* shelter. That entire thing is a vampire trap!"

Calaphase's head snapped quickly from side to side, sizing up the canyon around us. "The opening faces the rising sun," he said. "Think, Dakota! The trap is almost fifty yards away. How do you think he planned to get me into it?"

Good point. The master tag was too far away—probably. Surely it couldn't grab us all the way out here? I tensed, eyes seeking movement. Then I felt a prickling, goose bumps rising on my flesh—but it wasn't goose bumps. It was a flood of mana—but not from the master tag.

"Behind us!" I said, and we dove under the uncoiling whip of a serrated wire that trailed drops of glowing blood as it snapped through the air. Sure enough, there was another tag, a sprawled octopus snapping hungrily on the wall of a decayed tenement looming behind us.

On the cliff, the master tag's vines were now uncoiling, and we dodged back from them too, edging backwards, away from the tags, until we butted against the chainlink fence barring us from the parking deck's dark, twisted innards. Light flared from within, flashes in darkness, illuminating moving shapes which bore no resemblance to anything human.

"I think the tagger means for us to go to the tag," I said, "rather than it come to us."

"What do we do?" Calaphase said. "Run the gantlet?"

I swallowed. The tagger's playground was a box canyon of buildings. The black pavement stretched away from us, between the expanding rings of the master tag on the cliff and the waving wires of the coiled design on the tenement that had brought us here. Some of the twisted remnants of the swings and jungle gyms had tags on them, almost certainly traps. At the other end of the weed-strewn lot, forming the only opening in the box canyon, was a painted wooden fence, filled with hundreds of marks by the tagger.

Only then did I notice that the tagger was breaking the unwritten rules of the Atlanta graffiti scene: he had painted over the marks of other taggers. In my research, I'd found other taggers had immense contempt for paintovers and whitewashes; no one with any skill did them. I scanned the lot rapidly. The more I looked, the more I saw his tags almost desperately trying to plaster over his competition. The better the original, the harder the tagger tried to outdo it.

And through it all, woven through every design, was a quirky spray of wildstyle letters that I now recognized as the artist's actual 'tag', his signature: the word *XRYBE* over a stylized road snaking into the distance. At first I didn't get it, but then I saw older variants, the same road with all the letters above it still spelled out, still wildstyle, so I had trouble parsing it: S-T-R-E-E, then T, the X was actually a jammed-together S-C . . . and then I *got* it.

"*Streetscribe,*" I breathed. The name Revenance had warned us about. It was *everywhere*. "*Someone* is crying for recognition."

"Dakota!"

"What? No, no, we can't risk it," I said, glancing around. "The playground equipment is tagged. The far wall is tagged. This whole place is one big trap."

"Can we go back through the tag that sent us?" Calaphase asked.

I glanced up at it. It was weakening, spinning down, though it wasn't clear that it was actually going to shut off. "No," I said. "I think it needs to recharge—and besides, do you have any idea how to work that thing? Because I sure don't—not yet, anyway."

He glanced around. "We can climb the fence there, try the parking deck—"

"He'll have tagged the cars," I said—and then a solution hit me. "He'll have tagged everywhere he could—so let's go where he can't."

There was a narrow gap between the parking lot and the tenement. I ran to the corner of the chainlink fence and peered through, seeing a long parking lot and a ruined carousel covered by old graffiti. The fence was strong, the chainlink newer, and rings of razorwire guarded its top twenty feet above—and it held no surface for the tagger. Little tags lurked at its base, squealing sausage monsters like blind piglets, but they were too simple to pose real danger. I paid them no mind, spinning round over them as I built up mana and cried: "*Striking serpent, open a door!*"

My newly-inked asp tattoo reared to life and struck the fence once, twice, three times. Chainlinks popped with ringing cracks, then squealed away as Calaphase tore into the opened links with his hands, peeling the fence away in layers.

Then a horrible wail drifted from the far end of the lot.

"Keep pulling," I said, turning around. "Use your strength on the fence, and I'll use my magic to watch our backs."

Calaphase cursed and pulled at the fence. I could hear it tearing—but that noise was drowned out as the tags over the far end of the fence rippled with a massive wave of mana I could feel all the way back here, seventy yards away. There was no movement and almost no light; there was no *way* that could have been built up from the mana in old rotten boards.

So much for the mold theory.

Zipperface slid out of the tag, rolling out in style on a skateboard. Over his shoulder he carried a baseball bat; around his waist were strapped a set of spray cans like Batman's utility belt. His face was barely visible beneath his vast floppy hat, but even from this distance, the steel tabs of his jagged mouth glinted, a vicious grille spreading beneath glowing white eyes.

Then the eyes narrowed. The mouth frowned. And then that wide olive face peeled back open as Zipperface screamed in rage, a long, ropy tongue snapping out as Calaphase tore the second layer of the fence away. I tensed, not sure what form the attack take or how I might defend against it; but defend us I would.

Then Zipperface raised his arms, and a long low line spread across the base of the wooden fence behind him, a sparkling sliver-like light peeking underneath a door. I recoiled as the line lit up into a rainbow wall of graffiti flames.

Oh, hell. Fire. Defend us, I wouldn't.

"Dakota," Calaphase said, jerking at my shoulder. "Dakota, we gotta go."

Zipperface threw down his arms, and the fire shot out along the edges of the canyon, screaming towards us on both sides. The graffiti wasn't just reaching for us: it was *spreading*, cracking out over the pavement in jagged blocks, turning it into a sea of lava.

We turned and ran, slipping through the clinging wire of the fence, darting through the chasm between the tenement and the garage, putting on a burst of speed as the lines of fire met behind us and exploded through the gap in a blast of flame and mana.

We ran down the sidewalk, full tilt, Calaphase almost flying, dragging me behind him as I poured my all into it, ignoring the explosion of pain in my knee. But as fast as we ran, the fire ran faster, sliding along the foundation of the tenement, rippling up its side in waves of flame. The running tongue of fire shot past us towards the end of the lot, impacting a low brick fence, boiling up in a torrent of flame that cracked the pavement and cut us off.

Driven sideways by groping tendrils of fire, we dodged out across the asphalt, leaping over glowing red cracks in the pavement shooting out beneath us, aiming for a squat cinderblock building next to the carousel as yet untouched by the tags. Calaphase threw his shoulder at the door and knocked it off its hinges, dragged me inside, and slammed it shut behind us.

The flames roared behind us, trying to batter the door open. Calaphase wedged the bottom of the door shut with a dented metal pot the size of a tub, and I slid a broom handle through holes in the wooden slats around the top of the frame.

Desperately we looked around the blockhouse. Despite the musty darkness of our little prison I could see it had once been a kitchen, the back room of a hot dog stand or burger joint. There were no other doors or exits; the next best bet was a barricade of rotten wooden planks nailed over the broken remnants of what had probably been the front serving window.

I peered through the slats and could see the edge of the carousel, a black strip of pavement, and then a blissfully green tab of grass, wet by a sputtering sprinkler. I tugged at the boards, but they were stronger than I expected. Calaphase reached to help, but recoiled as the flickering light of magic fire rippled past the edge of the slats.

But the flames did not immediately tear inside; they retreated. We relaxed, but only for a moment. Then light began to creep in through cracks in the base of the cinderblocks all around us. Calaphase cursed and began looking around, tearing the place up looking for a fire extinguisher.

I whipped out my cell phone and dialed 911. It started ringing, but before anyone picked up, flames surged against the blockhouse walls: we didn't have much time. Through the cracks in the door and in the window we could see the fire rising up around us, cooler now but more elaborate, lazy licks of graffiti flames climbing the walls of the shop around us. Coiled wires and vines and roses were now visible in the flames, along with other motifs that I didn't recognize. The graffiti was tackling this building too.

I could hear the tinny voice of the dispatcher now, but the rising roar of the flames drowned it out. I lowered the phone, and Calaphase and I looked at each other.

"Dakota," Calaphase began.

"Don't you dare," I said. "Don't you dare talk like we're going to die!"

"We're going to get out of this," Calaphase said. "I want to *live*, because I've had a taste of a life that's better—and I don't mean your blood."

I was speechless. Calaphase stepped forward and took my hands, a Greek hero cast in bronze, flickering in the rising golden light around us. "I'm sorry I bit you. I regret that. But everything that led up to that—I'll never regret. Not for one minute."

"Calaphase," I said, squeezing his hands in mine.

"Dakota," Calaphase said. "I'm so sorry."

And then he grabbed me and *threw*.

Rotted boards exploded about me. I screamed as I was engulfed in flames. It felt worse than normal fire: hotter, more tenacious, biting at me as I flew through the boards, snapping at me as I sailed over the tagged pavement and onto the cool grass. I landed and rolled, winded, dazed—then caught myself, lurching to my feet as Calaphase prepared to jump after me.

The entire parking lot had been consumed by graffiti. What had been pavement was now a illustrated nightmare landscape of cracked black rock floating on hot lava. But it was no longer cartoony: it was eerily real. Like a street painting that fools you into thinking there's a hole in the sidewalk, the graffiti had dimension, making the blockhouse seem like it was supported on a crazy Jenga stack of flaming boulders, tottering over a lava field a thousand feet below.

But unlike a street painting, this was no forced perspective: it was *magic*. No matter which way I moved, the tower moved with me, and the chasm stayed between us. There was no way to bridge it. The blockhouse itself had become a torrent of lazy fire too bright to look at, climbing to the sky in a column of hate. Calaphase hesitated, flinching back from the snarling flames eating at the hole in the rotten wood barrier.

"Jump, damnit, *jump!*" I screamed, watching flames curl over the top of the blockhouse, a flue of vapor spreading over the roof just like the blue haze that flicks over a log a second before it lights. "For God's sake, Cally! *Jump!*"

Calaphase disappeared, then burst forth from the opening in an incredible burst of speed, sailing through the opening, the flames. But the flames grabbed at him, tripped him up so he tumbled and fell short, fell into the parking lot, fell into the *tag*—

And fell a thousand feet to his death below.

34. TRICK OF PERSPECTIVE

Calaphase stared up at me, lifeless, body broken on the tagged parking lot in a vast splash of blood. I couldn't believe it. He'd just jumped from the broken window of the little hot-dog stand, tripped as magic flame caught his feet, and pitched face down in the pavement—but instead of hitting the pavement, he'd seemed to fall forever into the vast chasm depicted by the tag, disappearing into the painted distance in some horrible trick of perspective.

But it wasn't just a trick, it was *magic*, and seconds later Calaphase had splatted into the pavement right in front of my feet with more force than if he'd fallen from an airplane. I stared down at him from the safety of my strip of grass, stared at the twisted body that had been so strong in my arms, at the broken fangs that had sipped my blood, into the lifeless eyes that an hour ago had stared back into mine as he told me he loved me.

His body twitched, and for a brief moment I felt a flicker of hope: maybe blunt trauma wouldn't be enough to kill a vampire. But then the vast splash of blood gurgled obscenely and began sinking into the pavement, blotted up by the graffiti, draining into the cracks painted in the rock, turning the glowing lava blood red. *There* was the power of the graffiti—these monster marks were feeding off of vampire blood, literal *blood rocks*. How dare they. *How dare they!*

My nostrils flared, and I looked up.

Zipperface stood at the far end of the parking lot, his misshapen head canted beneath his huge cap, his tiny eyes glowing, holding his baseball bat down and out like a sword in challenge. My face flushed with rage as I read more and more clearly off that exaggerated body language one clear emotion: saucy, self-satisfied glee. Suddenly a jagged, cartoony grin spread across that inhuman face, and he swept his paint can across the air in a clear gesture: *I tagged you.*

"Like hell," I said, stalking out across the grass towards him.

Zipperface raised his hands, and flames surged from the blockhouse, a wash of mana driving cracked lines out across the parking lot, extending the lava landscape that had killed Calaphase. No matter—I was still going to kill him. But I'd have to get past the lava to do it—and then I realized the magic was reaching my skin before the heat.

I spread my hands wide, testing the air, feeling the mana like an electric charge. Normally I built up mana, then activated the tattoos to spend it. But now I stepped up to the edge of the lot, threw my arms wide, and soaked up mana like fresh spring rain. The tag spreading across the lot began to lose definition, no longer an active menace but just a few inked lines. I was astounded that the tag could not just move, but spread itself; but I had no time to think about that now. The mana was flooding my body, filling me with heat and light, more than I could safely take.

Lacking real skindancing training, I once again borrowed moves from Taido, twisting round once to draw in the mana, then surging forward in a high-stepping stomp that punched both hands forward and hurled the mana out in a fiery ball. Dazzling and impressive, yes, making Zipperface jump back; but improvised and weak, too. Zipperface swung his bat and struck the ball of mana full on, making it pop into multicolored fireworks.

I stalked out over the pavement, throwing my arms wide to suck more mana out of his tag. The air was cool now. We were far enough from his playground that I could keep him from creating new flames as long as I kept his tag drained. But Zipperface was not out of tricks: he snarled, drew his spray can, and began drawing lines in the air in a complicated pattern.

The vast tag began to shimmer again, the lava regaining its glow, the rocks regaining their depth and falling away, one by one—but I was having none of that this time, and began sashaying to pour my own magic into the mix. I whipped off my jacket and let it flap away over the spreading chasm, exposing the unfinished wings of the dragon on my shoulders, already glowing with the mana my walk was pouring into it. Unfinished as it was, it couldn't defend me—but it could still help me kick this freak's ass.

"*Spirit of air,*" I murmured, "*give me wings.*"

Twin wings erupted from my shoulder blades just as the last rocks fell away beneath my feet, leaving me floating forward over the vast gulf like a glowing angel. This was beyond even my power, but the surge of mana rippling off the pavement buoyed me up. The more Zipperface fed magic into the chasm, the higher I flew—and the closer I got.

Zipperface's white gleaming eyes were fixed on me, and I stared straight back at him. I saw his logic now: he was a *projectia*, an image created by a magician operating somewhere else. Normally that figure replicated the image of the caster as closely as possible, but this figure was inspired by graffiti's love of distorting an image into a cartoonish parody.

I had a good idea of how to use my vines to disrupt his image and short-circuit his magic, and if the feedback didn't kill him it would at least leave me with a huge, living master tag I could study and use to track him back to his source.

But Zipperface, snarling, drew on the air again, spray casting runes that began draining the mana back out of the lava. I drifted lower and lower as the piece on the pavement grew duller and duller. My feet struck ground and I strode forward, twisting my arms to gather the remaining mana in my wings and shoot it forward into a net of vines that would disrupt his projection.

Zipperface tensed, watching me approach, canting his head further—then abruptly he drew three quick arcs in the air with his can. My eyes narrowed. The cartoony little sigil began to solidify, taking shape, looking familiar—and then I saw it. It was a baseball.

Zipperface swung his metal bat with a ringing crack, and the ball shot out and landed in my gut, knocking the wind out of me. My wings sagged around me, their mana surging back into my body like fire. I gasped for breath, trying to say a word of power. But Zipperface didn't wait. He stepped forward, gripping the bat with two hands, preparing to take off my head.

But then I remembered: in magic, pretty words don't matter. All that matters is intent.

"*Gaaah!*" I gasped, thrusting my hand out at him. A coiling vine leapt and entangled Zipperface's bat. He leapt back, trying to tug the bat out of my tattoo grip. I grinned and *pulled*, as my brand new asp curled up the vine and began sliding towards him.

Zipperface's snarl rippled across those metal teeth like a wave. He switched to a one-handed grip and pulled out his spray can again, drawing a pair of shears in the air. I leaned back, unfurling the vine, drawing my hand back in just as the shears sliced the vine in two.

Tension released, I fell back to the pavement, gasping for breath. In moments Zipperface was standing over me, a glowing cartoon parody of a man, white eyes gleaming, lowering his bat and spray can as he savored his moment of triumph.

I clutched my stomach, struggling for breath, and Zipperface raised the bat again, hefting the coiling tattoo vines trying to find purchase on its surface, preparing to hit me with a roiling ball of my own magic. Finally, I drew just enough breath to squeeze out one word. "*Sucker.*"

The snake in his half of the vines struck at him, and the vines themselves uncoiled, whipping around his head, crushing his cap, tearing into his face. Zipperface tried to toss away the bat, but the vines coiled around and caught his hand, pinning the bat to him. He dropped the can, trying to wrestle the bat away from his eyes—then snarled and thrust both arms wide, breaking all the vines into pieces, crushing the snake in his hand.

I laughed weakly. Tattoo magic wasn't graffiti magic: the broken marks couldn't just be reduced to dust like a sandblasted tag. Tattoos are alive, and tenacious. The remnants of the vines and snake dug into Zipperface's 'skin,' interfering with the magic, disrupting the projection. Zipperface began to melt, to cant over, becoming even more misshapen.

But he didn't fall. He held his bat out like a sword, holding me off, snarling, long tongue rippling out of his metal mouth. Then he stamped his foot and summoned his skateboard out of the ground. When the board fully materialized, he skated off, sliding back into the lines he had created against the wall of the tenement, merging back into them in a rainbow spray of mana.

I sagged back against the pavement, watching the glow fade from the graffiti. Long after Zipperface had disappeared, I gathered enough of my breath and strength to stand, and began to hobble back towards Calaphase. Even though I had seen what happened to him, my mind didn't want to accept it. Maybe he wasn't dead. Maybe he was just stunned. Maybe, with vampire regenerative abilities, he would roll over, smile, and be just fine.

Before I even got to him, I knew I was just lying to myself. Calaphase's body was drained, charred. After the magic tag had sucked him dry of blood, it had set him on magical fire. Slow streamers of rainbow flame lifted off his body, like slow-motion animation; beneath the flames was a smudge of blackness that was barely recognizable as a man.

Damnit. Damnit. Damnit! I stood there, face screwed up so much it hurt, mouth covered with my hands so no one would see, eyes squeezed tight so I wouldn't have to either. We were friends, we'd became lovers, seemingly moments ago—and he was gone. *Gone!* No more walks. No more talks. No more riding to my rescue in the middle of the night with donuts and that confident yet oddly bashful charm. Gone.

Finally, after how long I had no idea, I began to shiver in the cold, and turned away, looking for my vestcoat. I found it a blackened, smoking ruin atop a graffiti'd image of glowing rocks. I snatched it up, cursing as the hot cracked leather burned my skin—but as I grabbed it, my fingers had brushed pavement and found it cool. Magic, again.

I tossed the remains of the jacket into the crook of my elbow and began massaging my singed hand. The burn wasn't too bad, no worse than all the minor singes, dings and scrapes I'd picked up in our ordeal, but as I looked at my skin, it looked different somehow. After a moment, I realized why, and cursed again, more quietly now, at another loss.

"My dependable snakes," I said. Emotions welled up in me, and I clamped them down, inspecting the bare skin that until minutes ago had borne one of my best smaller designs, figuring out how to replace it. I needed the distraction of planning to fix what I'd lost. I needed to focus on *anything* but what had just happened. "I'm going to have to tattoo *another* one."

Flashing lights caught my eye and an Atlanta black-and-white shot past the end of the tenement, running silent with lights blazing. I waved hopefully, gratefully, and the car turned into the lot and screeched to a halt well short of the graffiti image of the molten lava. I ran towards it, and my heart leapt as Rand stepped out, flanked by Horscht and Gibbs.

"Rand, thank God," I said. "Calaphase and I were just attacked by magic graffiti—and it killed him. And I think the graffiti is using vampire blood for power—Rand? What's wrong?"

Rand stared at me, jaw clenched. Then he spoke the last words I expected.

"I'm sorry, Kotie. You're under arrest for the murder of Christopher Valentine."

35. LOCKUP

Beloved stage magician Christopher Valentine, AKA the Mysterious Mirabilus, had been famous for challenging "fake magicians" to perform a feat he couldn't replicate with ordinary stage magic. In twenty-three years of issuing the Valentine Challenge, he'd never failed.

Until me.

The real reason for his perfect record? In secret, Valentine was a *real* magician, using his Challenge to flush out and kill other real magicians—like me. I decisively met his Challenge to ink a real magic tattoo; that ended me up on Valentine's sacrificial altar, moments from death.

Karma is a bitch, though. The moment Valentine took me seriously as a threat, his flunky Transomnia realized I was powerful enough to destroy the tattoo that enslaved him—and literally stabbed Valentine in the back, distracting him long enough for me to release the Dragon tattoo.

Released from my body, my precious masterwork tore Valentine to pieces. So it *was* true: I killed Christopher Valentine with magic. In theory, a serious crime—but I thought there was enough evidence to demonstrate to anyone's satisfaction that it was self defense.

Rand knew this. He'd been there, or at least had helped pick up the pieces. But he showed no sign of it now. He just Mirandized me, cuffed me and stuffed me in the back of the cruiser, where I had to wait alone for half an hour until another unit could arrive . . . for Calaphase.

Calaphase. I couldn't believe he was really gone. Even though I'd *seen* him die, had *confirmed* it, some part of my brain refused to accept it. I just sat there in the car, hands cuffed behind my back, eyes tearing up, face hot and red. *Fuck.* This *sucked.*

Rand opened the door and sat down beside me. "Kotie, I—why are you crying?"

"What?" I said, unbelieving. "Rand, I just watched my . . . my friend die—"

"Your *friend?*" Rand said, eyes bugging. He slammed the door. "Oh, hell, I knew it—you hooked up with that *fang.*"

"His name," I said, chest unexpectedly tight, "was *Calaphase.*"

"God damn it," he said, turning away in the seat. "Gibbs, drive. Just—drive."

"Rand . . . what the hell is wrong?" I asked, as the car pulled out. "I know you don't think I did it. You *know* what happened with Valentine—"

"I know, I *know,*" Rand snapped. "Boys . . . take a virtual walk."

"Huh? We're driving," Horscht said, confused.

"How about them Braves," Gibbs said, flipping off the video camera.

"I'm a Falcons fan, not a—oh, oh, yeah," Horscht said. "Virtual. I get it."

Rand turned to me, apology and anger fighting for control of his face. "This is a conflict of interest. I could get fired, understand?" Rand said. "Your 911 call was incoherent, but we were able to get your location—and your number was flagged with an outstanding warrant."

"They send the cavalry to arrest me for a paperwork screw up of epic proportions?"

"There is no mistake. Fortunately there are a lot of people on the force who still owe your Dad and remember you. My friends in dispatch put Horscht and Gibbs on it, who pulled me in so we could make this easy on you. But when I find you? You're crying over a *dead vampire*."

"Rand," I began, a dozen quick, angry retorts on my breath. But then I realized Rand had just told me that he'd put his career on the line to keep me out of trouble, and had found me in a bigger stew than he'd ever expected. I drew a long, ragged breath, then let it out slowly.

"He is—was a good friend, and he's just died. Can we let it . . . him . . . rest right now?" I said, closing my eyes and trying to refocus on my new problem. "Thanks for coming personally, but . . . tell me about the warrant. This is bullshit. They can't prove murder, because it *wasn't*."

"All right," Rand said. "You know you're innocent, and *I* know, but . . . a couple of days after you killed Valentine there was an election. The turnover was an earthquake, and your file got dumped on the desk of Paulina Ross, a hot new prosecutor—an import from Birmingham—who decided her new job was to make an example of people who kill with magic."

"Oh, crap," I said. "Cops just *love* people who kill with magic."

"Oh, crap, exactly," Rand said. "With all the deaths and disappearances and suspicious fires we've had over the last month, everyone on the force is on edge. That's why I decided to make sure I was the one who picked you up. I wanted you to arrive in one piece."

"But," I said, "Misuse of Magic? No one from the DEI said—Philip never said—"

"Your boyfriend can't help you," Rand said. His eyes were boring into me, staring at my neck. I reddened—he had to be looking at the bite marks. "Or is that your ex-boyfriend?"

"He is, in fact, my ex-boyfriend," I said. "We split last week—"

"That's a shame. You're going to need all the help you can get," Rand said. "The murder charge isn't even the worst of your worries. Your use of magic is on the record."

"So?" I said. "I was defending myself . . . "

"But Misuse of Magic is still a crime—a *Federal* crime," Rand said. "So the assistant DA is working with the U.S. Attorney to put you away for Felonious Misuse of Magic. The murder charge is just a way to get to her real agenda. If Ross can't prove murder, she might go for felony manslaughter—and then the U.S. Attorney can still get you for Felonious Misuse."

I found I was shivering on top of the churning. Misuse *was* a Federal charge. I'd spend a *minimum* of five years in Federal prison, become a felon, and lose the right to vote. Even if I ever did get out of jail, I'd never tattoo again. Not magic, not legally, not in the States.

Worst of all, I'd never get Cinnamon back.

"This *sucks*," I said.

Rand opened his mouth, then closed it. "You're telling me."

"*I'm* telling *you?*" I asked. "*I* was tied to that table, having to defend myself."

"That wasn't your fault, but why were you there in the first place?" Rand said, glaring at me. "What sequence of events led up with that? What crowd were you running with? What were you involved in? *You* may be in trouble, but *I'm* the one who has to tell my best friend that I can't help his little girl, who regularly plays with fire and finally got burned. Speaking of which, *stop showing up at magical fires.* You're a *whisker* away from being brought in for arson."

I looked away. Only then did I notice the little details cropping up around us: billboards for lawyers, bail bondsman's offices, and broken looking people. This was a part of downtown I avoided for good reason: we were pulling up in front of the Fulton County Jail. I swallowed.

"I-I don't remember this," I said. "I thought we were going to the Atlanta City Jail."

"You haven't been arrested in a while, have you?" Gibbs said. Apparently his virtual walk was over. "They've been sending state charges to Fulton for years."

"I've never been up on a state charge before," I countered. "Misdemeanors go to City—"

"Damn it, Kotie," Rand exploded. "I bounced you on my knee! You had bows in your hair! It was bad enough that you became a tattooed freak with bite marks on your neck, but how did you fall so far that you know where they take you when you're arrested?"

My mouth hung open. Rand was absolutely enraged. I didn't want to set him off further—but he'd really stepped over the line there. No matter how much I didn't want to piss him off, there was no way I could let that stand. Finally I spoke.

"Maybe I've done some bad things," I said, "but defending myself is *not* one of them."

Rand just sat there, steaming, until the car pulled to a stop. "I won't be involved in the investigation," he said tightly, stepping out as Gibbs opened his door. "Conflict of interest. But I'll find a lawyer for you, save you a phone call—"

"I *have* a lawyer," I said. "Helen Yao of Ellis and Lee."

Rand froze at the door, eyes glaring back in at me.

"I *had* to," I said. "They're trying to take Cinnamon."

Rand cursed, leaning his hands on his knees. "Helen Yao, of Ellis and Lee," he said at last. "I'll call her. You . . . you stay safe in there, Kotie."

"I will," I said, and then blurted, "Don't tell my dad."

Rand glared, then slammed the door.

Gibbs leaned in after Rand left. "Don't take it too personal, girl," he said. "He loves you like you were his *own* daughter."

"I got that," I said, shifting uncomfortably. It was nowhere near as fun to ride in handcuffs as I had first thought. "But it still hurts, because *I didn't do anything wrong.*"

"I know," Gibbs said, rubbing his dark crewcut. "You ready?"

"As I'll ever be," I said.

And I let Gibbs help me out of the car—and put me in the pinball machine.

I really haven't been arrested enough to feel comfortable with it, and all the procedures at Fulton County were different enough from Atlanta City to leave me completely disoriented. They shuffled me from room to room in a careful corral of one-way doors that left prisoners always at the mercy of a man behind a glass controlling the buzzer.

I was interviewed, photographed, fingerprinted, and then dumped in a massive waiting area with chairs that looked like they were from McDonald's. After what seemed like forever my name was called, officers scooped me up again, and I was searched, examined, and even bandaged—a sharp-eyed cop had noticed wounds I'd gotten during the fight with Zipperface, perhaps when Calaphase threw me through the boards. After an officious nurse patched up my face, neck and hands, I returned to the pinball machine. Given what I was in for, at first I thought they might put me in some special cell designed to hold magicians, but I just ended up in a bland white holding cell with peeling paint, wedged in with a dozen other female prisoners.

I swallowed, trying not to show fear. There were druggies and drunks, clean-cut young women and well-worn older ladies. A small gaggle of tough-looking chicks were talking in one corner, glancing at me, but I actually found one rail-thin, ghost-pale woman more intimidating than any of the others, as she stared at me unblinking with cold black eyes. I found a seat, leaned against the outer bars, and stared out into the hallway of the jail, thinking just one thought.

Fuck.

"So, what you in for?"

I looked up. One of the tough chicks had detached from her klatch and come to tower over me. She was a fattie Bettie Paige, butch but not lesbian, with a devil-may-care, I'm-gonna-getcha grin in her eye—almost like she wanted to pick a fight. A big bruiser with a lot of muscle under the fat, she was maybe three hundred pounds, and a couple inches shy of six feet tall.

I slowly stood up.

I like being tall. I enjoyed watching her face as my eyes met hers—then rose four inches above them. I relished watching the confidence drain from her as she realized I wasn't just tall, but muscular, tattooed, and edgy. And just when she realized she was showing weakness, bucked up and tried to screw in her courage, I dropped the bombshell.

"Murder," I said.

"What?" she said, eyes flicking up to mine in fear. Then her smile quirked up, like she'd found another weakness. "But I betcha didn't do it, right?"

"Wrong," I said coolly. "I waxed that murderous son of a bitch before he had a chance to stick his diseased prick in me. Waxed him good."

That threw her, but she gamely recovered her smile. "Oh, hey, you're all right," she said. "I-I mean, good for you. Was he your pimp?"

"No, he was a serial killer who skinned women alive, raped them, then killed them." I mean, he was, really. I don't need to dress that shit up. In fact it was easy to lather it on. "Murdered one of my friends right in front of my face. Any other fucking questions?"

"Holy fucking shit," she said.

"And what are *you* in for?" I said.

"I, uh, led a 'squat in'" she said, embarrassed, as if it was somehow better to be in for murder—but wait a minute. A squat in? I stared at her more closely—she looked familiar. "I got a whole crew sitting tight to protest their evictions, but I found out you can't fight City Hall."

"You with the Candlestick Twenty? The renters the city is trying to kick out? Now *you're* all right," I said brightly. "So how did you end up in Fulton?"

"They got me for fraud," she said, now even more embarrassed.

"*Fraud?*" I said.

"Look," she said, "we were basically squatters. Our landlord burned half a mill in repairs trying to save his occupancy permit, but the city revoked it anyway. So *genius* here decides, let's move people in and use critical mass to force the city to change. But all I did was get screwed."

"Let me guess," I said. "The yahoos you moved in didn't want to pay rent."

"Worse," she said. "When I tried to get 'em to pay up, one of 'em ratted me for subletting the place without a permit, and some shmuck in the DA's office used it to scoop me up."

"Atlanta is just *filled* with schmucks in the DA's office these days," I said. Apparently werekin weren't the only people chewed up by the gears once the machines started rolling.

"Yeah, well, I don't think they would have tried it if we were still in the news, but the media got bored. They always want to have their new story," she said bitterly. Then she shifted. "So, anyway . . . your tattoos are awesome. Who did them?"

I blinked. Then laughed. "Is *that* why you came to talk to me?" I said. "*I* did."

"*You* did?" she said, eyes widening.

"Except for this one, this one, and this little design right here," I said, holding up my right hand and showing one of Kring/L's designs. "These were by one of my colleagues at the Rogue Unicorn, but the rest were by yours truly, Dakota Frost, best magical tattooist in the Southeast."

Her eyes lit up a little more, scanning my tattoos, now seeing the movement. "Wow," she said. "I mean, wow. When you said magic—oh, wow."

"You know, I'm relieved," I said, flexing my wrist so the gems embedded in the vines sparkled a little. "I thought you were coming over to try and kick my ass."

She shrugged, a little nervously. "Sorry I butched up. I was afraid to talk to you."

"*You* were afraid to talk to *me?*" I asked. Maybe Rand had a point about me being a tattooed freak—I loved them so much I forgot they could scare other people.

"I mean, I dunno, I've never been in Fulton, and you look like you gave as good as you got," she said. At my puzzled look, she indicated the bandages on my cheeks, arm, and shoulder. "Looks like the cops beat the shit out of you when you were arrested."

"What? No, the cops were princes. I got these bruises fighting magic graffiti, on a totally unrelated case," I said, shaking my head and staring out at the bars. When had I started thinking of my life in terms of cases? And thinking of *Cally* as a case? *God.* The really sad thing was, it *was* a different case.

My life was fucked up. "This is all some crazy misunderstanding. I *reported* the killing, when it happened, but somehow it got fucked up in the DA's office . . . "

I trailed off when I saw her face. She'd gone white.

"Fighting . . . magic . . . graffiti," she said thickly.

"You know what I'm talking about?" I said, and she nodded. "You've seen it?"

"Yeah," she said, swallowing. "At the Candlesticks. And these new tags are *nasty*."

"Can you show me?" I asked. "I mean, when we get out of here?"

"No way," she said, backing off. "One of them fucked up a friend—"

"And killed four of mine," I said, taking her arm to stop her. "Wait, please. I *need* to see a *live tag*. I've been fighting it for weeks,"

"Frost!" a voice snarled. "Let go of her and step up to the grate!"

36.   A LIKELY STORY

I looked over to see a pair of officers standing at the grate, frowning. I took my hand away and raised my hands placatingly to the guards.

"I don't want any trouble," I said. "We were just talking."

"A likely story," the officer said. "Now step up to the grate!"

I stepped to the door, glancing back at my cellmate. "I meant what I said," I said quietly, as the guard opened the door to the cell. "I need to see a live tag—"

"We usually paint over it," she said, "but . . . yeah, I can find some."

"If you can find any when you get out, call the Rogue Unicorn in Little Five," I said, as the guards started to take me away. "Ask for Dakota Frost."

"All right," she said. "Hey, my friends call me Ranger."

"See you on the outside, Ranger," I said.

One of the guards snorted.

My first expectation was that my right wrist would end up handcuffed to a steel ring in a metal table in some dull grey cop-show interrogation room complete with mirrored glass, where some charmingly idiosyncratic investigator would come use personality-flaw judo to eke out a confession that not only had I killed Christopher Valentine, but also John F. Kennedy.

Instead, the guards took me to a vampire trauma nurse, following up on the bite mark they'd seen when I was bandaged. He took samples from my bite wound, dressed it up with a garlic derivative, then dressed me down about safe sex with vampires and "bite safety," while at the same time reassuring me it was very unlikely I'd turn from just one bite, especially if the vampire in question was dead.

Jesus. I hadn't even thought of that: I just didn't want to give blood. I knew Darkrose had a long-lived human servant . . . but Saffron had been turned quickly. How many bites *did* it take? Slowly it sank in. I hadn't just dodged becoming a vampire's servant, I'd dodged becoming a vampire. But right now I wished I had become a vampire, rather than having watched him die.

A dark-haired, chocolate-skinned woman in a trim business suit strode through the door carrying a large manila folder. The black eyes behind her thin rectangular glasses found me and sized me up. Then she motioned briskly and the officer guarding me left without a word. The woman sat down across from me, opened the folder, and scanned it in silence.

She was fascinating: I noticed slight purple highlights in her otherwise businesslike haircut, and I found myself wondering whether she was black, Hispanic or Middle Eastern. Then she glanced up from the folder and stared straight into my eyes.

"Assistant District Attorney Paulina Ross," she said, eyes flickering over my hair and bandages before zeroing back on my eyes. "I'm told you haven't lawyered up, Ms. Frost."

"They're on their way," I admitted. Her eyes had no distinct pupils and irises, just cold blackness, and I found it difficult to meet her gaze. "But I can't imagine how they can help. I cooperated with the police fully the first time. Heck, I *reported* the death of Mirabilus—"

"Of Christopher Valentine," she said, voice halfway between correction and clarification. "Only *you* identify him as Mirabilus."

"It was his stage name," I said coldly. "I'm sure ten minutes with Wikipedia would—"

"I meant—" she said, then cut herself off. Her eyes studied me for a moment, then she continued, "Only your *story* has Valentine claiming that Valentine was not his real name."

"What he called himself isn't relevant," I said, now getting angry. "He was going to rape me and kill me, and his cold clammy hand on my ass spoke for itself."

"In *your* story," she said. "He can't tell us his side of the story. But his dead body, killed by your magic, speaks volumes."

My jaw clenched. "And what about the fingerprints on the knife that killed my friend?" I said. "Don't they have a voice?"

"They say that an old man fought off a werewolf," she responded, and then, clearing her throat, "That an old man with a Jewish mother fought off a fugitive Nazi war criminal who'd transformed into a monster and already murdered six other Jewish people that night."

"I hadn't known—why are you telling me this?" I said, confused. "If you want to get me, shouldn't you be playing your cards close to the chest?"

"Prosecutors shouldn't hide anything. It all has to come out in discovery," Ross said, still pinning me with those dark eyes. "But this is the last chance we will have to speak without an intermediary. I had to give you the chance to tell me the truth."

"I told the truth *at the time*," I said. "I was defending myself from a serial killer."

"Only *your* testimony ties him to that crime," Ross interrupted. "The man was a national treasure. He took a bullet for you in front of live witnesses. And you killed him. With *magic*—"

The door burst open.

"This interview is over," a thin, hawk-nosed man said, sweeping into the room with Helen Yao close at his heels. The man looked young, but his temples were graying, and he was wearing a suit that looked as expensive as Philip's helicopter. "I'm ashamed of you, Miss Ross, interrogating a witness without counsel."

"She didn't request I wait for you," Ross said, followed slowly by, "Counselor Lee."

The man I now recognized as Damien Lee, the more prominent partner of Ellis and Lee, glanced at me sharply. "She didn't?" he said. "How interesting. Helen."

Helen twitched, then opened her briefcase and pulled out some forms. "I have here—"

"Oh, give it," Ross said, motioning for the papers and scanning them quickly. Suddenly she held the papers out and stared at them, incredulous. "Now that's a very interesting gambit, Counselor." Next she stared at me with those piercing eyes. "We can resume this later."

"We're done here. Let's go," Lee said. He turned, then paused and turned back, staring at me dumbfounded in my chair, actually putting his hands on his hips. "Unless . . . you *want* to spend the night in jail, Miss Frost?"

There was surprisingly little paperwork to be handled. They just ran me through an exit room, clicked a few buttons on the computer to mark me released, and returned my effects. As I walked out of the processing room, Lee and Yao scooped me up and began ushering me out.

"Isn't there a side door?" Helen asked.

"For people the *DA* wants to keep under a lid," Lee said, punching numbers into a cell phone. "As for us, we take our chances. Barker, it's Lee. You ready? We're coming out."

"What's going on?" I said, confused—but with a definite sinking feeling that things were about to get worse. Lee started walking, holding out his hand to indicate the hall, and I quickly followed, Helen falling in on my right. "Why the cloak and dagger—"

"Miss Frost," Lee said, glancing at me hurriedly, "we've got to hurry before news gets out. Barker's pulling up in a black limo. When we go out those doors, we'll run straight down to it. Don't stop for anything."

And then we reached the outer doors, Lee and Yao opened them for me, and I stepped outside . . . into a sea of flashbulbs and microphones.

The media had their new story, and I was it.

37.   AN UNUSUAL STRATAGEM

I admit it: I'm an exhibitionist. I love attention. I walk around with a deathhawk every day and with my long, tattooed arms bare nine months out of the year. And it's for a purpose. No, really! Just a month or two ago, I would have relished the chance to stand before a crowd of reporters: think of the business it would bring into the shop.

But now all I could think of was Cinnamon, and how hard it would make our case.

The questions of the reporters were a dull roar, the flashbulbs scattered shots of lightning. *Did you kill Christopher Valentine? FOOM. Did you use magic? FOOM. Did you use your tattoos? FOOM. Is tattoo magic dangerous? FOOM. FOOM. FOOM.*

In a daze, I followed my lawyers, who fended off reporters with practiced ease. They'd clearly put thought into it. Lee took the left with his arms spread wide, soaking up questions like a sponge, dodging, deflecting, denying. Yao took the right, nonchalantly swinging her briefcase wide, between them clearing a path for me to walk unimpeded.

But they hadn't counted on my height, and even with me scrunched down, Lee wasn't a tall enough man. When he stepped down the next set of risers, one of the reporters shoved her microphone straight into my face and shouted, "Is it true that you've confessed to the murder?"

"Miss Frost," Lee said, trying to interpose himself between me and the mike, "has always fully cooperated with the police, but has not confessed to anything, much less murder."

"But in November you claimed to have killed him," the reporter pressed, still talking directly to me as we tried to press past her. "In your testimony—"

"Miss Frost's testimony has been misrepresented—" Lee said, trying to come between us.

"So she was lying?" the reporter said, talking over him. "Were you lying, Miss Frost?"

I stopped on the steps, glaring into space. Lee looked back in alarm and reached to grab my arm, but it was too late. The reporter shoved her mike in my face again and asked, "Don't you feel any remorse for killing a man who saved your life?"

My nostrils flared. Valentine had *staged* that shooting.

"No, I don't," I snapped, and the reporter's eyes gleamed.

Lee twitched violently. "Miss Frost," he said loudly, "doesn't mean to imply—"

"That she killed him?" the reporter asked. "You *are* saying that you killed him?"

Lee raised his arms, shouting something, but was drowned out as the reporters surged in. Flashbulbs flashed. Cameras pressed inwards. As Lee and Yao tried to fend them off, I got angrier and angrier. I wanted to belt out that yes, I had killed him, and no, I wasn't sorry. And it was true. But saying it would torpedo any chance I had of getting Cinnamon back.

Finally I could stand it no more. I straightened up, looked out over Lee and Yao, and picked out a reporter standing on the steps just beyond them. I made direct eye contact, and he shoved his microphone over Lee's head and into my face. I leaned in and spoke clearly.

"Everyone, please, step back, you're obstructing the stair."

Then I walked straight forward between Lee and Yao, gently moving the reporter aside with my hand as I passed. I heard scrambling and splutters behind me, but I just kept moving and hopped right into the open door of the limo. Moments later, Lee and Yao followed.

"Drive," Lee said, slamming the door. He settled into the backwards-facing seat opposite me. "Damn. That was a hell of a trick."

"I used to date a musician," I said. "She taught me a few tricks about working crowds."

Helen covered her face as Lee choked a little. "She . . . ah . . . well," he said. Then he recovered. "Still, let me do the talking from now on. You can't go around torpedoing yourself—"

"Have you been briefed?" I said. "Was I not completely honest with the police?"

"We had been hoping to quash that testimony," Lee said, now openly glaring. "We can't claim that your confession was coerced if you're going around corroborating—"

"My confession *wasn't* coerced," I said. "So your argument was going to be that the jury should trust me now because I was lying before?"

"Trust won't have anything to do with it—we're going get as much evidence thrown out as we can and argue self-defense, but *without* you testifying," Lee said. "Innocent people look terrible on the stand, but the unrepentant look worse—"

"I-didn't-do-anything-wrong," I said, gritting my teeth.

"So *you* think," Lee said. "But you don't seem to have realized that your own approval of your actions is meaningless if a prosecutor disagrees—and she can convince a jury."

"But Valentine was a serial killer."

"He was never arrested and prosecuted," Lee said. "He just died, by your hands, via magic—and Paulina Ross just loves making examples of people who kill with magic."

I leaned back in the limo as Lee went on. I wondered how much this was going to cost me. Surely they weren't going to take a criminal defense on spec the way they had done with the lawsuit by the Valentine Foundation. Then the bigger problem came back to me.

"What is this going to do to my custody case?" I said. "It can't look good."

"Oh, hell, Miss Frost," Lee said, frowning, "you're right, it certainly can't help."

"That's not our most immediate problem with Cinnamon," Helen said. "Earlier tonight I contacted the foster parent, Jack Palmotti, and it turns out he was frantic. Apparently Cinnamon brought something home that was meant for you, and he didn't know what to do with it."

"What's happened?" I asked, mouth dry.

"Cinnamon's getting kicked out of the Clairmont Academy."

38. A PROBLEM STUDENT

I bore down on the glass doors of the Clairmont Academy, watching my reflection loom large in the glass, Doug at my heels. I was *not* in the mood. But I couldn't leave Cinnamon's fate in the hands of a foster parent I'd never met and school administrators who didn't care. Then the doors slid aside, once again revealing Catherine Fremont, looking—relieved?

"Oh, thank goodness," she said. "I'm so glad you're here."

"What the hell is going on?" I asked, glaring down at her. "After all the effort we spent to get her into this school, I'll be damned if I see you just boot her out—"

"That's *so* refreshing," said a male voice, and I looked over to see a shag-haired man in a red-checked shirt limp towards us from the waiting area. "I didn't think you were going to show, but I'm so pleased you actually came here to fulfill your parental duties."

"Jack!" Doug said sharply. He wasn't just my ride; he'd been Cinnamon's tutor since . . . heck, even when she was in the hospital. But I'd not expected him to know more about what was going on than I did. "That was *completely* uncalled for. Dakota's a devoted parent."

"Doug, please," Jack said, "you haven't dealt with these parents like . . . I . . . "

He trailed off as I glared at him. "I don't believe we've met," I said coldly.

"Jack Palmotti," he said, extending his hand. "I'm Cinnamon's foster father."

Fremont shrank back from the two of us. After a moment, I extended my hand to him.

"Dakota Frost, Cinnamon's adoptive mother," I said. "Pleased to meet you."

Palmotti glanced between us. "So, Miss Frost . . . what is your relationship to Doug?" he asked. "It's low to circumvent a court order by sending a friend in the guise of a tutor."

"Doug is the fiancé of my best friend," I snapped, "and I resent the insinuation—"

"Please, please, everyone," Vladimir said, appearing from nowhere, stepping up between us, touching both me and Palmotti on the arm. "We're all here for one reason: Cinnamon."

I sighed. He was right. "Mister Palmotti, where are my manners?" I said. "It is my pleasure to introduce you to Doctor Yonas Vladimir, Cinnamon's math instructor. Yonas, please meet Mister Jack Palmotti. He's taking care of Cinnamon while the court case is resolved."

Vladimir and Palmotti froze for a moment. Apparently I'd broken their 'let's get everyone angrier' script by apologizing and introducing them politely. That was nice. Perhaps I should try it more often. Finally it was Palmotti that spoke, directly to me.

"So you know her math teacher," he said, with a half smile. "That's encouraging."

"Thank you," I said. "I'm sorry I was snappish. I . . . just lost a close friend."

And then I choked off, staring into the distance. Doug put his hand on my shoulder. And then Palmotti put his hand on my arm tenderly. I glared, through the edge of tears, but instantly I could see that he'd lost someone—I guessed, from the pain and the sympathy, his wife.

"I am *so* sorry," he said. "Please forgive me my suspicions. I wasn't trying to make it harder on you right now. And I *know* it's hard on you—believe me, I understand."

Our little group was admitted to Dean Belloson's office, a double-sized version of Fremont's office at the end of the row, containing a youngish, pudgy man with thick glasses who I first took to be Belloson's secretary before I realized there was no office beyond the one in which we now stood. There, the five of us sat in a semicircle of chairs opposite the Dean.

"I understand this may seem precipitous," the Dean said, "but young Miss Frost has skipped nearly a dozen classes this week, totaling almost three full days of class time."

"I'm sorry," Palmotti said, "I just can't make her do anything, much less go to school."

"Don't beat yourself up, it took *me* a while," I said. "And precipitous is precisely the word I'd use for kicking a new student out after only a few days of absences."

"Did you not read the Guide for Students and Parents?" the Dean said. "Didn't my staff explain it to you at the entrance interview? This is *not* a public school, open to all comers. We have *very* high standards. Three consecutive days of unexplained absences—"

"*Unexplained?*" I said. "What do you call that business with Burnham? You can't expect perfection when she's just been taken from her mother—wait, scratch that. Why is this even an issue with all that I'm paying you? This is a disciplinary issue between me and Cinnamon."

"Miss Frost," Dean Belloson said, taking off his glasses and rubbing his forehead, "it isn't that simple. This isn't a warehouse, and we're not storing Cinnamon for a monthly fee. She's a person, and a student, but not your typical student. Handling her takes extra effort."

"You knew when you took her she was an extraordinary needs student," I said. "Are you or are you not equipped to deal with werekin?"

"That's not it," Vladimir said. "Dakota, Cinnamon needs a *lot* of special tutoring."

"You also knew she had little prior education, which you personally said was OK," I said. "And I thought I explained to you we only just discovered she might have Tourette's."

"Oh, she's almost certainly got it," Vladimir said quietly. "I've suspected since she called me a clown in the entrance interview. She was immediately mortified and tried to distract us—"

"Or," the Dean said, "she could be an uncouth, but clever little—"

"She was mortified," Vladimir repeated. "Corprolalia—dirty speech, the symptom most famously and a bit exaggeratedly associated with Tourette's—is not just cussing. It can be inappropriate comments which are hard to bottle in, but don't reflect how she feels."

"I've seen that," Palmotti said suddenly. "I've almost certainly seen that."

"I have too," I said. *Damnit.* "At least twice earlier that day, in fact."

"Taken from her home? School shopping? A death of a friend? The more stressful it is, the harder it will be for her to keep a lid on it," Vladimir said. "But corprolalia often fades past the teens. Tourette's is more than that—facial tics, for example. On that note, that steel collar of hers—can we lose it? Tight collars can worsen the tics, but I understand it's locked on."

"I'll ask, but I suspect the answer is no," I said. "It's sort of her vampire visa."

"*Vampire* visa?" Fremont and Palmotti said in surprised, worried unison.

"Aha!" the Dean said, putting his hand to his head with an expression of disgust. "I *knew* I recognized that 'S' seal from somewhere. That's a vampire passage token, isn't it? House of Saffron, correct? The Vampire Queen of Little Five Points?"

"Why . . . yes," I said. "How did you—"

"My apologies, Miss Frost," he said. "If you'll pardon the pun, young Cinnamon's been bitten by vampire politics. One thing in her file that forced me to escalate this was a complaint from a parent—but that parent is in the Gentry, vampires in dispute with the House of Saffron. Lord Iadimus's wife may have seen Cinnamon's collar and decided to make trouble for her."

"Charming," I said. The last thing I'd expected was that the Dean was up on vampire politics—and if Cinnamon simply attending the same school as a child of the Gentry was causing problems, I couldn't imagine what Saffron was having to deal with working with the Gentry face to face. "And the collar only protects from physical, not political assault."

"Let's not lose perspective," Vladimir said gently. "The parental complaint was *not* the only thing in her already large file. And it isn't just tics or cussing, it's willful behavior. Her corprolalia, and I do agree she probably has it, only explains part of her smart mouth."

"How can you tell?" I asked sharply.

"Cussing out of the blue *might* be a verbal tic," Vladimir said, "but if it sounds like she meant it, she probably said it on purpose. But, honestly, our teachers are professionals. We can handle a few f-bombs. It's the acting out. It isn't fair to all the other students in her classes."

"Well, we're here," I said. "What do you want of us?"

"You have to convince her to attend and to behave herself," he said. "The Dean's right. I've seen this a lot with special needs students—it isn't that they're not capable, it's that they don't see how school is relevant to them. Cinnamon can be . . . *particularly* colorful."

I sighed. "All right," I said. "I am more than willing to talk to her, but as I understand the court order, it will have to be here at school, supervised. After school she has to stay in the custody of the Palmottis, and I can't *imagine* how hard this is on them."

"Thank you," Palmotti said, very quietly.

"I'll go further," the Dean said. "You have to convince her to take class seriously. We care about Cinnamon, we really do, but we have *many* hardworking students here—"

"All right, all *right*," I said. "I'll get her to show up, and at least be quiet in class. And I'll lean on her—but in the end, I can't force her to learn."

"That's not good enough," the Dean said. "Our one-on-one and small group resources are limited. It isn't fair to our special topics teachers if she's blowing them off."

"She's that far behind?" Something was tickling my brain, something Vladimir said that I had missed. "But surely there's time to catch up. She's only been here a little over a week."

"Yes, but that's not the problem," Vladimir said. "She's got special educational needs above and beyond being a werekin."

"Special needs?" I pressed. "Is she dyslexic, on top of the Tourette's?"

"Maybe a little," Vladimir admitted. "We're doing more tests. But the real problem, if you can call it that, is her brain. Maybe it's the werekin influence, maybe it's just natural, whatever that means. Regardless, she learns differently than the rest of us."

"Oh, God," I said. She'd shown such promise, in so many ways, but I'd feared exactly something like this. With increasing horror, I realized what I'd missed was that, just minutes ago, Vladimir had called her a *special needs student*. "You're saying she's . . . *mentally disabled?*"

"Quite the opposite," Vladimir said. "Cinnamon's a genius, on the level of *Gauss*."

39.   REMEDIAL CLASS

When Carl Frederich Gauss was ten, his teacher punished his class by making them add the numbers from one to a hundred. Before most of the other students had started, Gauss handed in his slate with the right answer. Mathematicians now think he started picking off pairs of numbers from each end of the sequence: one plus a hundred, two plus ninety nine, and so on— fifty pairs of numbers, each adding to a hundred and one: five thousand and fifty, *bam!*

Cinnamon was *that* fast.

After our meeting with the Dean, Vladimir had let Doug, Jack and I sit in on the math club. Six sets of problems were written on the whiteboards. I took a lot of math in college before I dropped out, but I recognized none of it other than the occasional sigma-for-sum or geometric symbol. Vladimir was before the board, lecturing to five of his star students sitting around him in a circle, all trying to pay attention to him . . . and to ignore Cinnamon.

And Cinnamon? My precious baby girl—who I'd missed so much, who I hadn't seen in so long—barely *reacted* when she saw me, and focused instead entirely on the class, if focus you could call it. Cinnamon *orbited* the other students, bouncing around the room, sometimes leaning on the wall, sometimes squatting on chairs, watching like a cat—but most often standing by the window, staring outside, tail twitching, face spasming, occasionally cussing . . . all the time with one cat ear visibly cocked to Vladimir's every word.

Vladimir was telling them how important this part of the 'competition' was; then he stepped aside and let the students attack problems written on the board. Cinnamon cursed and stomped up to the board, cocked her head at it, then grabbed a whiteboard marker in her fist and began scrawling answers before the other students had even started. She drew rectangles and arcs littered with symbols, and I understood her answers even less than the question.

"I thought this was a remedial class," I murmured to Doug.

"For math PhDs, maybe," Doug said. "No wonder her assignments looked so hard."

Vladimir handed over the math club to one of the students and motioned us into his office. Unlike the spacious windowed affairs of the administrators, Vladimir's office was apparently a converted storage closet—long, narrow, and surprisingly cozy.

"Keep your voices down; never underestimate werekin hearing," Vladimir said, sitting on the corner of a desk facing a wall covered with photos of forests and clippings of math articles. "Cinnamon doesn't understand. She thinks that because she's in the special class, it must mean she's stupid. The truth is the opposite—she's so smart she's not used to really having to work."

I sighed. "Maybe this is too much too soon," I said. "Maybe we need to track her back into a normal class, let her develop more stable peer relationships."

Vladimir raised an eyebrow at me. "Your mother was a teacher, I recall? Your intuitions are good, but she's bored out of her gourd in normal classes and gets *very* disruptive. You see what she's like when she's interested. We need to push her, hard, just to keep her engaged."

"Well, maybe it's the after-school tutoring," I said. "Perhaps tutor her during hours—"

"Actually, the math club is one of the few things she's almost guaranteed to show for," Vladimir said. "Every single day this week, in fact, even on days she ditched school entirely."

Doug was looking at some of Cinnamon's homework. "I find myself agreeing with Dakota," he said. "Doctor Vladimir, the physics of magic requires a lot of math, but I have to confess, speaking as her tutor, some of these assignments gave *me* a headache. I can see pushing her, but if you challenge her so hard she can never succeed, of course she'll feel stupid."

He held up the paper. The answers Cinnamon had written were scrawled so badly it looked like she'd been writing with crayons. Half the numbers were upside down, backwards, even rotated, and the answers seemed wrong. I was no expert, but it looked like dyslexia.

"Ah," Vladimir said, taking the paper gently and staring at it like it was a treasure. "This was my 'aha' experience. You don't take points off for a right answer just because it's in nonstandard notation. Join me at the board, let's see how she's doing."

In the classroom, Cinnamon was staring at the last problem. She'd scrawled several numbers down—a three, a backwards five, what looked like an upside down seven, and the number eight in a box with an arrow beneath it pointing to the left.

"Very good, Cinnamon," he said. "But you can't write it the way you came up with it."

"*Your* way is square," she said, eye flickering back at me, catlike. "*Uff!*"

"My way people will recognize," he said. "Now, the three is already right. What about the others? How do we write the bass-acwards? What's the right way to write upsy-downs? And do you really want to put an eight in the box? What's the smallest box you gots?"

She scowled, then wrote **-5** on the board, followed by **7i**. After squinting at the eight, she wrote **-√8 = -2√2**. "Satisfied?" she said, head snapping aside in her sneezy tic. "Hah."

"Holy cow," I said. "She came up with her *own notation* for imaginary numbers?"

"It gets better," Vladimir said. "Cinnamon, show us the path of the swirling brickies."

"Sure," she said, shrugging. She raised the marker, and then paused, her pupil nailing me out of the corner of her eye, triangular, so like the eye of the tiger I'd seen in the cage. "*Mom*, for the love, don't hover. Fuck! You makes me nervous."

I stepped back from the board. "Sorry."

Cinnamon drew a rectangle on the board, tall but not too narrow, like a squat door. Then she divided it in two with a line across its middle. That left a square on its top . . . and another door-shaped rectangle at bottom, same shape as its parent, but smaller and turned on its side. She divided the new door with a new line, making an even smaller square and smaller rectangle—and kept repeating it, smaller and smaller each time, a brick road curling in.

"That's the *golden spiral*," Doug said, leaning forward suddenly.

"Isn't it pretty?" Cinnamon said, drawing an arc curling in through each square that looked like the turns of a nautilus shell. "The brickies goes rounds and rounds, and the path swirls through them, all the way downs—"

"I *know* this," I said. "No wonder it looked like a door—that's the *golden ratio*. Artists use it to make their compositions look pleasing. It goes all the way back to the Greeks—"

"And as far as I can tell," Vladimir said, "she reinvented it *herself.* Cinnamon, do you mind if I show your mother some of your notes?"

"Sure, I guesses," she said, shrugging. "They're stupid. Why would you want to?"

Vladimir took the three of us back into his office. After some digging, he found a folder, filled with page after page of photocopies of painfully scrawled notes in Cinnamon's hand. "Her answers looked wrong, but *consistently* wrong," he said, pointing out flipped and tilted numbers in her notes. "She was writing backwards for minus and upside down for imaginary—"

"Doc," Cinnamon said, "you makes me look bad."

"No, Cinnamon, this is *amazing,*" I said, taking the folder and paging through her notes, which went from painfully scrawled to largely incomprehensible as she incorporated more and more traditional math. "We've got to jump on this right away if she really is this smart."

"Fuck," Cinnamon said. "You just wants to give me more work!"

"Cinnamon," I said, touching her shoulder. "I know schoolwork sucks. I hated it too. But even when I fell in love with tattooing, I had to work at it, *hard*. I don't recognize *half* of this, but, if I'm reading these equations right . . . you must enjoy the *heck* out of math."

She grinned despite herself, and so did I.

"I'm so glad you're enjoying math, but I have to be straight with you, Cinnamon. The Dean called us all down here because you've been skipping your other classes," I said. Her ears folded back, and she looked away. "We've talked it over, and they've agreed not to kick you out, for now, but you're going to have to do your part. You're going to have to show up—"

She hissed, twisting her head, pulling at her collar. "The other classes *suck*."

"I wish I could tell you that it gets better, but it doesn't," I said. "And I know it seems like math is easy to you now, Cinnamon, but it's going to get harder, too, and you need to learn to deal with it now. You're going to *have* to learn to work at things. It doesn't matter *what* you want to do, Cinnamon. If you *want* it . . . you'll have to . . . work at it . . . "

I trailed off, staring at the notes. Then I stood up. I was wrong. I *did* recognize this.

"Mom?" Cinnamon asked uncertainly.

"What's this?" I asked, pointing at a diagram showing a rectangle—and a pentagram.

"It's nothing," she said defensively. "I was just looking for more paths of the brickies."

"The golden ratio shows up in many figures," Vladimir said sharply. He looked as defensive as Cinnamon. "*Including* the pentagram. There's nothing demonic about it."

"I never said that there was," I said, showing the folder to Doug. "Look familiar?"

"Yeah," he said, taking the sheets. "This a lot like graphomancy. In fact, this set of golden rectangles is very similar to what's used by the tagger."

"And *this* shows a one-to-one mapping to a pentagram," I said. "Nothing demonic, but there's a reason white magic uses circles and black magic uses pentagrams. In graphomancy, a circle is a shield to keep things out, whereas a pentagram is a receiver to draw things in."

"Meaning?" Vladimir asked, still looking a bit defensive.

"Cinnamon has figured out," I said, "how a pentagram maps onto a pattern of golden section rectangles. And our friend the graffiti tagger uses similar patterns in his magic. I'm guessing that's how his graffiti gets so much power. It's built like a magical receiver."

"Uh . . . can I get a photocopy of this?" Doug said, turning the sheet back and forth. "I'm working on a similar problem with Dakota and this . . . this might help me."

The door opened, and Jack Palmotti gestured to us. He'd gotten a call a few minutes earlier and had walked out to take it. "Miss Frost," he said, "Can I see you outside?"

"Wait here, honey," I said, and followed Palmotti out into the hall. "What is it now?"

"I hate to be the bearer of bad news," he said, "but that was Margaret Burnham. She called to let me know about some developments in the case, and it slipped out that you were here, trying to do the right thing by Cinnamon," he said. "I'm so sorry."

"No good deed goes unpunished," I said. "Technically, I'm not in custody of Cinnamon, but the court order doesn't say I can't be in the same—tell me there's not a new court order."

"There wasn't until just now," Palmotti said. "When you were arrested, it was apparently all over the news. The prosecutor saw it, and asked the judge to issue a restraining order."

"They've barred you from seeing Cinnamon *at all* until the case is resolved."

40.   THIS ONE THING I COULD DO

Calaphase was gone . . . and I couldn't see Cinnamon.

That left me in a daze. I sat numbly through my lawyer's briefings, answering their questions when asked. It seemed to go on forever, and by the time Doug came to rescue me and dropped me off in front of Calaphase's house to get my car, it was a quarter past noon.

I'd hoped the police would be done with the crime scene by the time that we got there, but instead I found a swarm of them still there, examining the house, the tags, the graffiti—and my Prius sitting smack dab in the middle of the carport of a man who didn't own a car.

Before we could pull up, the siren of a fire truck drove Doug to the side of the road, far short of the house. As it sped past, I leaned back in the seat. I was tempted to come back later, but there was always the chance they might tow my car. Finally I hopped out, shooed Doug off, and trudged towards the house to try to get them to release the blue bomb to me.

The fire truck stopped right in front of the house, and I could now see smoke curling up from behind it. Great. The tag on Calaphase's house had caught fire too. Hopefully they'd caught it in time to save the house, but so much for the hope I could take a look at it.

And, similarly, so much for the hope I could quickly get my car. Before two words were out of my mouth, I was stopped, questioned, and detained. By now, I was learning how this worked: *these* cops hadn't been at the scene of Calaphase's death, and had to do their jobs based on what was right in front of them.

So I gritted my teeth . . . and cooperated.

At first it didn't seem to help. At this crime scene I had no allies. Rand was nowhere in sight, and Philip didn't magically come to my aid. But I *had* reported Calaphase's death, and that was in the system. So eventually Lucia Bonn, the detective in charge, got the story from downtown. But that just turned the questioning from suspect to witness.

"Thank you, Miss Frost," Bonn said, reviewing the statement form—they were becoming depressingly familiar. "I don't need to impound your car," Bonn said at last. "You can go—and for what it's worth . . . I'm sorry about your friend."

I thanked her, trudged back to the blue bomb and stared at it sadly. The tagger had keyed it, fucker, and then I noticed he'd defaced it with a few stripes—apparently Calaphase and I had interrupted him vandalizing my car when we came to the door.

My eyes tightened as I realized that the cops had not noticed the graffiti on it—they were not as elaborate as the tag, and from the right angle could have been mistaken for streaks of paint. I thought about just going, but then I tromped back and told Bonn what I'd found.

"Oh, *damnit*," Bonn said, rubbing her forehead. "Insult to—Jack, go take a look. Thanks, Miss Frost. You are the most cooperative so-called murder suspect I've ever seen."

Great, my fiendish plan was working. Yay me.

"I didn't do anything wrong, so I have nothing to hide," I said heavily, feeling my neck. Beneath the bandage, the bite from Calaphase was starting to itch again. "Anyway, if you, or more likely somebody in the DA's office, really wanted to railroad me, well, you're the cops, you can do it, whether I cooperate or not. Trust me on that."

Lucia Bonn suddenly looked very sad. "Yeah," she said. "You're right. We can."

"Not that I'm accusing you of anything," I said quickly. "You're just doing your job, tracking down the guy who killed my . . . uh, boyfriend. I can't control how you do it. The only thing I've got control over is myself, and I don't see why I should make your job harder."

"Miss Frost, take my advice," Bonn said, taking my arm and speaking quietly, but firmly. "Talk to your lawyers, and take *their* advice. Because no cop cares how nice you are. We all just want to catch the bad guy and move the fuck on."

It took an hour for the crime scene technicians to get back to the car, and then *another* hour to take all the pics and samples they wanted. While they worked, I took a walk down the pretty little suburban street, but then realized this was *his* neighborhood. We would have taken walks here. First, at night, then, maybe, someday, by day. I couldn't take it; I trudged back, plopped down on the sidelines, and tried hard not to pick at, or think of, my itchy neck.

Or think of my daughter, trapped in foster care, unable to see me.

It was well after one when they *re*-released the blue bomb to me. Without even time to stop for a snack I spent the next three hours at Ellis and Lee, where my lawyers worked me over on everything from Valentine to Cinnamon to Calaphase. Finally I trudged back to the Rogue Unicorn and steeled myself for the fallout of my stunt on the steps of the jail.

But there was none; Kring/L was supportive as always, and none of the staff gave me grief. They all knew what I'd been through. In fact, Annesthesia pulled me aside and confided that we'd gotten a few customers who wanted graffiti-based tattoos, and that she'd been turning them away. I thanked her—and not just because I didn't like the look of graffiti art on human flesh. Instead, at this point, I was raw enough about Calaphase that I was afraid that on the spot I'd do something I might regret.

Then, my day got even better. A cute, pigtailed college student came in looking for a 'Frost bite.' I smiled and told her she'd have to settle for a tattoo.

I love tattooing. I love talking to the clients, picking out the design, fitting it to the skin, feeling the smoothness of the canvas before I make the first mark. Even the prepwork—setting up the tattoo gun, the needles, the flash—has a pleasant rhythm to it, busy enough to make me forget things for a while. And when we get into the studio, just me, my tools and my client inside the protective barrier—well, they don't call it a magic circle for nothing.

She chose a simple design, a butterfly atop a long-stemmed rose. *Butterflower #4* was one of Jinx's best designs, with simple, potent magical lines easily customizable for body shape and skin color. She wanted it in a "safe" place, someplace where it would look good in a bathing suit but hidden under normal clothes. I knew the type: I had *been* the type, long ago, before I got addicted to tattoos. So I gave her her first "bite" curling over her shoulder blade, so she could try out her rebellious streak before committing to changing her life.

The warm vibration of the gun rippled up through my hand, and I imagined the sharp, scratchy pleasure of the needle on the other end. I frequently wiped away the ink and blood so I had a clear view of my canvas, but as I drew the gun closer to the more sensitive skin near the ridges of her bone, I put the cloth down briefly and put my hand on her other shoulder to calm her, talking more loudly to keep her attention as I went over more sensitive skin.

Magical ink is trickier than mundane tattooing; you have less ability to recover from your mistakes, and have to learn how to really focus to get it right the first time. But *Butterflower #4* was a small, simple mark, as magical marks go, taking little more than an hour, and after it was done I ran a little mana through it to make sure it worked.

The girl cried in delight when the butterfly stirred, then cooed as its wings lifted up into the air, throwing off little fairy sparkles of mana when, against my instruction, she touched it gingerly with her finger. No harm was done, though, so I coaxed it back into her skin so it could bond properly, bandaged it up to keep it safe from prying fingers, and sent her on her way with a stern but friendly warning—one more satisfied customer.

As I cleaned up, I felt good. At least there was this one thing I could do. Then I remembered Helen's warning about the suitability of my profession, and I cursed. There was a good shot they were going to take this from me too, either because of the murder case or the custody case—that is, assuming there was anything I could do to get Cinnamon back at all.

"You have a call," Annesthesia said, as I stepped out of the front inking room.

I checked the clock. "Almost nine," I said. "A bit late for Rogue business."

"She called twice while you were tattooing," Annesthesia said, "but I didn't want to interrupt you. It was only on the third call that she actually said it was urgent."

"Oh, hell," I said. My first thought was Helen calling with bad news about Cinnamon—but any kind of urgent call from Jinx or, worse, Saffron would be bad news right now. "I'll take it in my office," I said, stomping back to my desk and picking up the receiver. "What the hell's happened now?"

The line was silent for a moment. "Dakota Frost?" the voice said uncertainly.

"Best magical tattooist in the Southeast," I snapped, "but no-one ever needs an urgent tattoo—" At that last bit I stopped myself. First, I knew from experience that it wasn't true, and second, it was no way to treat a customer. "Sorry, it's been a bad day—"

"Well, given that your day *started* in jail," the voice said, laughing, "I can believe it."

"Ranger?" The Bettie Paige knockoff from the jail—who needed my help with graffiti.

"Still want to see some magic graffiti, Dakota Frost?"

My jaw hung open. "Oh, *do* I," I said. "When and where?"

41. SPEAK OF THE DEVILS

The Candlestick Apartment Complex was in the West End, an inaptly named area of Downtown Atlanta even closer to the heart of the city than I was in Little Five Points. Even at ten at night, a fair number of the homeless milled around, which made me uncomfortable, which itself made me *more* uncomfortable. At a traffic light, I took a moment to make myself actually look around me, and saw the area was quite nice, with clean sidewalks, beautiful trees, and friendly people. Maybe I'd have to turn in my liberal do-gooder card.

The Prius told me to turn, and I turned, crossing train tracks and ducking under bridges, winding through smaller and smaller side streets whose broken pavement made Moreland seem as smooth as Georgia's gas-tax highways. Graffiti began making more than its usual token appearance, and the tags got more and more elaborate—some of them looking suspiciously familiar, not the tagger's exactly, but something I'd seen before.

I sighed. Some of the graffiti was beautiful, but a lot of it was just crap. There were clearly masters trying to do larger pieces here, some of them quite clever, especially a guy who kept drawing a kind of subversive Mickey Mouse smoking a joint. But for every masterpiece there were a dozen 'toy' taggers throwing up scrawls and gang signs, sometimes right on top of the masterworks, *tsk tsk*. Made both the masterpieces and the tags look like junk. No, not junk—unsafe. Like the people who lived there didn't take care of what they had.

And then I was there, pulling up at the gate of a World War II ammo dump converted into apartments that, until only a few months ago, had housed hundreds of people. A lighted sign that had clearly once read "Candlestick Apartment Complex" in warm inviting letters now had an amateurishly-made banner draped over it, trying to legally rebut that claim by screaming "CANDLESTICK WAREHOUSES" in bold block letters.

I drove up to the iron gate and found the keypad had been broken open and hotwired. There was a notice from the city, a "POSTED: NO TRESPASSING" sign, and haphazardly duct-taped atop it was a piece of cardboard shouting: "WE STILL LIVE HERE, ASS!"

I stared at it, wondering if I should bail. This was *not* how I lived my life. I mean, I know I'm tall, tattooed, and edgy; but I keep my nose squeaky clean, and that includes staying in *legal* housing. If the city really was rolling the landlord to rack up fines, squatting wouldn't fix it. It was more likely to get everyone arrested for trespassing. And I was in enough trouble already.

Then I thought of Calaphase, and Revenance, and Demophage, and Lord Delancaster, and the three dead werekin at the werehouse whose names I never had the chance to learn. When had I started cutting slack to werekin that I no longer extended to humans? This was the only housing most of these people could afford. It was Ranger's right to fight back if the city tried to screw her or her landlord—and I had to learn what Ranger knew.

I hit the red button, waited for the gate to creak open, and drove the blue bomb inside.

The Candlestick Apartment Complex was a maze of concrete canyons: long, barren lanes of pavement wedged between high white walls topped with black gutters. There were a few signs of graffiti, but many of the warehouse walls were recently whitewashed, and on a fair number of the older ones splashes of paint covered some of the tags.

So the residents were fighting it. Good. But I saw a few larger pieces untouched—not the magic tagger's, but something else entirely: tall, narrow artworks covering the walls from top to bottom with designs that were both artistic and hauntingly familiar. So the residents *weren't* whitewashing everything—they knew *what* to fight. Even better. I could learn from that.

I finally found unit A6 on a rollup door in the middle of one of the long canyons. I squeezed the blue bomb in between a rusty old van and a paint-covered pickup. Once out of the car, I started to notice more signs of life: bicycles, window boxes, cat food bowls.

From the unit to the right of A6 I could hear faint thumping music, and out front there was a shiny big-rimmed SUV painted with an ad for "Tha Peeplz Recordz." In the unit opposite A6, the rollup door was up, and I saw a welder at work on a dented old VW bug, covering it with pointed metal leaves that made it look like a great big artichoke.

"Dakota Frost," came a voice. I turned and saw Ranger leaning against a smaller door next to the rollup. Something kept scratching and bumping at it behind her, but she leaned harder, keeping it firmly closed. "Didn't think you were going to make it."

"Wouldn't miss it for the world." I said, and followed her inside.

A6 was a deceptively long warehouse, easily five or six times as deep as it was wide, that someone had converted into multi-level lofts. The upper lofts were apartments and artists' studios, Ranger explained; the bottom had been an art gallery.

Now, however, the maze of white walls of the gallery was filled with sleeping bags and piles of cardboard boxes—a makeshift refugee camp for the evicted apartment dwellers who were the Candlestick Twenty. There were actually almost a hundred holdouts in the complex, but the only ones that the media cared about were the ones Ranger had taken in.

The strange scratching noise proved to be a giant galumphing dog, which immediately started scrabbling around us on the cement floor trying to lick us to death. Waving us off, Ranger collared the slobbering menace and dragged it barking (playfully) back to her upstairs apartment while she barked (*not* playfully) into her cell phone. When she returned, snapping the phone shut, her face was red and her hands were shaking.

"That call was *another* hundred bucks down the drain," she said. "I *hate* lawyers."

"Tell me about it," I said. "But you didn't call me here for legal advice."

"No," she admitted, drawing me behind a few makeshift walls into a kitchen near the front end of the gallery. While I leaned against the kitchen table, she pulled a few glasses out of the sink, rinsed them cursorily and poured a couple of Cokes.

"Thanks," I said, staring at the smudged glass skeptically.

"All this started," Ranger said, drinking from the glass as if the germs from the skanky sink wouldn't kill her, "when we had a fire and the city did an inspection. But all this shit is thick World War II concrete. We never *had* fires until the graffiti showed up."

"Damnit," I said. "That's consistent. Can you show me the latest tags?"

"I didn't see this one, but I've called the guys who did—speak of the devils."

My eyebrows raised as Keif and Drive walked past the kitchen window. Moments later there was a knock on the outer door. "Hey Ranger," Keif's voice called. "Let us in!"

"Speak of the devils, indeed," I said.

42. CANDLESTICKS AFIRE

The four of us sat down in the kitchen. Drive started going over a map of the facility while Keif and I stared at each other across the table, me with my arms folded, him scowling at me from beneath his crown of dreadlocks, hands clasped tightly on the table.

It was entirely too suspicious that Keif and Drive hit it big just when magic graffiti began spreading over Atlanta, that their marks had showed up on the tagger's playground, and that now here they were again. And while Drive was blathering on about the Vaiian significance of this and the Niivan significance of that and his theory that the tag placement itself was a kind of graphomancy, Keif was actively sweating under my gaze.

You didn't need Sherlock Holmes to put two and two together. Keif was involved, in which case he was probably the one that tagged the building that burned, and would never fess up. Or . . . something else was bothering him.

"I'm not here to finger you guys, if that's what you're worried about," I said, eyes fixed straight on Keif, who glanced away guiltily. "I'm not a rat. I walk the Edge. Your secrets are safe with me. But I have to know *everything*, Keif. I need what you learned from the tagger."

Drive abruptly stopped and stared at Keif. After a moment, Keif sighed.

"Look, we call ourselves *writers*, not taggers—but yeah, I know the guy," Keif said. "Not personally, but from his pieces. Super technique, great caricaturist, but he switched up, doesn't do figures or signature tags anymore. Back when he did, he did these fat-hat little devils and signed them Streetscribe, written with X-R-Y not S-C-R-I—"

"That's the guy," I said. "Go on."

"He's got himself a three man crew now, from the looks of it," Keif said. "An apprentice and a toy—no, that's harsh. The *senior* apprentice just copies, but he's got real skill with a can. The *junior* apprentice is still real sloppy, lots of drips, but he's got a flair for new designs."

"The two-and-a-half Siths theory again," I said, and Keif grinned. "But what about you? What have you learned from him?"

"Look, I've never met him, or any of his crew," Keif said, smile fading. "Not that I'd know if I had. But . . . you asked what my secret was earlier. I use walls that have mold, just like the Streetscribe, but that's not all of it. I've been biting his designs."

"Aha!" Drive said. At my baffled look, Drive explained. "Keif means he's been reverse-engineering the Streetscribe's pieces. You sly dog, I've been wondering where you've been getting some of your better circuits."

Keif looked away. I stared at him. He was still acting like he had something to hide, but for the life of me I couldn't see why he'd want to hide studying the tags. Or maybe it wasn't something wrong from his perspective—the Streetscribe was a killer, after all.

"So why is that a secret?" I said. "You afraid copying his art will piss him off?"

"Copying?" Drive said. "Circuits are one thing, but don't tell me you're a cribber—"

"I'm *not* cribbing his art," Keif insisted, staring at the table. "I'm not! I'm biting his *designs*—a *lot* of other magical writers are too—but I am *not* ripping off his *art!* I want to make a name for *myself*. I can't do that if I'm spending *my* time throwing up *his* pieces. Streetscribe and I are both representational artists—artists!—with our own styles. I do-not-crib!"

I stared at him. Maybe he was telling the truth. Maybe he wasn't a cribber. Maybe he was as artistic as he claimed. But he still looked embarrassed—and he'd just admitted that he and the Streetscribe were competing for the same walls. I decided to toss a line out and see if he bit.

"Let me guess," I said. "You're not above whitewashing his tags if he's taken prime wall space. You're both targeting special surfaces for your largest tags, and he's nailed all of the best ones first. And since you can't ink magic directly over magic . . . you're wiping his out."

Keif let out his breath in a sharp hiss, but he didn't deny it.

No one said anything. After a moment, Drive stood up. "A crossout is one thing, but an actual whitewash? What were you hoping to do, learn his tricks, wipe out all the evidence and take credit for them as your own? Man, that's low," he said, and stalked out of the room.

Keif glared up from his clenched hands. "Happy now, Nancy Drew?"

"I prefer Encyclopedia Brown," I replied, "but if you'd just been up front about what you knew, then I wouldn't have had to expose you."

"Why the hell are you butting into this?" Keif said. "Why can't you let it alone?"

"*You* popped up when this started going down, and I had to know why," I said. "And now I know—he's a giant, and you're standing on his shoulders, using his work as your canvas."

"Who cares?" Keif said. "That's how graffiti works. You don't build your own damn buildings to mark, you mark what's already there. Who cares if I'm doing it atop his shit?"

"I told you his shit killed one of my friends, right?" I said. "Did I tell you the total body count is nearing twenty, including two close friends, one of them *more* than close?"

Ranger went pale and put her Coke down. "Is that what went down last night?"

"Yeah," I said quietly. "Almost got killed, but I made it. My . . . friend wasn't so lucky."

"Aw, shit, man, why are you doin' this to me?" Keif said, staring up at no-one in particular. "This was a good gig—"

"You kill anybody?" I interjected.

"What? What? No!" Keif said, raising his hands. "My tags don't have that kind of juice."

"Then I don't need to tell anyone anything," I said. "I can keep this quiet, but I've *got to know how the graffiti works*. Looking at images has helped, but both me and my graphomancer are stumped. It crucifies vampires, tears up werewolves, and can catch buildings on fire even after you paint it over. It can create wide area effects, like wind. It can be triggered remotely—it's powered from an external source. Tattoo magic can't beat it. I need to know how to short-circuit it, before the tagger snaps his fingers and sets half Atlanta ablaze."

Keif was silent for a second, eyes scanning the air.

"How many tags are there in the Candlesticks?" Ranger asked abruptly.

"I get it, I get it," Keif said. "I'm thinking. To answer Dakota's question, Streetscribe's blackbook, his library of designs, is very complex. I don't fully get it. But there are some base patterns that serve as conduits of power. Call them spreading throwups, doorway tags, and octopus roses. Those last ones are his real masterpieces, and they're the most dangerous."

"*Thank* you," I said. "But how do you use his magic if you don't understand it?"

"I'm a leech," Keif said bitterly. "Normally, you can't write magic over complex magic unless you know it inside out. But remember you said you already knew whitewashing doesn't destroy the magic? So I whitewash the underlying tag to lock it down, then lay down new circuits on the same lines to power my own designs."

"Like magical induction," I said.

"Yeah," Keif said. "Though the rules aren't so simple as electromagnetism. Even figuring out what parts of the design are the power elements is tricky. Unless you know graphomancy in and out, it's hard to follow."

"I know a witch who can help me out with that," I said. "But *you've* worked with his designs enough to know how their power flows. Is there a way to short-circuit them?"

"*Maybe*," Keif said, eyes closing, head moving as if he were tracing circuits from memory. When he opened his eyes, he said, "Never thought about how to make his designs *less* effective, but I'm sure I could come up with—"

"That's great," Ranger said, an edge in her voice, "all this is fucking great, but, Keif—you never answered *my* question. How many tags are there in the Candlesticks, that you've painted over, that may catch on fire?"

Keif sighed. "About a dozen pieces, most painted over, by me or others."

"Jeeezus," Ranger said. "What triggers it? Are these just ticking time bombs?"

I thought about that a moment. "Maybe," I said. "It isn't quite clear yet. At first I thought they catch fire because they're painted over, but today I learned that wasn't true."

I stared at Keif, hunched over, dreadlocks spreading out like a porcupine; at Ranger, frowning over her Coke, at Drive, lurking just outside the door, listening with a disgusted look on his face. This was about more than just unsightly graffiti. "Anybody die in those fires?"

Ranger nodded. "Seven in the first fatal one, then fifteen in the second."

"*Twenty-two people?* Jesus," I said, leaning back in my chair. Count all the vamps and werekin who'd vanished or died, add in humans who died in suspicious fires, and you got a total body count of almost forty people. "Let's assume the tag's magic will be disrupted if painted over with a new tag, and diminished under a whitewash. Sound reasonable?"

"Sounds . . . reasonable," Keif said. "It might depend on the original purpose of the tag. Maybe yours were stronger. Intended to kill. The Candlestick tags may just be routine shit."

"All right. Then the right thing to do now is go to the new tag, photograph it, then figure out how to shut it down. If it works, we repeat the process here, first on any remaining whitewashed tags, then on your own. When they're defused, we whitewash them."

"I am *not*," Keif said fiercely, "going to whitewash my *own art*—"

"You've got to, or you'll go to jail. We can't clean up the whole city by ourselves," I said. "We can't. We've *got* to tell the police. I can keep your name out of it, but my pull won't help if your tags are plastered all over the city while you're hanging at Michael C. Carlos."

"Aw, shit," Keif said, face strained. "Damnit, we shouldn't have taken that show."

"What? No," Drive said, leaning against the doorframe. "*You* gotta clean up your act."

"Yeah," Keif said, hunched over so far his dreads flopped forward. "I'll think about it—"

"You'll *think* about it?" Ranger said, standing, tossing her Coke in the sink. "I'm gonna get evicted or arrested or killed because your shit is burning up our home? *Hell* no. You're not going to think about it—you gotta clean it up starting now!"

"Yeah, sure," Keif said—and then glanced up in surprise to see all three of the rest of us standing. "You mean, like right now?"

"Like *now* now," I said. "The tagger moves fast."

Keif got to his feet. "All right," he said. "All right. No time like the present, I guess."

We followed Keif out. He wasn't the healthiest of boys; he had a distinct penguin wobble and I started to worry he wouldn't make it. "How far are we going? Should we take my car?"

"Nah, it's not far, but I gotta run by the studio and pick up my paint," Keif said, pointing at a door on the opposite side of the white canyon. "And I want to go pick up my camera."

"Wait. Something's different," Ranger said.

I felt mana tingle around me. I whirled, inspecting the scattered pieces of graffiti. At first, I didn't *see* anything different; there were some tags, but our tagger hadn't shown up and sprayed a new masterpiece while I'd been drinking my Coke.

But then my eye caught movement, low and furtive along the warehouse wall. At first I thought it was a mouse or a bug, but then I caught it again, long, spindly, like the shadow of a hand. My eyes didn't want to see it at first, but then I had a brainflash. This is what it felt like when *other* people tried to catch *my* tattoos moving. I tilted my head.

"Oh, Jesus Christ," Keif said. "There's a spreading throwup along the wall!"

A long line of black graffiti slithered along the base of the wall: spidery black shapes, boiling up in waves, a scribbled animation of a swift river running just beneath the edge, only surging up when the dark channel below could no longer contain it.

I started backing up. I saw at once why Keif called it a spreading throwup—simple, fast to ink, and self-replicating—but it wasn't just mold-powered graffiti. Maybe that factored into it, but there was no way that long, narrow rivulet of hate could generate that much power from that little surface area. This *had* to be a magical receiver: somewhere, folded up in that nasty scribble, something like Cinnamon's pattern of golden rectangles was receiving power.

"Everyone stay away from the walls," I said. The graffiti was backing up at each of the doors, bunching up in a squiggle with oddly precise curves and angles before spilling up and around the doorframe or curving around the sill. "We need to move back, take cover—"

"Oh my God," Ranger screamed. "What the hell *is* that?"

I looked up, and saw Zipperface stepping out at the other end of the canyon. Even from this distance I couldn't see how I'd ever mistaken him for human: head too wide, arms too thick, legs too short. He was a walking caricature of a man, grinning and evil.

We faced each other briefly; then he raised his glowing, misproportioned arms and graffiti exploded up the walls. Long thin lines leapt up, curving arcs slid through them, the graffiti wove into itself, creating a grid, then a moiré pattern—then filigreed flames.

Zipperface stood there at the center of a spiderweb of graffiti—then he ripped open those metal teeth and belched out a spray of flame which rippled out through the spiderweb, caught along the walls and began screaming towards us, turning the alley into a canyon of fire.

"We're totally exposed here," I said, backpedaling towards the door. "Everyone, back inside, let's go out the back way—"

"Don't!" Ranger said, tackling me just as I got to the door. We rolled aside just as the flames screeched around us and coiled around the door in a tongue of flame. She grabbed me around the waist and lifted with surprising strength, half pushing, half dragging me away from the entrance and around my car. "There *is* no back way out!"

"But all the squatters . . . " I said, horrified, as the flames roiled around the door, licking out at my car, trying to reach around it to get us. "They're trapped, we have to get them out."

"This used to be an arms warehouse," Ranger cried. "The walls are a foot thick. There's no way out but the front. Going back in is suicide—oh, Christ, my *dog's* in there too—"

"Jesus," I said. I looked around, ran to A6's window planter, picked up a pot and hurled it through it through the plate glass window. "Fire! Fire! Everyone out! EVERYONE OUT!"

Ranger grabbed my hand and pulled, jerking me back from the window as fire leapt from the door to the window frame. A window to our left smashed open, a metal towel rack complete with toiletries flying out and scattering on the ground. A naked man, damp with shower water and hair still filled with suds, leapt through and tripped, bright arterial blood spraying out from his leg where the glass cut it. Keif was screaming, holding his hands to his face, a horrible flickering light beaming through his fingers and the seams of his clothes while Drive whapped him with his motorcycle jacket, trying to put it out. The door to A6 opened, and there were screams inside as the fire leapt inside the unit. And then the fire wrapped around my car.

My Prius exploded in a yellow ball of flame, a loud clap hammering my ears an instant after the hot wash of heat stung my face. A yellow fireball roiled up into black smoke, there was the vicious sparkle of evil magic, then the battery caught, fire and magic, blasting the hatch out, slamming into the opposite wall in a blue-white bolt of magic that was half fire, half lightning.

We were knocked back off our feet as broken glass fell from shattered windows up and down the alley. After a dazed moment, Ranger hauled me to my feet and yelled something.

"What?" I said, barely able to hear her over the ringing, the flames, the screams. Then it sank in. "My car! He blew up my *car!* I should never have called it the blue bomb."

"Forget it! Get out of here," Ranger said. "He's after you! He'll kill you if you stay. He'll kill *us* if you stay! Go now, while the confusion lasts!"

"But the people inside—"

"*I'll* save them," Ranger said, "if I have to drag them all out myself! You get out of here—go on! Before he catches sight of you again!"

I stared past her into the confusion. Between the smoke, the flames, and the people spilling out into the alley, I couldn't see Zipperface; ergo, he couldn't see me. I took one glance into Ranger's eyes, then turned and ran. In shame, in fear, in hope that I would get away. I ran.

Not just from Zipperface, though; because Ranger was right—and Counselor Lee was right, and even Detective Bonn was right. The worse things got, the more that people would start looking for an answer to stop it—and the day I had been freed, in both places the police would know that where I went, the fires restarted.

You didn't need to be Sherlock Holmes to put two and two together.

The first person the police would look for would be me.

---

43. NO SAFE HAVEN

I stumbled back to Lee Street and the nearest gas station I could find and called for a cab, then ducked inside the restroom to wash up. God. Whoever was behind Zipperface—he'd killed my car. He'd killed my car and my friends—and he'd almost killed me. Twice now.

My hands were shaking as I splashed water on my face. As the water trickled down, I heard police sirens and fire trucks, and stayed put. Only after someone knocked impatiently on the bathroom door did I nervously slip out and skulk among the cola cases until my ride came.

As the West End receded and the driver rode quietly on, I started to think I was paranoid: of course the police were called to the scene. After the cab dropped me off at the hotel, however, I went with my gut, quickly grabbing toiletries, my riding gear and helmet, then hopped on my Vespa and took off, just before a police car swooped up to the hotel, sirens blazing.

I figured using my credit card would be a dead giveaway, so I drove up far north up I-85. I felt that magical tingle again as I passed the Perimeter, but I kept going, all the way to the Mall of Georgia, and withdrew as much as the parking lot ATM would let me.

While it was spitting out money I called Dad. He didn't answer, probably zonked out on the recliner, so I left a brief message. Then, the moment the receipt was in my hand, I hopped back on my bike and headed back south. With any luck, they'd think I was fleeing to South Carolina—when instead I was going to ground in the city, *my* city, Atlanta.

I rode the first few miles on the highway to get some distance—always a danger even when the police weren't *specifically* looking for me, as the Georgia

Highway Patrol sometimes pulled me over just to try to figure out whether the Vespa was a motorcycle or a moped. But by the time I reached Gwinnett Place Mall I knew the area well enough to take the surface streets, slipping off onto mini-mall infested Pleasant Hill before finally escaping to the wide pine-lined lots, wooden fences and aging split-levels that dotted sleepy Old Norcross Road.

I was still OTP—outside the Perimeter—but the suburbs were well trafficked enough that I didn't worry about trolls. Soon, I found a Waffle House where Old Norcross crossed Buford Highway, swallowed my pride, and settled at the counter to take stock.

No one noticed me. Wearing old jeans, a brown bomber jacket, riding gloves and a bandana, I didn't look much like myself. In fact, with the bandana covering both my deathhawk and the tattoos on my temples, I looked *normal.* It was an odd, good feeling. I found myself enjoying *not* being stared at, swigging sweet tea, and having a damn good waffle.

In theory, they couldn't pin the fires on me, but I was already accused of one crime I didn't commit, and everyone had warned me juries simply didn't understand magic. So I needed my freedom of action, at least a little while longer, until I could either figure out how to cut off the graffiti's power source, or find the prick who was orchestrating it, or both. And to do that I needed a place to crash, snag some Internet, and make some phone calls.

But who to call? I *really* wanted to leave mundanes out of it. Half my friends had nearly gotten killed trying to take on Valentine, and I didn't want the karate club getting burned alive by Zipperface, or Michael Bell arrested for aiding a fugitive.

The Edgeworld was also cut off from me. After the werehouse fire, I had tried and failed to contact Lord Buckhead, the werehouse itself was gone of course, the werekin now hated me, my contacts at the Oakdale Clan were dead . . . including Calaphase. *Damnit.*

Thinking more broadly, there was the Underground, the network of tunnels under the city. But it was werekin territory, and Philip had mapped all of the Underground that *I* knew, so he could find me, if he was forced to. Being a fugitive *sucked*: like walking a minefield, there were many places to step, few of them safe, and no way to tell which from which.

Finally, I swallowed my pride and called the Vampire Consulate. After all, it was a Consulate; who knows what that *really* meant, but maybe Saffron could offer me some temporary protection until the police sorted out I was innocent.

"Junior Van Helsing Detective Agency," a sweet voice answered. "This is Nagli."

"Hello, Nagli," I said. "This is—"

"I know," Nagli said quickly. She sounded strained. "Caller ID."

"Ah," I said. "Actually, I was calling on Consulate business."

"I know," she repeated. "Each number has its own line."

"Uh-huh," I said. This was damn peculiar. "That's good to know."

"Your discretion is appreciated," Nagli said, voice suddenly hushed. "Don't—"

And then there was commotion in the background, a new voice talking. Nagli started to respond, but there was a sudden racket, as if the phone had been ripped from her grasp.

"Who is this?" said the new voice—Saffron. I didn't respond, and she said, "Frost."

"Yes," I said.

"Darkrose is *gone*," Saffron said, voice acid. "Went hunting for three other vampires gone missing—and never came back. You were too busy with your new friend apparently."

"I'm sorry," I said, but I couldn't leave it at that. "Calaphase is . . . gone too."

"I know," Saffron said, some of the acid leaching away. "I'm sorry . . . *Dakota*. And I heard you were arrested." She paused, then asked, "How are you holding up?"

"Fine," I managed, "until I was attacked again."

"When?" Saffron said.

"Just now," I said, and told her. "I left the Candlesticks on fire. It happened less than twenty four hours after I got out of jail. And a fire started when I went back to Calaphase's to pick up my car. I think the police are looking for me."

"Almost certainly," Saffron said. "Since you got out, fires have broken out all over the city. Dozens of people have been killed. The media's talking about a *plague* of arson, which is bad enough . . . but I'm just waiting for someone to break out the *t*-word."

"Terrorism," I said. "Oh, flying fuck me. Saffron . . . I may need some help here."

"Damnit," Saffron said. "I can't take you in. You're not wearing the collar."

"Can't you—" I said, and then let the words hang there. "Forget it."

"I . . . I took you off the roster," she said, embarrassed. "The police can't search the Consulate without a warrant, but if someone saw you, if they get even a whiff, they can get one. If you were a vampire, I could actually give you asylum, but for human ser—uh, don't take this the wrong way, Dakota, but for human servants, there's negotiation involved. If the police come knocking, unless you're *already* on the roster, I'd have to give you up."

"And they *will* come knocking," I said—I knew how this worked. "You're my ex."

Saffron was quiet a moment. "Look, Dakota. I can't aid you. I'm a public official. I *have* to follow the law. It will raise a stink if it even *sounds like* I told someone to help a fugitive. And I think you should expect the police will be watching all of your friends too."

"Damnit," I said. I needed to go *completely* off the radar. "All right. Look . . . I should go."

"All right, Dakota," Saffron said. "Well, then . . . good luck."

She hung up.

44. QUANTUM MAGIC

There was one more person to call: Jinx. I didn't immediately get an answer, but then I realized I knew one person who was *technically* a mundane, but was as deeply involved in the Edgeworld as I was, if not more—and through him, I'd get access to Jinx for free.

"Doctor Zetetic!" Doug said happily into the phone. "*Guten morgen* to you! Thanks for calling so early, I know it's the crack ass of dawn in Berlin—"

"Doug?" I said slowly. *Doctor Zetetic?* It took me a moment, but then I got it: Zetetic was the original name of the *Skeptical Inquirer*. Doug was covering my identity. Of course the police would talk to him. One of my known associates. *Great.* "You know who this is?"

"Yeah, yeah, yeah," he said breezily. "Anyway, I did talk to Finkelstein about your problem, and it's tied to the Bekenstein bound. Care to talk some loop quantum gravity?"

"Sure," I said, even more slowly, "if you're free to talk."

"Oh, yeah, yeah," he said. "What you're dealing with is a quantitized bijection between disjoint manifolds—I'm sorry, am I bothering you guys? Sorry. Hold on a minute, Doc."

"Sure," I said, hearing voices, then some bumping around. The line got a little more quiet, and I asked, "Doug? You still there?"

"Yeah, Doc," he said, voice tense—and he was still coding the conversation. "I'm going to take a walk outside. I was over at my fiancée's, but the police are questioning her."

Oh shit. They'd *already* gotten to my friends and family. "I hope it's nothing serious."

The line was silent for a moment. "I'm afraid it is," he said grimly. "Remember she was attacked last year? Well, the police have reopened that case. It may be related to a rash of arsons that's hitting the city. The last was a warehouse fire, easily killed twenty-five squatters."

"God have mercy," I said. "All those warehouses, with only one exit."

"Yeah, it was pretty fucking horrific," Doug said, his voice a bit shaken. "They're making a huge deal of it. I expect they'll interview anyone even remotely involved."

Damnit, damnit, damnit! "Well, Doug . . . thanks for the heads up."

"No problem," Doug said. He sighed with relief. "OK, I think it's safe to talk."

"Thank God." I filled him in on the details of last night's attack, and Calaphase's death—how we fell through the graffiti, how Calaphase fell into it—and how his blood was sucked out by what should have been marks on the pavement. "Please tell me you found answers."

"Oddly enough, I cracked it helping Cinnamon with her homework, though the answer ultimately involved loop quantum gravity," he said. "But it's easier to think of it like . . . like a magic door that shows distorted images of both its source and target."

"Doug, don't patronize me," I said. "I know what it's like, but I need to know how this thing works to fight it. I dug into the literature, and there's no such thing as a magic door outside of a fairy tale. We're dealing with deeply hidden magic that's never surfaced in the Edgeworld."

"And I think I know why," Doug said. "Have you heard of the Bekenstein bound?"

"Doug, I read *Scientific American* more than *you* do," I said. "It's something to do with the holographic universe, right? Somehow, deep down, we're really two-dimensional?"

"Right. Deep down, *you are your interface*," he said. "In quantum mechanics, if a thing acts the exact same way as another thing, it *is* that thing. According to Bekenstein, you have no way of telling the 'real me' from a surface that absorbs and transmits the same particles."

"So if you had a magic cave painting, there could be a whole world behind its surface," I said. "*If* you could paint it. But no one could paint a whole world down to its particles."

"But they do in the movies, armies of Wookies on alien worlds," Doug said. I started to protest, but he said, "In the computer, procedurally generated—simple rules that can be applied over and over again to populate a whole crowd and forest. But it takes millions of steps—"

"He can do that, and he doesn't even need a computer," I said, with a tingly 'aha' feeling. "He's created graffiti that can draw itself—a self propagating intent, we'd call it." I explained I'd seen it first with fire at the tagger's playground, then at the Candlesticks.

"I strongly suspected that," Doug said. "Lines of graphomancy that use mana to make *more* lines, one idea leading to another, a recursive pattern, unfolding forever, an infinite conceptual field. There's no *limit* to how far magic can build on magic—"

"If you have the mana," I said. "But he'd never get enough to create a whole world."

"That's where I'm going," Doug said. "To link space, I think he's using magic to create a 'spin network.' But a magic cave painting that held a whole world would take as much mana as creating a small universe. But if the cave painting mapped between two spaces—"

"If it was a gateway," I said. "It's a magical gateway."

"Exactly," Doug said. "If the painting is mapping points in one space to another, then there's no need to create a whole world. All the geometry of the painting would need to do is create the map. That spin network could be atomically thin, *magically* thin."

"That sounds like surface-to-surface link," I said, "but Calaphase and I seemed to travel through an actual space, if a distorted funhouse version of one."

"You can create *arbitrary* geometry with a spin network," Doug said. "He could create a twisted little pocket space propped up by several tags. In fact, I'm guessing *all* the tags are connected together, like a network—and it will get stronger the more that are plugged in."

"Jeez, Doug, that's heavy grade magic," I said. "How am I going to fight this shit? This guy is a Michelangelo of the genre. According to Drive, he could make his tags look like anything if he wanted to. Any reasonably sized tag could be one of his traps."

"No," Doug said. "You *can* fight it, because I can tell you what to look for. Jinx and I think the spin network will show up as some repeated pattern, like a grid or a spiral."

"There *is* a spiral that's *like* a grid," I said. "There are coiling vines and barbed wire that showed up in almost every tag, looping tightly at the center to make a grid like a sunflower's. It's the vines, Doug, the spiral of vines. That's your spin network."

"Maybe," Doug said. "I thought of that, but they don't seem to cover the whole tag."

"No, they don't," I said. Damnit. Every time I thought I had figured out how the tags worked, I ran into a brick wall. We thought it was graphomancy, quantum physics, whatever, but there were always missing pieces to the magic, like something . . . hidden beneath the surface.

And then it hit me. "He's using multiple layers! I thought it was oil chalk, but Officer Horscht found an aerosol spray can. Spray painted graffiti isn't like tattoos. It's layers of paint."

"I thought tattoos had layers too," Doug said. "I've seen you go over designs—"

"To build up colors, but it all ends up as plaques of pigment in the dermis—a single layer that's magically active. But we already know the graffiti doesn't work that way." I explained what Keif had explained to me about whitewashing the tags and using induction. "He can use several layers of paint to build up a pattern as complex as needed and we'd never see the whole of it—except the spiral of vines, which *have* to reach outside the canvas to pull someone in."

"Right. And look for echoes. If it *is* a gateway, you'll see echoes of your environment in the tag, and maybe distorted pictures of the target on the other end."

"Like ghost images in a two-way mirror," I said.

"It's more like a television. The idea is simple, but the implementation is *not*," Doug said. "There is *too much* physics involved. There is *no way* a backwoods graphomancer cooked this up on his or her own. None whatsoever."

I was silent for a moment. "Like I said, maybe it's hidden knowledge. Some ancient wizarding trick, developed in secret, hidden for centuries—"

"Maaaybe," Doug said. "But I looked, Jinx looked, even you looked, and the three of us found bupkis. Now, maybe you're up against an ancient cult of wizards, with magic beyond anything that I could find at the Harris School of Magic, or maybe some modern wizard with access to a physics lab. Or maybe, just maybe, it isn't even human knowledge at all."

"Not . . . human," I said. "You mean like . . . vampire? Werewolf? Fae?"

"No," Doug said. "The answer to your question combined thousands of years of magic and decades of study of the output of two-mile-long particle accelerators. I strongly, *strongly* doubt anyone just stumbled onto this on their own just dicking around. It would be like finding the design of a solid state laser in da Vinci's notebooks, centuries before quantum theory."

"Go back to the *not human* part," I said. "If it's not human knowledge . . . "

"The graffiti links two spaces," Doug said, "but the other side doesn't have to be *ours*."

---

45. THE DETECTIVE FROM SPACE

I spent the night in a box under a bridge halfway to Macon, Georgia. I had woven my way through the heart of Atlanta on surface streets, then risked exiting the Perimeter again on the highway, heading to Macon but intending to cut back towards Blood Rock.

The tingle as I went OTP was invigorating, but by the time I passed Stockbridge I was flagging. I turned off a few miles later, wound through smaller and smaller country roads until I found an industrial looking area with a small bridge running over a creek. I didn't see any signs of trolls or other Edgeworld nasties, so I pushed the Vespa under the bridge, stole a box out of a nearby Dumpster, crept back under the bridge and into the box, and went to sleep.

Early, early the next morning, a truck running over the bridge woke me. I stretched, sore and cramped, and stood up. My neck hurt, my back hurt, and then both hurt more when I abruptly ducked down as I heard voices. After a moment the voices faded, and then I saw a couple of workmen walking down the road, turning in to the very place I'd stolen the box.

I leaned back against the bridge and took stock. I expected to feel sorry for myself, but I didn't. Sleeping in a box had been cold and uncomfortable, but it had ended in a new day. Even the dingy, trash-strewn underbelly of the bridge was brightened by sun flickering off the burbling water. I saw a little scribble, near the abutment, stared at it curiously, and pegged it as a hobo sign—a graffiti precursor—that marked this place as a good rest stop. And it was indeed.

This too would pass, like the water slipping by in the stream.

"I can sleep in a box under a bridge," I murmured to myself. "I can do anything."

So my next step: get real help, and with all of my other contacts dry, that meant Arcturus. Of course, he didn't answer, not after any number of rings, not after three calls. I don't know why he even had a phone. And I certainly couldn't call Zinaga.

I considered trying to slip in uninvited, but if my 'banishment' was real, the last thing I needed to do was show up at Arcturus' door with a horde of vampires and vampire thugs on my heels. Heck, even if I did make it, the first thing Zinaga would do would be to sell me out.

Come to think of it, there was no guarantee Arcturus would receive me. Zinaga had tried to poison the well. What I really needed was something to get in his good graces. And for the man who eschews material goods . . . the best currency I could think of was a favor.

So I needed to get into Blood Rock . . . and to get on Arcturus' good side.

There might be a way to do both at the same time. Two birds, one stone.

I thumbed backwards through my text messaging log. January, December, November—and then I found it. I swallowed. I *was* going to do this. My thumb hovered over the call button; but I wasn't that brave. Instead, I *texted* . . . the vampire Transomnia: **<<Need to talk. Coming to Blood Rock. Be cool.>>**

There was no response. I wasn't certain I'd get one. It had been months since he'd texted me after kidnapping Cinnamon, and he could have ditched that phone. Even then, he was an old-school vampire, probably asleep. I stared off into the distance, thinking.

Then the phone rang, and I nearly dropped it. I answered immediately. "Transomnia?"

"I don't want to know why you'd think he'd be calling you," Philip said coldly.

"Philip!" I said, brightening. After all the static he, McGough and Rand had given me, I hadn't even thought of actually *calling* him. "Look, I didn't know who else to turn to. I—"

"Dakota," he said firmly. "I understand why you ran. I might even have done the same thing. But I can't help you, except to tell you—*turn off your phone. We can track you by it.*"

I hung on the phone, stunned. "Philip, you know I didn't do it."

"I know, and I know you're probably working the problem right now, but you're wanted for murder and arson. So hang up, and *turn off* your personal tracking and recording device," Philip said. "You spent a *hell* of a long time on the phone last night—I'm surprised they didn't pick you up already. If I could find you, it's only a matter of time before someone else will."

"But Philip—"

"Between Stockbridge and McDonough," Philip said. "Under a bridge, it looks like."

"Damnit!" I said, killing the call, then powering off the phone. *Damnit, damnit, damnit!* I *knew* cell phones were insecure, and had gone and been a fucking *amateur* anyway. Quickly I gathered my things and pushed the Vespa out into the street, started her up, and hit the road.

I puttered up State Road 20 until I got close to Conyers, then pulled off and got some food, again at a Waffle House, tucked just off the highway. I got directions to the nearest library from the waitress, and headed down there to try to get some Internet.

The library was larger than I'd expected, a two-story affair with large triangular roofs and a little gazebo-like structure near the entrance. I got an out-of-state visitor's pass so I didn't have to use my library card, fired up a computer, and started to figure out how to find Transomnia.

That's right. That was the first stage of my brilliant plan: go straight up to the door of the bad guys and knock. The green-haired vampire, Transomnia's apparent second in command—what was her name, Nyissa?—had snarked that I didn't know where I was, but I hadn't lied: there were only so many roads in Blood Rock.

And as for what house on what road? They'd held me in a big room, but not a warehouse: more like a furnished basement. That meant a multi-level house, possibly new, which in turn ruled out most of Blood Rock, which was primarily single-storied and falling apart.

They'd been threatened by my presence, which mean they were near Old Town. They *also* had the Sanctuary Stone, which means they had to be close to the Rock itself—if not right on top of it, nearby, on a ley line intersecting the Rock.

That left a lot to look for, but I had satellite and aerial imagery from MapQuest, Yahoo, Microsoft and even Google to help me out. So, feeling like a detective from space, I zoomed in on Blood Rock and started looking for Transomnia.

My real goal was ultimately Arcturus, but MapQuest showed there was no "back door" to Arcturus' pad: just steep hills and deep creeks. I was no woodsman, nor did I want to get shot cutting through backwoods Georgia, much less find myself stumbling around in a ravine while vampires tracked me down.

At the front door, I was pretty sure that I'd be spotted by Steyn or his peons. In the short time I'd been in town last, I'd seen Steyn twice. And now, Steyn could do more than turn a blind eye to the vamps or run me out of town: he could turn me over to the APD.

So I had to approach the vampires directly, hands up. I looked for what felt like hours, and was about to give up when, absently closing a window I was done with, I saw it.

Inadvertently I'd created two windows with two different views of the same area, side by side. It was the top of Blood Rock hill proper, zoomed in on the new complex of houses that I'd seen on the map. The complex was half built in one set of pictures dating from a year ago, nearly complete in the other, six months later—with something that looked like a mansion or clubhouse off a narrow access road, not visible on any street map, but clear as day from the air, especially in the shots taken during construction.

I tilted my head, looking at the complex of roofs, barely visible in the trees. It felt right: new, multistoried, on the Rock itself. And then I pulled up the map of ley lines: the building was smack dab at the crossing of three of them, with the most powerful line going through the Rock itself.

"Gotcha," I murmured.

I wrote down the address (and two or three other likely candidates) and closed up shop, much to the relief of a young college student waiting on the machine. I found a nearby Chic-Fil-A, gratefully chowed down, then hopped back on the Vespa and headed to Blood Rock.

It was nearly dark by the time I found my way through the winding roads to Blood Rock. Once again I felt a tingle as I passed the boundary . . . and then, a slowly growing headache, just like when Nyissa had banished me. I'd looked into the magic: it wasn't enough to hurt me, but, like Nyissa had said, if the vamps still had the Sanctuary Stone, they'd know I was here.

But I didn't let that stop me. I just drove to the new subdivision atop the Rock, where I found my path barred by a simple, unmarked gate with an equally simple buzzer and camera. I stopped a few feet short, nerving myself to drive up and press that buzzer.

Before I did, a car passed me on its way to the gate. A hand reached out and pressed the button. Moments later, the gate slowly slid back. I debated tailgating. Transomnia's guards might take that as a threat, but the point of driving all the way to their door was to force an audience. On the other hand, I might have guessed wrong and could be tailgating a man into his home.

And then the man in the car looked back at me: not a vampire, not a thug, just a pleasant good-old-boy Georgia businessman in a black suit. He didn't have the hard look people get when strange women on motorcycles are sitting outside their driveway waiting for them to come home. In fact, he actually smiled, staring at me, curious, then started to turn forward.

"Hey, bud," I called. "I'm a bit lost, and I'm wondering if I'm at the right place."

"All right, let's see if we can straighten you out," the man said, in such a classic Georgia accent I imagined 'Bud' was probably his real name. "Looking for Stone Rose Sanctuary?"

My eyes widened. Good Lord, the vampires were brazen: the seals on the Sanctuary Stone *were* roses. They certainly weren't trying to hide. "That . . . sounds like it."

"Applying for a job?" Bud said, looking me up and down. "Or are you a client?"

My mouth opened. I had no way to translate what he was saying into something I understood. Finally I managed, "Looking up a friend who works here. And you?"

"Oh! I'm not, you know, staying at the, ah, inn," Bud said. His face reddened a bit, then split into a wide grin. "Just here for the food. Great restaurant. Follow me in."

He rolled the car forward, and I started the Vespa up and followed.

As I rode through, the gate squealed shut behind me. So this was it: I was heading through creaking iron gates towards a mysterious chalet nestled deep in the woods. My Vespa would be taken away by mysterious valets just as the sun would set, trapping me to dine under candlelight under the watchful eyes of predatory vampires, served by black-garbed waiters trained not to notice when their masters started noshing on you instead.

Or not to notice when Transomnia had me dragged out and shot.

Either way, I was committed. I was going to ask for help from my worst enemy.

46.   BEARD THE LION

"My name is Dakota Frost, but I doubt I'm on the guest list," I told the maître d', tucking my gloves into my helmet. "I'm just here to see Lord Transomnia."

The Stone Rose Sanctuary was plantation-style rather than Victorian, new rather than old; but everything else was as I expected. A valet did indeed whisk my Vespa and Bud's Volvo away, a doorman opened a door onto a plush red foyer, where a black-garbed maître d' ushered Bud off to join his party before returning his attention to me. He stared at me, not really seeming to comprehend. Apparently I wasn't dressed fancy enough to overcome the language barrier.

"Lord . . . Transomnia?" the thin, hawkish man asked. His face was lined, and he had a long shag of graying hair, almost a mullet; but his eyebrows were dark and his eyes sharp, making him look far younger. "I'm afraid I'm not familiar with that name."

"Really?" I said, hopes falling. But this place had been here for at least six months, back when Transomnia had been trying to hide from Valentine by playing junior wharf rat at the Oakdale Clan. At least one of his people had been here. "What about the Lady Nyissa?"

At *her* name, the maître d' rankled. *Jackpot.* "The proprietor of the Sanctuary," he said crisply, "prefers her privacy. The Stone Rose Café has a policy not to mention her, *or* her associates, by name. If you are a client of the club, however—"

"As I said, I'm not a diner or a client," I said, glancing around the foyer. "I'm here on personal business with one of the associates of the proprietor of the Sanctuary."

The front door opened, and a charming older couple walked in, a cheerful, vaguely Asian man and an older woman with hair strikingly dyed half black, half blond. She smiled at me, then murmured to her companion, and a gold nose ring sparkled as she turned her head. Interesting.

"*Please*," the maître d' said quietly. "Are you a friend of the proprietor?"

"No, I'm her worst enemy," I said, and the headache I'd been nursing suddenly got a little worse—probably the effect of the Sanctuary Stone. *Interesting.* "Well, technically, the worst enemy of her master, the Lord, uh, 'T'. I called ahead. They should be expecting me."

The maître d' stared at me, then the new couple. He raised his hand to them for a moment's grace, then leaned forward to me. "Ma'am," he whispered, "the proprietor and her associates are not . . . disposed . . . at this time—"

"I understand they may not be up yet," I said, smiling. Messing with this guy was turning out to be quite fun. "I can wait in the throne room like last time."

"Theme rooms are reserved for *clients*," the maître d' said, his confusion and reluctance shifting into stern suspicion. "If you would like to reserve one on an ad hoc basis—"

"Excuse me," said a dark-suited man, stepping out of a side room to catch the maître d' by the elbow. "The Lady informs me we have another, um, trespassing situation, like we did a couple of weeks back, so the guards will need to—"

"Hi," I said, waving my fingers at him cheerfully.

The dark-suited man looked up at me briefly and did a double-take. "Holy sh—" he said, hand going to his breast pocket, then freezing there as he caught sight of the couple behind me. His eyes flickered between me and the couple. He made a strangled noise.

"Dakota Frost," I said, even more cheerfully. "We met in the van last week?"

"What—yeah," he said, relaxing slightly, hand still inside his jacket. "Uh . . . yeah."

"I can wait in the throne room until you guys figure out how to fit me into your schedule."

"Uh . . . yeah," he said. He couldn't take his eyes off my tattoos. "Let's do that."

"Should I put up my hands?" I asked.

His eyes flickered again to the couple. "No, but . . . put the gloves and helmet back on."

"Uh, sure," I said. "I guess I am more dangerous naked."

I wished I had a picture of the maître d's mortified look as the older couple laughed. I smiled at them, popped my gloves back on, then the helmet.

"I hope you guys enjoy your meal this evening," I said.

"Oh, we're not here for dinner," the woman said, smiling. "We're here for the club."

And with that last word, it hit me. *That* was how vampires made their money: prostitution. Vampires were dark, edgy and attractive, and their bite was damn near orgasmic. That vampires traded in sex didn't surprise me, but there was more to it than that: there was the club, the clients,—and despite their trash talk, Transomnia's band of vamps had done little more than scare me. After the initial assault, they hadn't done me physical harm.

The reactions of the guards seemed to confirm my perception of their reluctance. In a side room, three surrounded me while the first man searched me thoroughly, but not a one of them drew a gun. That was encouraging. That they were all packing, not so much.

"Damn, she's taller than she looked in the video," one of the new guards said.

"And throws a hell of a punch, too," said another, bearded guard, glaring at me—and I recognized him as the tough bruiser who'd attacked me first on my last trip to Blood Rock. He looked considerably different cleaned up and in a suit. "For a girl, that is."

The new guard chuckled, and I glared. "Would you like a demonstration?"

"Settle down," the first guard said, as he finished patting me down.

"I told you, I'm not armed," I said. "Not so much as a toothpick."

"We'll see about that," he said, pulling out an airport-style scanning wand. It made a *wzzowing* noise as he ran it over my jacket, and he pulled my cell phone out of my pocket.

"Do *not* turn that on," I said. "I'm on the run. The police can track you with that."

His mouth quirked up. "You really think they're tracking you?"

"Certain," I said. "My source in the DEI called to warn me."

"*You* have a *source* in the DEI?" he said, laughing.

"Ex-boyfriend," I said.

His face hardened. "Ah," he said. "Good contact to have."

The bearded guard cleared his throat. "This is nuts," he said. "We should just—"

"We should just what?" the first guard said sharply.

"Eat right, and practice clean living," I said.

"Unbelievable," the first guard said, motioning with his hand.

I kept the same smile plastered on my face that I'd had since walking in the door. They had kicked the shit out of me earlier. But I was here to ask for help, so I sat on my anger.

They led me down a winding stairway, then down a well-appointed corridor with many doors on each side. And then I was back in the throne room I'd seen before: dark curtains, elegant couches, the same metal chair in a lowered area of flagstones, and the same steps rising to a medieval style throne . . . and behind it, the Sanctuary Stone—*wailing*.

This was magic I understood: a single resonator inscribed with graphomantic runes, charged up by the intersection of three ley lines, and activated by blood magic. The great disc of stone was humming, glowing red, brightening visibly as I approached. The guards clearly could see it—the first one actually looked shocked—but clearly only *I* had trouble looking at it. I wondered if this is what vampires felt looking at crosses.

And then I realized the Stone *did* work on the same principle as crosses and vampires: it was feeding my own hostility back to me. But I didn't need to be hostile to Transomnia, didn't *want* to be hostile to him. I was coming to him for a favor, but after all he and his had done, it was hard to let go of the anger.

How had Saffron defused that cross, with something like a breathing exercise? What had Darren and Rory said about breathing? The bridge between your conscious and unconscious? I drew in a breath, let it out. Let it go. The Stone began to calm. I felt for the thread of anger, released it. The throbbing glow faded; the sound receded, as did my headache.

"That's better, now," I said, stepping forward to stand before the throne.

"Holy living fuck," the bearded guard said. "Did she just turn off our early warning system by *breathing?*"

"Something like that," I said, smiling. I was forcing the smile, but I held onto it, forced myself to try to believe it. They still looked wary, so to head them off before they decided to club me or something, I said, "Relax. It only works if I mean you no harm."

Now that I could think, I glanced around: rich curtains, muted lighting, and comfortable chaise lounges, each with a view of the pit where I stood. The chamber shifted in my eyes from the throne room of a citadel of vampires to a performance space in a well-appointed private dungeon. Of course, I knew that in Saffron's case, those were one and the same.

All this wasn't the work of Transomnia. It *couldn't* have been; it was being built while he was ostensibly the thrall of Mirabilus, and playing flunky of Calaphase. That meant that, like the maître d' had implied, technically, this was *Nyissa's* pad.

Transomnia wasn't setting up a criminal empire in the backwoods of Georgia. He was laying low from the police at Nyissa's bondage-and-discipline bed-and-breakfast.

"Weren't you just here?" a female voice purred. "Didn't you pledge not to come back?"

I turned, and as expected, saw Nyissa, the deliciously pale, green-eyed, purple haired vampire who had threatened me before, leaning against the throne, twirling the metal poker she carried as if it was a riding crop. Can you say *DOM-in-a-trix?* "I had no-one else to turn to."

"*You* need *our* help?" came a male voice. The goateed vampire I had seen last time now stepped out from behind the other side of the throne. He didn't quite fit the B&D B&B theme, but then he might be one of Transomnia's imports rather than Nyissa's co-dom. "Really?"

"Not precisely," I said. "I need to speak to Arcturus, my old master. So I'm here to beg permission to return to Blood Rock."

"Here to beg? Wonderful," Transomnia said *just behind me.* I flinched as he stepped around me and climbed the steps to the throne, where the Stone was glowing again. "Absolutely wonderful. Please, have a seat in the chair. But where's your suit, Dakota Frost?"

"She did look good in it," Nyissa purred, glancing curiously at the Stone.

"My . . . suit?" I said, calming my breath. Then I remembered the awful getup they'd stuck me in when they'd first brought me here. I started to hit back with a smart remark, then realized the truth was even better. "Probably burned to a crisp when my car exploded."

And then I pulled off my helmet. The vampires and thralls immediately snarled, and one of the guards reached for me. "Oh, relax, everybody," I said, setting the helmet on the floor beside me. "I *can't hear* in that thing. You don't like it, shoot me. I'm not here to fight."

"Such insolence," the goateed vamp said. "We do not permit that here—"

"And yet she speaks the truth," Nyissa said, surprised, seemingly at herself. "I don't think she could even stand before the Stone if she meant us harm."

"Whether she means us harm or not, she cannot speak to us this way."

"Enough," Transomnia said firmly. "Everyone, shut up, unless I owe you my life."

All the other vamps and thralls froze, uncertain, and Transomnia said, even more firmly, "That means, everyone except Dakota Frost. Please, sit down. How did you find us?"

"Google Maps," I said, sitting. There were choked laughs, and I shook my head. "You were threatened by my visit—and you had the Stone. That meant you were close to the center of Blood Rock. This room, on the other hand, is large, and underground, and perhaps new. Most of Blood Rock is small, single-storied, and falling apart. Really, it wasn't that hard."

"Do the police know?" he said.

"I didn't tell them where you *are*," I said, raising my hand. "But you made me late for a court appointment, and the judge made me make a statement to the police."

"Damnit," Transomnia hissed. "Frost, we had a deal—"

"They know what happened to me," I said, raising my hand, "but not what I deduced from it. If they haven't found you already, they're probably not looking. Tracking down the crazy story of a murder suspect is probably the last thing on the police's agenda."

"A murder suspect?" Transomnia said. "*You?*"

"Valentine," I said.

"Valentine!" Nyissa hissed. "How could they accuse you of murdering that sick fuck?"

"No good deed goes unpunished," Transomnia said, frowning. "There is no way they could know what really happened in that room. I took the security tapes."

"Of course you did. So it's my word against a dead man," I said, rubbing my forehead. "A national hero—look, could you please turn that off? It's giving me a headache."

"Turn . . . off?" Transomnia said, baffled—then he looked back at the Stone, which was humming and glowing again. "But if you do not mean us harm, then why—"

"If you think I'm not pissed off at being charged for murder, you don't know me."

Transomnia laughed. "I don't think I know you," he said, "but do it."

"My Lord," Nyissa said, protesting.

"Oh, come on, unbanish me already. The spell takes, like, a minute. You can always rebanish me later," I said. Nyissa glanced at Transomnia, who nodded. Then she tromped up the stairs and began waving her hand over the Stone. Almost immediately, my head felt better. "If you please," I said, "I need to mention some names you've asked me not to."

Transomnia's eyes gleamed red. "Go on," he said.

"Calaphase is dead," I said, and Transomnia's mouth quirked up into a smile, then faded into a frown. "Murdered by magic graffiti, along with Revenance and one or maybe two more vampires of the Oakdale Clan. The Gentry has reported—oh, heck, I've lost count . . . "

Transomnia's face grew carefully neutral as I continued. Nyissa finished her spell and the Stone faded into quiet silence, and yet still I kept going through the list of attacks. Nyissa herself pretended to scowl as she descended the steps towards me, but I could see she was spooked.

"The werehouse itself was destroyed by magic graffiti, as was the Candlestick Apartment complex," I said, racking my brain for any other incidents. "Oh, that last one was part of an attack on me personally, the second in as many days—"

"And yet none of this has touched the House Beyond Sleep, or any of the other clans or houses outside the Perimeter," Transomnia said thoughtfully. "Why have you brought all this to my doorstep, Dakota Frost? To spread the curse to us?"

"*No*," I said. "Look, my friends are dying. I've got to stop this, but I have no leads. The police know nothing. Despite weeks of hunting, I've learned next to nothing. I need to speak to someone who has real hidden knowledge. I need to speak to Arcturus."

"And I've forbidden you to come to Blood Rock," Transomnia said slowly, "so you came to *me* . . . to ask for safe passage?"

"For *permission*, like a good little girl," Nyissa laughed, sitting down on the chair arm so her thigh closed the cuff on my wrist with a sudden clank. "How delightfully obsequious."

"Unbelievable," Transomnia said, as Nyissa stretched her poker out and closed the cuff over my other wrist. "You could have tried to sneak past us, ran straight to Arcturus—"

"Oh, that worked so well last time," I said, clanking my wrists experimentally. The cuffs were not locked—but then she glared, and I sat still. "Your little stunt nearly cost me my *child*."

"What?" Transomnia asked sharply. "You don't mean . . . Stray?"

"No—yes, oh, never mind, I'll explain later," I said. "The point is, you're being used. Zinaga, Arcturus' current apprentice, wants him to herself. So she ratted me to you, you made me miss my appointment with him, and that got me on Arcturus' shit list—"

"Back up. Ratted you out . . . to *us?*" Transomnia said, raising an eyebrow—then raising his eyes to Nyissa, who shifted on the arm of the chair. "And again, you did not think to tell me your contact with the skindancers was the master's current apprentice?"

"When you sent me here, you ordered me to establish relationships with the locals," Nyissa said. "And we have *both* survived by keeping our associates compartmentalized."

"True enough. So, Dakota Frost," Transomnia said, eyes returning to me, "what can you offer me in exchange for permission to visit your old master?"

"I didn't come here *just* to ask for permission," I said, and confusion spread among the vampires. "I want a favor too—and I can't offer you anything worth what I'm asking."

Transomnia scowled, and his eyes glowed red. "What favor? Out with it."

"Return the Sanctuary Stone," I said, "and make peace with the tattooed in Blood Rock."

47.   DEAL WITH THE DEVIL

Transomnia sat there stunned for a moment. "You want me to *what?*"

"Rescind the ban on skindancers and their ink in Blood Rock," I said, watching his eyes glow brighter and his lip curl into a snarl. "And return the Sanctuary Stone—"

"What? No. No!" Nyissa said. "The Stone is *mine*."

"Return it to the Stonegrinders," I repeated, "and let Arcturus know I'm behind it."

I flinched back as the other vampires snarled at me and Transomnia just glared. It was easier not to look him in the eyes. He was a vampire, after all. It wasn't safe to look in his eyes. It was easier to look away, to admit that I feared his gaze, that he had me cowed, damn it.

So I looked up and held his gaze, and immediately his eyes blazed. I started to flinch as I felt his aura expanding, challenging my shields; but that's as far as it went: my hackles didn't rise; my knuckles didn't tingle. Apparently the scary vampire mojo could go off like a reflex.

"I'm sorry, Dakota, I didn't quite catch that," Transomnia said, fangs fully visible. "It sounded like you just asked me to roll over before a magician of the brand that enslaved me, and open my gates to his legions. Perhaps I misheard you. Care to run it by me again?"

"All right," I said. "Arcturus is deadly serious about his shit list. I'm in Coventry or something, which basically means I'm exiled until he feels he's pissed on me enough. Even with your permission, I need to get back into his good graces, or he'll just turn me away."

Transomnia stared at me, then laughed. "And so he will turn you away."

"With our permission, of course," Nyissa said, sweetly with an edge of venom.

"*Zinaga* will turn me away," I said, uncomfortable with her so close, "and then promptly rat me out. If she finds out you've given your permission, she'll just turn to Steyn, and I'll be lucky if he just arrests me. Steyn's more of a piece of work than you guys are. I need to bring the both of them something which will make them take me back into their good graces."

"I will *not* return the Sanctuary Stone," Nyissa growled in my ear, and I leaned away from her, best I could in the chair. "This is the Stone's *home*. I *built* this place for it.

"I thought . . . the Stonegrinder's Grove was its home," I said, still leaning away.

"The Grove!" Nyissa said, leaning back in disgust. "It's three miles from the Rock! It barely *works* there! I didn't design it for that distance! I only gave it to them for safekeeping."

"But clearly, Dakota didn't know that, because the Stonegrinders did not tell her," Transomnia said. "Remember the trouble we had retrieving it from the Grove."

"Rescuing it, you mean," Nyissa hissed. "Treated my work like their *birthright*—"

"I'm sorry!" I said, trying to raise my hands, only to have them clank against the cuffs. "I wouldn't have asked had I known it was yours. My request for a treaty still stands, though."

The vampires were silent for a minute, and then Gregor laughed. "Very well," he said. "What does that sound like, my Lord? A four-pint request?"

"No," Nyissa said. Gregor was amused, but she was still *angry*. "No amount of blood, no matter how sweet, is worth shifting the balance of power."

"And yet we must consider the suggestion, once heard," Transomnia said.

"Why?" Gregor said, followed a half second later by, " . . . my Lord?"

"This *is* a vampire court," Transomnia said, steepling his fingers. "There are protocols to be observed when supplicants petition us. All right, Dakota Frost. You had to know we wouldn't take this well. I assume you had a good reason for asking. Let's hear your argument."

"People are dying," I said. "*Vampires* are dying—"

"Yes, yes, and you're the only one who is fighting it, or can stop it?" Nyissa said, and I looked sidelong at her. "You bring us this ridiculous story of remote attacks on other vampires by graffiti, of all things, and then ask us to turn our backs on the real threat right here."

"And yet, we *had* heard of the disturbing attacks on other vampires," Transomnia said pleasantly. "Now why is it, Nyissa, that when you argue with her I feel like taking *her* side—her my worst enemy, and you my most loyal servant?"

While she froze, I leapt in. "No, my *master* is the last best hope to stop it. He's a real old-school magician with hidden knowledge, and we need to get him *involved*. So I need you to do *him* a favor on my behalf, something spectacular, so he'll forget I . . . I blew him off."

Nyissa looked at me with sharp amusement. "To make him forget you stripped your mastermark, you mean," she said, eyes narrowing at me. "According to Zinaga, Arcturus considers it a personal insult. Our favor would need to be spectacular indeed."

"Honoring her request would be spectacular . . . and in the apprentice's interests as well," Transomnia mused. "It would make it unlikely she would rat you out to the authorities."

"Can we not order the apprentice to silence?" Gregor asked.

"Threats to the apprentice will not endear us to the master," Nyissa said, "and are not likely to be effective. Zinaga's powers are growing."

"Look, this . . . plague affects all of us," I said. "And, yes, I am effectively the only one fighting it. The police are tripping over themselves because they can't involve magicians in the investigation. The Consulate can't help because they're vampires, and this stuff will eat them alive. Even you can't help—directly. But you can help me try."

Transomnia frowned. "Assuming I wanted to help you fight this plague," he said, "why should I allow an army of my enemies to flourish in my stronghold?"

"They aren't your enemies. You, personally, have a bad *history* with skindancers," I said. "So you banned skindancing magic here. But this town is *known* for its tattooing, and by acting like gangsters, you've pissed off a townful of people, half of whom have magical powers."

"What does that matter?" Gregor said. "We have the Sanctuary Stone—"

"It's a burglar alarm, not a defense system," I said. "If Nyissa built it, she knows."

"We . . . we could still take them," Nyissa said, resentful and almost . . . pouting?

"I know you're vampires," I said, trying to remain patient, trying to remain calm with her on the arm of my chair. "You're tough, experienced and powerful. You might win the battle, but if it came to that, you'd almost certainly lose the war—you'd have to flee Blood Rock."

"Well, aren't you the peacemaker," Transomnia said, still smiling pleasantly, but more mocking. "Shooting for a secretary of state position in the new administration?" The vampires laughed at me, and I said nothing. "Do you have any suggestions, Dakota Frost?"

"Start with an olive branch to Arcturus," I said. "I need him in this fight, and more importantly, we all need to be on the same side. Send him the message that you're laying off the ban on exposed tattoos, that you're willing to talk. He's respected in Blood Rock."

"Would you like Nyissa to deliver this olive branch for you?" Transomnia said.

"Me?" Nyissa said, standing. "My Lord, what have I done to deserve—"

"Nyissa," Transomnia said. His voice was strangely . . . gentle, almost like he was dancing around a difficult subject. "You may not be powerful, but your personality is strong. No one will mistake delivering a message for weakness. I want the townspeople to start thinking of you as an authority figure, and not just the pretty madam of the brothel."

"I was *right*. This *is* a brothel, a B&D B&B," I said. Were all the vampires like this? Little things Calaphase had said started to add up—all the dates he went on, how cagey he was about his source of income. Even some things Saffron said now sounded suspect; did she have a stable of human clients as well? "For what it's worth . . . I'm sorry you have to live this way."

"Don't be," Transomnia said. "Hiding here beats being a lackey for a serial killer."

"Or running a protection racket," Nyissa said.

"Like the Oakdale Clan was running with the werehouse," I said.

"No," Transomnia said. "We served a valuable function, keeping the werekin hidden. I picked the Clan . . . I picked *Calaphase* because he was an honorable man."

"Yes, he was," I said, eyes tearing up a little. "You made a good choice."

Transomnia's eyes narrowed. He rose from the throne and walked down to me. I squirmed in my chair, trembling, as he turned aside my head to stare at my neck. My heart started beating in my chest as he kept staring at my bite marks.

Finally I said, "It's not an open invitation."

Transomnia smiled, full fangs, and I looked away. "Look at me," he said.

Unwillingly I looked up, eyes off center from his glowing red pupils. All the other vamps were staring down at me hungrily. Now that they had started to think of me as willing meat, you could see them calculating how they might get their own bite of the pie.

"How did you get that wound, Frost?" Transomnia said, relishing the moment.

"I seduced Calaphase," I said, and Transomnia flinched. "Then he got carried away."

"*You* seduced—" Transomnia began, scowling—and then his face softened. "You seduced him, he bit you . . . and then he died right in front of you."

"The same night," I said, staring at the floor. "That same hour. He saved my life, then had the blood sucked right out of him by magic graffiti."

Transomnia stood there. "I wanted to kill him," he said, his hand falling to my shoulder. "Just like I wanted to kill you for causing my exile from the clan. You'll never know how much. Being the thrall of Mirabilus was . . . *horrible*. You saw how I acted under his geas."

"I'm sorry," I said. Mirabilus skinned his victims alive—and Transomnia had acted like his sick little protégé while under his spell. I couldn't imagine what he'd made Transomnia do—and didn't want to. "I never meant to get you kicked out."

"Calaphase was attracted to you and overreacted," Transomnia said. "But how could he have known what exile would do to me? I couldn't betray Mirabilus's secrets, not even with Calaphase's aura protecting me from the worst of the geas. I don't blame him . . . anymore."

His hand squeezed my shoulder. I shuddered at that easy familiarity. I didn't like him that close, either physically or emotionally. But . . . some part of me appreciated that brief second of comfort. Transomnia wasn't just someone who assaulted me, or who had hurt my daughter. He was someone who knew Calaphase and regretted his passing.

Transomnia released me, then turned and ascended to his borrowed throne. "No matter our disagreements," he said, sitting, "I do not think I can let him go unavenged."

"I'm glad to hear it," I said quietly. "How are we going to do that?"

"Thanks to you, Dakota Frost," Transomnia said, "I'm going to do nothing. I'm now known to the police as the dangerous minion of a serial killer, rather than third flunky to the left in an obscure vampire biker gang. I can't even go by name in public anymore."

I swallowed. I *would* never know everything Transomnia had lost. "So . . . "

"So I am going to *let* you do this for me," Transomnia said. "Let you, you understand? I will allow you to return to Blood Rock, and even extend an olive branch to your old master, so you may learn what you need to learn to fight this thing. But this is a favor I am doing for you."

After a moment, I nodded. "I understand. Thank you, Lord Transomnia."

Transomnia stared at me for a long time, then his mouth quirked up in a smile. "If I do this thing for you, one day I may ask you for a favor," he said, miming a hoarse old Italian accent. "That day may never come—"

I laughed—I couldn't help myself. I quickly choked it off, hoping not to piss him off; but while the other vampires were unamused I could see that the guards found it quite funny. Finally I managed, "One wish at your command, Don Transomnia."

"Excellent," Transomnia said. "Get her a token."

Nyissa sighed, climbing the steps. "Yes, of course, my Lord."

"She's still *the enemy*," Gregor said, somewhat perplexed. "*They're* still the enemy."

"Oh, shut up, Gregor," Nyissa said. "Why do we keep you around?"

"I seem to recall I'm good with figures," he replied.

"If Arcturus *can* help her, Frost's next step will likely be to go to the Consulates for aid," Transomnia said, very calmly, lecturing *without* sounding like he was talking to a child. "If she petitions with our backing, and the Vampire Queen accepts her help, our standing will be enhanced, and this overture can be followed by another. If they do not, we can plan accordingly. So we shall give her a token to remove any doubt about our backing for Frost."

"I hate to say this, Trans," I said, flipping open the cuffs and standing as Nyissa stepped behind the throne. "I really do. But being in charge has done well for you."

"And getting the shit kicked out of you has done the same," he responded. "You've developed quite the backbone to go along with that bravado."

Nyissa returned with a small gold amulet on a chain and held it out to

Transomnia. "What did I say?" he asked. "Give it to her." When she hesitated again, he said, glancing at me, "Lady Nyissa, Dakota is . . . family now, so I'll tolerate this. But if she was a representative of the Consulates, or, the dark night forbid it, the Gentry . . . "

Nyissa straightened. "I understand," she said. "You could not be so lenient."

"*I* was going to say, we must present a united front," Transomnia said. "If discord leads to actual harm, however . . . I assure you, I cannot show lenience."

Nyissa walked down the steps of the throne to stand before me. "Please accept the sign of the House Beyond Sleep, Dakota Frost."

"Thank you, Lady Nyissa," I said, taking the chain and slipping it around my neck. "Far more convenient than the sign of the House of Saffron, and classier than a laminated ID card."

"Calaphase didn't give you one of those silly things, did he?" Transomnia asked.

"Yeah," I said. "About the only thing I have left from him."

Transomnia frowned. "Go in peace, Dakota Frost," he said. "Talk to your old master, make your case to the Consulates, the Gentry, to whomever you have to, and the House Beyond Sleep will protect you, for what good that will do. But remember one thing."

"What's that?"

"The balance sheet has changed, Dakota Frost," Transomnia said. "Now, *you* owe *me*."

---

48.   A DROP OF BLOOD AND A QUARTER

The limo slid through the hairpin turns and rickety bridges of Blood Rock. I sat in the rear seat, staring forward, at Nyissa, who sat opposite me, green eyes blazing, her shag of violet hair shimmering against her porcelain-white skin. Her corset-topped dress-like coat flared open on the seat around her to expose leggings and riding boots, and she had woven strips of cloth into her outfit, accentuating her curves with a dangerous Mad-Max-meets-steampunk air.

Knowing that she was one of the Sanctuary's professional dominatrices should have made her less threatening, but she didn't carry a crop: she carried a metal poker. She'd threatened to *blind* me the last time we met. And I was alone in the car with her.

Her eyes blazed at the gold coin around my neck.

"I'm sorry about the Stone," I began. "I didn't know——"

"I don't care if this makes political or strategic sense," she interrupted. "Vampires survive by being disciplined. By following the *rules*. Those who violate the rules must be punished, and yet he has rewarded you."

"I'm sorry to offend you," I said. "But I called ahead. I was willing to walk away . . . ”

"That is not the point. Normally, to win protection, a client must offer . . . tribute," she said, rolling the poker in her fingers. "Blood, and money, the occasional service."

"That protection racket again," I said.

"An act of submission," she countered. "Clients, after all, come to us—as you did."

"Not willingly," I said. "Only because I had no other option. And I'd have thought twice if I had known a favor required a pound of flesh."

She laughed at me. "Surely a vampire has demanded service of you before," she said. "Were you not under the protection of the Vampire Queen of Little Five Points?"

"She never asked anything of me—" I said, then stopped. That was not quite true.

"She had to take blood, or she could not have protected you," Nyissa said, eyes boring into me. "If you were too skittish for a bite, perhaps she demanded a cut."

"A pinprick," I said. "One of those little medical finger pricks."

Nyissa nodded. "How sanitary. I use them myself. And what toll did she require?"

"I didn't want her help," I said hotly. "I just needed safe passage—"

"Past my master, Transomnia, who asked for blood as his toll," she said. I squirmed, and she smiled. "Yes, I know your history. You refused his toll, and paid another price."

"Are you vampires or trolls?" I asked. "He got kicked out over that."

"And yet we must live, and so even passersby must pay the toll," she purred, twirling the poker in her hands. "Unlike humans, vampires need not kill their prey to feed, so the arrangement worked well for centuries, until you Edgeworlders upset the order."

"We never intended to starve you," I said, staring at the poker. The light from her eyes was actually reflecting off its metal surface, which somehow made the glow more real. "We just wanted to use magic freely, and all the stuffy old rules just sounded like excuses."

"Understandable, but now you know our secret. Vampires trade in sex and blood. We demand submission and tribute from our favored clients, and grant them safety in return. For those not so favored, there is the toll of passage."

I sat there frozen, acutely feeling the blood pound in my throat.

Her eyes gleamed. "I think I shall make you pay the toll."

"Transomnia gave me his protection," I said.

"From external threats, but not from me," she said. "And your ignorance is no longer an excuse. If you refuse me, you will pay another price. I will not help you. In fact, I will throw this olive branch in Arcturus' face. When I'm done, he will rather *die* than help you—"

"Transomnia ordered you to help me," I said.

"And what if I disobey him?" she said, leaning back in the seat and thwapping the poker against her palm. "We have seen what he does to those who break the rules. I will likely be rewarded. What a coup, to make his enemy my client for a drop of blood and a quarter."

"I'm not going to give you blood," I said, mouth dry as paper. "And I have no money."

"Not a drop? Not even a quarter?" Nyissa said, smiling viciously. "That *is* all I demand for my clients to claim protection. Just a token of the traditional toll of blood and money. That's all you'd have to give up. Just a drop of blood . . . and a quarter."

"That . . . " *sounds so reasonable*, I thought, but it also sounded like a deal with the devil. I didn't know what being her client meant, and given that she was a vampire dominatrix I had no desire to find out. Well, very little desire. Still . . . "That's *so* not going to happen."

"I *shall* make you my client," she said more firmly, mouth opening until I could see her fangs. "But not yet. For now, you *are* just a passerby. Nothing more than a toll would be appropriate. But what toll could I demand that would give you the taste to return?"

She pulled her dress apart father, and my eyes went wide.

"Now," she said, planting one foot in the middle of the limo, "kiss my boot."

I stared at her for a moment. Then I laughed. "I have far too much self-respect—"

"You will kiss my boot," she said imperiously, "or I will not help you. *That* is my toll."

"But . . . Transomnia *gave* me his *protection*. He *ordered* you to help me," I said, voice sounding unpleasantly petulant. For her part, Nyissa arched an eyebrow and tilted her head in an effort to look imperious. "I don't think he will approve of you adding conditions."

"But Transomnia is not here," she repeated, "and he need not know."

I just stared at her, wearing her boots, her corset, with her poker, so like a crop.

"You know you want to," she said, eyes burning at me.

"Are you . . . *hitting* on me?" I said, eyes tightening. Her lips slowly curled into a smile—and then mine into a snarl. "Oh, you insensitive *bitch!*"

I don't think it was possible for someone as pale as Nyissa to actually blanch, but her eyes widened and her eyebrows shot up, accomplishing the same thing. "Well," she said, scowling, "whether you want to or not, you must lick my boots, or I will not help—"

"I'd rather die!" I snapped, leaning forward, and as I did so I felt a flush hit my cheeks and a ripple of mana go through my tattoos. "The hell with you and your toll! You can go shit on Arcturus' doorstep for all I care, and sort it out with Transomnia!"

Nyissa froze. "My apologies," she said carefully, her eyes tracing my tattoos, no doubt following the mana still trickling through them. "Given the stories that are told about you and the Maid of Little Five Points, I thought you would find that appealing."

"Have you lost your mind? Were you not listening?" I snarled. "My lover was just murdered, and here you are, treating me like a side of fresh meat."

Nyissa put the poker down and abruptly leaned forward, putting her hand on my knee. I jerked back, unsure of whether I should take her hand off or whether she was about to take my head off. Then her hand squeezed me briefly, not unlike how Transomnia's had.

"My *sincere* apologies," she said. "I was not thinking. I had heard . . . well, that you were once the submissive of the Vampire Queen, before she was a vampire," she said, eyes flashing at me with equal parts lust and embarrassment. "Now that you have permitted us to bite—"

"First Saffron, now you," I said. "What is it about being a vampire that makes you so pushy?"

"Our diet, and auras," Nyissa said, withdrawing her hand. "We have to be pushy to satisfy our . . . desires, and our auras give us a sense of when someone is . . . receptive."

I glared at her. "You really think I'm *giving off signs?*"

"No, no," Nyissa said, raising her palms. "I apologize. I *sincerely* apologize. I can see how that would sound insulting. You are not giving off signs. It is more a sense that your blood is compatible. If the donor is in any way willing, a vampire's aura . . . greases the wheels."

"You're trying to sway my mind," I said, looking away.

"Not trying, exactly, it's just a reflex," she insisted, and I remembered Calaphase saying the same thing. "But skindancers are different. Your reflexes naturally keep us out. You sense our auras against your skin and deflect the energy."

"I don't think so," I said. "I've been almost rolled by a vampire."

"When he bit you," she guessed. I reddened, and she nodded. "During sex, when your nervous systems were in full contact, interpenetrating." Her eyes glinted as I squirmed. "But normally, the only time a vampire comes in direct contact with your nervous system is when you look them eye to eye, exposing your retinas to their auras. You probably think by looking away you're safe. But it isn't that simple. A vampire's aura is always on, always hungry for life. I can teach you how to recognize it. How to defend against it."

I looked at her, not directly in the eye as I had before. "Why—"

"If I make you my client, I must give you protection," she said. "But protection has many forms. Teaching you to defend yourself would protect you, even if I was not here. Isn't learning how to do that worth becoming my client? Look into my eyes—"

"No," I said, looking even more off center. "You're just trying to sway me."

"I would *love* to," she said, licking her lips. "But . . . I am not a powerful vampire."

My eyes narrowed. She was right: she *wasn't* a powerful vampire. I guessed she'd been a vampire for at most thirty, maybe forty years. Saffron, in contrast, had matured in a few short years into some kind of cross between a vampire Terminator and a force of nature.

What determined a vampire's power? Clearly it wasn't age. I had no idea.

"You have little to fear from me," Nyissa was saying, "and in truth I can offer you little physical protection. But I can easily teach you how to defend yourself. I know how to thwart a vampire's aura—I *was* a wizard before I was a vampire, after all."

"Really?" I asked. "Isn't that some kind of no-no?"

"I *am* lurking in rural Georgia," she said, smiling wryly. "Still, what of my offer?"

"Sounds great," I said. She *had* designed the Stone, after all. She probably had a lot to teach me. "Very generous. But I'm *still* not going to look you in the eye."

She looked away, the frown returning to her expression as her eyes searched the air. "No, I suppose not," she said. "I don't guess I've earned that yet, have I?"

"Not by a long shot," I said. "And I don't like that language 'yet' . . . "

"Very well," she said, picking up the poker again—and once again planting her boot in the center of the limo. "That still leaves the toll."

I glared at her boot. "Like hell. I am *not* going to kiss—"

"Please," Nyissa said. "Vampires who control territory must exact a toll. I've already lost my position at the Sanctuary by allowing Lord Transomnia to come in without a toll."

"Then why did you let him *do* that?" I said.

"I owe him my life," she said, and I found myself with nothing to say. "Now, please, *Lady* Frost, play along. Kissing my boots *is* the toll I am known for, and being able to claim I exacted it from *you* will not only enhance my position, but also reestablish some respect for the law within the House Beyond Sleep, rather than the rule of Transomnia's whims."

Damnit. Now the crazy psycho vampire with the metal poker was talking law and order to me, *and* giving me a chance to throw something in the face of Transomnia he couldn't easily take umbrage at. I struggled on the seat for a moment. Then I broke down.

"*Fine*," I said. "I'll kiss—*peck*—just *one* boot. You have to pick which one."

Nyissa smiled, her face breaking out with little dimples when she did so. She stared off in the air for a second, holding the poker by her cheek like a fairy wand, then leaned back and pointed the poker at her extended right boot.

Swallowing, I slipped off the seat and knelt on the floor, then went forward onto my hands and knees, cheek falling aside Nyissa's boot. I could smell the leather, feel the soft, plush carpet beneath my feet, hear her breathing as she leaned down over me.

The car screeched to a halt and we were both thrown forward, me flying between her legs and landing on top of her. Her eyes were thrown wide in total shock as I awkwardly tried to push off her and nailed her breast.

Then the tires squealed and we were thrown forward again as the driver hurled us into reverse, a hail of gravel and dirt roaring beneath the limo as it awkwardly fishtailed, trying to back up from whatever had brought us to a stop.

Nyissa pushed me off her, her hand nailing my breast this time, and I tumbled back into the floor. I flexed and brought my vines to life. Nyissa's eyes glowed, she raised the poker, and we crouched back to back, staring out the windows as the limo rocked from its hard stop.

The squealing and rattling stopped, but the tires were still spinning. Nyissa and I were thrown onto each other as the limo drunkenly slewed around, lifting into the air. Flickering red light began creeping up under the cracks of the doors and climbing the sides of the windows.

"Oh, God," I said. "It's the tagger—"

"Oh, no," Nyissa said. "He's going to kill us—"

"That's far enough!" a voice screamed. "I'll make you regret coming to Blood Rock!"

---

49.   A TORRENT OF RED AND GOLD

"What the *hell?*" I was certain I recognized that voice, and reached for the door.

"No, don't," Nyissa said, grabbing my arm with irresistible strength. "Don't challenge him. Let him rage, maybe he will tire of it and let us go."

"Let go of my arm," I said. Nyissa shook her head, and I asked, "This client thing, is it feudal? You protect me in exchange for tribute, but I can also be called on to protect you?"

Nyissa blinked, then squealed as the car rocked. "Y-yes," she said, shrinking back from the flickering orange light now roaring around all the windows.

"Then let go of me," I said. "It's my time to protect you."

The car rocked again, slewing around, and she released my arm. Quickly I tore off my jacket, unzipped my chaps, exposing as many tattoos as I could. Then I opened the door.

A torrent of red and gold leaves whipped around the car, like a tornado made by the spirit of fall. Giant vines weaved through the storm, not unlike my own, but thick as tree trunks, snapping like giant snakes—and then one struck the car and knocked me flying.

"*Whoa!*" I cried, arms windmilling. A 'spirit of air' haiku it wasn't, but my cry captured my intent and my panicked movement spread the mana I had already been building, making the half-finished wings of my new Dragon erupt from my back in a flare of purple feathers.

Wind caught under them, braked my fall—I wasn't quite flying, or even falling with style, but managed to twirl downwards like a maple seed, buffeted by the roiling tornado of tattoo magic around me, but not quite knocked from the air. As I stabilized, I saw him.

The wide, strong figure of Arturo Carlos "Arcturus" Rodriguez de la Turin danced in the road, legs moving quickly around the points of a pentagram, arms waving in counterpoint with the grace of a Tai Chi master. His shaggy white hair tossed in the wind of his power. The tattoos of his bare arms and chest didn't just glow, they *blazed*, sweeping out around him in a tornado of leaves and vines that swirled beneath the limo, lifting it thirty feet up into the air. From his back, a huge serpent uncoiled, rising up, growing larger, preparing to strike.

"*Spirit of vengeance,*" he snarled—and then he saw me. "Frost?"

He paused his quick dancing steps, and the torrent began to abate.

"*Friends of the earth, ease my fall*," I murmured, and my vines coiled out and below me, cushioning my fall as I touched down on the dirt road, which he'd nearly blasted back to the clay.

"Frost!" he cried, happily, stepping forward. As he did so, Zinaga, who had been leaning against a tree and watching the show with an unconcealed grin, suddenly scowled and turned her back. Arcturus, as usual, did not notice. "I can't believe it—Dakota Frost!"

He looked genuinely surprised to see me. I wondered what, if anything, that I'd said that Zinaga had passed on to him. Probably just enough to cast me in the worst possible light. Then I looked over my shoulder, up and at the limo, which was now tottering and sinking as the tornado began to break up. Arcturus saw it too, grimaced, looked at me, then grimaced even more. He struggled with something; the glowing snake twisted, reared. Then Arcturus cursed.

"*Spirit of vengeance, spare them my wrath*," he said, bowing slowly, throwing his hands wide. The limo began to settle gently to the ground, the leaves dispersed, the vines recoiled, and the snake resentfully sank back down into his back. At the precise moment he completed his bow, all signs of his magic dissipated— and the limo's tires gently touched the Earth.

"Always the showman," I said quietly, letting my own wings and vines fade.

"Good Lord, Frost, what are *you* doing riding with the vampires?" he said, rubbing his hands together. Little glowing sparks erupted where flesh met flesh—the mana-capacitor yin-yangs on *my* palms were based on *his* example. "And why are *they* riding straight into the heart of Old Town? I told both you *and* them to stay away until you learned better manners."

I stared at Arcturus, taking him all in: Hispanic features, English accent, that slightly aristocratic air which always made me want to kick his teeth in. I reflected on what Nyissa said. I thought about how to best handle the situation. Then I opened my damn mouth.

"Damnit, Arturo, you didn't tell me anything because you don't answer your phone."

"The telephone," Arcturus said archly, "is not a universal feature of the human condition. For the bulk of history, people have spoken without electrical intermediaries—"

"I'm not finished," I said. "Any message you had for me was *not* passed on by Zinaga, who just as clearly hasn't passed on to you half of what I told her. She's probably holding out on both of us for the same reason she sold me out to the vampires: she's jealous."

Arcturus' eyes bugged out and he whirled on Zinaga. "You betrayed my *star pupil* to the vampires?" he said. Zinaga flinched at 'star pupil'—meaning she and her years of service were, what, chopped liver? No wonder she was jealous. "A serious accusation. Defend yourself!"

"Of course I didn't sell her out," she said, shrugging her shoulders with a cocky 'I can get away with it' air. "And if I had, would she be here?"

"Actually, I get on famously with vampires, after their fashion," I said. "Which answers Arcturus' first question. I had grovel to them before I could come grovel to you."

The limo door opened, and Nyissa's booted foot planted itself in the road. She followed it out, twisting her poker in her fingers, features composed, assured, hostile. The layered, nuanced woman was gone, replaced by the scary psycho bitch I'd seen in the court of Transomnia. Her game face was on, and she strolled straight up to Arcturus as if she was not terrified.

"Oh, it's *you*," Arcturus said dismissively—but beyond that, was he a tiny bit . . . *embarrassed?* "Sorry about the light show. I thought you were your boss."

"Think nothing of it," she said, staring straight at Arcturus. "The Lady Frost is correct. We intercepted her earlier based on a tip from Zinaga, with whom I have maintained a . . . private relationship . . . to keep the line of communication between skindancers and vampires open."

"She's lying!" Zinaga said. "I never called her!"

"I never said you *called*," Nyissa said, withdrawing a cell phone from the folds of her dress-coat, "but . . . you did."

Nyissa thumbed through listings on the phone, then held it to Arcturus. He stared at it, cursed, then glared over at Zinaga, daring her to contradict. She just slumped back against the tree, looking away. "Return to the shop," he said. "I'll decide your fate later."

"She should stay," I said. "I want her to hear this."

Arcturus glared at me sharply. "See now, Frost, you're in Coventry already—"

"Because we forbade the Lady Frost to return to Blood Rock," Nyissa said.

Arcturus squinted at Nyissa. "Well, if she didn't have the fortitude to defy you," he said, glancing at me sidelong, "she should have just stayed away."

"*No one* has the guts to buck them," I said. "Not even Zinaga, and she's their ally. You don't know that because you spend all your time holed up in your studio, but everyone in town is running scared. Go downtown tomorrow night and you won't see one exposed tattoo."

Arcturus winced . . . then snorted. "Who cares," he said, though he was grimacing. "Anybody with *my* ink could take them, if they had chests—"

"But, as she said, no one has any guts," Nyissa said. "Everyone in Blood Rock fears the House Beyond Sleep . . . which brings us to the Lady Frost's proposal."

"Proposal?" he said. "What proposal?"

"The Lady Frost has convinced us," Nyissa said, "that our fear of skindancers has created the very conditions we wanted to avoid: open hostility. She has suggested that we should lift the ban on skindancing in Blood Rock . . . and we have agreed."

Zinaga stood up straight, leaning away from the tree with her mouth hanging open. Arcturus stood there in the road for a moment, swaying, then said, "Again, why should I care? Anyone who doesn't have the guts to stand up to you—"

"Stop being an ass, Arturo," I snapped.

"No, you stop being an ass," Nyissa said. "You are not helping."

"Look, you—"

"Are you not my client?" Nyissa asked. "Do you not want my protection?"

"Technically no," I said, "and not really, no."

She raised an eyebrow. "So you *want* all vampires to consider you free game?"

I stared up into the night sky, then let out my breath. "No."

"Then as my client," she said, "you will learn to hold your tongue."

"I'd pay good money to see that trick," Arcturus said.

"I only need a minute of silence to make my case," Nyissa said. "This town was a haven for skindancers first, before the vampires came. You and I had our disagreements, but we were civil. It was my master who feared skindancers, and my master who imposed the ban. Frost was one of the skindancers he feared, and she convinced him that fear was not warranted."

"Oh really?" Arcturus said. "You don't think we could put the hurt on you?"

"So could a posse of pissed off townspeople with shotguns," Nyissa said. "Frost's suggestion is to stop pissing you off, starting with rescinding the ban on displayed ink."

Arcturus cocked his head. "And what do you get out of it?"

"My Lord Transomnia would like you to extend his apologies to the people of Blood Rock," she said, "and my client, Dakota Frost, would like you to accept my apology for interfering with the legitimate business she had with you."

I let out an exasperated breath. "Oh, you're just loving this."

"Zip it," she said. "And don't forget, you still owe me a drop of blood and a quarter."

Arcturus looked at her, then me. "This vamp your new girlfriend, Dakota?"

I rankled—and so did Zinaga; how interesting. "Now, look—"

Nyissa licked her lips and looked at me. "Why, that's—" she began—and then her face fell. "That's a flattering suggestion, but poorly timed. Miss Frost's romantic companion was just murdered, by magic. I believe that's what she's here to talk to you about."

Arcturus stiffened. "Murdered? By magic? Not skindancing—"

"No," Nyissa said softly, so I didn't have to. "Magic graffiti. And her friend is not the only victim. This plague has claimed dozens of vampires, werewolves, and normal humans."

"Damnation. And I'm sorry to hear about your friend," Arcturus said. Clearly Zinaga had told him nothing. His eyes scanned me, then narrowed. "But the vamps have picked the wrong horse to back—you'll be useless in a fight, now that you've stripped your masterwork."

"I'm inking a new Dragon," I said.

His eyes narrowed further. "Those wings you used? Show me." I turned so Arcturus could look down the back of my shirt, which left me facing Nyissa. She smiled sweetly, and I shuddered. "Hard to get a whole picture," Arcturus said. "Could I pull this up a moment?"

"Not with Miss Predator figuring out where to sink her teeth," I said.

"Or plant her tongue," she said sweetly.

"Ew," I said, folding my arms in front of me. "Look, you can see the wings over my shoulders, and between them the head of the Dragon, or the start of it, anyway. Those aren't isolated marks, I'm redoing the whole masterwork to a new design—"

"So you are," Arcturus said, and despite my warning, lifted the back of my shirt to inspect my inking more closely. After a moment, he said, "Impressive. I thought you'd have gotten sloppy, running all that commercial ink. But you've gotten better."

"I love my work."

Arcturus released me, and I turned back to face him.

"Tell me, Frost," he asked, "are you ready to learn to fight this thing?"

"Yes," I said. "Do you have anything to teach me?"

"Oh, *do* I," Arcturus said, his eyes glinting. "I don't have secret knowledge about graffiti, but there's a *lot* about skindancing I didn't teach you before you quit."

"Damnit," I said. Actually I *had* hoped Arcturus would have some secret knowledge, but there would be no silver bullet. "I don't have time to get bogged down with dancing lessons."

"You don't have time *not* to," Arcturus said. "Tell me all you know about the graffiti, and together we'll work out how to take it apart. Then I'll train you to do it, using improvements to your library of tattoos and specific moves to use your new tattoos to defend yourself. Deal?"

I blinked at him. "Now *that's* what I'm talking about," I said. "All right. I'm in."

---

50. NO EASY ANSWERS

The fires in Atlanta petered out after a few days, according to the news, but I was *not* relieved. The attacks had stopped for a week after the werehouse fire—then we lost Calaphase. Now we were a little over a week past that round of fires—and running out of time.

But I had *no* idea how I could be working any harder or faster.

"Understand me. This is no Yoda nonsense," Arcturus said—*again*. He moved his arms in a slow arc, which I mirrored with difficulty—and increasing frustration. "Fuck 'do or do not, there is no try.' No. Try and try again, piece by piece, until each piece is right. Then puzzle the pieces together, over and over again, until the big picture is second nature."

Since I'd arrived, each day had been devoted to skindancing until I could barely stand, and each night to graffiti analysis until we could barely keep our eyes open. Yet, deep in the night, trying to drift off in the musty chill of the spare room, I often lay awake, worrying about Cinnamon, mourning Calaphase . . . or dreading what disaster was coming next.

I sent Cinnamon a postcard through Doug, but I was too paranoid to call directly. I was off the radar and planned to stay there. I did try emailing her through an anonymous proxy—I remembered a *few* tricks from my days volunteering in the Emory computer lab—but got no response. Heck, I didn't know if Palmotti was letting her use the Internet.

When I logged in, however, I found my secret admirer had no problems with his Internet connection. Based on the press clippings he'd flooded my inbox with, Arcturus and I estimated the *new* fires had killed at least thirty-five people. Also, a werekin lawyer disappeared at the same time, and I suspected a transportation attack like the one on me and Calaphase.

Counting everything, the death toll from magic graffiti had nearly hit eighty. It got worse each time: a handful of people around New Year's Eve, twice that many after Revenance died, and another doubling after Calaphase died. I *was* dreading what was coming next.

At least I was making progress on skindancing. Arcturus had showed me a technique to remove the curdled ink left in my burn, then helped me design a better asp I inked in its place. We also added a few defensive marks that might help if I ran into Zipperface again.

As I carefully inked the design to Arcturus' impatient direction, I guessed why he had let his own marks get so crude. If you tattooed yourself repeatedly, only to pull them off so you could ink new ones, I could see how you could start focusing on the magical lines over the artistry. I love my work, though, and when I was done, even Arcturus was impressed.

But, as my new arsenal healed up, Arcturus didn't let me rest on my laurels. Instead, he gave me a crash course in skindancing logic—first, with a refresher of the basic moves, and then a review of the Dances—what in karate would be called a hoke or a kata.

We practiced beneath the trees on a big hexagonal sand pit behind his wooden split-level home, a crisp January wind making the shadows of the branches dance with far more grace than I could manage. Strangely, the regular exercise seemed to be helping my knee: maybe I had been pushing myself too hard at the dojo. Regardless, being in less pain didn't mean I made fewer mistakes. Soon, I stumbled again, sand kicking up from my foot where I caught myself, and Arcturus broke his form and stood beside me, watching me move.

"Pathetic. Back to the Dance of Five and Two," he said sharply, walking beside me, correcting my arm here and there, occasionally cuffing me upside the head as I stumbled through the motions. My feet drew out a pentagram, forward, back left, right front, left front, back right, forward again, then repeated it again, switching right for left. I felt like I was falling over my own feet with every little J-step. But at the end Arcturus grunted, pleased.

"Not bad," he said, rubbing his chin. "Thought you'd abandoned your practice?"

"Rarely doesn't mean never," I said. "And I do martial arts. They're similar."

He laughed sharply. "Not likely," he said. "What's your most similar move?"

I thought a moment. "Not so much a move, as a form—*semay-no-hokay.*"

"Means nothing to me," he said. "Show me. Or must you put on jammies to fight?"

"It's not a fighting form," I said. I knelt, bowed to touch the sand, and leaned back up. I exhaled completely, lifted up on one knee, extended my hands—then pulled them back in, inhaling, and started windmilling myself through *semay*.

Its movements weren't that difficult; the really taxing part was its elaborate pattern of controlled breathing. Soon everything else was pushed out of my mind. Arcturus, despite his protests, seemed to instinctively get the form, even correcting my hands once.

"Not bad," he said, with the same little grunt. "Doesn't sum like the skin dance, but you're going over many of the same moves. I can see why it helps. Let's take a break."

He poured some lemonshine for us from a pitcher on the picnic table and took a swig. When I tried, I gagged, half from the alcohol and half from the lemon. I'd forgotten how strong he made it. "Gaah," I said, "worse than ever. Is this lemonade or a margarita?"

"Can't quite make up its mind, can it?" he said, grinning. "Zinaga has been feeding in limes along with the lemons. That and the tequila gives it quite a kick."

I stared at the drink, suspicious of anything prepared by Zinaga. But *I* had convinced Arcturus to forgive and forget, so I had to put my money where my mouth was. I grimaced through another swallow, and set it down. "Gaah. All right. How bad am I doing?"

"Terrible. Rusty as all getout. It will take a month to get you back to fighting form."

"We don't *have* a month," I said. "We've got to figure out how to defeat the graffiti before it starts killing people again—"

"Dakota, we've spent almost a week and a half looking at graffiti, and neither of us have made headway because there's no headway to be made," Arcturus said. "Trust me, there are no secrets to be found looking at more pictures or drawing more diagrams."

"Then we're not looking hard enough," I said. "There has to be some weakness—"

"What is this, the Star Wars theory of battle?" Arcturus said, plucking an M&M out of a jar on the picnic table. "Hoping to find that small exhaust port just below the main port?"

"Don't mock me," I said. "I need to find out how the tags work so I can beat them."

"Dakota, *you can't beat the tags*," Arcturus said. "You can't. He can spray one as big as the side of a barn, with a thousand layers, and all you have is two square meters of skin. If you go toe to toe with that, it will burn you. You need to learn to beat the *tagger*."

I sat down on the picnic table. As soon as he said that, I knew he was right. I closed my eyes, running through the math. Doug once called magic conceptual physics: the part of the world affected by pure ideas. Well, it wasn't that simple: a magical intent is only as strong as the mana that powers it. Against stronger magic, that intent can pop like a soap bubble.

Ignore for a moment *where* it was getting the power, and just look at the surface area, at the layers. At a rough guess . . . the magic that a large tag could put out could be a thousand times as much as that put out by a person. And the source of the mana? If he painted enough layers, it could be the world's best magical capacitor, storing up the trickle of magic put out by the living mold underneath for hours or days before releasing it all at once in a torrent of mana.

No wonder I hadn't been able to shield against the graffiti.

It was like trying to stop a bullet with tissue paper.

Inside Arcturus' basement studio, the phone began ringing, and I started to get up to answer it, just like I always had when I'd been his star pupil.

"Leave it to Zinaga," Arcturus said, stopping me with a hand on my shoulder. "Why so quiet? Trying to use all your college maths to figure out how it beat you?"

"Yep," I said. "Actually, I've pretty much nailed it."

Arcturus sighed. "Cocky as ever. You keep thinking you understand magic, but calling it mana is no better than calling it qi and looking for chakra. Everyone tries to reduce magic to laws they can understand. But magic doesn't obey the laws of nature. Magic is *super*natural."

"Supernatural doesn't mean anything," I said, staring out at the patterns in the sand as the phone went silent. "It's just a word we use for the 'vitamins' of nature, the parts you can't assemble out of smaller pieces unless you've already got the material to work with."

"By that definition *radioactivity* is magical, or damn near close to it," Arcturus said, rubbing his hands together. When the roughly inked yin-yangs on his palms came apart, a glowing pattern spread between them, a cat's cradle of light far more delicate than anything that sprung from the finer lines of my tattoos. "But you know better than that. Magic is more than just a rare spice. It's the spice of life—living, breathing life forms."

I stared at the dance of light between his fingers. I knew the graphomantic patterns that made the form possible, could gauge his intent, maybe even measure his mana, but there was more to it than that, something just beyond my reach, elusive and tantalizing.

Then the phone started ringing again.

"Let me shoo whomever's on the phone," I said, standing.

"Don't," Arcturus said firmly. "*Don't* answer it."

I stared at him, as the phone kept ringing, and ringing, and ringing.

"Answer your own phone on your own time," Arcturus said. "Leave my phone alone. No one has any business calling my phone. If I wanted to talk, I would call them."

"That won't *work* if *everyone* has your attitude," I said, as the phone kept ringing.

"I am not everyone," he said, ignoring the noise. "I am Arcturus. I'm a skindancing master. And I'm with my star pupil, trying to beat some sense into her."

"That's *incredibly* annoying," I said, pointing at the ringing phone. "I need to concentrate. Let's at least take it off the hook."

"Learn to ignore it," he said. "Would you stop and answer a cell phone during a fight?"

"We're not in a fight," I said. "And what if it was important—"

"It is *never* important," he said.

"My *daughter* was *kidnapped* last year," I snarled. "They called to tell me what to do. What if I hadn't answered the phone? They might have—"

"They were not going to kill your daughter just because they couldn't get you on the phone," Arcturus said quietly. "They took her because they wanted something. Killing her wouldn't get it from you. They *will* find another way to deliver the message."

"How do you know that?" I said.

"Trust me," he said, even more quietly. "I know."

I just stared at him, as the phone rang, and rang, and rang. Arcturus was an aristocratic Chilean, educated at Cambridge, hiding out in the backwaters of rural Georgia in a cabin filled with pictures of a wife and daughter I had never met and he had never spoken of.

As usual, dumb old me never thought to ask why.

"Arcturus," I said softly. "Who was on the phone the last time *you* picked it up?"

"What?" Arcturus said blankly. "What? No! Not kidnappers, if that's what you're asking. I have picked up the phone since then, Dakota. Last time for my brother, I think." Then his face clouded. "But . . . yes, once it was. And the experience left me with an aversion."

"I'm so sorry."

He shrugged, turned away. "Waters long under," he said, pulling out his sheaf of notes. "Back to the here and now. Back to the sound. On the other end of that phone, a person is looking for you, but they can only find you if you pick up. The sound is just an alarm. It can't hurt you. It doesn't oblige you. But it can distract you. Realize that, then learn to ignore it."

"Ignore what?" I asked.

He smiled, picked out a diagram, put it in front of me. "And now something else to ignore: chakra, smakra, mana, qi," he said, smoothing the paper out. "All pretty words for the flow of magic, for the loci where it collects in the body. To fight the tagger, you must master that power—not intellectually, but intuitively, as an instinctive reaction without thought.

"Your martial arts have done you well. You have maintained your skill at concentrating magic in your loci, maybe even improved it a little. Now you must learn how to concentrate more coordinated patterns of magic and use them to generate more complex spells on the fly."

But I was staring at the diagram: it was the Pentacle of the Dance, a pentagram that showed how the five different kinds of magic used by skindancers related to each other. I'd seen it, drawn it a thousand times: walking the pentacle was a fundamental tool used to check the magic of flash to make sure the magical circuit worked as advertised.

But this one was different. Overlaid on the pentagram was a square, then a circle, then a naked, spreadeagled human figure: the Vitruvian man, the iconic figure drawn by Leonardo da Vinci five centuries before I was born. *This* Pentacle, Arcturus explained, showed how the human body itself was not just a source of magic, but a component in its logic.

"Oh, God," I said, flashing on Revenance's spread-eagled form, on Tully, suffering in the vines, even on Cally, broken body splayed out in a crude X as his life's blood spilled out onto the tag. "It *is* skindancing. The tagger is using skindancing logic with graffiti magic."

"Now how is he doing that, Frost?" Arcturus said. "There is no dancer—"

"The writhing of the victims. Hence the barbs, the sawing, the prolonged *torture.*"

"Frost!" Arcturus said. "We went over that. Random movements wouldn't sum—"

"It would if there's a ratchet, like a self winding watch," I said, staring into the Pentacle. "What if it's not just a receiver, but a *transmitter?* It traps people, kills them, and beams the harvested magic elsewhere to power . . . something else. Do you have a map of Atlanta?"

Arcturus froze, then went out to the garage, yelling for Zinaga while I got the graffiti pictures. When he returned with the map, I tamped it down with the pitcher and M&M jar and used M&Ms to mark where graffiti had been found or where fires had been reported.

In moments the picture emerged. Our data was not complete, the diagram not perfect, but there were enough little bits of candy to see the beginnings of a great pentacle spread over the whole of the city of Atlanta, just like the Pentacle of the Dance on the Vitruvian Man.

"It's a city-sized resonator," I said. "No wonder the tags never seem to run out of mana. They aren't just powering themselves—they're powering *each other.* Mana building up in the mold capacitors all over the city gets beamed to the traps, which in turn use that power to torture more magic out of their victims. It's a . . . a *distributed necromantic network.*"

Arcturus' jaw clenched. "God *damn* it," he said. "And it will be more than just mana—it will transmit the tortured intents of the dying victims back to the source. It's not just a city-sized resonator. It's a city-sized harvester of pain. That is *foul.*"

I thought about Transomnia, Nyissa, and their auras prickling against my magical tattoos. "It likes vampires because their auras extend beyond their body," I said. "That triggers the magic and springs the trap. Shapeshifters can trigger it too, but anything alive could feed it."

"Vampiric graffiti using skindancing magic," Arcturus said. "Killing people as part of some far vaster spell . . . to do *what?*"

"Something *really* horrible," I said, pointing at a join on the network. Arcturus *had* taught me something new, just in this short week. "Look at the corresponding point on the Pentacle. This isn't a chi junction. It's an intent nexus. That's why the network transports people."

Arcturus stared at the map, then the Pentacle. "How do you figure that?"

"Extracting a person's intent is a short-range process," I said. "And these points on the Pentacle are points of pain. It moved Revenance—it moved me and Calaphase—to the place which needed the most pain to be applied. This network is collecting *suffering.*"

"God," Arcturus said. "We must *stop* this."

I laughed bitterly. "No argument."

He nodded a couple of times and took another swig of his limonshine. "I have to call the vampires," he said with distaste. "I don't believe this. *I'm* going to call the bloody vamps. I'm going to thank them for their gesture, then propose we work together to eliminate this threat."

My eyes widened. "You'll . . . you'll fight *with me* against the tagger?"

"What? No . . . I can't leave Blood Rock, Frost," Arcturus said, pained. "I can't afford to be outside the Sanctuary circle, much less appear in public. I am marked for death."

I stared back at him. "You've been here, what, twenty years . . . "

"It does not matter how long you hide," he said grimly. "If you kill the right person from the wrong family, you do not appear in public, ever. Not even to fight this. It's a rule."

"Who did you kill?" I asked, immediately regretting it.

Arcturus looked away, took another long gulp of limonshine. I followed his eyes. He was staring into the house, into the open sliding door of the den, staring at a small picture on the coffee table. I didn't need to get up to know it was a picture of his wife and daughter.

After what seemed like minutes, Arcturus cursed and set his drink down. "I cannot *think* with all this racket," he said, and stormed into the house. Then my mouth fell open as Arcturus picked up the phone savagely and snapped, "What the hell do you want?"

I swallowed. I had successfully tuned the phone out after Arcturus' speech. For him to pick up the phone, my questions about his family must have really rattled him. Or maybe it always rattled him, and he was putting on a brave face to forget what he'd lost.

"Yes, speaking. Who are—yes, right again," Arcturus said. He grimaced, then picked the phone's cradle up and walked over to the door, and I sat up in alarm. "It's for you."

"*How?* No one knows I'm here," I said. "Who is it?"

"God damned Bespin, sounds like."

"Bespin? I don't know a—" I said. "Oh. Where Luke went after he bailed on Yoda."

"Yeah," Arcturus said. "This is why I hate phones. If you take the call, you have to act."

I stared at the phone, then took it. "Hello?"

"Dakota," Philip said, a bit strangled. "God, I hope your line isn't already tapped."

"Philip," I said. "Oh, Philip, how did you—"

"I got your cell phone records, tracked your recent calls—and the last one got me Transomnia," Philip said. "To get your location, we had to trade some information. I told him to ditch his phone. He's probably gone to ground. He'll be harder to track now."

"It's all right, he's . . . not wholly evil," I said. "But why risk it? What's happened?"

"Palmotti's filed a missing persons report," Philip said. "Cinnamon has disappeared."

51.   THE HUNT IS ON

"Vladimir," I said, into a spectacularly disgusting gas station pay phone, "tell me Cinnamon showed up for her afterschool math club."

"Why, yes," he said. "She just left."

"Thank God, and damnit," I said, glancing around. I half expected an army of spring-loaded cops to descend on me at any moment. I know the drill. If the police can't find a fugitive, they let it be known that the suspect has won a prize—or that her daughter has disappeared.

"What's wrong?"

"She's gone missing from the Palmottis," I said. "He's filed a missing persons report."

"Oh, Jesus," he said. "And here I was thinking things were going better. She's actually *been* at school. Didn't Palmotti even think to call us?"

"Maybe he did," I said. "Who knows?"

"You haven't talked to him?"

"Not yet. And frankly, I'm scared to, and not because I'm forbidden to see Cinnamon."

"Why, Dakota?" Vladimir asked, voice filled with concern. "It isn't the police, is it?"

Oh, damnit, me and my big mouth. Instinctively I trusted Vladimir, and had been talking to him as if I'd already taken him into confidence. I hemmed and hawed; finally, I gave in.

"Yes," I said. "They started looking for me because I was on the scene of the Candlestick fire, and have been loose while fires have been ravaging the city."

"You're taking a risk even calling me," Vladimir said, even more concerned.

"Yes," I said, and explained how Philip had tracked me with my cell phone. "But a random payphone is probably safe, at least calling you. They've probably tapped the Palmottis's phone—my daughter is there—and maybe the phones of my close friends. *I* would."

"You're probably safe making one call per payphone," Vladimir said, after some thought, "if you're willing to hang up and drive for twenty, maybe thirty minutes after the call."

"Vladimir! I'm shocked," I said. "I didn't mark you as devious lawbreaker."

"I read a lot of suspense novels," he admitted. "But if you're willing to spend one call, why not go for broke? Why not call the police directly, tell them you've nothing to do with the fires and ask for news about your daughter?"

"I take back my crack about devious, Vladimir," I said. "Switch to true crime books. The police won't believe me because I call and sound concerned. They won't believe anything short of me turning myself in so I can rot in jail while the tagger burns the city down to the ground."

"If you do turn yourself in, and the fires keep popping up, wouldn't that clear you?"

"Maybe, but I'm not going to sit on my ass in the Fulton County Jail while Cinnamon's gone to ground, probably to precisely the same places this werekin-eating graffiti is likely to be found. Turning myself in for something I didn't do is an absolute last resort."

"Jesus," Vladimir said, after a long pause. "What's that going to do to your case?"

I blew out a harsh breath. "Oh, hell, Vladimir," I said. "Nothing good, but I can't think that far. We need to find her and get her back to Mister Palmotti, or at least find her some other kind of protection, before she gets killed. Once she's safe, we worry about saving the case."

Vladimir was silent for a moment. "Dakota," he said. "You weren't this worried about her safety the last time we spoke. What's happened?"

Without thinking . . . I told him.

About Calaphase's death. About Revenance's death. About the attacks on Tully, on the werehouse, at the Candlesticks. I told him how hard the graffiti was to fight, what it could do—and how Arcturus and I had pieced together that it was part of a far greater spell, a citywide network of death, one Doug believed was beyond any magic or science known to man.

"Oh my God," Vladimir said. His voice was trembling. I'd forgotten I was speaking to a math teacher and not one of my normal Edgeworld contacts, and that taking someone into confidence didn't have to mean dumping off all my woes. "What are we going to do?"

"Don't be afraid," I said. "Focus on what we can do. Go after Cinnamon, if she hasn't been gone too long, and get her to wait for Mister Palmotti. If not, find a pretext to call him and let him know she's been seen—but *don't* mention my name. If you see her again—"

"I'll make her wait for Mister Palmotti," Vladimir said.

"*No*," I said. "Don't *make* her do anything. She's a werekin with a *large* beast. She can take a bullet, lift a car, and run like the wind. Don't spook her, or she'll go to ground."

"Maybe I'll just *ask* her to wait for Mister Palmotti," Vladimir said.

"Better," I said. "But more importantly . . . tell her she needs to keep away from graffiti."

"Sure," Vladimir said, "but, Dakota, as bad as everything you said was . . . it didn't sound like a Cinnamon-specific threat. Are you sure you're not borrowing trouble?"

I was quiet for a moment. He was right, but he didn't know the whole story. And I hated to violate her privacy, but . . . "Yes, I'm sure," I said. "She runs with . . . *dates*, in our language, this boy, Tully. He's another werekin, maybe a little older, not in school."

"Hoo boy," Vladimir said. "And you let her, unchaperoned?"

"Not on purpose," I said. "I'm not even supposed to know about it."

"And how do you know about it?" Vladimir asked, a smile in his voice.

"Because I'm a parent, and I did the same kind of thing before she was born," I said, and Vladimir laughed. "Before the werehouse burned, I'd pretty much gotten the picture. If she's not with me, not with Palmotti, and the werehouse has burned to the ground, she's running with him."

"Well, if he is a werekin," Vladimir said, "maybe he can keep her safe."

"No. She has a bigger beast, and he nearly got killed at the werehouse when they made him whitewash it," I said. "And he's a *fan* of graffiti, if not a writer himself. They're probably hiding out in precisely the same kind of places that the tagger would have hit, and they don't know a random-looking squiggle can unfurl into a masterpiece that can burn people alive."

"Hoo boy. All right," he said. "Look, I'm going after her, Dakota. She didn't leave fifteen minutes ago, and maybe she and her boy are grabbing a smoke behind the school."

"Oh, Lord," I said. "One more thing I'm not supposed to know . . . "

"You *can* confront your children about things they're trying to hide," Vladimir said firmly. "Like you said, you're a parent. It's your job."

"Yeah," I said quietly.

"One more thing—have you called to warn her?"

"Yes, but there's no answer," I said. "She may have let her cell phone die."

"No, I've seen her using it today. And her iPod. Look, I need to run after her."

And with that, the phone went dead. But it was OK. Without even knowing it, Vladimir had given me everything I needed to know to find Cinnamon. I opened my phone, turned it on, quickly checked my call history, then powered it down and made one more payphone call.

To Philip.

Twenty-five minutes later, I was pulling past a row of dilapidated homes into a ratty old cul-de-sac. No, cul-de-sac dignified it; the street just ended in a canyon of scraggly trees and fallen leaves. Where the sidewalk ended, a broken gate lay against a chain-link fence. Through the gap a narrow dirt path led into one of Atlanta's city parks.

I thought of parking there and walking, as not to spook my targets. Then I realized they would hear me on foot or on wheels. And *then* I realized I was a skindancer, and there was no reason for them to hear me at all—unless I wanted them to.

I didn't get off the bike, I didn't strip off my clothes, I didn't murmur a cheesy haiku. I just closed my eyes, drew in a breath, writhed sinuously in the seat of the Vespa in a movement Arcturus had taught me, and breathed out, focusing on the thought of silence.

Mana burned against my skin, then receded as my vine tattoos came to life and slowly began snaking out from beneath my sleeves, my pants, my jacket, my collar. Slowly, the sounds of the wind, the road and the trains receded. When all noises were gone, I opened my eyes.

My vines coiled around me, ghostly and silent in the sunny air. The trees waved in silence, and a train lazily slid by, just beyond the end of the park. One car was covered with wildstyle letters, colorful and splashy, but as it passed it made no sound. Satisfied, I started the Vespa up, and quiet as a ghost, bumped it down through the park and hid it behind the trees.

I tromped silently up to the edge of the park, where the grassy green space overlooked the railroad. This clothes on technique was too slow for battle, but my clothes trapped stray mana and made the spell last longer. Soon I found a squarish cinderblock structure, covered in graffiti, sitting in a kink of the railway lot. With all the underbrush, it was actually hard to tell whether it had been abandoned by the railway or the park service.

And then my breath caught, as I saw, on the side of the building where Philip told me Cinnamon was probably hiding, the distinctive graffiti marks of the tagger.

---

52.   PLAYING HOOKY

On my guard, I crept forward, gathering my vines like a shield. These marks were just quick throwups, a crude sketch of a snake by the junior apprentice, and a more assured mark by the journeyman—but with an unmistakable motif of a werekin ward rune embedded in it.

My heart fell. I stared at it in horror, hoping that didn't mean what I thought it meant. But as I watched, the rune changed slightly: a little tweak here, a little edit there, fleshing itself out so it grew a little bigger, a little rounder, the nubs of six tentacles appearing at the outer edge.

What Arcturus and I had feared was true: the city-wide master spell was feeding back even into simple graffiti. The apprentice's throwup was too simple, but the journeyman's had the right motifs. It was plugged into the circuit. He probably didn't even know he'd done it.

Maybe that was what had happened before.

No matter. I sized up the mark: no larger than a hand, it probably had days before it could go off. Once I was satisfied it wouldn't rear up and eat me, I leaned up a torn piece of chain link fence, stepped through, worked my way around to the door, and stepped inside.

Cinnamon was there, laughing, talking into her cell phone, sitting on an upended trash can in front of a table made from a weathered old door over which she'd spread her schoolbooks. Two schoolbags were tossed in the corner at her feet, positively bulging with books.

On the other side of the room, Tully was fretting over a battered old boom box. He turned to say something and froze, staring at me. His eyes flicked involuntarily at a battered backpack; rather than books, however, his bag bulged with cylindrical objects, like . . . spray cans.

I scowled. There was a reason Tully had been so good at finding graffiti. He was one of the taggers, probably the journeyman. Almost certainly he hadn't meant harm—certainly he hadn't meant to get *himself* almost killed—but there was so much collateral damage.

And if he was a tagger, then Cinnamon—*oh, God.* There was a reason Cinnamon's notes had been so useful to Doug— No. No, I couldn't deal with this now. I had strong suspicions—but no proof yet. I had to focus.

I drew in a breath, pulling in the mana and my vines. Then, slowly, sounds returned.

"—no, not longways, stupid, they'll buzz in all over us," Cinnamon said, laughing. "Just add the digits. *F—uhh!* No, add the digits, and if the *sum* divides by three, so does the original. Try it—eeek!" She froze like Tully, just staring at me, and I mimed closing the phone. After a moment, she said, "Mom wants me. Call you back."

I stared at her a moment. I felt my eyes narrowing. Clearly she was *not* trying to stay hidden, going to math club and calling friends. She was just ditching the Palmottis, unthinkingly jeopardizing not just me, but my chances of getting her back. And that wasn't even counting the awful *mess* I strongly suspected Tully had gotten her into. I pulled off my helmet.

"I'm very disappointed in you, young lady," I said, flashing on all the times Mom had said that to me. It felt more than learned: was there some motherly-daughterly DNA that made that particular sequence pop out, in any language? "The door wasn't even barred. What if I'd been Transomnia?" She flinched, as I'd hoped. I didn't really think Transomnia would go after her, but I knew she feared him from their last encounter and I hoped that would drive the point home. "And there's no other exit. What if I'd been Zipperface?"

"Zipperface?" she said, eyes widening.

I was glad to hear she had no idea who I was talking about—maybe she *was* innocent—but then I realized I'd never told her what he'd done. I'd never had the chance. "Zipperface is the punk with the nasty grill," I said. "The *projectia* of the tagger. He . . . he killed Calaphase."

Cinnamon stood there trembling. Then her eyes grew fiery, defiant.

"Cally died?" she asked. "Cally died and you didn't tell me! You didn't even call!"

I just stood there, stunned. She was right, and I had no defense.

"I calls you and calls you, and you never answers your phone—"

"Cinnamon," I repeated.

"Fuck you. My name's not Cinnamon!" she screeched. "It's Str—"

But she choked that off. Then her lower lip began trembling.

"Cinnamon, I'm so sorry I didn't tell you about Cally," I said quietly. I was relieved. Her surprise meant she almost certainly wasn't in deep, and Tully looked as shocked as she was. "I never got to talk to you in private, and before I knew it, I was on the run from the police—"

"Old *witch!*" she barked, immediately looking away. "You still could have called!"

I drew a breath and looked up into the air. That hurt, but not because of the witch crack. I could slough that off: it was just as Vladimir had said, caused by the Tourette's, something that had popped out under stress, not even in the same tone of voice as the very next sentence.

It hurt because her accusation was true. I *could* have called. Cinnamon had been wearing me out. It was hard being a mother. It was far more than befriending a kid and filling out a few forms. It was real work. And when all this nonsense had started, I had used that as an excuse. Not that I didn't need to be fighting the graffiti; of course I did. But I used it as an excuse to take a break from Cinnamon, and called it work. My mom, in contrast, had found time to call me almost every day—even on the day she died of cancer.

I looked down at my baby girl. Her lip was still trembling. She *still* thought, to this day, that I was trying to get rid of her—an impression she'd gotten from a few wisecracks I'd made the first day Lord Buckhead had cajoled me into taking care of her.

I frowned. My sharp tongue had left scars we'd have for the rest of our lives. Now my slack ass was an inch away from reopening those wounds and pouring in a whole shaker of salt. Like it or not, I was going to have to take the reasons I'd not called her and defend them.

"Cinnamon," I said firmly. "I'm sorry I left you in the dark, but I'm on the run. I had to cut everyone off—they're trailing all my friends, not just Saffron, but even Doug and Jinx. And I had to turn off my phone. I *had* to. The police can track you with your cell phone."

Cinnamon dropped her phone like it had stung her, but Tully just laughed. "Don't listen to her, Cin, she's just tryin to weasel," he said. "They can't track your cell phone."

I spread my hands. "And yet, I'm here," I said. "They may seem like it at times, but cell phones are not actually magic. They've got little radios in 'em. They talk to cell phone towers. Each phone has a chip with its own little number so the tower knows the call is paid for, and who to beam the call back to. How could they *not* track a cell phone? They wouldn't *work!*"

Cinnamon leapt out and turned off her phone.

"Damage is done at this point," I said. "I'm here."

"Why?" she said sullenly, twisting her neck in its collar.

"You disappeared," I said. "I wanted to know you were safe."

"*You* disappeared," she shot back. "You tossed me off on the Palmottis and *ran!*"

"I was forbidden to see you," I said.

"If you cared, that wouldn't have mattered!" she shrieked.

"If I violated a court order, I might never have seen you again."

"That law is stupid," she said. "If you cared, you would have called!"

"I couldn't," I said. "I was—I *am*—on the run from the police."

"For what?" Tully snorted. "Run a red light in your little blue car?"

I glared. I wanted to bite his head off, but I decided to keep my insights to myself until I knew more. "No, for arson, you ingrate. For the fire that blew up the little blue car."

"You blew up the blue bomb?" Cinnamon said, paling.

"No!" I said. "The tagger did."

"It's writer," Tully said.

"Thanks for cluing me in, Tully," I said, glancing at him in bitter triumph. *Writer indeed.* "Anyway, they're going after me because the fires started right after I got out of jail."

"Why . . . why did they put you in jail?" Cinnamon said.

I sighed. "They charged me for killing Valentine."

"Valentine?" Cinnamon said, turning white. "But . . . but you saved me from him!"

"Yes," I said. "Yes, I did."

Her mouth set. "So . . . so you knows the law is stupid, you're on the run from it, and yet here you are to take me back to the Palmottis! What, did he *fink* me, and you called your square ex-boooyfriend to sniff me out so you wouldn't look bad?"

"She never said she was going to take you back," Tully said.

"No, she's right, down to the ex-boyfriend part," I said. "She's a genius, remember?"

"Cin, a genius?" Tully laughed, and she hissed. "Then why's she in the stupid class?"

"It's Special Topics, not Special Ed," I said. "Tully, think for a second. Here you are, on the run, hiding out, free to do whatever you want, and what are you two doing? *She's* doing number theory while you're banging on an obviously busted stereo."

Tully's brow furrowed, and Cinnamon said, "The speaker wire, doofus."

Tully turned the stereo over, found a wire hanging loose from the speaker, broken off. "Aw, man," he said. "When were you going to tell me?"

"Give me that," I said, as Cinnamon giggled. I flipped the stereo over, pressed the red and black tabs that released the wire from the back of the speaker, and handed it back to him. "Strip that, then plug it back into the same holes."

"Wow," Tully said. He popped a claw and picked at the wire, then pulled a switchblade and started making real progress stripping the insulation off. "Where'd you learn that?"

"You learn a lot in college," I said, "trying to make do."

Cinnamon was still giggling, but then her face fell.

"Stop it. You . . . you can't fool me!" she said, glaring. "You don't— *fffuhh!*—you don't cares about me. You didn't even care enough to mention you just found out I was with a boy."

"I didn't *just* find out you were with a boy," I said. "I've known for weeks. He's sweet on you, knows your new name, uses it often enough to shorten it, hangs around enough practically to hover, and you're not even swatting him away."

Her mouth hung open, then set, trembling. "Shut up!"

"It was easy to figure out," I said. "I'm your mother."

"You're . . . you're not my *real* mother," Cinnamon said. "We only just met . . ."

"I am too your real mother," I said, opening my arms. "I've always been your mother your whole life. We just didn't know it yet."

That got her. Cinnamon's lower lip started trembling again. Then she pounced.

"Oh, Mooom," she said, crushing the life out of me. "My Mooom. I'm sorry."

"Can't—breathe—" I said, hugging her back as best I could. "I'm sorry I left you."

"What are we going to do?" she asked, head jerking a little as she did so.

I sighed, leaned back, put my hands on her shoulders. "We're going to fight," I said. "Which means we have to play the game their way, at least a little."

"But whyyy?" she asked. "I don't wants to go back to the Palmottis. We could run—"

"And live like this?" I said, extending my hand across the shed.

"It isn't so bad," Tully said.

"Tully, you live in the margins," I said. "You're always hiding in an unused warehouse or broken down shed, where someone can come along and shoo you away. But you should have your own place, with full rights. You should be able to turn into a wolf in a public park and run free. And the only way to do that is to engage the world, head on."

"That kind of thinkin' gets a werekin shot," Tully said.

"Maybe so," I said. "But that's why there are Edgeworlders. We straddle two worlds for a reason. We don't just want to be free to visit your world. We want you to be free to visit ours."

"So what does we do?" Cinnamon asked.

I dinged the ring on her collar. "We take you back to the Vampire Consulate," I said. "You're under Saffron's protection—you have the right to claim asylum. From there, you can call Ellis and Lee, and hopefully they can work something out."

Cinnamon looked like she'd swallowed a prune. "Do I gots to stay there?"

"Maybe. Maybe you'll have to go back to the Palmottis, maybe not. I'm just hoping that you exercising your legal right to asylum will neutralize the effects of Mister Palmotti's missing persons report, at least as far as our case is concerned."

"Fuck!" Cinnamon said, then bit her lip. "I made things worse, didn't I?"

"Don't worry about it," I said. "Let's go make things better."

Cinnamon and Tully rode with me all the way to the Vampire Consulate, Tully barely hanging on to the back of the Vespa. I don't know how we didn't get pulled over—two fugitives, another minor, and only one helmet between us. But we kept to surface streets, and eventually made it to Auburn Avenue, where we found the deconsecrated church that was the Lady Saffron's home— and the old Victorian that held the Consulate offices.

"This is stupid," Tully said, wavering. "We don't needs to do this."

"Yeah," Cinnamon said slowly, looking at him for support. "Maybe we can—"

"No," I said firmly, hopping off the scooter. "Pep talk's over. You're a missing person. I'm wanted by the police. Technically, I'm not even allowed to see you, and if I'm seen *with* you it will get you into trouble. So. We're going into the Consulate, where you legitimately have the right to claim protection, and where Mister Palmotti can pick you up."

They looked at me, uneasily, and I glared. "Cinnamon, I love you, and Tully, I can tell you love her, but the two of you don't know how much trouble you've made," I said. "Now let's go inside and hope that between Saffron and Ellis and Lee, we can sort this all out."

I took two steps across the street—then the Victorian *exploded*.

53.   COFFINS AFLAME

A flash of heat against my face. Purple flashbulbs dancing before my eyes. My body flying through the air and impacting the pavement, skull cracking against the curb. The squeal of tires, Cinnamon's screams, Tully's cries, rough voices shouting. I started to lift my head, opened my eyes—and saw the heel of a boot slam down into my face.

Ow.

When I came to, I was sitting in a long, low chair, in an elegant dressing room done all in yellow and sepia, like a picture in a faded newspaper. At first I thought something was wrong with my vision; then I saw a blue egg on the desk beside me, and picked it up.

The glass felt reassuringly heavy in my hand, very real, at the same time it held dreamy sweeps of subtle color. In the light it shifted from blue to purple to red, and I could see it was dotted with little white and yellow bubbles.

Clearly, nothing was wrong with my color vision, and I set it down on the table. It was the lampshade that was yellow glass; that, the drapes, the wallpaper, and the *pictures*—old newspapers, aging photographs, lithographs, pages of ancient books.

"Welcome back, envoy of the House Beyond Sleep."

I looked over to see a man, all in black, sitting on an ottoman, hunched like a vulture, staring at me. His suit was exquisite. The gleaming tourbillion watch on his wrist looked more pricey than my dead car. His cropped black hair was styled into thin frosted spikes. He ground a toothpick between perfect human teeth—but his eyes were dead black points.

"I'd say back to the land of the living," he said, hands parting briefly, then clasping back together in a wringing motion that made him look even more like a vulture. "But, you know."

I glanced around me, then at myself: my feet were actually propped up on an ottoman like the one he sat on. Groaning, I tucked my legs down and kicked the ottoman forward so I could sit up. As I did so, the chain holding Transomnia's pendant bounced against my chest.

"Good eye," I said, staring down at it. "You or your men."

"Or women," he said, flat and uninterested. "Sexism in such a day and age."

"Yeah, yeah, if you do have any women working for you thugs, I'll apologize in person," I said, feeling my face. I was sore, but not too bruised, and I felt back to find not one but two tender, swelling lumps on the back of my head. "We marking time until I'm conscious?"

"Yeah."

"I'm conscious. Where's Cinnamon?"

"Safe, though a little better off than her wolf cub," Velazquez said, standing briskly. A bit of metal flashed inside the coat as he did so, something nasty in a shoulder holster. His hunched posture had hidden the weapon while keeping it in easy reach. "Can you stand?"

"What do you mean, better off than—ow," I said, wincing. "Was he hurt—"

"He's fine . . . for now," Velasquez said firmly. "Sorry about the boot, *Lady* Frost. You did a good job going to ground; bandana-and-biker jacket doesn't fit your description. If you hadn't wandered into our little trap—"

"Trap—the *Consulate?*" I said, struggling to stand. "You blew it up to get to *me?*"

"Overkill, I know," he said, spreading his hands. "But we're tired of dicking around with you folk, and my mistress seemed to think you would be easier to capture if . . . disoriented."

"I think that building was on the register," I said, wincing. "You *bastard.*"

"The name's Velazquez," he said.

"You get everyone out before you blew it up, *Velasquez?*" I said, rubbing my head. He shrugged, and I cursed. "Then I'll still keep calling you *bastard.* Who was still in there?"

"I didn't take attendance," Velasquez said, still flat. "You have a problem with our methods, take it up with the Lady Scara. I'm just your escort, envoy. Can you stand?"

I stood up and my head was whirling, and not just with dizziness: what had happened to Cinnamon, to Tully, to everyone in the Consulate? I swayed a little, and he stepped forward to steady me. I towered over him. He couldn't be over five-six, but when he checked me out it was more of an appreciative glance than an 'oh shit you're tall,' which I liked.

"You," Velasquez said, "are in the court of Sir Leopold, vampire lord of Atlanta."

"Lord Delancaster is the vampire lord of Atlanta," I said.

"Only in his mind," Velasquez said. "And on TV. The real power in Atlanta isn't Lord Delancaster or his puppet queen at the Consulate. It's Sir Leopold, and the Gentry."

The Gentry. Ever since this started, Saffron had been talking about static from the Gentry, and Calaphase had filled in the details—wealthy, ancient vampires who saw humans as little more than food. I even had a list of the Gentry vampires who had died. They were mad enough to have caused trouble at Cinnamon's school just because she wore Saffron's collar. They had a real stake in this—and yet I hadn't given them any real thought. Why?

With a certain degree of horror, I realized that after I'd heard Calaphase call them old-school, I'd dismissed the Gentry as conservative yahoos who should get with the times—stupid of me, for two reasons. First, I should have learned from dating Philip that people were more than just the political (R) or (D) after their names—I should have made them allies in this fight.

And second . . . old-school implied forgotten knowledge: the precise kind of knowledge that I had looked for but Doug had dismissed. Could the *Gentry* be the source of the graffiti's magic? It seemed unlikely, but regardless, forgotten knowledge was incredibly dangerous when the group kicking it consisted of people who'd lived forever and accumulated power for centuries. Against a two thousand year old undead Emperor Nero, me and Rush Limbaugh would be fighting on the same side. That thought scared me more than even the Gentry.

"—so Sir Leopold has eagerly awaited an audience with you," Velasquez was saying. "And, as it turns out, he's also curious about an envoy of a House of vampires he has never heard of. It's best not to keep him waiting when he's eager or curious. Let's go."

He motioned to the door. Suddenly I was remembering how many other vampires—Saffron, Calaphase, even Transomnia and Nyissa—had dropped nasty hints about the Gentry, and I *really* didn't want to go through that door. "You first," I said. "Lead the way."

"Don't get cute," Velasquez said. "Move it."

"Look," I said, kneading my brow, not precisely stalling for time but gathering my thoughts. "First, do I have any weapons? You searched me, right?"

The toothpick whirled in his mouth. "You're unarmed."

"I knew you felt me up," I said, and the toothpick twitched as his mouth quirked in a smile. "*Busted.* So I'm not a threat to your bosses. Second, do you have magic bullets?"

The toothpick stopped, but only for a second. "Silver hollow points," he said slowly. "Dipped in wolfsbane."

"Feh," I said, folding my arms. "Not a threat. You know kung fu, or box, or anything?"

Velasquez shifted slightly, in a way which somehow, indefinably, made him more menacing. "Do you really want to get shot, Miss Frost?"

I stared at him coolly. "No, but I have been, twice recently, and here I still stand. So we're both effectively unarmed, and I've got fifty pounds, six inches of reach and two different martial arts up on you. Lead the way, sweet cheeks."

He laughed. "You think you can actually stop bullets?"

"Oh, this damn conversation again," I said, slipping my hands into my jacket pockets and casually letting out my breath to activate my shield. "*Phooo*, yeah, yeah, yeah, I can stop bullets. I could even show *you* how, though it takes years of training and a *shitload* of magic tattoos."

"Huh," he said, the toothpick twirling. "I may take you up on that."

"Dial the Rogue Unicorn, ask for Dakota Frost," I said.

"You are unreal," Velasquez said—and then he smiled grimly. "And it *would* be a big fucking insult for an envoy to go in unannounced—and Sir Leopold definitely wants me to announce you as an envoy. Time to face the music, *Lady* Frost."

He opened the door on a room the size of a small banquet hall, with heavy stone walls and flickering gas lights. Someone had tried to add a civilizing touch—there were long yellowed curtains and brown tapestries, and even the huge wooden beams across the ceiling added to the sepia tones—but the huge stone blocks left an unmistakable impression of *fortress*.

Then my vision focused on the people in the room, and I stopped short, trying to grok what I saw. In that moment of speechlessness, Velasquez introduced me. "Lords and Ladies of the Gentry," he said, "it is my pleasure to present the Lady Frost, Envoy of the House Beyond Sleep." When he finished, I started forward, alternately enraged and horrified.

They looked like giant art pieces: two huge wine bottles wrapped in blood red cloth, each standing beneath a giant ice pick. Then the cloth twitched, and the scale shifted in my eyes. They were man-sized cages shrouded in red curtains, standing beneath huge metal spikes.

The curtains twitched again: someone was inside each cage. My gaze lifted from the hidden prisoners to the cruel metal spikes, each taller than a man and thick as my wrist. Atop the spikes were *massive* stone weights, dangling precariously from single ropes rising to the rafters.

Those thin ropes each led to a winch on either side of the hall, each guarded by a black-suited man. A simple pull of a lever would end the life of whoever was imprisoned within—and then the stones could be winched back up for the next victim.

Between the execution cages, steps led up a raised dais towards three thrones. Lord Delancaster sat regally to the left of the center throne, blond tresses flowing down behind him. Cinnamon sat on the right, visibly trembling, head snapping periodically.

A black-suited man stood behind her, silver-quarreled crossbow at the ready. Behind Lord Delancaster, a similar black-suited woman stood, wooden stake in her crossbow. On the center of the dais, Tully lay bleeding, bound in silver barbed wire, between a tall white man and a short black woman—both in formal dress, both pale for their race—and both eyeing his blood.

Physically dominating the center of the room was a massive freestanding chunk of wall like the one at the Michael C. Carlos Museum, ensconced within a magic circle. But dominating my attention was a flaming coffin—and standing before it, a withered vampire lord. But the fires rippling up behind him were not yellow and natural: they were artistic, rainbow graffiti flames.

Oh, *shit*. The Gentry *was* in control of the graffiti.

The lord of the hall was all that I imagined a vampire would *really* be like. His skin was white as bone, infinitely wrinkled, almost corrugated, and yet so gaunt his features were little more than a skull. His ears were huge, misshapen, at once batlike and distorted as a cauliflower; his nose was a huge, hawkish beak that came down almost to his lip, a thin excuse that peeled back over a massive set of fangs, half piranha, half Rottweiler. Black rivulets of hair were slicked back over his nearly bald dome; beneath his wrinkled brow, two caterpillar eyebrows guarded the pits of his eyes, and their twin points of white flame.

When he moved, he crackled, like the rustling of aged newspaper or the cracking of an old book's spine. I *knew* this condition—I *had* read Saffron's paper. His human cells had been completely consumed by the vampiric fungus: he was *truly* undead, a lich.

The lich walked the length of the black enameled coffin, lit eerily by the wall of rainbow fire roiling up behind him, then he turned to me, bony claws clasped before him, voice a breathy hiss. "So . . . Dakota Frost," he said. "The black widow wanders into our web at last."

"Excuse me?" I said, baffled. I had not expected that. "Black *what?*"

The lich's burning eyes bored into me, an odd amusement spreading over his face. "Surely you know the term—a lethal lover," he said. "You *are* Dakota Frost, in public the paramour of the so-called queen of the vampires—and in secret, I'm told, her slayer."

"I'm *not* her paramour," I said, now offended, "much less her slayer."

"*Someone* has assaulted the Gentry," the vampire hissed, "and who stands to gain more than the vampire queen? And who stands at the queen's right hand? An illicit peddler of magic meant to be hidden, a meddler in the ways of werewolves—and a slayer of wizards!"

"I'm never going to live that down, am I?" I muttered.

"Why would you want to? Any vampire could only dream of having such a formidable human troubleshooter. And yet . . . " the lich said, turning to glance at the vampires on the dais, "Velasquez tells me you bear *other* tokens . . . one of a House I have never heard of, and one of clan that is destroyed. Can you not make up your mind where your loyalties lie, Dakota Frost?"

"I . . . " I began. "I really *don't* know what you are talking about."

"Don't you?" He stepped aside, extending his claw towards the coffin of flame. My heart spasmed—he had mocked Saffron, his men had destroyed her Consulate: maybe he'd killed her. The flames seemed to surge as I stepped forward. Cautiously, I edged towards the coffin.

A vampire lay within the black enameled casket, his body half consumed by slow swirls of wildstyle flames. His burning head was tilted away from me, and half his face was eaten by the graffiti'd flames, but I still recognized him: it was Demophage.

"Thus ends the Oakdale Clan," the lich said. "You were also their troubleshooter, were you not? I do not think I would hire you based on *this* reference."

I took another step forward and felt the shimmer of mana. I looked down to see the edge of a clumsily marked magic circle barring my path. It was surprising it even worked: the magicians who built that ham-handed circle could never have inked the graffiti.

I looked over at the lich, then back down at Demophage. This made no sense. Then I realized the massive misshapen shape beyond the coffin was a huge section of cinderblock wall, covered with shimmering graffiti contained by a clumsy magic circle. As the tag pulsed, I could feel surges of magic leaking through the shoddy magic barrier containing it, even stronger than the sporadic leaks dribbling out from the nearer, shoddier barrier around the coffin.

The vamps didn't control the graffiti—they were studying it too. These were *samples*.

"Oh, *crap*," I said, horrified as I realized how shitty the magic circles were. So much for the ancient knowledge theory—these guys were *yahoos!* In fact, the tags were within an inch of breaking free and killing us all. "This is terrible!"

"Why, yes, I think it is," the vampire lord said, stepping around the coffin to smile at me from behind the flames; beyond him the two vampires began to approach, while, Cinnamon and Delancaster remained frozen on their thrones. "But I am curious. Why do *you* think it so?"

"I thought you controlled the graffiti," I said, "but *you're* more in the dark than *I* am!"

54.   POWER, FIRE AND ICE

The vampire lord's smile deepened—and then he laughed.

"I can see at first glance how you might think that, given how we have enshrined it," the lich said, gesturing at the freestanding wall, "but you understand the situation. *Excellent.*"

My mouth quirked. I couldn't help it.

"You watch the Simpsons?" I asked. "You'd make a great Monty Burns."

The vampire's smile vanished, with the slightest hint of befuddlement. "As insolent as your werekin brat," he said. "But only human . . . and human insolence can be burned away."

And then the white points of light in his eyes *flared*, expanding to eat the world.

"Jeez! Stop that!" I said, flinching. I wished I'd taken Nyissa up on her offer to learn how to fend off vampires. The religious symbols on my knuckles were tingling as the lich expanded his aura, but I didn't feel the fire I'd felt when facing Saffron's rage. This vampire had control and an agenda: simple crosses would not thwart him. "Velasquez, do you have any Advil?"

Velasquez made a choking sound. Then the vampire hissed, and Velasquez snapped an order. "Sir," he said, as a minion darted off, "I think that the Lady Frost was making a joke."

"I am aware of that," the vampire lord said icily. "In a moment she will need it."

I swallowed.

"Why are you humoring her?" asked a strong woman's voice. Heels clicked closer from my right, and I glanced cautiously aside to see a black ballgown, a broad, matronly African-American face, and two blazing points of eyes beneath ponytailed salt-and-pepper black hair. *Now* the crosses on my fingers felt like they were *burning*, and I jammed my hands into my pockets and glanced away as she said, "Why have you brought this human before us as an Envoy? She is free game, fairly caught as part of pruning the branch of Delancaster—"

"Fairly caught as part of an assault on the *Consulate*," a cultured male voice said. This new vampire stepped from the shadows behind one of the killing cages. Tall, blond, regal, in a textured grey business suit with a banded-collar shirt, he moved towards us in velvet silence, a physical chill the only sign of his power. "Never mind your vendetta against Delancaster—it was useful for us to have a public lever. Now you have destroyed that."

"My little trap caught the paramour, did it not?" the black vampire said, and I swallowed. Had she really destroyed the Consulate, killed Saffron, just to get to me? "Stunned a *formidable* witch enough for Velasquez to scoop her up like so much cat litter, with no loss of life."

"No loss of *our* lives," the new vampire said, pale blue eyes flashing.

The evil Oprah hissed at the evil James Bond while the lich just cackled, a dry croak that would have done the Emperor of the Sith proud. Oh, God. This wasn't good. My collar was gone, *Saffron* was gone, and I stood between three vamps: power, fire, and ice personified.

I swayed there in the nexus of their magic; then a tanned white hand appeared, holding two little pills. I stared at it a moment, then looked back to see Velasquez. I was glad he had taken me seriously, and the lich had proved right.

"Thank you," I said, and cautiously slipped a hand out to reach for the Advil.

The black vampire struck Velasquez's hand and sent the pills flying. "You mock us!"

"Such treatment of our guests," the lich said, "does not become you, Lady Scara."

"You are worse than Iadimus," Scara snarled. *Oh, crap.* She was the enforcer Calaphase had been afraid of, and her idea of a 'little trap' was blowing up a whole building. "*I* caught this criminal. Why have you called a full council and paraded her before us as a guest?"

"Because those are the rules, my dear Lady Scara," the lich said, extending a claw towards my chest. "She bears the token of the House Beyond Sleep."

"True, but it is a House we do not recognize, headed by a Lord we have barely heard of," said the blond ice vampire I presumed was Iadimus. "The Lady Scara has a point, Sir Leopold. Why *did* you have Velasquez bring her before us, rather than question her in private?"

"And do *not* say as an envoy," Scara said, with a rough laugh that was little different than a snarl. "Ridiculous. Free game, caught fairly, is still free game, even with the brand of an upstart vampire unwilling to face us. She did *not* come here on a mission, she has no protector—"

"I *am* on a mission," I said hotly, "and I *have* a protector, the Lady Nyissa—"

Then it all happened so quickly.

Scara leapt upon me, blindingly fast. My hand popped up in a block, agonizingly slow. Her teeth and blazing eyes surged upon me just as my upraised hand struck her chest. Magic flared with a clap of thunder. She screamed and batted me away, spinning me round. Out of the corner of my eye I saw Iadimus, looming close, then flinching in turn from my flailing, blazing hand—and then my eyes refocused to see Velasquez, standing before me, drawing his gun.

I had no time to think. I just gasped and thought *shield.* All the mana built up from my sudden twist and from the feedback from Scara poured into my tattoos. And then Velasquez opened fire, the bullet ricocheting off my shield, knocking me back into someone's arms.

I sagged back as Velasquez blinked in shock. Red blood started seeping out of his expensive white banded shirt, his mouth opened—and then he toppled forward.

The teeth of a T-Rex loomed large in my peripheral vision, and I realized I had fallen into the arms of the lich, who had actually caught me and now leaned over my shoulder, snarling, as his best man bled out upon the ground. "No!" he snarled, and tossed me away.

I stumbled towards Scara, who was staggering backwards, patting a burn mark on her chest with one hand, something glittering held in the other. She looked up and snarled, and without thinking I surged forward, her swinging claws sliding off my upraised arm, my knee popping up to shield me and then stomping down on her instep as my other arm shot out and landed all my religious tats under her chin.

With a satisfying flash and clap, Scara fell backwards like a log of wood. The glittering thing tumbled out of her hand—Transomnia's token, complete with its chain. When she'd leapt upon me, she must have ripped it off—but I didn't have time to think about it. Two crossbow-armed guards surged off the dais, and I slid backwards, feet dancing sashaying J-steps, thinking *shield, shield, shield!* With a twang the guards loosed their bolts, one bouncing off my chest, the other skimming my temple, staggering me backwards towards the graffiti'd wall.

I stumbled, my magic-filled skin recoiled from the magic circle barrier and I caught myself leaning against thin air. The guards moved in, I slid back to my feet sinuously, building up power, re-establishing my shield—but I had to get this jacket off!

I glanced aside, making sure Iadimus wasn't about to pounce upon me. But he was not moving: he just stood there like a pillar, staring down at the lich, who cradled Velasquez in his arms, holding him like a child. Then the lich let him fall, and turned his blazing eyes on me.

In less than a blink the lich was on me, seizing my throat, lifting me bodily, snarling. I gagged. I choked. Then my vines erupted from my skin and tore my jacket apart. I shot my hand out, and my vines whipped out across the chest of the vampire and sank into his flesh.

"You killed one of our best men," he snarled. "I'll tear out your throat!"

"You killed one of my oldest friends!" I said. "I'll tear out your heart!"

The lich's eyes burned on me, furious—then curious—then amused. "Tear out *my* heart because Scara killed . . . who? Your little vampire queen, perhaps?"

"But," I said. When Iadimus said no loss of our lives, I'd thought he meant the Gentry, not vamps in general. "But . . . prune the house . . . Scara blew up her Consulate."

"Oh, Dakota Frost, you fool," the lich laughed. "Thinking you can fight with us like we were common street thugs. We are not pugilists; we are strategists. *Uncover the cages.*"

The guards at the winches, who had not moved an inch during the battle, now stepped forwards. The golden tassels were pulled; the red shrouds fell. And inside the killing cages I saw Darkrose . . . and Saffron. Darkrose looked all right behind the bars, just worn and tired; but Saffron looked like . . . like she had become a vampire.

Her ruddy skin had gone pale, her curvy cheeks had become drawn, and one hand gripped the cage, bony and white. Only her flaming hair had held its color, but had an odd luminous cast to it that made it seem unreal. She raised her head to look at me, eyes pinpricks of light.

"You're starving her," I said, choking it off as the lich tightened his grip.

"Yes," he said, "and we will be killing her, unless you release me."

"You'll kill her anyway," I said, gripping his wrist. It was like a bar of iron, and I concentrated, letting out my breath, murmuring words of strength to protect my throat.

"You don't know that," he said, tightening his grip, choking me again. "You do know we'll kill her—or her companion, or perhaps your daughter— *gak!*"

My vines tightened about his chest, and I had the distinct feeling that they had penetrated that chest, that they were curling about his heart. I found the twisting knot rolling underneath the tendrils of my magic and squeezed, and he snarled and choked harder.

"You—so much as—break my daughter's iPod and I'll be most irate."

"You'll do nothing," he snarled. "Or she and her friends all die by *inches*—"

A roaring blast tore through the room, striking my face with the sting of a full backhand mixed in with the hot breath of a dragon. Broken splinters of a wooden door sailed past us and clattered off the wall. Guards began dropping around us, red flowers blossoming in foreheads and chests under a hail of silenced machine gun fire.

Just like that, Iadimus was gone, just gone, and I gripped the arm of the lich tighter as he stumbled back, still suspending me in the air, moving away from the smoke and dust rippling out from a side entrance that had exploded. Secondary explosions and more gunshots echoed through the room, and the remaining guards retreated behind columns and doorways that gave them cover. One ducked out to fire and took a bullet straight to the face. I looked away, squirming in the lich's grasp, trying to see who was storming through that door. Was it SWAT? Was it the DEI? Was it the remnants of Darkrose's crew?

No. It was just one man—one *werewolf*, eyes glowing green and lupine as he darted out of the roiling smoke, silenced machine pistol in one hand burping death as he took cover behind the flaming casket, silvery rapier in the other deflecting crossbow quarrels as he rounded it and moved in, fluid and unstoppable, black body armor deflecting another crossbow as he stepped up to us and placed his rapier against the lich's throat.

"Hello, Dakota," said Doctor Yonas Vladimir. "I see you've found Cinnamon."

55.   A LIFE FOR A LIFE

"*What* the *fuck?*" I said.

"Lords and Ladies of the Gentry, if I may have your attention," Vladimir said, voice ringing out across the hall. He no longer looked like the crippled math teacher: his thin hair rose like a dark halo, his eyes glowed like twin emeralds, and his body moved with the grace only possessed by werekin. "Forgive my entry without an introduction, but no one living knows me by sight. Except, of course, Sir Leopold—who can tell you all that I am Vlad the Destroyer."

"Oh, sweet merciless night," Lord Delancaster said, voice filled with horror.

"You all know my rules," Vladimir said. His dark body armor gleamed where Kevlar mesh met exotic composites, and night vision goggles and grenades and widgets hung from the ballistic straps crisscrossing his body—armed and armored like a werekin Nick Fury. "I walk alone in secrecy and peace. If either is disturbed, I destroy everyone who has seen my face." He smiled, and I felt a shiver in the lich's grip. "You remember, don't you, Leopold?"

"There is no need for such measures," the lich whispered, head tilted ever so slightly back from the point of the blade. "We have not disturbed you."

"Ah, but you have, Leopold," Vladimir said, glancing past us. "When you attack my friends, you become my enemy."

"Thank you, Yonas," I croaked. "But how did you even know—"

The lich laughed. "Oh, you do not know Vlad the Destroyer, Frost," he said. "He could track a ghost across the steppes of Russia, even before all the toys of this modern age."

"Don't take this the wrong way, Dakota," Vladimir twisted the blade back and forth, and I could see it was made of bands of two different metals, one steel, the other . . . silver? "But I would not break cover and destroy a great House just for you. I'm here for Cinnamon."

"Cinnamon?" the lich asked—then snarled. "That foulmouthed little *stray?*"

Vladimir dug the point in. "Never use that word," he said, smiling up at me, very, very grimly. "She *goes* by *Cinnamon.*"

Scara stirred. I started to speak, but the lich tightened his grip on my throat. Scara rose to her feet. I kicked, seemingly uselessly, but really building up mana to shield my throat. "Vladimir," I choked out. "Behind—"

Vladimir just kept smiling at me, but his gun moved, just a flickering blur, *phut-phut*, and Scara went down, screaming, blood spurting from her shattered knee. "You coward," she roared, fangs fully exposed. "Drop the guns and face me."

The gun spat again, and Scara tumbled over, bleeding from her hip and arm. "Not likely," Vladimir said. "No duels, no contests, no facing off in the pit with the rules stacked against me. I am a *warrior.* I do not fight for machismo or tradition. I only gird my loins to go to war."

"You have no honor!" Scara snarled, trying to right herself.

"Honor?" Vladimir snarled, shooting her again, knocking her other arm out from beneath her so she faceplanted on the stone floor. "Is it honorable to kidnap a vampire because her lover was too powerful? Is it honorable to burn a young girl alive because she was loyal?"

"Burn to . . . oh no," I said, still struggling on the end of the lich's arm. They'd left Nagli in the Consulate, oblivious, even after they'd booby-trapped it. "You did kill someone in the Consulate—Nagli! She was practically a child, still in college! You murderous *bastards!*"

Scara began trying to get up again, and the lich snarled at her. "Stay down, you fool," he said. "This *is* Vlad the Destroyer. You are lucky to be alive."

"You are all lucky to be alive," Vladimir said softly, digging the point of his blade into the lich's neck. "Now, Leopold—"

The lich cackled at him. "I will do nothing. By coming here and not killing us, you have proved yourself as impotent as Frost."

I kicked and writhed, and Vladimir snarled, digging the blade in further..

"Do not tempt me," Vladimir said. "I will kill even you, Leopold."

"Yes, but before I break her neck?" the lich said, squeezing harder. Surely he had noticed my shield was up, that any human neck would have already broken? "Before Iadimus cuts the rope on the cages? Before my guards lay their bolts into the heart of the werecat?"

Vladimir's eyes narrowed. "You will still die—"

"And you will still have lost your objective," the lich said, cackling softly. "And I will go to my grave knowing I have taken something precious from Vlad the Destroyer."

Vladimir did not move. "A truce, then," he said.

The lich's piranha grin grew wider. "Raising the white flag so soon?"

"Suggesting you lower the witch," Vladimir said, "before I remove your head."

The lich shoved me harder against the field of the magic circle, and I went still. He smiled, thinking I'd given up. I was thinking something else: *what* an *idiot!*

For a magic circle to have this much resistance, it had to contain an *immense* amount of mana. What if the circle broke and we tumbled inside? Didn't he care about what was trapped in there, something so dangerous its last kill was still burning with magic flame weeks later?

My eyes opened. Something was wrong with my theory of how the magic graffiti worked if it was *Demophage* who was burning. He was inside a magic circle. What was happening to him had to be the natural outcome of the magic, absent all other influences.

I glared at Vladimir and Leopold. They were arguing, politely, about the details of their little truce, about the rules they would follow. Vladimir looked like he was making progress.

Too bad I had had just about enough of all this shit.

"Perhaps I can let the death of Velasquez go," the lich said, "and you the Consulate secretary, if you agree your kills today balance those we made in Darkrose's army?"

Vladimir cocked his head. "That is . . . acceptable—"

"The hell it is!" I said, squirming against the lich's grip.

"Dakota—" Vladimir warned, as the lich squeezed and I writhed.

"Nagli for Velasquez," I said. "Darkrose's men for Velasquez's men. Deaths for deaths. Fair enough. But what about life for life? What will you give me for the life I spare?"

"Whose life will you spare?" the lich said.

"Yours," I said, and I released all my pent-up mana at once.

The head of the Dragon screamed out from behind my neck. The wings burst through the shoulders of my jacket. The tail tore through my rights pants leg and whipped out through the air. And my vines began emerging, from wrist and ankle and through every open hole.

The lich quailed, trying to tighten his grip: but his fingers slowly loosened as my vines inexorably expanded, and then Vladimir dug the blade in and the lich gave up entirely, slowly lowering me to the ground. I kept my eyes narrowed upon him, as much for concentration as anything else. The Dragon was not complete, the four segments were not connected, and without the crash course in advanced skindancing that Arcturus had given me the tattoo would already have disintegrated. This was a bluff, a grand bluff: but the lich did not know that.

"What do you demand?" he said, leaning back from the head of the Dragon, arm still on my collar *pro forma*, holding his other hand over his heart, where my vines still coiled.

"Free the hostages," I said.

"No," he replied.

"I could kill you," I said, and a rippling growl crackled out of the Dragon.

"*I* could kill *them*," he said, tightening his grip again. "You only offer one life."

I scowled. "Then free *one* hostage. Give me Cinnamon."

"No," the lich said. His eyes gleamed at me, obviously pleased, and I started to get scared. What corner was he backing me into? "I will not free the children," he said. "Without them, I have no leverage. The most I would do is . . . spare the life of one of the vampires."

"I don't want the vampires," I said. "*I want Cinnamon.*"

"Then you will not mind if both the vampires starve to death," he said.

My eyes widened. "Yes," I said. "I mind."

"Then spare my life," the lich said, "and you may feed . . . *one* of them. A life for a life."

"Leopold," Vladimir cautioned. "I can still kill everyone in this room."

"Do you not see what stands before you?" the lich asked, gesturing at me with his free hand. He no longer resisted my coiling vines; he actually leaned back into them, letting them cradle him, leaning back to appreciate the glowing head of the Dragon. "Frost could probably kill everyone in this room. So could I, or Delancaster, or Iadimus. One of us might survive, but if we fight, it will be a carnival of blood—and all those you hoped to save will surely die."

Vladimir just stood there, holding his sword. His eyes flickered to mine, then to the lich. I found myself looking between the two of them as well. We were all in agreement; none of us wanted to die, but the lich held the upper hand. A truce was worth a gamble.

I drew in a breath and concentrated, and the Dragon furled its wings and slowly began drawing back into my body. The lich loosened his hand. Vladimir took a half-step back. And then I let the vines go and slid away from the magic circle to stand by Vladimir.

"Guards," the lich said, gesturing at Scara. "Drag that off. Extract the silver bullets and feed her. This is her mess. She must regain her strength in time to see it cleaned up."

The guards twitched, unwilling to come out of cover. Vladimir and I glanced at each other warily. The lich raised a shaggy eyebrow at us, openly curious as to what we would do. Finally Vladimir motioned them forward, and two guards carried Scara out.

"Now, choose," the lich said. "She who left you, or she who took her from you."

"Actually, *I* dumped Saffron," I said. "And Darkrose and I get on fabulously."

The lich tilted his head slightly. "Such modern ways," he said. "In the old days she would have killed you for such a betrayal, for fear you would have returned with a stake."

"Now we just go on Jerry Springer," I said. "It's more painful."

The lich hissed. "Enough delay. Choose."

I swallowed, and stepped between the cages.

On the one side was Darkrose: stripped out of her catsuit and leggings, wearing nothing but a ragged shift that was little more than a burlap bag. She was drained thin, her black skin crackled and dry like she was covered in burned paper. She lived—at least she breathed—but a normal human would be dead after ten days without water, or half starved without food.

But she looked nowhere near as bad as Saffron. They couldn't have had her quite as long as Darkrose, no more than a week, but she looked little better than the lich: skin dead white, pulled tight over her bones, cheeks sunken until I could see her skull.

I looked more closely, then recoiled as I saw little white threads creeping over her skin. It was the vampiric fungus: the magical infection that powered vampires and animated zombies. You never normally saw it outside of a microscope. I knew what was happening—I *had* read Saffron's paper. Without normal human food, the delicate balance between living human flesh and undead vampire matter inside Saffron had been disrupted, the vampiric fungus was blooming, and she was sliding from daywalker into normal vampire.

Saffron opened her eyes at me, filled with hunger, and I looked away, feeling none of the love I had once felt and all the hate. This was precisely what I had feared would happen if she became a vampire. I glanced at Darkrose's pitiful form—but who was I kidding?

"I'm so sorry, Darkrose," I said—and turned back to Saffron.

I stepped to the cage, pulling back my sleeve, and extended my arm to Saffron. At first she didn't move, but then her brittle hands took it tenderly, and gave me a brief squeeze, as if she knew what this cost me. Slowly, tenderly, she kissed the skin above my hand.

Then her teeth sank in, her eyes closed in bliss, and Saffron took life from my wrist.

56. RETURN OF THE VAMPIRE QUEEN

There was a sharp pain, a near-orgasmic pleasure, and a terrifying sensation of blood flowing out through my skin, drawn by the suction of her mouth through an orifice that should never have been there, through which blood should never have gone. But beyond all that I felt mana: my own life force, built up in my skin and my body while I had been threatening the lich, just pouring out through this new conduit like a live electric wire.

Seconds later, Saffron ripped her mouth from my wrist, snarling, droplets of blood spraying out over the cage. I collapsed backwards, holding my wrist, as Saffron stood in one explosive motion, arms thrown wide, shattering the bars of the cage so they clattered out across the hall, ringing with the impact wherever they struck like deranged churchbells.

The huge stone weight snapped off its chain and fell upon her. *Her* arm swung up in a savage motion, breaking off the metal spike with a twang. Then she *caught* the stone, screamed with rage, and hurled it the length of the hall, where it impacted with a clap like thunder.

Saffron turned towards Darkrose's cage, and the guards tensed, raising their crossbows. One was too tense, and he loosed his bolt. Saffron caught it midair and crushed it in one hand.

"If starving me has taken my daylight, *you all die*," Saffron snarled, broken splinters dropping out of her hand one by one to the stone floor below. She no longer sounded human; she sounded worse than the lich. "If you kill my mate, I will *torture* you all to death."

"Such power, such fire," the lich said. "Most impressive, surely, but you have been listening. The calculus in this room has not changed—unless you relent. Recall my offer. We are willing to acknowledge your power . . . if you acknowledge ours."

Saffron glared at him, looked down, nodded.

"You planned this," Iadimus said. I couldn't pin down where his voice was coming from; if anyone was going to walk out of this alive, it was him. "You knew the Lady Scara would oppose so you had her taken out—and you knew who the Lady Frost would choose."

"Would it change your vote?" the lich snarled. "We have lost two elders to this plague. We have already discussed replacements. She was our first candidate. Shall we proceed?"

Iadimus was silent for a moment.

"No, it would not change my vote," he said. "And, yes, I think we should."

"Congratulations, my dear," the lich said, cackling. "You may sit at the big table."

"You pompous windbag," Saffron snarled. "You really think I will let this go?"

"Now now," the lich said coolly. "Don't be petulant, my dear. Delancaster has spoiled you. But the Gentry will not quake before you like leaves. Tantrums are unbecoming in well-groomed children." His voice hissed like sandpaper. "Don't make me take away your pet."

Saffron tensed. So did the guards around Darkrose. Then Saffron seemed to crumple, and looked up at the lich, who gestured to the throne where Cinnamon sat. When the guard's hand touched her shoulder Cinnamon hopped up like her ass was on fire. He led her to the edge of the stage, and she stood where he put her, holding her tail so it wouldn't switch back and forth. A little gasp escaped her lips, a rough cough and head snap, and the lich hissed at her sharply.

"Be silent, you foulmouthed brat," he snarled. "Even if you are Frost's daughter—"

"Leopold," Vladimir warned. "The child has a condition."

"Enough," the lich said, voice crackling. "She was warned. No more insolence."

Cinnamon nodded; then she looked at me, eyes pleading, neck twisting in its steel collar. Talk about stress—Cinnamon was one outburst away from setting the lich off again. How was I going to help her, sprawled on the floor amidst a pile of twisted metal rails and cracked stone?

"*Thank you,* Dakota," Saffron said, and I looked up to see her looking sadly down at me. "I never wanted to force that on you." Then she lowered her head, walked down to the stage, ascended the dais, and sat down under the crossbow of the guard.

"Uh . . . okay," I said, sitting up but still totally bewildered. "What just happened?"

"'The Gentry' means a clique of the most powerful vampires in a region," Vladimir said, bending down, examining my wrist. "This Gentry just offered 'acknowledgement' of Saffron's power. By acknowledging their power in return, Saffron gains standing among them."

"Wonderful," I said, wincing as he pulled out a tiny silver flask with a cross and poured a clear, fizzing substance on the wound—*holy hydrogen peroxide?* "A vampire country club."

"*Don't* think of your vestigial Western aristocracy," Vladimir said, pulling out a compact first aid kit. "Gentry is an *old* word, and the organization it represents is older still—"

"Enough history," the lich interrupted. "I have kept my part of the bargain. A life for a life, Dakota Frost. Now . . . I count four more. What do you have to offer me in return?"

"What do I have to offer?" I asked helplessly, as Vladimir bound the wound on my wrist. "I don't even know what you want."

"Scara was right," the lich said. "We did not bring you here just as the Envoy of a House we do not respect. And, as it turns out, neither did we capture Darkrose just to get to Saffron. You are a slippery woman, Dakota Frost. We captured Saffron to get to you."

"To *me?*" I said. "What do you want with me?"

"*Some* of us," Iadimus said, appearing on the dais, carefully staying out of direct eyeshot of Vladimir, "are not fooled by your protests and denials. You *have* to know why you are here: to stop your assaults on vampires."

It took me a moment to get it.

"Do *what?*" I said. "You think *I'm* behind the attacks?"

"The police certainly do," Iadimus said. "According to the Lady Scara's sources, the district attorney suspected you from the start."

"The district attorney is *not* the police," I said, "and if she suspected me, it's only because I was a magician at the scene of a magical crime—"

"With a history of killing by magic," Iadimus replied.

"The police called me to that crime scene," I said, inwardly cursing. McGough had been right from the start. I should never have been there. "They *knew* my history—"

Iadimus's eyes tightened. "Perhaps they wanted to see what you would do."

"Hang on, you're saying the police, my *uncle*, invited me to the scene of an assault hoping I'd turn it into a murder, and didn't arrest me on the spot when it did?" I said. "I don't think you know how *human* police work—or my uncle, for that matter."

"Perhaps your relative didn't want to see you for what you were," Iadimus said, pointing at Demophage's coffin. "After he let you walk, you *annihilated* the Oakdale Clan."

"Oh, you *didn't* just accuse me of killing my own lover," I said acidly.

"Bah," Iadimus said. Yes, he actually said *bah*, and it was all I could do not to follow with *humbug*. "You are a magician, with knowledge, skill and animosity towards vampires. Before you eluded the police, they confirmed your presence at several of the attacks."

"Because I was investigating them!"

"So the Lady Saffron claimed, but the Lady Scara's sources say otherwise," Iadimus said, holding up my Moleskine. "And you have *detailed* notes going back to the very first kills."

"Of course, *moron*," I snapped, "because Saffron assigned me that task weeks ago!"

"*Her* story," Iadimus snapped back. "Perhaps she is shielding you out of misplaced loyalty, or well-placed loyalty if she is using you to eliminate her competition."

"*Some* Edgeworlder *had* to investigate, because the police *clearly* don't trust us—"

"Don't trust *her*," Iadimus said. "After the Lady Saffron's *spectacular* lack of success dealing with assaults on the Gentry, the Lady Scara warned her contacts in the police the Lady Saffron might be attempting a coup, using you as her instrument."

"Gee, *thanks*," I said. "Now I know why I had to sleep under a bridge—"

"We warned the police, and the Lady Saffron publically disowned you within the *hour*," Iadimus said. "Yet she was seen working with you closely mere minutes later, when the safety of someone still under her protection was at stake—a crime for which we could have charged her."

I scowled at him. This was a conspiracy theory, deep rooted. It would not be easy to win them over. Heck, I was starting to question Saffron, and I *knew* I wasn't her hired killer.

"There was a brief lull when the police managed to bring you in on a pretext," Iadimus continued. "But you eluded them, and since then, *seven* more vampires have been killed."

"*Jesus*," I said, making Iadimus flinch. "That makes the combined toll, what, fifteen?"

"Sixteen *vampires*," he said, eyes narrowed to blazing chips of ice. "But not just vampires. Sixty-four of our human prey—*your* kind—have died, and four werekin—"

"*Fah*," Cinnamon said, flinching first at the death count—then at Iadimus's glare.

"*Not* my fault," I snapped, trying to refocus the conversation back on me. "Even when I was in hiding I was working to stop—"

"I do not believe you," Iadimus said stiffly. "And neither does the Lady Scara."

"I, however, *do* believe her," the lich said, smiling. "And Scara is not here."

Iadimus's mouth opened in shock, showing full fangs. Then he covered them, scowling.

"Irrelevant. The Lady Scara's argument holds. I still oppose you. The vote is tied."

"What about Lord Delancaster?" Vladimir asked sharply. "He's a vampire lord."

"The rebel does *not* get a vote," the lich snapped, and Vladimir and I looked at each other, baffled. Delancaster did not respond; he just sat on the throne, motionless. "His protégé, however . . . makes a quorum." And then the lich looked at Saffron.

Iadimus drew a breath. "Oh, you manipulative *bastard*," he said quietly.

"Protégé . . . *me?*" Saffron asked. The attention seemed to have rattled her, and her voice sounded one drop less like the lich, and one drop more like Saffron. "What about me?"

"You," the lich said, "are now in the Gentry. What say you about Frost's assignment?"

"You *know* what she'll say," Iadimus said icily. "What, did you plan this?"

"Planned the death of Velasquez, the assault of the Destroyer, the shaming of Scara? Planned Frost pulling a dragon from her back? Come now," the lich said. "But never waste a good crisis. Answer, child. Did you assign Dakota Frost the task of defeating the graffiti?"

Saffron just stared at him. "Yes," she said cautiously.

"So you would be willing to commit that to a vote? To a finding of fact by the Gentry, that this is the explanation for Dakota Frost's presence at all the graffiti crimes?"

"Yes," Saffron said, even more cautiously. I got this sinking feeling that we were being maneuvered into a trap. "Yes, I asked Da—I asked the Lady Frost to investigate them."

"I concur," the lich said.

"I do *not*," Iadimus snarled.

"Irrelevant," the lich said, smiling. "We have a quorum of elders, who have made a finding of fact that dismisses Scara's objection. In fact, we can go further . . . now that the Lady Saffron is in the Gentry, her request to Dakota Frost gains the force of command."

"Now wait a minute," Saffron began.

"No, I see no need to wait. You commanded her to act, and so far she has produced no results," he said. His eyes flashed at me. "Perhaps we can find new ways to motivate her."

"You mention Cinnamon's name again," Vladimir said, "and—"

"No need for threats, Vlad," the lich said. "I heard you when you said you came for Cinnamon and not for Frost. If the child holds her tongue, she can keep her head."

"I'm not going to let you take her mother," Vladimir said.

"And if you had to choose between them?" the lich said.

"Well," Vladimir began, his eyes flickering over at me. "I'd—"

"That's the same choice I would make, Doctor," I said, staring at Cinnamon. The mention of her name had rattled her once again, and she was biting her knuckle. What had she *said* to the lich to piss him off? I had to get her out of here, whatever it took. "Don't be ashamed."

"Excellent," the lich said, eyes focusing on me. "Then perhaps you will both agree that if I guarantee her safety . . . I can, in exchange, place you 'on the hook' for Saffron's command?"

I swallowed. Vladimir and I glanced at each other. Then we both nodded.

The lich's mouth parted in that piranha grin. "Dakota Frost," he said, his bony hand slowly extending towards the cinderblock wall, "you have been given a command by a member of the Gentry, and have failed us. Now, we give you one last chance to redeem yourself:"

"Dakota Frost, on penalty of death," the lich said, "stop this plague."

57. TOO SPOOKY TO PICK UP A PHONE

I stared at the wall. Then at the lich. "Wait, what? Stop *this?* That's . . . it?"

"That is it," he said, smiling evilly. "Though I doubt you will find yourself up to—"

"Get to the point," Iadimus said. "She does *not* understand what we're asking of her."

I stared . . . and then got what he meant. "Oh, I think I do," I said, feeling anger build. "Studying it for weeks, remember? I know you aren't asking for a sandblasting job."

"Quite right," the lich said. "We are commanding you to kill the tagger."

"No. No, you are *not*," I said sharply. Being strong armed into what I was already doing really pissed me off. "First, I'm *no one's* hired killer, sir. And second, Saffron's command was to stop the graffiti attacks. You are not commanding me to kill the tagger, but to *defeat* him."

"But if you kill him, wouldn't that—" the lich began, perplexed.

"Why do you think killing him will stop the attacks?" I said, waving at the tag. "*Look* at that thing, growing in power. Is the tagger here? Is he hiding behind one of the curtains, orchestrating it? Who are you to tell me how to fight it? What the fuck do you know?"

"Watch your tongue, Frost," the lich hissed. "I will not tolerate—"

"*You* will not tolerate?" I interrupted. "You have no idea what you've done! How long have you had this tag? How long have you had Demophage?

Days? *Weeks?*"

The lich's scowl slowly faded, became uncertain. "Over two weeks."

"*Damn you!*" I said. "That was before *Calaphase* died, before dozens of others! You had a *live sample* of the graffiti and kept it hidden when you *knew* I was fighting it?"

"We did not believe," the lich said, "you *were* fighting—"

"All this *pointless* death, destruction, and brinksmanship, when all you needed to do was make *a phone call!* I would have broken *the speed limit* to come take a look at this!"

"You are not an easy woman to find," Iadimus began.

"You *idiots!*" I said. "I only went into hiding, like, ten days ago, and I only did *that* so I could stay free to fight the graffiti. I've spent *weeks* crisscrossing Atlanta trying to find a way to defeat it. I have been *desperate* to find a live tag."

Glaring, I turned to the most perfect—and most safely contained— sample of the tagger's artwork that I had seen. This is what I'd needed all along, and the bastard had withheld it from me—and Calaphase had died. I wanted to whip out the Dragon again and take my chances.

As I stared, watching the tag elaborate itself further, watching it lift from the wall like a bas-relief, I felt my skin tingle, then heard the crackling of paper. My eyes started to tear up, and I looked over to see the lich standing six inches from me, eyes white points of flame.

"Buzz off," I said. "You're making my eyes water."

I felt Vladimir move to my other side, growling softly.

"If you two are going to fight, take it outside," I said.

"It took *considerable* maneuvering to get the Gentry and the Consulates united behind you in this fight," the lich hissed. "But even still, I will not tolerate insolenc—"

"Save it. We've lost weeks and people, all because you all were too proud or spooky to pick up a damn phone. So we're all now weaker while this thing is getting stronger—every second. You'll note the tag has become more saturated and dimensional *while we've been talking.*"

I felt a movement from Vladimir, as if he was looking at the tag. But the lich just nodded. "Yes. It has been growing with power since we . . . caught . . . it. It was little more than a crude cartoon with the slightest movement. Our wizards think Demophage fought his way free before he died, as his corpse was not burned beyond recognition like the others, but instead *continuously* burned, with a non-consuming magical flame."

I scowled. "It harvested enough blood and suffering to *start* the spell," I said, "but not enough to finish it, whatever the spell actually is."

"Our wizards . . . concur," the lich said carefully. "We brought the wall and Demophage here for study, but soon we found the link was not broken, and the tag was still growing."

"I've seen that before," I said—earlier today, outside Cinnamon's and Tully's hideout. "With the right core logic, even simple tags could elaborate into full-blown masterpieces."

"The magic circles stopped the process for a while," Iadimus said, "but almost from the moment you arrived, it accelerated. You can see why we thought we had the master tagger."

"Fallout from our fight," I said. "When the lich shoved me against the magic barrier, it weakened it. Releasing the Dragon couldn't have helped matters."

"Regardless," the lich said, "After Vlad's assault, it accelerated even more. Now . . . "

We looked at the tag, at the familiar design: the whorl of barbs, the rounded hillside with its eerie golden leaves of grass, the black outline of the city behind a sky of fire. This tag—this *master piece*—was a thousand times more detailed than the one that had killed Revenance. It had to be feeding on the carnage. It stood off the wall like a living sculpture now, and its movement was so supple and fluid I felt like I was watching an animated film.

But there was something more. I leaned in. My eyes tightened. In the center of the whorls was a repeated pattern, wrapped over with barbed wire: six stone pathways, arcing into the center of the whorl. But they weren't pathways: they were distorted images of columns. The six stone columns that held up the roof of this very room—an echo of our environment.

I looked from the graffiti to Cinnamon, trembling, and Tully, suffering.

There might be a way out of this after all.

I shoved my hand in my pocket. "Look, Sir Leopold, I'm—sorry I backtalked you in front of your fellow vampires," I whispered. "I understand that looks bad and you can't allow it. But this menace doesn't care about your pride or politics. It feeds off living vampire flesh. It murdered my friends. I will do everything in my power to help you take it out."

The lich's face contorted into a pleased grimace, in a way worse than his rage. "How . . . magnanimous of you, Dakota Frost. And how do you plan to . . . take it out . . . so you can avenge your lost friends, and save the lives of your remaining friends?"

I stared at the tag, my eyes running over its lines, its logic. Now, close up, not just photos, I could see the receiver lines that gave it power, pick out the intricate woven elements that made it a spatial bridge. "I have a plan," I said. "But it's going to be risky and unpleasant."

"Unpleasant?" the lich asked. "For whom?"

"For me," I said. "And my assistants. I'm going to have to take the fight to the tagger."

"So you *do* accept your burden," the lich said. "What assistance will you need?"

"*Assistants,*" I said. "I need Cinnamon and Tully to defeat the tagger."

The lich stared at me, then began laughing. "Such a childish ploy—"

"This is real," I said; my quickly-hatching plan could be trading the frying pan for the fire. "You have to decide what's more important to you, defeating the tagger or keeping one hostage for each of the Gospels."

The lich just kept laughing, then gave a little bow. "Very well, you can have one assistant," he said. "*I* will choose this time. We both know who you would pick—"

"I'd pick Tully," I said loudly, "*if* I was willing to take a half-assed stab at this in the hope that dying in the attempt would prompt you to let the hostages go. But I have no intention of dying and no faith in your mercy, so I will need both of them."

The lich drew himself up out of his bow. He was no longer laughing. "Pick one."

"I am not picking either of them. I am taking both," I said softly. "Understand me clearly. This isn't negotiable, because it isn't a trick. *It's part of the procedure.* I need them both: Tully has seen more of the tags than anyone, because he worked with the tagger."

"I did *not*," Tully cried, twitching in his hogtie. "I'd never—"

Iadimus snatched Tully's bag from the side of one of the thrones, strode forward and opened it up atop him. As I had expected from the bulges in it when I'd seen it in their little hideout, oil chalk and rechargeable paint cans tumbled out. The tagger's tools rained down on Tully, and he cried out, writhing in the barbed wire.

The lich glared at Tully, lips curling in a feral snarl. "Iadimus, how long were you planning on keeping this from us?"

"You are not the only one who withholds information to his own advantage."

The lich raised his hand. "Guards—"

"You kill Tully now, this won't work, and the tags take over the city," I said. "And second, I need Cinnamon because she has analyzed the logic of the tags for me. She may not be a fully trained graphomancer, but her mathematical skill more than makes up for it."

"Mathematical skill?" the lich said incredulously. "What skill has a street cat?"

"Cinnamon," Vladimir said loudly. "Come down here. Show us why you're precious."

Nervously, Cinnamon left the throne, and I stepped back from the tag. She tried not to look at anyone, not the guards, not the vampires, not Darkrose, and especially not the lich. Then she stopped right in front of me, still holding her own tail, head snapping periodically.

"Cinnamon," Vladimir said, "how many cinderblocks are in that wall?"

"*Hahh*," Cinnamon barked, then tilted her head. "Two hundred and forty three."

"Is that a lonely?" Vladimir said. "A prime number?"

"No," she said, disgusted, face twitching. "It's a *fffuhh*, a f-five threes tower."

"Oh," Vladimir said, a bit crestfallen. "Three to the fifth power. So it is."

"Of course it is," Cinnamon said, tilting her head the other way. Her head was still snapping, her mouth still twitching, but she was a bit calmer now that she was talking. "The closest lonely's two forty one, skip down two, also a lonely, the first lonely."

"So three to the fifth power," Vladimir said, "is the sum of two primes?"

"*All* counts pass three are the sum of two lonelies," she said. "Isn't it obvious?"

Vladimir let out his breath, then grinned. "Goldbach's Conjecture, obvious? No, but . . . when all this is over, I'd very much like you to explain it to me," he said, tousling her hair. "In fact, write it up for Monday's class. Consider it makeup for your missed test, young lady."

"O-OK," Cinnamon said nervously, re-adjusting her headscarf with one hand. "Fuck. *Everything* turns into a test . . . "

Vladimir looked at the lich. "Get the point?" he asked.

The lich looked at me, and I flinched away. "Do you really need her?"

I sighed. Steeled myself and looked up at him, eye to eye. It hurt, like staring into two twin suns, not in my eyes, but behind them. "No," I said. "You shouldn't let me take them."

"Do not lie to me!" the lich snarled, and the buzzing between my ears grew worse—then quickly faded. "Ah," he said, drawing his hands before him like a praying mantis as my wooziness faded. "Ah. I see. Well played. You really think you are going to die?"

"There's every possibility," I said—and Iadimus straightened in salute. "The tags are *very* strong, and the tagger is inventive and artistic. Alone he'd wax me. But Tully knows his patterns, and Cinnamon knows how his magic works. Between the three of us, we can do it."

"You will have my best men backing you," the lich said. "Of those that remain."

"No," I said. "We do it alone."

The lich smiled. "Do you really think I will let you walk out of here—"

"We're not walking anywhere," I said, gesturing at the wall inside the magic circle. "We're going to take the tagger on *right here*."

58. INTO THE MAW OF MADNESS

The lich's mouth hung open . . . then widened into that grotesque parody of delight.

"Ah!" he said, clasping his hands together. "You and your assistants are going to do a little magic trick, and just make the problem disappear?"

"Something like that," I said.

"This is ridiculous," Iadimus said, still standing straight, but the subtle respect in his stance gone, replaced by wary mistrust. "She's clearly planning a trick."

"You've threatened to kill me if I don't stop the graffiti. But how do you imagine that's going to work? Do you expect me to mix up a potion, or break into the Georgia Tech Physics of Magic lab, spin up their magic accelerator and perform an incantation?"

"Well—"

"I'm a *skindancer*," I said. "I ink magic tattoos and dance to bring them to life. I've spent the last week learning the logic of the tags, improving my skindancing skill, and repairing some of the tattoos that were damaged in previous battles. *I'm* as ready as I'm going to be."

"If you are so ready," Iadimus said, "then why have you not yet destroyed them?"

"I won't lie to you," I said. "These tags have damn near killed me, four times. Each time it was because the tagger chose the time and the target, and either I was the target or I was blundering in to save the target. Now, things are different. I'm ready, I have Cinnamon, I have Tully, I have an intact tag without a trapped victim, and I have a hell of an incentive."

"Your life," Iadimus said, "and the lives of your friends."

"Yeah. But not in the way you think," I said. "The real reason is that your magic circle is total crap, and the tag is about to bust free and kill us all. Quiet, everyone, and listen."

The room went silent. In the sudden silence, you could hear a rushing sound, as of a terrific wind. I let the sound rush over me, relished the horrified looks on the vamp's faces. Then I turned to look at the tag. The whorl was spinning, and the flames behind the city were beginning to rise in a rippling wall of rainbow flame. Beyond it was the source of the noise: within the magic circle containing Demophage's casket, magic fire was rising in a tornado of flame.

"The tags are both batteries and generators, transmitters and receivers," I said loudly. "Their magic feeds on not just blood, but pain and death, then stores it up. Even through your crappy magic circle, it was able to absorb enough power and pain from the carnage of Vladimir's assault to finally activate. Once activated, it can power magic fires."

Iadimus appeared and consulted with two sycophants, a man and a woman. Scowling, they looked over at me—perhaps they were the magicians that had laid the magic circle I'd just called crap. Well, fine: it *was* crap. Then Iadimus asked them a question in low tones, and both of the mages nodded— one reluctantly, the other vigorously. Both were scared.

"I'm sure they've told you that if the fire breaks out, it will destroy this building," I said. "But just as clearly you can see that there's no more material to burn in there. That fire is being fed magically from an exterior source. To stop it, I'm going to need to go into the magic circle, take on the tag and sever that connection. The tagger uses a graffiti-based *projectia*, so he's plugged into the circuit. The feedback of destroying this tag will almost certainly kill him."

The last sentence was a lie, but Iadimus looked at his mages, who slowly nodded.

"Very well," the lich said.

They bought it.

"Release Tully and give him back his backpack," I said. "And give me my cell phone. It's in Velasquez's breast pocket."

"Why, so you can call for help?" Iadimus asked.

"And provoke you to kill Darkrose?" I said. There was no one manning the rope at this second, but any guard with a gun or crossbow could do the job in a heartbeat. But then Vladimir stepped forward, and I smiled. They wouldn't dare kill her while he—

"Or provoke me to kill all of you?" Vladimir said darkly. I swallowed, and Vladimir looked at me pitilessly. "I want to help you, Dakota, but I survive by preserving my privacy. Do not involve the police, or I will wipe this place out, move on, and start over."

I stared at him. I hadn't expected that; I'd thought we were on the same side. Perhaps the lich was right; I really *didn't* know Vlad the Destroyer. "Good to know," I said finally. "In any case, I'm on the run from the police. I'm not going to even turn it on unless I have to."

"And why would you have to?" Iadimus asked.

I struck the magic barrier with my hand, and a hollow sound echoed through the hall. "Because these are damn near soundproof. Listen to that fire: it's raging, but you can barely hear it through the barrier, and if you can barely hear that you won't hear me. If I need you and your magicians to do something I'm not going to play fucking charades."

"If it's soundproof," Iadimus said, "how do you know your phone will work?"

"You can *see* it. Obviously it's transparent to electromagnetic radiation." There were blank looks. "You know, light, radio waves, two parts of one spectrum—"

"Dakota, quit showing off your knowledge," Vladimir growled. "And the rest of you, quit dicking around. Leopold, give her what she asks so she can get on with it, or quit this place before the fire escapes and kills you all."

"Just us? Not you?" Iadimus asked.

"He will not die," the lich said, motioning to his guards, "not even in a fire."

Moments later, Tully appeared beside Cinnamon and me, left hand squeezed over his bloody right wrist. "The barbs were silver," he said. "The bleeding won't stop—"

"Keep pressure on it," Vladimir said. "The touch of silver may have damaged the outer layers of cells, but it won't have poisoned you."

"What are we going to do?" Cinnamon asked fearfully, tugging at her collar.

I took Tully's refilled backpack and my cell phone from one of the guards and knelt down before the two of them. "I'm going to take us inside the magic circle. Once inside, I'm going to perform the Dance of Five and Two, which will highlight the lines of the tag. Tully—"

"I didn't do anything—"

"Regardless, you know graffiti magic," I said, and then, since I knew it would irritate him, I said, "you know it because you're a *tagger.*"

"It's *writer,*" he said, and bit his lip.

"Yeah, gotcha," I said. "Once the lines of the tag start to glow, you, Tully, will need to identify the mana cycles—the magical power circuit. Then Cinnamon can tell me which points to destroy in what order to create maximum feedback."

"But I don't knows how—" Cinnamon said.

"It's a simple logic problem," I said. "You'll know it when you see it. It's why you're precious, remember? I don't need you to explain it. Just see it and tell me. Remember, *stay close to me* while I'm doing the first dance, then as soon as I tell you, step straight back to the edge of the circle while I'm working. If anything goes wrong, Iadimus's magicians will pull you out."

"We will not," the female magician said.

The lich raised his hand. "Do as she says. We must question them if she fails," he hissed. "And you must be on hand in case the circle is broken when she takes them through the barrier."

Reluctantly, the two magicians stepped forward. The lich stood behind one of them; Vladimir stood behind the other. I put my hands on Cinnamon and Tully's shoulders and led them forward, straight up to the edge of the magic circle.

"How will you stop it from grabbing us?" Tully asked fearfully.

"Arcturus, my master, taught me how," I lied. "Ready?"

"Yes," she said, swallowing. "Fuck!"

"All right," I said, "let's do this."

I raised my hands and stepped right up to the edge of the field. I stared at the spinning whorl, at the six arcs of stone, then closed my eyes. For the moment, the magic of the tag was a distraction: I needed to feel the magic of the circle first.

I heard the surging of the magic barrier as it tried to contain the magic within, the muffled roaring of the flames, and beyond that, like a hidden baseline newly noticed on a familiar song, the humming of the spinning whorl as it gathered its power.

I spun, then began shimmying my arms up and down, harmonizing myself with the field. Then I slowly lowered my hands, placing them on Cinnamon's and Tully's shoulders. I couldn't believe I was going to do this, to take us into that torrent of magic.

But hopefully it was better than where we were.

I tugged Tully and Cinnamon forward and leapt with them through the field, shattering the magic barrier. The tag surged out hungrily. No time for fancy dances or subtle intents; I just lunged forward and screamed: *"Web of space, take us to your heart!"*

The whorl expanded. Its tentacles reached out—and *pulled us inside.*

---

59. THE TRUTH WILL SET YOU FREE

Second time through, Streetscribe's Happy Fun Ride was much more manageable. There was the initial shock as mana flashed against my skin, worse than before as this tag was more powerful and my skin had grown more sensitive. But I sloughed the pain off, and with it the buffeting of color and the torrent of wind screaming around us.

Even with training, I couldn't help being jerked, twisted and buffeted: it was like riding a roller coaster in a hurricane. But I once rode the Mindbender at Six Flags Georgia five times in a row, and had been through this before. So when this kaleidoscope ride came to an end, I landed head up, boots down, with legs coiled for impact, and then straightened right up to standing.

Cinnamon and Tully fell into the water at my feet, their screams turning to spluttering as water splashed up into their lungs. I reached down and collared them both, hauling them to their feet. Tully looked fine, if a bit rattled, but Cinnamon was dry retching—I had forgotten about her motion sickness.

While she struggled upright, I took stock.

We were in a dark stone tunnel, lit only by the magic of the tag behind us. It was a cruder version of the masterpiece we'd seen in the lich's lair, and I realized there was a brief window when they could come after us—or that the tagger might have a secondary trap, like the one that took Revenance. The werekin were still stunned, but I was going to take no chances. "Move," I said, and dragged them down the corridor away from the tag before anything happened.

When we were fifty yards away, it was so dark I pulled out my phone and powered it up, using the light to guide us into a small cubbyhole in the tunnel. I pulled Cinnamon and Tully inside and positioned myself at the edge, watching to see if anyone else came through the tag, or if any secondary tags had triggered. After a few moments, however, the glow of the tag died out.

"Whew," I said.

"What," Cinnamon said, gasping. "What the *fuck?*"

"We're in the Underground," Tully said, staring up at the masonry. He was right: the tag had transported us somewhere into the vast network of ancient tunnels that crisscrossed the city. Legend had it that they dated back to the Civil War. From my time down here, however, I suspected they were actually far older. "How did we get into the Underground?"

"I was hoping you would tell me," I said, "but in case the tagger didn't fill you in on that part of his magic, the tags can act as magic doors."

"I don't knows the writer that did the tag," Tully said.

"Whatever," I said, dialing a number.

"What are you doing?" he said fearfully.

"Calling Vladimir," I said. It buzzed several times, then picked up.

"Hello, Frost," Vladimir said. "What the hell—"

"Sorry to keep you in the dark, but it was necessary," I said. "I was afraid the lich and his buddies wouldn't let us proceed if he knew what I planned."

"You've got that right," he said, "They're demanding to know where you are."

"Tell them we're wherever the blood goes when a tag drains a vampire," I said, glancing around the dank tunnel around me, flickering in my own light. "Tell him I think that's somewhere in Underground Atlanta—and I don't mean the tourist trap downtown."

"I think he got that from context," Vladimir said, laughing. "What are you doing there?"

"Exactly what I said we were going to do," I said. "We're taking the battle to the tagger."

Vladimir was silent for a moment, then he relayed what I said. "Sir Leopold is asking how you plan to do that?"

"The doorway tags transport victims to traps," I said, "but they're not one-to-one. It's more like a subway network. I used my magic to guide us to its heart. With any luck, there's a central tag within a few hundred yards—and along with it, hopefully, the tagger."

"So you really are taking the battle to him," he said. "The lich is impressed."

"Good. So tell him hands off the hostages, or when I get back I'll be most irate."

There was a squawking on the phone, and Vladimir laughed. "I think they heard you."

"Vampire hearing, right," I said. "Well, Lords and Ladies of the Gentry, next time you hear from me, I'll either have dealt with the tagger—or will be calling the cavalry. Frost out."

"Frost out?" Tully said. "Can't you just say goodbye like a normal person?"

"Oh, come on, lighten up," I said. "We're deep underneath the city, about to go on a mission. All we need are walkie talkies and flashlights."

"*We* don't needs either," Cinnamon said.

"True enough, but I will," I said. "Give me your iPod."

"Why?" Cinnamon said, mirroring Tully's fearful tone. "I didn't do anything wrong."

"I'm not taking it to punish you. I'm going to use its light as a flashlight so I can turn off my phone. I don't want Philip butting in and getting Darkrose killed," I said, and she relaxed. "But, strictly speaking, you lied, Cinnamon. You *have* done something wrong."

She just stared at me, eyes wide. "I-I'm sorry I ran away from the Palmottis—"

"You know that's not what I'm talking about, Cinnamon," I said, kneeling down so I could look her in the eye. "You need to come clean."

Cinnamon looked at me in fear. "Wh-what about, Mom?"

"You can't hide anything from me," I said. "I know you're the third tagger, honey."

"No, Mom," Cinnamon said, shaking her head. "I'd never paint anything that hurt—"

"I know you would have *never* hurt Revenance," I said. "You hiss and swat like a cat, but inside you're just a little old softie. I don't think you meant for any of this to happen—but as far as doing graffiti, come on. I bet you were tagging walls before I ever met you."

"But Mom," she said. "You don't understands. I didn't do it—"

"She's right," Tully said, looking at me with a cocky *I-can-get-away-with-it* look, aimed straight at good old me, the big square—the big square who, unbeknownst to him, got away with all he did and more back in college. "She didn't do it. Neither did I. Sure, I'm a writer, but I didn't have anything to do with this shit, and you can't prove—"

"Oh, come on! 'They hit us *really good?* 'Don't you want to *see it?* And 'Right under my nose?'—*that* nose? Give me a break!" I said. "I admit, after the tag turned on you I crossed you off my list, but what did I find today on the outside of your little hideout? A werekin ward rune written with the tagger's logic, slowly rewriting itself into one of the tagger's traps."

"So that's why it turned on me," Tully said—and realized I'd nailed him. "Oh, crap!"

"And as for you, young lady," I said, turning to Cinnamon. "You want me to look at your drawings, but don't want me to recognize them scrawled over the walls? You want me to check your homework, but not recognize your number system woven into the tags? I didn't want to believe it, but Doug used *your* notes to pick apart the tag's design—and you run with Tully."

"Oh crap," Cinnamon said. Her ears folded and drooped, she hunched up, and her tail wrapped around her. "Oh crap oh crap oh crap! Mom—I-I-I'm *sorry!*"

And there we had it. All the admissions I needed to hear.

"S'alright," I said, sitting on a shelf in the alcove. "Really, it's all right. Come here."

Fearfully, Cinnamon sat down in the other corner of the alcove. Tully remained standing, defiant, putting his hand on her shoulder. She jerked away and muttered something, and he sighed and went to sit down in the other corner, sullen. I looked at her expectantly.

"We—we were just having fun," Cinnamon said. "All the other werekin were doing it. Not just the kids. The werekin have been bombing the werehouse since its earliest days. Gettyson taught me my first marks, the symbols we uses to stake out territory."

"I've seen them, before I even met you, on the very first day I went to the werehouse," I said. "Magical runes. The most they'll do, though, is glow, or give you a mild shock if you stray where you're not supposed to be. How did you get into writing? Tully?"

"Not just me," Tully said defensively. "A lot of the cubs are writers from wayback, at first simple stuff, names and warnings. But after we saw the living marks, we started copying them. I was the best. I learned how to do them right. At least, I thought I did . . . "

"Until it turned on you," I said. "Whatever this thing is, not only did it try to kill you, it killed Cinnamon's old guardian and my boyfriend. It's fair to say it's completely out of control. I'm not blaming you. There's no way you could have known it would lead to this. But I need to know how it started, who's behind it—and how it works, so I can fight it."

"All right," Tully said. "All right. She doesn't know. I just thought . . . it would be fun, you know, something to do on our runs. We made it a game, to run out into the city and spread the coolest looking lifemarks as far as we could—"

"Oh, hell," I said.

"Don't look at me like that," Tully said. "We didn't mean to hurt anyone! It was just a big old adventure. And after it started, it was too late to fess up. You heard the vamps—they wanted to kill us. No one will believe we didn't know what this shit could do!"

"You're right, they won't," I said. "But *I* know you couldn't have known copying his designs would make them stronger, or that one tag could receive information from another and elaborate itself. Later, we can have the lecture about not copying magic you don't understand."

"*I'm not a cribber!*" Tully snarled furiously, his eyes glowing. "And I do *too* understands, though I got way more than ever I bargained for—"

"This is complicated magic," I said. "You can't grok it without training."

"I *had* training," Tully said defiantly. He dug into his pants and pulled out a battered pocket notebook. My eyes bugged. "I got it straight from the source."

"I'm the Streetscribe's apprentice," Tully said, "and he gave me his blackbook."

| **60.** | **TALE OF THE TAGGER** |

I took the blackbook in my hands like it was the Holy Grail. It was a small, battered old black Moleskine with the tagger's XRYBE road sign scratched into its cover. Inside, I could see hundreds of tiny drawings, precise as a graphomancer's, annotated in an immensely tiny Portuguese script. As I flipped through it, Tully spoke.

"Streetscribe came from Sao Paulo," Tully said. "Tall, lean, good runner. He's a were, but I never found out what kind—I thinks a leopard, but he kept to himself when he changed. He wrote as Streetscribe, but face-to-face, he called himself the Painter of Night."

"The anti-Kinkade," I said. Tully stared at me blankly. "No one appreciates me. Go on."

"Painter wasn't born in Sao Paulo," Tully said. "He came from some hick town hacked out of the rain forest near the border of Peru. But his family came from the rain forest itself."

"A displaced tribe," I said grimly. "Pushed out by *logging*."

"If only," Tully said. "A displaced pack. Hunted down by *vampires*."

I stared at Tully, suddenly aware of the cold water soaking through my boots.

"Painter was in school in Sao Paulo when the fangs attacked his town," he said. "Wiped out his whole family. He tracked them back to Acre, trashed some of them, but got pretty trashed in return. That convinced him to never tangle with fangs. So he started lookin' for a weapon."

"His family was really old-school—old weres, with old magic and old gods," Tully said. "Painter had learned some of the old ways, so he wandered out into the rain forest, across the border, looking for his family temple. He found it, or somethin' like it—"

"Oh, *Jesus*," I said.

"—and holed up in the tunnels below. He found some cave paintings, or somethin', and figured out how they worked with schoolin' he'd picked up in Sao Paulo. Eventually, he cracked their code, and learned some dark magics to use against the fangs."

"Oh, Jesus," I said. "So this *wacko* found an equivalent of Atlanta's Underground, not underneath Sao Paulo but under some lost Mayan . . . no, *Incan* temple, *maybe*, deep in uncharted forests between Brazil and Peru, where we're still finding uncontacted tribes to this day?"

"Yeah, I guesses," Tully said.

"So, in the deepest heart of the rain forest, under an ancient temple built by an unknown culture, the Streetscribe found even older secret places he thought *might* be related to his family gods, and started reverse-engineering random magics until he made something *really* nasty?"

Tully nodded, swallowing.

"And why are we dealing with this here," I asked, "rather than reading in the comfort of own homes about how Sao Paulo was wiped off the face of the Earth by an explosion of magic so horrible that the faithful rightfully interpreted it as the wrath of God?"

"He *tried*," Tully said, and swallowed again. "Painter went back to Sao Paulo, began writing again, this time as Streetscribe. But he was too bold, and soon the police were after him—and then the vamps. So Streetscribe fled north—and kept going."

"And now he's here," I said quietly. "His new home."

"Still fighting the vamps," Tully said. "Sounded like a good idea. You gots to trigger the traps, see, and until . . . until he took Revy, I thought he'd just use them against *bad* vamps."

"Bad vamps?" I asked. "I thought werekin used vampires as their *protectors*."

"At the full moon," Tully said with disgust, "when rich jerks comes out to play. The rest of the time, vamps prey on us lifers, for blood or money. There are *plenty* of bad vamps."

"Including the Oakdale Clan?" I pressed. "Who decides who's a bad vamp, Tully?"

"Fuck!" Cinnamon barked. "*Trans* was a bad vamp."

"Yes, baby, but not as bad as you might think, even given all the bad stuff he did," I said, staring at the blackbook. My point was that the tags couldn't tell good vamp from bad vamp, but I didn't have time for that argument. "Why'd Streetscribe give you this, Tully?"

"I—I told you," Tully said. "We—*he* wanted to set traps for . . . for bad vamps. So he gave me his blackbook . . . and told me to make copies."

I looked up in horror. "And you gave it to . . . "

"Other werekin. The kids, the lifers," he said. "*We're* the ones the vamps hassle. But what does it matter? He didn't teach anyone else how to make the masterpieces."

"He didn't have to," I said. "The tags are part of a larger spell—a city sized resonator. If you throw up a tag of the right design at the right point, it will plug into the circuit, elaborate itself like the one the Gentry had, and, eventually, attack—just like yours did with you."

"Oh, crap," Tully said. "Oh, *crap*. He mentioned tags powered each other, but I thought . . . I thought you had to paint traps *deliberately*, thought you had to prime them to spring—"

"Well, clearly you thought wrong, or he deliberately misled you," I said. "All you really need is a photocopy of his notes, and you can spray paint your very own murder machine. How many copies of that *nuclear fucking weapon* are floating around, Tully?"

He swallowed. "I—I gots no idea."

We sat in silence. Then I flicked on Cinnamon's iPod and shined it over the blackbook's pages. Most was gobbledegook, but the few English scraps were chilling: *Let the graffiti get the upper hand* and *I wish to become a living scream so all the world can feel my rage.*

The magic was clearer, but still elusive. I concentrated. Whatever the Streetscribe had copied, it wasn't precisely Incan, and was even less recognizable now that he'd regurgitated it. It was hard to get a firm grip . . . on what he was trying to do . . .

"Blood rocks," I said, with sudden inspiration. I turned to Tully, who stared at me, baffled. "He was at school in Sao Paolo? Like, at college? Like, a *chemist?*"

Tully nodded.

"Blood on rock. The arsons are unintentional, or at least a side effect. The flames are a *desiccant*," I said. All this time, the answer was in me—three years of chemistry at the best university in the Southeast. I flipped through the blackbook, which made more sense with each page. "They evaporate all the remaining blood, make sure it's harvested. The vapors get sucked back through the magic door, and the particulates are blown away . . . resetting the tag."

Cinnamon and Tully just stared at me.

"The Streetscribe's more than a magician. He's an engineer. Everything in these tags has two purposes," I said. "The background is transmitter and receiver. The whorl is trap and transport. The flames clear the tag of its victim, and prepare it for . . . for what?"

"For the next victim?" Tully said.

"For the next part of the spell," Cinnamon said.

"To receive the magical intent of whatever spell the harvested blood is fueling," I said, flipping through the pages. "More vampire traps? But these spells, they're not just for vampires. There are glyphs for weres and humans too. It attacked you, Tully. But *why?*"

"Can I?" Cinnamon asked, holding her hand out for the book.

"Sure," I said, giving it to her. "I thought the tagger attacked you for whitewashing his art, but that's before I knew it was yours, and you his protégé. Would he have turned on you?"

"No," Tully said. "The Painter understood I had to whitewash my own stuff. But he never warned me about the tags turning on me. And they never evolved like that before."

"So," I said, "you either gaffed the tag so it picked up something it shouldn't have, which I seriously doubt would have worked, or the trap sprung on you because . . . it was *supposed* to?"

"No!" Tully said, uncomfortable. "He'd never do that . . . and if he had, he would never have told me. He had to know I'd never attack other werekin. He had to know!"

"But it had to attack a werekin," Cinnamon said, lowering the book and staring off into the distance. "It *had* to. It needed a were. I *knew* it the instant Iadimus gave the counts, and the Streetscribe's book backs me straight up. The deaths, they're all towers of fours. It's a diet."

"What?"

"Carbs, protein and fiber," she said, "only it wants weres, vamps, and humans. It needs them to balance the magic—mostly Niivan blood from vamps, a little Vaiian blood from weres—and lots of human suffering from burnt sacrifices washes it down, like fiber."

I stared at her. "You learned about macronutrients in school?"

"We gots, *hah,* we gots a nutrition class," she said proudly.

"So, tell me," I said, "what's this diet?"

"Counts, squares, cubes," she said. "For each new were, it can eat its square of vamps, but it gots to wash it down with a cube of human deaths. Once it's topped off, it stops, until a trap's sprung again. Then it gets hungry, and eats until it balances out again."

"Cinnamon, are you sure?" I said.

"Before it took Cally, thirty-nine people died, a tower of threes—three weres, three by three vamps, and three by three by three humans," she said, showing me a sacred geometry construction in the blackbook. "After, it kept eating till it got a tower of fours—four weres, four by four vamps, and four by four by four humans—totals, that is, not skips forward."

"The trap has to have a balance of fuel," I rephrased slowly. "And each death of a were exponentially increases the requirements for other victims. So if it eats one more were—"

"It can take its square," Cinnamon said. "Skip forward nine more, twenty-five vamps—"

"And a hundred and twenty-five humans total," I said. "More if takes both of you—"

"Wait . . . why would it take *us?*" Tully said. "I don't understands. He only hated vamps! Why would he want to hurt us? I—I don't wants to go in there if he's turned on—"

"In *there?*" I asked, following the involuntary jerk his head had made when talking. "*That* where you smell the most paint and blood?"

"Oh, God, oh *God*—"

"Oh, don't worry, Tully," I said. "The tagger doesn't want to hurt you. He wants vampires. The occasional werekin is just a vitamin pill—*humans* are the green salad."

"Mom," Cinnamon said. "There are *thousands* of vamps in Atlanta."

"And only a few dozen werekin have to die to clean them all out—along with tens of thousands of human deaths," I said. "He's building himself a werekin paradise enforced by magic graffiti, hungry for any vamps or humans that stray within the Perimeter."

"God," Tully said, sitting down, putting his hands over his ears. "That's awful!"

"Welcome to the party, Tully," I said bitterly.

"He never told me," Tully said. "I swear, he never told me what they really did!"

"You should have figured out what they *really* were when Revy died, or at least when it attacked you," I said. "If you'd just stepped up, maybe Cally . . . "

And I stopped with that. Slinging blame wouldn't help us now.

"Mom," Cinnamon said. "We gots to stop this."

"A-agreed," Tully said. Then, more strongly, "And I wants to help."

"You can *help,*" I said, "but only from a distance. If he kills you, hundreds will die."

"But Mom," Cinnamon said. "He'll *kill you.*"

"No, and no buts," I said. "I need your help, but I have to fight him myself."

61.   MANO A MANO, FACE TO FACE

"I could turn invisible," Cinnamon said, peering down the tunnel. "Scope it out—"

"No!" I said, pulling her back. "Your tattoos, they're werekin magic. Activating them will put out an aura stronger than a vampire's—and if this thing is as hungry for werekin as it is for vamps, that will set the tags off like a bear trap."

"Well, what then?" Tully said. "Just barge straight in?"

"Right—same plan as before, for real this time," I said, slipping off my ruined bomber jacket. "We go in, *fast*, examine the tag, figure out how to kill it, and you two step as far back as you can while I disable it. If the tagger shows up, or the tag goes wild—run. Don't try to save me, don't try to fight him—just run. And *don't* run in the same direction."

"No!" Tully hissed quietly. "I gots to stick with her, protect her."

"Fucking *coward*," Cinnamon blurted, scowling and looking away. But Tully just shoved at her, almost playfully, and she swatted at him. "You wants *me* to protect *you*, little wolf—"

"Shush!" I said. "More than our lives are at stake here. Werekin are the sacrifice he needs to activate his magic. If, God forbid, he gets one of you, the other will most likely escape, and over a hundred vamps and humans get to live a few more hours."

"A hundred and two," Cinnamon said.

"For the love," I said. "Just . . . move in with me, and fall back quick. Ready? Let's go."

We ran out into a vast, domed grotto whose crumbling stonework walls were laid thick with intricate graffiti, like centuries of glowing Technicolor cobwebs. The floor was half water, half land, a snaking pool and cracked paving stones making a yin-yang, complete with a little island and a tiny pool to make the dots of contrasting color in the black-and-white design.

Beyond the snaking pool was a hillock of debris that looked like a tumbled down gazebo . . . and beyond that, was the largest master tag I'd ever seen, with swollen cracked tombstones the size of MARTA buses, a giant wheat-covered hill the size of a circus tent, and a slowly spinning whorl painted like a galaxy, glaring down upon us like a giant all seeing eye.

"All right," I said, planting myself in a ready stance. "Tell me where to go."

"I'm looking, I'm looking," Tully said, turning round and round.

"Something's not right," Cinnamon said.

"The magic feels different," I said. "Guard yourselves."

But nothing prepared us for what happened next: nothing. I put my hands up in a Tae Kwon Do stance, then shifted to Taido. Cinnamon and Tully crouched behind me, making a defensive triangle. We waited—still nothing.

"Maybe we gots the wrong place," Tully said at last.

"Maybe," I said, relaxing slightly. "Maybe I screwed up."

"The logic's right," Cinnamon said. "That's *the* master tag. But . . ."

I squinted at the far walls. Tully shifted. I heard Cinnamon swallow.

"*Hahh*—what's the sticky stuff on the walls?" Cinnamon said. "It's giving off light."

"What's the brown?" Tully said. "That's not paint—oh, *fuck* . . ."

Stains of dried blood seeped from filigreed marks running the entire circumference of the hall. A white sticky substance, like cobwebs but thicker, coated the walls beneath it, glowing like moonlight, gathering itself up into bulbous masses like a frozen froth of boiling water.

"Blood rocks, indeed," I said.

"Why do I knows what that shit is?" Tully said. "I can't put a name to it."

"You've lived around it for most of your life," I said, turning round and round to follow the foul growth around the rim of the hall. "I've dated it, twice. We've seen it almost every day. It was standing all around you in the room, cackling, threatening to end our lives."

"It's the Niivan fungus," Cinnamon said. "It's what gives vampires their life."

"Their *powers* . . . and thirst," I corrected. "So . . . it's literally a vampire tag."

"Not just vamps. It uses Vaiian organelles too," Cinnamon said. At our baffled looks, she explained, "The stuff in werekin blood that makes it magic. You learns about it in school."

"Go, Clairmont Academy," I muttered. "Apparently *I* need to go back to school."

"Vamp blood carries pain, human blood is fuel, but werekin blood builds the furnace—and the furnace is about done," Cinnamon said, pointing. Up from the dried blood, green roots climbed the dome like sick ivy. "Six werekin will complete the design. Then it won't need us anymore. Just humans and vamps, which it eats up to kill more humans and vamps."

My eyes widened. Four werekin had been killed already. I needed to get one of the two of them out of here. If the tag took them both it would complete the construction.

Then my eyes traced down from where she was pointing.

Beyond the gazebo, where the vampiric growth was thickest and most intricate, mingling with streamers of werekin roots, the material . . . *detached* from the wall. The growth became a glittering spiderweb of green and white, dancing through the air, converging behind the gazebo on a point we could not see. Cinnamon swallowed, and Tully shifted. They'd seen it too.

We looked at each other. Then, wordlessly, we edged around the wreck of the gazebo.

Someone had made their home there—and long abandoned it. Boxes and bags and bones were scattered about, along with food wrappers and fungus and foulness. The smell was ghastly. There was a large safety cage—grimy, rusted, and all bowed out as if battered from within. Beyond it, we saw broken art tables, plywood canvases, paint cans—and a slumped figure.

"Painter?" Tully asked, starting forward. "Painter? Are you all right. . . "

I held him back. "He's gone," I said.

The Streetscribe lay sprawled in a chair before an eight by four piece of plywood, paint can still held in one hand. The beginnings of a new design covered the board before him, grids and whorls of black lines, a variant of the tag traps, more elegant, more deadly.

But something had gone wrong: sticky strands had erupted from the board and enmeshed him, thickening into black, rotted ropes that converged into his mouth, nose and eyes. Out through the back of his head, the strands exploded, spraying forth in a delicate spiderweb.

I followed the spiderweb up, up, a thousand tiny lines that grew into a fantastic array like the rigging of a ship, white ropes and sails coated with a green Sargasso slime. The magic had used his brain as a camera obscura, projecting the design across the upper surface of the hall.

"There's your answer, Tully," I said quietly. "Whatever discretion the Streetscribe had, it's gone. All that's left are his designs, working as intended without restraint."

"Oh, God," Cinnamon said. "He's still breathin'."

"Jesus," I said. I couldn't hear anything, but after a moment I saw his chest move. The man was half-rotted—*maggots* were crawling on him—and he still breathed. "Werekin healing, or vampiric reconstruction? Some side effect of the tag?"

"It's keeping him alive," Cinnamon said. "I knows it—"

"The hell with this," Tully said, pulling his switchblade from his bag.

"What are you doing?" I asked.

"I'm gonna cut him out of that shit," Tully said. "He's a were. Maybe he'll heal—"

"It's in his brain, Tully!"

"I—I don't cares," Tully said, nervously stepping forward. "I *owes* him . . . "

I'd love to say I said *Don't!* or *Hey!* or *Maybe we should think this through.* But I wasn't on top of my game, and I didn't. In fact, all that I could really clearly think of was that putting the Streetscribe out of his misery was probably a good thing.

Then Tully's hand touched the web, and we found out how wrong that was.

Tully jerked back as the Streetscribe twitched and a silver sheen rippled up the web. Rumblings and light echoed through the cavern. Deep images seemed to move in the darkness beyond the surface of the walls. Then the walls glowed, brightened—and Zipperface exploded out of them and began sailing through the air on a skateboard propelled on a trail of fire.

"Oh jeez, oh jeez, that's his self portrait!" Tully screamed. "His spirit was consumed by his avatar! *His spirit is in his avatar!*"

Zipperface screamed along the outer edge of the wall, and I readied myself. Arcturus and I had gone over this. There was an *immense* amount of power in the master tag, more than we had ever anticipated, but it was all being channeled through one small mobile projectia.

So this was it: mano a mano, face to face, me versus Zipperface.

Could I cut Zipperface in half with my vines? Maybe, but he could burn them with fire. Use my Dragon's fire against him? Zipperface had no real skin, the flames would dissipate. Use a hawk projection? He could use the baseball. Go hand to hand? He could use the bat.

None of my standard tricks would work—so I had prepared new ones. I shimmied, drew an arm over my back, and plucked a newly-inked feather from the wings of the Dragon. Then I laid it down on a newly-inked mark on my forearm, clenched my fist, and brought both to life.

Zipperface's mouth peeled open into two glittering arcs of teeth. His ropy tongue snaked out as he hissed at me, and he pointed his bat at me and called me out. Then he looked down at his chest. Dead center, an arrow now protruded—though it had started life as the feather, before being shot out from the crossbow I had inked upon my arm.

Bits of down fluttered away from the wound, the slightest of glows shined through the hole, and then the arrow sank in and his shirt rippled closed over it. Zipperface looked up at me, his white eyes gleamed beneath his floppy hat, and he smiled. Then he leaned in, the skateboard banked, and he screamed down upon me, baseball bat cocked back to take off my head.

That mano-a-mano stuff? Two masters face off in an arena and fight for fifteen minutes? It only works in the movies, or when opponents are evenly matched. I knew I wasn't an even match before I stepped up to the plate. So, I'd taken precautions—using *his* own tricks.

Suddenly white light burst from every seam of Zipperface's design. All the mana pouring in from the tags all around us had finally activated the self-replicating pattern Arcturus and I had woven into the feather. With a sudden *pop*, Zipperface exploded in a cloud of glowing down, the body of the Streetscribe jerked and flopped, and the spray can fell from his half-dead hand.

The skateboard kept sailing forward, bounced off the ground a few times, and slowly rolled to a stop at my feet. I slowly lowered my hand, letting the crossbow merge back into my skin; a moment or two later, the skateboard itself dissipated.

"Damn," Tully said. "You don't screws around."

"I haven't spent weeks studying these things for nothing," I said.

"Fuck!" Cinnamon said, suddenly terrified. "Fuck, mom, something's wrong . . ."

I turned to follow her gaze. Some of the filaments embedded in the Streetscribe's skull were blackening, disintegrating, floating away. But instead of dying out, the giant tag on the wall was growing stronger. With each line that detached, the tag was more and more free.

"I was wrong," I said, as Cinnamon backed up into me. "Whatever discretion the Streetscribe had was the only thing that had been holding the tags back."

Suddenly five thick cables jutting from his skull were simultaneously broken, and the giant whorl on the wall began glowing, spinning, picking up speed. I remembered what Doug had said about reflections of the local environment in the image of the tag, and began to be very scared that the only 'reflections of the local environment' I could see were rivers of stars.

Then the whole cavern shook. The perspective of the tags changed. The ring of vampiric matter began to glow, and the circuits of werewolf blood began to blaze. The massive, bus-sized tombstones surged and cracked like real stone. The huge hillside behind the whorl loomed closer, then moved through the whorl, shattering it, so the great knobbly dome with its waving strands of grass was seemingly barreling right down on us.

Then the tombstones lifted up and *doubled over*, fat squirming worms blindly reaching forward, stretching out of the canvas, striking the ground one by one, their white chalky backs tipped by cracked wooden shields. No, not wood . . . *nails*. The tombstones were *fingers*.

And then the huge hillock, waving with giant stalks of wheat, lifted itself up. The wheat was *hair*, the hill was a *head*, and the sodden misshapen thing surged forward out of the canvas and glared at us with the two blazing pinpricks of fire that were its eyes.

Just as Revenance had warned us not to, we had awakened 'it'.

Then 'it' opened a mouth fifty feet wide and *screamed* graffiti fire down upon us.

62.   VINES OF FIRE

I shrieked in pain as rainbow fire tore at my hastily erected shield. I seized Tully and Cinnamon and dragged them back towards the pool in the center of the chamber. Behind us we heard a deep rattling, like a dragon drawing its breath. Then all three of us dove into the water as a second wave of flame swept over us, boiling off the surface of the water with a metallic hiss.

Multicolored flames danced above us, lighting the bottom of the pond with a shifting dancefloor light. I floundered, but Cinnamon dragged me forward with werekin strength, cutting through the water to the gazebo's counterpart, an island of broken masonry and rebar jutting out of the pool. In the sudden shallows we half-swam, half crawled, lungs aching, until we surfaced behind a jagged triangle of masonry that provided a shield against the fire.

Gasping, we planted ourselves against the wall. Another gut wrenching scream echoed through the cavern, and we all flinched back as a wave of heat bloomed from all around us, followed quick on the heels by another gout of multicolored graffiti flame.

"There!" Tully said, pointing. "Make for that exit, the air was freshest—"

"No!" I said, pulling him back. There was light in the tunnel he pointed at—and there hadn't been before. "A trap tag is active, you can see it."

"That's how it got Revy!" Cinnamon said, flinching as the monster belched forth another horrifying scream. "Forced him out into the tunnels, into the traps . . . "

"Of course," I said, falling back as another wave of heat flooded over us. "He warned us about it—so he came *here*, awakened it somehow, and got caught when he fled."

"We can't stay here," Tully said, as intricate flames swept past. Flickering tongues of color began wrapping around the edges of the wall, and I started splashing water on it.

"Wet the wall! Wet it before the pigment can take hold!" I shouted, and we all started splashing water up on it, desperately trying to prevent the tag from creeping around. Where the wildstyle flames had already crept, water boiled off with a screech; but where the water landed first, the tag's outlines became limp and indistinct, a fizzling nothing. "Keep going!"

"This won't work," Cinnamon said, leaning around the wall. "Everyone down!"

There was a wave of heat, we hunched back against the wall, and another gout of graffiti flame tore around us in a kaleidoscope of brilliant color. The deadly curls and blazing twists of fire were artful, wonderful, even *extraordinary*, and inspiration struck me.

I leaned around the corner, glaring at the potato-shaped monstrosity with starry eyes. It caught my gaze and glared back, misshapen mouth spreading into a wide grin, opening into a vast fissure lined with the cracked, grimy cobblestones that were its teeth. My eyes traced those ham-fisted lines, then compared them to the graceful barbs erupting from the Streetscribe.

I leaned back as orange light built up inside the monster's malformed maw. Moments later, flames tore past us, gracefully, *painterly*—and clearly, by the Streetscribe's hand.

"That thing isn't the tagger's creation," I said. "It's something that he let in, something that possessed him—but *it's still using his mind* to make the flames."

"Something that possessed him?" Cinnamon said. "Like a demon?"

"Like a demon," I said.

"I thought you didn't believe in demons," Tully said.

"I'm a scientist. I won't deny evidence right before my eyes, even if it needs a little . . . interpretation." Another hot flash, a gout of flame, followed by a terrible cracking noise. "Maybe it's a projectia of an evil wizard, a Lovecraftian Great Old One or a genuine Christian demon. Who cares? It *isn't by the same hand as the flames*, and we can use that to take it out."

"*Fuck* that," Tully said. "We can't take that thing on."

"That *thing* is a vampire," I said. "A cartoon of one, spirit of one, essence of one. I don't care. It feeds on the life force of the living. And we've just let it in. We need to stop it *here*, or the bodycount will make the tagger's vampire genocide look like a pretty little utopia."

"How the hell are we going to do that?" Tully said. "I never saw anything like that, and from the looks on your face neither have you."

I glanced over the wall, then ducked back down at another intestine-churning roar swept over us. We hunched down from the fire, and I concentrated on what I saw. Whatever was coming through wasn't yet physical:

it was still a construct, a projectia like Zipperface.

"God help us if we see the source for that self-portrait," I said, "but for now, it *is* just a portrait. Whatever that thing *really* is, it's on its side of the door, what we're dealing with right now is a *projectia*. A construct obeying the rules of magic, of graphomancy."

"How does that help us?" Cinnamon asked.

"You have to do it, Cinnamon," I said. "*You* have to break the circuit."

"Me!" she said. "I'm not a graphomancer."

"Cinnamon, you're a genius," I said. "You're the smartest mathematician I ever met."

"Fuck! *How* does that *help* us?" she asked.

"Magic is mystical, magic is special, magic can break the walls of space open and let the bad ones in—but the logic of magic is *just math*," I said. "You studied tattoo magic under the Marquis and graffiti magic under the Streetscribe. If anyone can find a weakness, it's you."

Cinnamon stared down at her hands. Then she pulled out the soaked copy of the tagger's blackbook from her back pocket and began carefully flipping through its damp pages.

"You knows," Cinnamon said, "I listens to more books than anyone. Reading's like slogging through someone's garbage. Listening's like, *hahhh*, like they're talking to you."

"That's . . . nice, Cinnamon," I said; the flames had paused for the moment, but there was a slow crackling, *splintering* sound rippling through the cavern. "But how—"

"I got to talk to Marcus Aurelius," she said. "Emperor of Rome, and he gots the same problems in court I gots in the lunchroom. I wants to reach out and hug him, but he's gone, two thousand years, eleven twos standing up, more or less, and all I gots left of him is one little bit of his soul, talking to me, telling me everything is all right. But it isn't the listening that puts me in touch with him; that just makes it easier. It's the book. *Books* holds bits of people's souls."

We just stared at her, as she stared down at the tagger's notebook.

"The tagger isn't gone," Cinnamon said. "We gots one little piece of him left." She looked up at us. "We gots to destroy the blackbook."

"Easy said, easy done," Tully said, reaching forward, but Cinnamon hissed.

"For the love, go slow," she said, jerking it away. "There's a plan."

The whole cavern shook, another deep cracking sound echoed above us, and a giant chunk of masonry fell, splattering water and debris a dozen yards out into the pool. "For the love, hurry," I said. "Sounds like it's breaking loose from the wall. We don't have much time."

"Shreddin' it won't do it," she said. "And we can't really use its magic against the tag—he's gone beyond the blackbook and the tag's loose anyways. But the tag is all his ideas—and his book is filled with his ideas. One can link to the other, like sympathetic magic." And then she stared right at me. "Mom, *you're* gonna need to short out that link."

She explained her plan, and I nodded grimly. This was not going to be pleasant, but the hot flashes of the tagger's fire had resumed, hotter now, and it was clear we had no more time.

Cinnamon explained the designs to me as Tully tore out rebar from the piled masonry; then we divvied up Tully's remaining markers. They took the spray cans; I took the oil chalk—just two, one to draw and a spare in case the first broke. Hopefully I would need only one.

I reached up against the triangle of the wall and began drawing a row of unicursals, little hexagrams with X's through their centers that began sparking magic almost as soon as I finished them, shorting out the creeping graffiti flames and leaving me room to work on the big design.

"Ready?" I said, as Cinnamon muttered to herself and Tully tensed.

Then the flames died, Cinnamon said, "It will work," and we *moved*.

I leapt up atop the pile of debris and screamed "Hey asshole!" The shapeless thing on the wall screamed and shot out a barbed tongue that cracked against the pavement just as I leapt back behind my triangular shield of stone. Then another gout of flame ripped past its edges.

I was now alone behind the shield. Good. Cinnamon and Tully dove into the water in opposite directions when I leapt, and by now were each halfway to shore. I pulled out the oil chalk—*God*, I loved the tagger's materials. This was going to be so much easier than the way I'd marked magic circles before—and began drawing on the rough surface of the brick.

The geometry of magic at first seems simple. The circle I drew would act as a shield, keeping the magic of the flames off me for a few crucial moments. The five pentacles Cinnamon and Tully would spray would act as receivers, drawing more magic away.

I began drawing the next arcs. Combining symbols is where simple turns deceptive. A circle around a pentacle acts like an insulator, shielding it from our world, turning it into a receiver for good and evil spirits from other planes. But draw the circle a shade smaller, so its circumference touches the tips of the pentacle, and you've created a magical diode that lets mana pass through only one way. The circle still protects whatever is inside it from *your* magic, but the intersecting points enable it to project its magic out upon *you*. And so the careers of your wannabe demonologists often end before they ever begin.

But I wasn't drawing a pentacle inside my circle. I was drawing a unicursal hexagram, a Star of David with the two horizontal lines crossed. It was a magical short circuit, a receiver that lets magic flow freely out of its center. The centers of the tiny versions I'd drawn to short out the graffiti flames creeping over the rock were going off like sparklers. With all the mana in this cavern, stepping to the center of my big unicursal would be suicide.

A tremendous crash shook the vault, and I saw dust and water splash up from the impact of a foul, twisted hand that had torn free from the painting and slammed into the floor. The gripping mass of white, wrinkled flesh was bigger than the body of an elephant, attached to an arm thicker than ten trees; but there the resemblance to any plant or animal I knew ended.

Arteries of neon and veins of mercury surged through flaccid, fungal flesh. Muscles bulged in frantic lumps like boiling water. A skin like tattered canvas frayed and reknitted as I watched. Jagged edges of its skeleton were briefly visible, more like thorny vines than bones. The great nasty thing surged forward in waves, pulling and stretching, ripping and reforming, tearing itself out of the painting, piece by painful piece.

The monster screamed, rattling my teeth, and I briefly wondered what kind of thing it was. What kind of thing the Streetscribe had drawn on. What kind of thing led him to build magic that collected the intents of tortured people, trapped and struggling to get free. Concentrated intents that it could use . . . for what? Perhaps, to break free itself?

Whatever it was, we had to stop it.

A gout of fire leapt through the air at the far wall, and I saw Cinnamon leap out of range of the flames, a high curving arc, tail flickering. Snapping tentacles whipped at her, but she dodged and dodged, ducking behind a pillar as another blast of flame swept over the area.

When she moved again, gleaming arcs and lines of graffiti began wrapping around the pillar and rippling out over the floor, a self-replicating pattern of Cinnamon's own design. I raised an eyebrow: the werekin moved fast. They'd already given me the five pentacles I needed, and had moved to the next stage of the plan: distraction.

The new design began climbing the wall, leaping up into the vampiric matter, leeching its power. At first, the monster didn't seem to notice, but as the tiled kites and darts began growing, they began interfering with its magic. Cinnamon had called them Penrose tiles: self-replicating, but never precisely repeating, disrupting the regular pattern needed for the monster's design.

Realizing the danger, the thing screamed at Cinnamon, but then turned its head to blast fire at the opposite wall, where Tully had started two more self-replicating Penrose tilings. Curling graffiti flames rippled over the growing tiles. They began to flicker and burn out under the Technicolor barrage, and the monster gathered itself, preparing to fire again.

It had forgotten about me. Now was my moment.

I closed my eyes.

Deep beneath the water, the tattooed vine extending from my wrists snaked towards shore, guided by a tiny bird projectia gripping its branches in its beak. Through the bird's eyes I saw the vine burst through the surface. Using the bird's wings I guided the vine through the fallen stones, out of sight of the monster. With the bird's tiny feet I landed upon the rotting body of the Streetscribe—and let myself merge with him.

I shuddered. Long before whatever had happened, the Streetscribe had been corrupted by his own magic. He was neither alive nor dead, neither werewolf nor vampire. Arcturus was right: all of my classifications were useless. There was something mystically unwholesome about joining the bodies of the living and the undead with a magic tattoo, and I felt my soul being drained by the great void left where the Painter of Night had disintegrated.

I seized the book. I was cold. I detached the vine from my other wrist. I began to shiver. I let the vine coil around the book, then let it merge with the leather of the cover. Now I was freezing—merging with tanned hide was even *more* draining. I couldn't keep this up long. I screamed and kicked the wall where Cinnamon and Tully had undermined it, and the jagged triangle of stone toppled forward. I leapt up onto its bottom edge as its point splashed down into the water, exposing me—and my unicursal magic circle—to the monster.

"Come on!" I shouted, teeth chattering. Actual frost was creeping back up the vines, tiny bits of ice dancing in the air around me like sparks. *"Heat me up, you bastard!"*

The thing refocused its will on me. Now I could see its misshapen pentagonal head, the metal sheen to its cobblestone teeth, the twin points of fire in its eyes, the roiling tongue. It was Zipperface, writ large. Zipperface may have been the Streetscribe's *projectia*, but his magic was built after *this* model. Why? Who knew? Streetscribe was gone, his book all but destroyed. This *thing* was all that was left, and in a moment the answers would be gone forever.

Then the monster opened its mouth wide and belched fire at me.

I stepped right to the very edge of the magic circle, folded my arms, leaned forward, and merged with its shield. Then I unfolded my arms and spread them wide, expanding the circle as I expanded my arms, shielding myself with it just as the flames hit.

The magic bubble bent and bowed under the assault of graffiti fire, coiling around it, sweeping over me. But by the time the flames touched me, they were cool, just flickering light. Their power was being leeched into the circle, shorting out at the cross of the unicurse at its center in a blazing bonfire of raw magic.

The smell of ozone wafted into the air. Cracks spread across the stone. Mana buffeted my skin. A few more seconds and that power would blow the circuit, shattering the magic circle. The feedback would kill me—but I didn't need more than a few more seconds.

"Spirit of life," I cried, *"bring this monster down!"*

And I threw the blackbook through the shield into the heart of the unicurse, letting my vines flow off with the book like a green cable of life, freely detaching them from my body—but *not* from the Streetscribe's.

The blackbook whacked against the heart of the twisted hexagram and blazed with power, a circuit of mana flowing from the monster to my magic circle, through the book, back along my vines to the tagger, rippling out through the spiderweb along the walls of the cave, and finally feeding back into the monster.

It screamed, its power draining out along the magical conduit of fire it had created, its essence beaten back by the destructive intent that it had projected. Then the feedback leapt onto that torrent of fire itself, a vicious circle that began ripping the monster apart.

I leaned back as far as I could, trying to hold myself at the rim of the shield, where the flames died but before the raging magic storm began. And for a moment it worked.

But when I released the vines on my arms, I had forgotten that *all* the vines on my body were connected. The vines I had extended bloomed and flourished along the vicious circle of the conduit, a lightning bolt made of leaves, sucking backward from the book to the tagger to the monster and back again—whipping past me, and taking the rest of my vines with it. I screamed as the torrent of vines followed the current, ripping off my body, spinning me like a top.

———ʗ

Then all the energy in the cave converged with a clap of thunder.

63.   POSTMORTEM

I stared up into blackness. I smelt acrid smoke. I felt incredible pain. Shimmering auroras of blue and red drifted before my eyes, like the churning Rorschach images you get if you squeeze your eyes far too tight.

Then Cinnamon's worried face appeared against the red, upside down and staring at me, ears poking out of her wet headscarf, eyes wide and scared. "Mom?"

Tully's face appeared too, at my left, tilted at an odd angle. "Miss Frost?"

I blinked. The shimmering redness was in the ceiling, glowing blue fungi and flickering red embers, shimmering in and out as smoke drifted across them. Cinnamon and Tully were quite real, and I sat up, wincing in pain.

The master tag was destroyed, a huge blackness of soot licked by a dying streamers of real flame. I couldn't see the Streetscribe, only burnt embers of the spiderweb that had enmeshed him, half obscured by an oily column of smoke. Beyond the mound, a vast misshapen mass was sinking into the ground—the head of the monster, lopped off when the tag short-circuited.

I winced again in pain, and held up my hand: my hand, my forearm, my whole body was red, sore and burning—and my vines, my beautiful vines, *all of them*, were gone. I felt my hand, my skin, frantically. I was burned—but not badly. I rubbed my forearm with my thumb, then winced. Actually, that was a good sign: a really severe burn would have killed the nerves.

"Stupid!" Cinnamon said, biting her knuckle. Then she said, "I means, don't pick at it."

"I know, I know," I said, feeling my other hand, more gently this time. Then I looked around. Most of the cavern ceiling was cracked and sooted, and plaster and masonry fragments were fluttering down like confetti everywhere I looked. "Give me your knife, Tully."

"S-sure," he said, fishing out the switchblade. "What . . . "

"Both of you, walk the perimeter of the cave, make sure that none of the tag is left," I said. "Spray over anything that's left—but if you start to feel woozy, *head for the exit*. The fire may have eaten the oxygen. I don't want to beat this thing only to die of asphyxiation."

"W-what are you going to do?" Tully asked, staring at the knife.

I opened it with a *snikt*. "Make sure the Streetscribe is dead."

Cinnamon and Tully both stared at me for a second, then ran off to the wall of the cave. I shook my head, and turned towards the wall that had held the tag. At its base, the decapitated head of the monster was disintegrating, fluttering away in giant leafy embers, like flakes of burnt newspaper drifting out of a fire. I then inspected the wall itself. After scanning it for a minute, I convinced myself that whatever had been there was well and truly gone.

Then I walked around the mound and made sure the same was true of the Streetscribe.

When I returned, Cinnamon and Tully were waiting at the shore of the little lake, near where they dove in to avoid the flames. Their eyes grew wide as I approached.

"Gaah," I said, wringing my hands to try to rid them of the black grease. I spied an old piece of burlap atop the debris and picked it up. As it peeled away from a mound of white powder, it cracked and crumbled in my hands, but there was enough left to get the gunk off. I wiped off Tully's switchblade, tossed the rag, snapped the blade closed, and extended it to him. "Thanks."

"Y-you can keep it," he said, horrified.

"Thanks," I said, slipping the blade into my back pocket. "Let's go."

"Mom," Cinnamon said. "Mom, your face. You've gone . . . hard."

I stared at them both a moment, and they both backed up a little. I wanted to tell them it was a hard thing to cut off a man's head and have it flop out onto the earth beside your feet—and it didn't make it any easier that it was a blackened corpse. I wanted to chew them out, to list all the people who had died, to scream at them that this wasn't over.

But there was no point. There was no way, even with a solid knowledge of magic, that they could have known that spraying a little graffiti could have led to all of this. The real sinner was the Streetscribe—and he'd paid for it in full.

"This was a hard day, Cinnamon," I said. "And I had to do some hard things. But all that matters now is you're all right. You too, Tully. We made it. Thank you."

Cinnamon grabbed me suddenly. "I'm so sorry, Mom," she said. "I'm so sorry . . . "

"Don't you be sorrying me, little Cinnamon," I said, patting her head. "It's all over but the shouting. There will be shouting. Now let's get the hell out of here."

We wove our way out of the cavern, found our way to the dark stone tunnel (after three tries) and tromped back through the sludge to the archway. Half the graffiti was scorched and blackened, but the other half was barely touched—some of it, disturbingly clean.

But when we got to the arch, my hopes fell. The gateway looked like it had been sprayed with a flamethrower, and in spots was actually still smoking. There was nothing left of the tag, which had burst with such force even the stones of the arch were cracked and splintered.

"Well, *fuck*," Cinnamon said, kicking a fallen archstone away.

"Great," Tully said. "A ten mile walk through the Underground."

"I think we should have expected this," I said, staring at the blackened arch. The stones were warm to the touch. "Tully, you know the tagger's magic—do you think that all the tags will have been destroyed along with the master tag?"

His brow furrowed. "N-no," he said. "Only the gateways, the ones plugged into the . . . the master circuit. All the freestanding tags will still live."

"Do any of them have designs like the one we just destroyed?" I said, and at a glance to his face knew the answer. "Oh, damnit, you little fool."

"I'm sorry, Miss Frost," he said nervously. He glanced around. "But—but I knows these tunnels, I thinks. I wasn't lying about that. We can get out if we follows this one."

"No," I said. "Actually, I think I know a shorter way out. If we backtrack a little and go one level up, there's a passage that comes out at Cabbagetown, right near Grant Park."

"That's . . . that's the lair of the lich," Cinnamon said. "No, Mom . . . "

"No way," Tully said, jerking back. "No *way* am I going back there."

"You're right, no way," I said. "Not after all we just went through to get you *out* of their hands. First, we get you safe. Then, I go deal with the lich."

"Mom! You can't go back there," Cinnamon said. "Your-your vines are gone. Those were your shield! The vamps will be able to—"

"Darkrose is in a cage!" I said. "Delancaster and Saffron are prisoners. And no matter how tough Vlad the Destroyer is, I don't think he'll stick his neck out to save them."

"Don't you understands," Tully said. "*They're going to kill you.*"

I stared off into the distance a moment. Then I drew out my cell phone.

"Maybe if I play their game," I said, "but not if I play *my* game by *their* rules."

---

64. STORMING THE FORTRESS

"The deal is the same," Nyissa said, eyes wide, fingers gripping the poker so hard her knuckles had turned white. "You can have my protection for a drop of blood and a quarter."

I was back in the limo again, asking a favor of the House Beyond Sleep. But this time, the tables were turned. I was calm and *Nyissa* was terrified.

Nyissa didn't want to help at all. As Philip had predicted, Transomnia had skipped town shortly after Philip had called him. The Stone Rose Sanctuary was once again hers. But Arcturus had convinced her she had to do her part in the larger battle—to help free Saffron and Darkrose.

"It is a token of the, of the *traditional* toll of blood and money," Nyissa said thickly, "an amount of blood too small to object to, and an amount of money too small to count as consideration under the laws of Georgia."

"I'm not sure you've got the law right on that last one," I said wryly.

"There is a thin line between vampire dominatrix and outright whore," Nyissa said, "but I like to keep it drawn. So a token toll is all I demand for my clients to claim protection."

I stared at her, twisting the poker in her hands. She was scared out of her wits. Then I reached forward and put my hand on her knee to comfort her, as she had on mine . . . when we were last in the limo headed towards a confrontation. This was getting to be a habit.

"You don't have to do this," I said. "And I'm not asking you to physically defend me."

"You're asking me to walk between the Gentry and *Vlad the Destroyer*," she said. "The Gentry is unpredictable. You don't know what they're capable of. The Destroyer is all too predictable. You have *no idea* how powerful he is. He's slain entire armies."

"He's not so bad, he's . . . " *Cinnamon's math teacher.* But could I say that? Was that betraying the privacy of a man who could slay armies? "He's, well, he's not so bad, but that's not the point. I'm not asking you to fight for me. I'm asking you to give me legitimacy. Weapons won't save Darkrose. I want to walk into that room with something far more powerful: an idea. The idea that someone not in that room, an unknown quantity in power and capabilities, cares about the outcome. The idea that a *fellow vampire lord* has authorized me to speak for him."

"But," Nyissa said, "Transomnia is not here."

"They don't need to know Transomnia has skipped town," I said. "And we're not going to tell them the House Beyond Sleep is three vampires in rural Georgia missing their lord. You are the second of a great house, their emissary, and have every right to take this stand."

Nyissa stared at me. Then she said, "Take out a quarter."

I dug in my pocket, found one, held it up.

"Lick it clean," she commanded.

"Ew," I said. "That's gross, it's money, you don't know whose hands—"

Her mouth quirked up. "Do it," she commanded. While I did, she pulled out an ornate finger ring spike and slipped it on. "Now hold out the quarter, and extend your other hand."

I held the quarter out in my right palm, then extended my left. She pricked my left index finger with her metal claw, then guided the welling drop of blood atop the quarter. Then she gripped my right hand softly, took the quarter from my palm, and slipped it into her mouth.

I disliked that image, a twisted communion. That was a bit much, even for a lapsed churchgoer like me. But, for the purposes of the magic, my religious discomfort didn't matter. When the blood touched her tongue I felt a tingle shiver up my whole body, and then Nyissa released my hand, falling back into the seat in bliss. After a moment, she sat up, took the quarter, and slid it into her bosom.

"I have tasted your blood, felt your aura."

"Yeah, yeah, you'll know if anyone spoils me," I said.

"More importantly, an experienced vampire will know we are linked," she said. "When I present you, I may touch you to emphasize that. That may be a bit gauche since you just lost your boyfriend, but it will help sell it. Please don't be offended."

"It's all right," I said distantly, as the limo started to slow down.

"We're almost here. Damnit. If they try to sway your mind, squint, like down to slits," Nyissa said. "It sounds cheesy, but your retinas are part of your brain. Vampires hypnotize people through their eyes by extending their aura, establishing a brain-to-brain link . . ."

"I love it when you talk science to me," I said, and the limo stopped. We were in one of the oldest neighborhoods in Atlanta: Grant Park, not a stone's throw from the Park proper, a tree-lined valley that held Zoo Atlanta and the Cyclorama. Here, one side of the street was lined with houses over a century old; the other was dominated by a looming fortlike building built after Sherman took Atlanta. "Grant Park was a guess on my part. You're sure this is it?"

"Based on what you saw, and what I know of the Gentry, this is where you were taken," Nyissa said, peering out the window. "Besides, did not your lover in the DEI confirm it?"

"Philip is my friend, not my lover. Hell, I'm not even certain he's my friend," I said, "and just because the other end of my call to Vladimir ended up in this area it doesn't mean anything. It wouldn't surprise me to find an empty room with a signal repeater."

"No," Nyissa said. She was trembling. "I have not taken you to an abandoned warehouse. This is the Gentry's stronghold. We shouldn't even be here; the Gentry does not like to be approached. In the olden days vampires were staked for merely showing up uninvited."

"And this is their stronghold, guarded by Scara," I said. I stared off into the distance, thinking. Then something on the other side of the street drew my attention. At first I couldn't put my finger on it . . . and then it hit me: one of the old mansions was a bit too shuttered, and had several black vans parked in front of it. Something was tickling my brain, a bit of Civil War trivia I'd learned from Michael Bell. "But maybe there's another way. Vladimir gained entry, somehow, through a point relatively undefended—and I think I know just where that is."

Nyissa followed my glance. "What are you suggesting?"

"Some of the generals who moved into Atlanta after the Civil War built houses with underground passages, crossing the street," I said, struggling to remember what Michael had told me, years ago. "Vladimir came in from a side entrance. I'm betting he used that as his entrance to the stronghold. When we left, he was still standing there—it was his exit. If we enter that way, we can avoid fighting our way through armed guards just to deliver my report."

"You *really* think there's a back entrance over here?" she asked dubiously.

"Worst case scenario," I said, "it's not, and we apologize for waking someone up early."

"Or late," Nyissa said, drawing up the hood of her cloak. "It's almost dawn."

"I take it you're not on the Saffron diet," I said. "Oh, hell. Let's do this."

We got out of the limo and approached the house. The black vans looked all too familiar, but I'd had enough jumbled encounters with black vans and boots flying in my face that I didn't trust my memory. But when we stepped up to the porch, the front lock was busted.

"Now, that's blatant," I said. "I expected Vladimir would have more subtlety."

"Maybe he was in a hurry," Nyissa said. "Or maybe this home is being burgled."

"Then the two of us get to play superhero," I said. "Either way, I think you're up."

Nyissa glanced at me from beneath her hood. Then she rang the bell.

A spinsterly old black woman came to the door—but not half-asleep in her bathrobe, or irritated. Instead she was alert, in haute couture, and wary. She looked *almost* perfectly made up, but her hair was a touch disheveled, and she had a bruise on her forehead. "Yes?"

"I apologize for waking you," Nyissa said carefully. "I am the Lady Nyissa of the House Beyond Sleep, and this is my client, Dakota Frost."

"I know who she is," she said, glaring at me. "And you know you did not wake me."

"Ah," Nyissa said. "Then you know we would like passage to see Sir Leopold."

"Go to hell," the woman said. "After what your wolf did to my poor boys."

"My apologies, ma'am," I said, spreading my hands, "but it's almost dawn, and it's like an armed camp down there. I'd like to deliver my report while he's still awake, and I don't have time to negotiate my way in through the front. We would like to use the tunnel, please."

"You bitch," she said, staring between the two of us. Then she opened the door. "You know I can't stop you. I can't even call to warn him, with what your wolf did to my phone."

We entered into a picture book from the Atlanta History Tour. Victorian furniture was decorated with art deco lights. Yellowed pictures climbed horsehair plaster walls. An ancient violin leaned against a Victrola phonograph. And a corridor jetted forward into the house, right through its center, towards a parlor in the back where I could see stairs up—and down.

But we didn't get that far. A dark-suited security guard was standing by one of the corridor doors, openly holding a crossbow. He saw us—he had clearly been watching the door the whole time the woman had been speaking—and he touched his finger to his ear and murmured.

"Oh, hell," I said, glaring at the older black woman, who was smiling viciously. "Figures that the unguarded back door was a trap."

The low voices speaking in the room behind him stopped—and then the door burst open, and the Lady Scara stomped out towards us, two guards on her heels. "Well, well," Scara said, baring her fangs in an equally vicious smile. "Look who we've caught sneaking in, trying to mount a rescue. Dakota Frost—"

"My client is not here to mount a rescue," Nyissa said clearly.

Scara scowled and stomped up to Nyissa. "And who the hell are you?"

"I am the Lady Nyissa, Second of the House Beyond Sleep," Nyissa said imperiously, twirling her poker. I have to admit, when she was on, she was good. There wasn't the slightest crack in her act. "My client, Dakota Frost, is here on behalf of Lord Transomnia to—"

Scara moved with a blur, seizing Nyissa behind the neck and forcing her to her knees. Nyissa jerked and twisted and swung the poker, but Scara effortlessly batted it away, gouging a chunk out of the horsehair plaster walls.

Both the guards behind her moved forward instinctively, but Scara snarled at them—then reached out, seized one of their crossbows, and jammed it against Nyissa's chin. She angled the crossbow downward, shoving Nyissa's mouth open, breaking one of her fangs.

"You talk too much," Scara said—and fired the crossbow into Nyissa's mouth.

65. THE CENTER CANNOT HOLD

Blood splattered everywhere. Nyissa fell to the carpet, jaw forced wide open by the end of the silver crossbow bolt protruding from her mouth. She flailed, and I had a horrific image of the bolt jutting out of the bottom of her mouth and into her voicebox.

"Oh my God," cried the woman, running back into the house. "She shot an ambassador!"

Scara looked at me, then threw the crossbow down and smiled. "Looks like you are going to need a new protector," she hissed. "What toll shall I make you pay?"

She stepped towards me, eyes glowing, sending a prickling sensation rippling through my skin. I flinched in fear, drawing up my energies, but I could tell that I'd lost too much ink. My shield would be useless. Her hand reached out—

And then Lord Iadimus was standing between us, straightening his suit. It was like a magic trick. One moment she was advancing on me, the next he was standing there, Scara flinching back. The prickling sensation disappeared, replaced by icy cold emptiness.

"What is going on here?" Iadimus demanded. No one answered, and after a moment he knelt and examined Nyissa, on her back on the floor, choking to death on her own blood. He tilted her head up, then hissed. He gently rolled her over onto her side.

"Who is this vampire?" Iadimus asked.

"She called herself Nyissa," Scara said contemptuously. "Frost's protector—"

"Don't task me, Lady Scara," Iadimus said sharply, examining the bolt. "Miss Frost, does the Lady Nyissa have guards?"

"A driver, waiting in the limo," I said.

"Guards, request the presence of her driver," Iadimus said, withdrawing a white handkerchief from his suit pocket. "I want her attended by her own people."

"Yes, sir," one of the guards said.

"Lady Nyissa," Iadimus said gently. "I am going to remove the quarrel."

"What are you doing?" I hissed. "Call a doctor—"

"No time. The quarrel is silver," Iadimus said quietly. "It is killing her. Removing it will hurt, and perhaps damage her, but she will have a chance to heal. Lady, are you ready?"

Nyissa's head moved slightly. Perhaps it was a nod. Then Iadimus wrapped the end of the bolt in his handkerchief, got a good grip, and pulled it out in one swift motion. A new spray of blood splashed out along the floor, followed by a horrible sucking sound as Nyissa fought for air. But even as she flailed, I could see the blood flow stopping, see her begin to recover.

"Get her to a bed," Iadimus said, standing, letting the guards move in. "Get her blood, as soon as she's able. Find her fang, put it in warm milk, and call my dentist."

Then he turned on Scara.

"How dare you, Lady Scara," Iadimus said, oh so mildly—and a terrible coldness began to spread through the room. I swallowed, and backed up against the wall.

"She was impudent," Scara said defiantly. "Thinking she could offer protection—"

"You *staked* a fellow *vampire*," Iadimus roared. I, the guards, even Nyissa flinched from that ice cold rage, and Scara's face sagged in fear as the larger, taller vampire towered over her. "You assaulted her under truce! You staked her without trial!"

Scara twitched. "I—I—"

"Go back to the Council Chamber or die where you stand."

Scara hesitated only a moment, then turned and quickly retreated down the corridor.

Iadimus stood there, perfectly still—then abruptly was standing right before me, elbow extended. "*Lady* Frost," he said stiffly. "My apologies for my colleague's boorish behavior. I should like the honor of escorting you to court under my protection."

"Thank you, Lord Iadimus," I said cautiously. "Do—do I have to pay another toll?"

Iadimus glared down at the patch of blood on the carpet. "Enough blood has been shed," he said curtly. "Consider me . . . the Lady Nyissa's stand-in, while she is indisposed."

I took his arm, swallowing. "Thank you."

"We shall take the tunnel," he said stiffly.

I followed him in through the long narrow passage cutting straight through the center of the house. It was like walking through a museum, with thousands of ancient artifacts and pictures arranged beneath high cove ceilings. In one room, the glass was shattered, bullet holes marred the hair plaster, and behind a piano was a pool of blood. Vladimir had *not* been subtle.

I half expected the tunnel to be artfully hidden behind a trick door, but near the back of the house, a well-lit stair curved down into to a full-sized basement, holding a parlor that was similar to, but more intimate, than the one where the vampire held court. A big-screen TV dominated one side of the room; even the ancient vampire was turning into a consumer.

Glass lamps lit either side of a columned entranceway, with a heavy door that looked not unlike the front door of the house we'd just entered. It had been splintered clear of its hinges. The light grew dim in the hallway, provided by widely-spaced bulbs that barely illuminated the yellow wallpaper. Iadimus led me forward through a century and a half of history splayed over the walls in the form of old photographs, from daguerreotypes through digital prints.

Bloodstains began appearing in the hallway, but Iadimus didn't stop, not even when we encountered the bodies of two more guards, dead on the floor. We emerged in another parlor, this one filled with scattered bodies. I shuddered, but Iadimus kept walking, climbing the stairs into another room, all the doors but one blocked off with tossed furniture.

Iadimus cleared his throat, then led me through the door and into the vampire's parlor.

"Thanks for the heads up," Vladimir said dryly, leaning against the doorjamb.

"Do not mention it," Iadimus said stiffly.

"You left a lot of bodies on the deck back there," I said quietly.

"You can't make an omelet," he said, staring over my shoulder at Iadimus. "But I don't think it will matter. Consider it payment for all of Darkrose's men Scara killed."

"As you offered before—a fair proposal," Iadimus said. "I am inclined to seek agreement with you, so we may salvage something from this catastrophe."

"I am inclined to let you all live if you behave," Vladimir said.

"Excellent," Iadimus said, releasing my arm and turning to face forward. "Sir Leopold, Lords and Ladies of the Gentry," he said, with a gracious bow, "on behalf of the Lady Nyissa of the House Beyond Sleep, may I present her envoy, the Lady Dakota Frost."

I nodded to myself. Then I turned and faced the vampire court.

Everything was more or less as I had left it: Saffron and Delancaster seated on either side of the lich's throne, Darkrose still in her cage. Scara sulked at the edge of the dais, and everyone else looked grumpy and uncomfortable. Even the vamps' guards were seated, except two fresh ones around Darkrose, one guarding the rope, one guarding the cage with a crossbow.

Only the lich seemed alert, bright, animated. He prowled around the chunk of masonry, brazenly walking past the now-broken magic circle, touching with an occasional cackle the blackened surface where the tagged gateway had once stood. Demophage's coffin still flickered with slowly dying rainbow light. *Interesting*—though the lich seemed not to notice.

"I did what you asked," I said. "Now release my friends, and let's put this behind us."

"We can clearly see you dealt with the magic marks," the lich said, hand extended to the cracked, blackened ruin of the tag. Chuckling, the lich returned to his throne and sat down. "But what of the rest of what you promised? What became of the tagger?"

"Dead. I short-circuited his magic to kill both him and what he summoned." I turned to give Scara the full force of my words. "Then I cut him free of the graffiti, pulled what was left of his brain through the hole the tag had made in his skull, cut it into pieces, and stomped on 'em."

Something flickered over Scara's face, but she did not respond. The lich, however, did. "Well, well, well," he said. "Our little Edgeworld witch has shown herself to have a spine—"

"And *then*," I continued, "since he seemed to have such an affinity for vampire magic, I rammed a wooden stake through his blackened corpse, and cut his head off with this." I pulled Tully's closed switchblade out and tossed it at his feet. "I couldn't quite get off all the goo—and while I'm not a vampire, I'm pretty sure you can smell that's burnt human, well, werekin fat."

The lich just sat there in stunned silence. After a moment, Saffron spoke.

"Yeah," she said. "*That's* what I'm talking about."

"Nuke the site from orbit," I said. "It's the only way to be sure."

I glanced at her, and she nodded. Neither of us was smiling, or happy, or even really friends again, but it was a truce, of sorts, a shared bit of sentiment in the face of adversity.

But then Scara spoiled it. "Lead us to them, and we will put them on trial," she said, spinning around, talking to the hall. "One of the delightful farces all you precious children value so highly. If we find them innocent, we find them innocent; if we find them guilty—then we will kill the wolf, and leave to Vlad the Destroyer the duty of killing his own pupil, or the guilt of sheltering a murderer—"

"God *damn* you," Vladimir said.

"That sounds like a *great* idea—go to hell, Scara!" I said. "I did what that the Gentry asked, and *this* is the thanks I get? I don't believe for a minute that you plan to hold a fair trial, and I'd die before I turned over Cinnamon."

But at that, Scara whirled and jabbed her hand out at me.

In hindsight, I don't think she intended to strike. Her mouth was open, as if she was making a point, a gesture I recognized half a second too late. Too late, because in the first instant her hand shot towards me, I instinctively sashayed back and murmured *shield.*

Mana flooded out over my body—but my vines were gone. Magic surged into what was left of my tags, especially the Dragon, my *unfinished* masterwork, with unterminated graphomantic circuits spreading out over my whole body. Without the vines to ground them, they dumped all their mana back into my skin in concentrated points, and I *screamed.*

My body flailed. More mana built up as my skin stretched and living blood surged through millions of capillaries running beneath billions of cells, feeding back into my tattoos and then back into my body. It was a living feedback circuit, like the one I had used to destroy the monster—but the only place for the magic to go was back on myself.

Slowly, inevitably, the pieces of the Dragon came to life—and began tearing me apart.

---

66.   DAKOTA RISING

I screamed again. I hunched over. And I concentrated, as hard as I could, at holding the Dragon together. It was still in four major components, each with open circuits meant to be connected together. If any of them fully detached from my body as they were, they would dissipate—and spew mana all over me as it did so. God knows what that would do.

But I held it together, gritting my teeth in pain. The wings of the Dragon erupted and flapped, smashing into the cinderblock wall and knocking it over. The tail snaked out and flipped over Demophage's coffin. And the head and neck lifted from my own neck, rising, rising, eyes opening to show me the room through the Dragon's eyes.

Saffron's distorted image stood before me, eyes wide with fear, shouting something. Vladimir had fallen back, Iadimus and Scara had fled to corners, even the guards had scattered as plaster and wood fell from the ceiling under the relentless beating of the Dragon's wings. But Saffron stepped up straight before me, in the eye of the storm, shouting my name.

"Dakota, please," she was crying. "Calm down! The rafters! You'll kill us!"

And then I realized: they didn't know this was unintentional. Here I was, seconds away from dying at the hands of my own magic, but to someone from the outside it looked like a skindancer had whipped out a monster and was laying waste in her wrath.

Pain rippled through me, and I snarled. I staggered, but played it up, shoving my hands out like vicious claws. That actually helped, the tattoos on my knuckles filling in for the magical points of the Dragon's unfinished hands, and I drew the wings in around me like twin shields.

"Back up," I growled. Saffron did so, and I hunched over further, letting the mana bleed out into the religious marks on my knuckles. The other vampires flinched, but Saffron just stood her ground. "Give me a minute to calm down, and I'll hear your plea."

"Thank you, Dakota," Saffron said.

I couldn't tell whether she really believed she was in danger, or was playing it up for effect. Regardless, the mana streaming out through my hands started to balance the Dragon, and I began to straighten, drawing it in slowly, hands still shining with unearthly light.

The lich rose and stood by Vladimir, muttering something. Vladimir nodded, with a light chuckle. After a few moments, Scara and Iadimus rejoined them, hanging a bit further back, shielding their eyes from the light coming from my hands.

"I now believe that she was capable of taking the writer," Scara said.

"Agreed," Iadimus said.

"Of course she took out the tagger," the lich said dismissively. "You should have known that when she teleported out of here, much less when the tag exploded."

I was now standing fully straight, but the head of the Dragon was still whipping about, giving me a headache-inducing double image of the room. The freestanding wall had been completely destroyed, the outer columns were cracked, even the ceiling was damaged.

Impressive. Time to play this up.

"I have a few things to say," I said, clenching my fists until the tattoos on my knuckles *blazed*. All the vampires flinched—except Saffron, and, interestingly, the lich. "First, get Darkrose out of that thing, right the flying fuck now."

Everyone stood frozen a moment, then the lich flicked his hand at Darkrose's cage. Guards began to free her. I was so glad that the Dragon hadn't knocked the weight down on her while it was flailing. Saffron smiled gratefully and ran to Darkrose's side as they got her out.

"Second," I said, turning my attention to Scara, "leave my daughter out of this. No one even mentions her *name*, and don't take that as an excuse to call her a stray, not ever again. She was never here, and had nothing to do with this plague."

"But," Scara said, clearly afraid, but unwilling to drop the matter—or drop her hand, which meant she still meant me harm. "But if she was a tagger—"

"I'm not finished," I said. "The master tagger was Tully's mentor, but duped him into drawing tags that were part of a master spell that required werekin blood. Tully was almost killed by one of his own pieces, which elaborated itself into a trap just like the one here on that wall."

Scara lowered her hand, ever so slightly.

"If you are really convinced of that," she said, "you must have some proof."

"I have proof, a copy of the tagger's blackbook," I said, counting on Tully to find me one. "A dossier of all the tags, my notes, and how I deduced there were three taggers but only one master. Even proof that I took out the Streetscribe. I can take your men to the cavern."

"Yes, of course," she said. "Once I have seen proof with my own eyes, I will consider the matter closed, and order my soldiers to dynamite the cavern to eliminate any remaining—"

"You'll do no such thing," I said firmly. "You will have to send trusted human witnesses, and if I catch a single stick of dynamite on a one of them I'm going to shove it up their asses."

"But," Iadimus said, "if we cannot see—"

"This is for your protection," I said tightly. "No vampire, vampire wannabe, or anyone who even *smells* of vampire is to approach the inner sanctum of vampire-draining magic."

"Agreed," the lich said. He seemed amused, even muttering asides to Vladimir as I spoke. "But what about the suggestion to dynamite it? Even you seem to think it is still a threat."

"Before we make *any* irrevocable decisions about the cavern," I said, relaxing the Dragon slightly, "we're going to collect enough evidence to tell us what we're left with. If *you* can't find an Edgeworld crew with skills to photograph it properly, we use my contacts with the DEI."

"We will *not* allow you to bring in outsiders," the lich said slowly.

"I'm not done," I said, flexing the Dragon's wings, "and I *do not* want to have to do this again next week having destroyed our best evidence. The tags were part of a *genocide* engine. Designed to exterminate vampires, using human and werekin blood to balance the magic."

"Is that even possible?" Iadimus asked, looking at his magicians.

"Oh, yes," the man said. He had gone pale. "Obvious, really, now that she said it."

Both Iadimus and Scara seemed to draw back, and I continued, "Bad enough, but the magic was corrupted, a misreading of forbidden Incan magic. The collected intentions of the victims were slowly incarnating a demon."

"A . . . demon?" Vladimir said.

"Demon, alien, small-g god, what have you," I said. "My scientists from Georgia Tech assure me this magic uses advanced concepts not likely to be hidden lore or backwoods graphomancy—it's more likely to come from another world or dimension."

"Your . . . scientists," the lich said.

"When I said I've been studying it for weeks, I meant I'd been studying it for weeks," I said hotly. "So we don't throw away our best chance to figure out what the hell it was and what it was trying to do before my scientists and your magicians have a chance to look at it."

"Agreed," the lich said, and Scara hissed, but reluctantly. Iadimus nodded.

"Agreed, then," I said. "And if we do decide that the cave is still a threat *and* that dynamiting it will help, we find out where the fuck it is before we blow it up—I have no desire to topple the IBM tower and kill fifty thousand people in Midtown."

"I do not care how many humans have to die to protect vampires," Scara said.

"You *do* care, because this is the twenty-first fucking century and the DEI will *find* you," I said. "And when they do, they'll find that I've found you first and pulled your fucking heart out. I did *not* save your life just so you could go on a killing spree."

Scara's lips parted in a vicious snarl. "You did *not* save *my* life—"

"Be silent," Iadimus said. He looked over at the lich. "We were more stable at five—"

"Now now, not in front of our guests," the lich said, staring at me, wrinkled dead face smiling and amused. "You make a good point, Lady Frost," he said, voice velvety smooth, "but why, if you have destroyed the tag and the tagger, do you not think this is over?"

"Because only tags connected to the network will have been destroyed," I said, pointing at Demophage's body, which had spilled out of its coffin and yet still smoldered with glowing rainbow wisps. "Any other tags may still be active, and some of them have components of the spell. Worse, the tagger's designs are self-replicating, and self-elaborating."

"No," the lich hissed, recoiling from the magic flowing off Demophage's corpse. "No, we cannot have this again. We *must* destroy them—"

"*If* you can," I said. "But each and every one of them is like a Venus' Flytrap for vampires. You're going to need help: knowledge of the tagger's designs, and even photocopies of the tagger's blackbook, are now spreading through Atlanta's graffiti community."

Scara snarled. "We will not permit it! We'll track them down and destroy them."

"What? What did I just say about killing sprees, and now you're talking about sending vampires out against magicians who can use them as a *power source?* No," I said . . . and my idea took full shape. Very firmly, I said, "I forbid it."

"You . . . *forbid?*" the lich said incredulously.

"I forbid it," I snapped, flapping the Dragon's wings. "If you could have dealt with this you would have done so. *You* had to call *me.* You may rule the vamps, the Bear King the weres, and Buckhead the forest, but where the use of magic is concerned *I'm* in charge of Atlanta."

The lich just smiled and nodded. "A bold claim," he said. "I am prepared to accept it. But you do *not* know what a *mess* you are stepping into."

One of Iadimus' magicians cleared his throat. "My Lord . . . the Wizarding Guild will have something to say about that."

"Then let them step up and deal with the problem," I said, glaring at him. I'd never even *heard* of the Wizarding Guild before this. "Dozens of people died. My *friends* died. Thousands of people were put at risk by this, including any of the members of the Guild who live inside the Perimeter. If they don't like how I'm handling it, let them come to me."

The lich laughed, a delicious, vicious sound.

"And how *will* you handle it?" Iadimus said. "Kill all the taggers?"

"Sounds like a great idea," I said. "We should also stake all the vamps, and put a silver bullet in all the weres. And why don't we burn all the witches while we're at it?"

Iadimus sighed. "A puerile analogy," he said, "but you've made your point."

"Not yet," I said. "The police have been trying to stamp out graffiti for years, and short of putting cameras on every street corner like in London, they've not been able to do it, even though they weren't fighting people who can turn into animals and disappear."

"The police failed only because nothing was at stake when it was mere spray painting," Scara said dismissively. "We will succeed if we have the will to do what needs to be done."

"Aren't you listening? Half the taggers are weres. Their werekin friends will turn on you, just because you're vamps. You'll start a war—and I won't have that."

"*You* won't have—" Scara began, then froze when Vladimir stepped up to my side, turned around and growled at her, oh so softly. Saffron abruptly left Darkrose's side and stepped to the other side of me, folding her arms.

"Lords and Ladies of the Gentry, let me be clear," I said. "A lot of good people died recently—vamps, weres, your human servants, my good friends. But not all of them died at the hands of the tagger—many died as a direct result of *your* actions, Lady Scara."

She tensed. "I will not be held to account for defending my people."

"Nor do I intend to," I said. "That's over now. This was a terrible, dangerous situation in which many people acted out of fear—including you, *Lady* Scara. You murdered many good men and women at the Consulate, but I am prepared to forgive and forget—this one time."

"What are you *doing*, Dakota?" Saffron muttered.

"This is not the Wild West," I said. "This is not the Stone Age. This is the *twenty-first fucking century*, and tribal warfare stops, *now*. From now on, if you have a grievance, you bring it to the Consulate—open warfare between factions in the Edgeworld of Atlanta is *forbidden*."

Scara snorted. "And if I do not play along?"

"If anyone breaks the truce," I said, "then I will take them down."

"And I'll help," Saffron said.

"As will I," Vladimir said.

"As will *I*," the lich said, smiling.

Scara and Iadimus both turned on him, stunned. Then Iadimus snarled.

"Oh, you've been waiting for this, haven't you?" he said. "Damn you."

"If you have a grievance, take it up with the Consulate," the lich cackled. "If the Lady Frost agrees, of course. Unless . . . she *wants* to be judge and jury, in addition to executioner?"

"What? No, of course we should have a, a grievance procedure," I said, thinking fast. The vampires already had courts, didn't they? "We, ah, could begin with the Consulates—"

"No!" Scara said, her voice tinged with despair.

"Finally," Lord Delancaster said, relaxing into his throne, looking, for the first time, as if he truly belonged there. "Play acting no longer."

I stared at him blankly, then looked at Saffron. "What . . . what did I just do?"

"The Consulates," the lich said turning back to his throne, "are *my* project, Dakota Frost. An independent power structure to which even members of the Gentry may be held accountable. But there has not been enough . . . independent power to enforce this idea . . . until now."

"But . . . aren't you the big man on campus?" I said, confused and alarmed. "Didn't you always have the power to make him your lieutenant?"

"No!" Scara said. "No! You can't! I forbid it—"

"You cannot forbid anything any longer," Iadimus said. "Your allies on the Gentry are dead, Delancaster's protégé has replaced them—and your behavior has become embarrassingly erratic." He turned to Delancaster with an ironic smile. "I will support this plan, my Lord."

"You-you can't do this," Scara snarled. "To put *him* in charge—*you can't trust him!*"

"He remains a puppet, but it has been a century and a half, my dear," the lich said, sitting on the throne next to Delancaster. "And his protégé is one of us now. The Lady Saffron leads the Consulates, I will support her, and together . . . *we will support the Lady Frost.*"

Never waste a good crisis, indeed. "Uh . . . thank you for your support, Sir Leopold."

"Don't thank me yet," he said, staring at me. "How *will* you deal with the taggers?"

"Well, we have Tully, trained by the tagger," I said, thinking as quickly as I could, "and my contacts in Atlanta's human graffiti community are already working to defuse the tagger's tags. My team will teach other taggers these methods, and spread the word: eliminate the bad tags when you find them, and make no new tags designed to prey on the life of another."

"And if they do—"

"Then you catch them, you give them to me, and I give them to Philip," I said. "And let the men-in-black deal with getting enough evidence to make it stick."

"That's nonsense," Scara said. "We are vampires. The taggers are werekin. Neither of us can go to the police. We can only enforce your rules through violence, which you forbid."

"If only you had someone with recognized authority," I said. The lich's piranha grin was growing. "Someone to give me an appointment, and the power to make it stick."

"But . . . but I can't do that," Saffron said. "I can't make appointments."

"No you can't," I said. "Not at the city level."

Saffron glanced at me. Then she followed my gaze to the throne . . . to

Lord Delancaster, Vampire Master of Georgia, in his mind, on TV—and in the eyes of the State.

"If only," I said, "Lord Delancaster really had the power you've pretended to give him."

"No! You can't!" Scara said to the lich—like a scared little child. "You, you *promised*—"

"Lady Frost," Iadimus said quietly, and now *I* flinched back from the sudden icy cold and the unexpected hate in his pale eyes. "You have *no idea* what you have just done."

"But I—" I began, then stopped. He had sounded like he supported my quickly hatching plan, but now he was *angry*—and Scara was *terrified*. I really *didn't* have any idea.

"Things are not as simple as they seem," Iadimus said, glaring at me. But his eyes didn't blaze at me for long; he quickly turned to the lich, and the wave of frost intensified. "You *know* that, Sir Leopold. Do you really think you can maneuver us like little children?"

"I think I have," the lich said.

"Wait, wait, wait," I said. "Think about what I'm asking. This is in your best interests. I'm offering you a chance to get my help on tap. I'm trying to get us to work together."

"But—but—" Scara began, eyes fixed on Delancaster like a fearful cat on a challenger, afraid to look away lest the newcomer pounce. But she broke the glance, shook off her fear, and glared at me, eyes glowing cold red. "But what if we do not want to work with you?"

I stared at her, eyes tightening into slits. I felt her aura expand, felt her anger burning against my face, flooding past my skin. Then my vision began to double, as the head of the Dragon—which had never fully retracted—began to rise over my head again. I snarled as the feedback loop begin again—the pain was excruciating—and Scara backed up.

"Then I kill you where you stand," I said through clenched teeth, and Scara nodded.

"Enough, enough," the lich said, raising his hand for silence. "You have made your point, Dakota Frost—and even so, you will never know how close to death you came. Your designs have played into mine . . . quite nicely, I must admit. Still, I rarely tolerate such insolence in my presence. A thousand years ago I would have had your tongue cut from your mouth at the first insult. Five hundred years ago, we would have all fallen on you at the first sign of such magic in the hands of someone we do not control.

"But the world has changed, and while your diplomacy leaves much to be desired, your conduct is honorable, your power considerable—and your logic . . . plausible. Magic has been practiced in secret since recorded memory for good reason, but now that Pandora's box has been opened, we will need more than just hope to fight all the things fools like you have loosed upon the world. And since sometimes the best way to fight fire is with fire . . . "

And then he looked over at Lord Delancaster. The two eyed each other warily, and then Delancaster nodded heavily in agreement. He closed his eyes and raised one finger to his forehead, lips moving. Then he put his hand down and spoke clearly, like he was on TV.

"With the unprecedented spate of accidents involving magical graffiti in the recent weeks, it has become clear to me that greater regulation of *and* education in the use of magic is needed. Therefore, I am convening a Magical Security Council, including representatives of vampire, werekin and other Edgeworld communities, and I plan to petition the State of Georgia for official recognition of and empowerment of this body.

"Based on her work resolving this crisis, I appoint Dakota Frost the Council's chair."

67. THE HELL OUTTA DODGE

The Magical Security Council. Those words hung in the air. My ploy had worked: we would replace fangfights at the OK Corral with something more reasoned, more modern.

And *I'd* be heading up it all. *Oh, shit.*

"Well . . . is that it?" Saffron asked, voice ringing with unexpected authority. "Are we all now in agreement? Are we now done?"

"Of course, my Lady Saffron," the lich said.

"Thank you," she responded. "Then I am taking my people. All of them. *Now.*"

With Vladimir guarding our backs, Saffron, Darkrose, Delancaster and I picked our way out of the wrecked hall. The freed captives were gathering in the foyer: Delancaster's servants, Darkrose's bodyguards—and Nyissa's driver.

Then Iadimus carried Nyissa out to us, and Saffron flinched like she'd been slapped. Her gaze quickly bounced between me and Nyissa, face mottling with rage, and I realized she'd detected the link Nyissa had forged between us. But then, just as quickly, Saffron relaxed.

"The Lady Nyissa stepped up to defend the Lady Dakota," Saffron said, stepping forward, gently touching the cowl of Nyissa's robe, "and this was the thanks she got."

Iadimus stiffened, then let Nyissa down gently into Saffron's extended arms.

"My most profuse apologies, Lady Saffron," he said. "It will not happen again."

We practically mummified our vamps with curtains, then rushed them out to the limo. Even Saffron, covered in a heavy coat, hissed in pain as sun glinted off parked cars; but even after having been starved and forced to drink blood, she did not catch on fire.

We retreated to the Four Seasons Hotel, where Saffron booked a linked set of suites that made my hotel look as shabby as my cardboard box under the bridge. While a servant tucked in the nearly comatose vampires and Saffron called a doctor for Nyissa, I called Cinnamon.

"Mom," she said, voice brimming with relief. "Are you safe?"

"I am," I said, and explained what happened. "And are you?"

"Yes," she said. "We're with Lord Buckhead in the Underground. "

"Good," I said. "Cinnamon, honey . . . Vladimir's coming to take you back to school. After that . . . you have to go back and stay with the Palmotti's."

Cinnamon was speechless for a moment. "But . . . Mom——"

"Cinnamon . . . right now, you can't stay with me. I'm about to be arrested."

"No!" she said. "Mom, *fuck,* you saved the whole city."

"The police don't know that," I said, "and if they find you with me, they'll take you away. Is that what you want? Or do you want to stay in the Underground, be on the run forever?"

"No. I wants to come home," she said. "And I wants . . . I wants to go back to school."

I felt something relax deep within me. "Then go back to school, love," I said. "Vladimir will keep you safe until we work this all out. You can trust him."

"I trusts you, Mom," Cinnamon said.

We said goodbyes, I closed the phone—and then my jaw opened in shock. Saffron had walked out of the vampire's suite in her bathrobe, closed the door—and then dropped the robe and stalked towards the window, buck naked but for her bomber goggles.

"I can't thank you enough, Dakota," she said, passing me, flaming red hair over ghostly curves, stepping straight up to the window—and throwing the curtains wide. The bright morning sun streamed in, and she hissed and flinched. There was a searing sound, smoke rose from her skin—and then it began to dissipate, and she slowly turned her head towards the sunrise.

"Oh thank you, God," she said. "I'd just die if they had taken my daylight."

Something smart alecky, like *clearly not,* popped into my lips—but didn't pass them. I stood there watching her for a while, watching the sun gleam off that skin, reddening, first like a rash, then more like real color was returning. Part of me wondered how that worked, made me want to give the papers of the world's only vampire vampirologist more than a token read. The rest of me was just so glad she was alive.

"Dakota, my behavior's been *unconscionable,*" she said, stepping up to me, then giving me a huge hug in her birthday suit. "Tell you what. I'll forgive you if you forgive me."

"Uh . . . deal," I said, uneasily embracing her naked body. Can you say . . . *awkward!* But I knew her well enough to know that while part of her was deliberately tweaking me, the rest of her really did think nothing of it. Oh, *Savannah.* "Friends?"

"Always," she said. We hugged again, longer this time. "I missed you."

"I missed you too," I said. "I wish I'd realized sooner you never left."

There was a knock at the door, and Saffron cocked her head. "Room service," she said, mouth quirking up in a smile. "Oh, Dakota. I did miss you. I want you collared again, if you really are going to do this ridiculous Daniel-in-the-lion's-den thing——"

"Saffron," I began, but room service knocked again, and I gave up. "I'll think about it."

"Fair enough," she said, putting her hand on her hip, still standing there nude before me, the window, God and everybody. "Now . . . I need to sun and feed, I mean, get real *human* food in me, before the fungal symbiote destroys any more of the outer layers of my skin."

On the way down in the elevator, my phone rang, and I whipped it out. The number was PHILIP DAVIDSON. I clenched my jaw, found my wits . . . and put the phone to my ear.

"Oh, *hi*, Philip," I said.

"She said nonchalantly," Philip replied. "So, Dakota . . . vampires who haven't been seen in days or weeks are back on the radar. Savannah Winters charged a suite at the Four Seasons, and Lord Delancaster's office has called a *press conference*. And the DEI's remote viewers woke up screaming that something *mammoth* went down somewhere in Atlanta around four a.m. I can't see the whole picture, but I can tell this is all part of the same elephant. Fill an old friend in?"

"Oy," I said. "All right, Philip. Here goes." And I *told* him. Not in half measures, either. I talked, the elevator landed, I kept talking, I crashed in a comfy chair in the lobby and kept telling him as much as I could without giving away any confidences that would get me killed.

"Oy," Philip said. "You've cleaned up a mess, and created a bigger one."

"Not likely," I said. "You didn't see it. You have no idea what we were up against."

"Then you have to give me an idea," Philip said firmly. "You have to come in."

"Philip," I said. "I can't just drop by the DEI office. I'll be arrested on the spot."

"Right now, we all just want to talk to you," Philip said. "I can get them to hold off on any new charges at least until we debrief you—I play golf with the U.S. Attorney's husband. But I can't do that if you're on the run. You need to turn yourself in. Now's the time."

My eyes widened as a short, rumpled figure wandered in to the lobby of the Four Seasons—Detective McGough. "You aren't kidding," I said. "You sell me out?"

"Of course not!" Philip said. As if on cue, Detective McGough noted the phone on my ear, waved politely, and hung back as Philip denied having led him to me. "I wasn't responsible for the raid on the werehouse, and I'm not going to turn you in now. You can't do my job if you stab everyone you meet in the back . . . and besides, Dakota, you're a friend."

"Whatever you say, Philip," I said distantly. "See you soon."

I hung up, pocketed the phone slowly, and stood.

"All right," I said, proffering my wrists. "I'm ready."

"Ready for what?" McGough asked, jamming his hands in his rumpled coat.

"To turn myself in," I said, lowering my hands. "Isn't that why you're here?"

"No," McGough said, with a rough shake of his head. "That's something you need to work out with Rand. I heard through the grapevine you'd be here . . . and we need to talk."

"Heard through the grapevine? *How?*" I said.

"What, you don't think your guardian angel knows where you are?"

I stared at him blankly. For a moment I thought he was being completely literal; then I got it. "My mysterious benefactor in the APD, revealed at last." My mouth curled up in a smile. "What did you do, feed the texts through a friend in the National Security Agency?"

McGough's eyes bugged. "No, but damn close," he said. "How'd you figure—"

"Well," I said, "Mystery texts are all spooky, and it was a Fort Meade area code."

"Headquarters of the NSA," he said. "Not bad. Actually, it was an old college roommate, now in a CIA field office *also* in Maryland. Very good contact to have, like your Special Agent Davidson. I'm impressed you looked up the area code. Not many people would have done that."

"Not many people used to date Special Agent Philip Davidson," I said.

"That's not what I hear," McGough laughed. Then his face grew serious. "You did good with what I gave you, Frost, but I'm not here about the case— I'm here about the aftermath. *Especially* about that stunt you pulled this morning with the vamps."

"Well," I said, "once I—wait a minute. How *did* you know I did good with what you gave me, much less what went on last night? I haven't spoken to the police yet . . . "

"I'm not here on police business," McGough said. "This is strictly Wizarding Guild."

68.   THE GIFT THAT KEEPS ON GIVING

"*You're* working for the Wizarding Guild?" I asked. "While working on the APD? Isn't it a huge no-no to have a practicing magician on the Black Hats?"

"Yes, yes, and no—and I'm not a practicing magician," McGough said. "I have only the barest hint of a magical bloodline, and hardly do any magic at all."

My brow furrowed. "Then . . . why are *you* in the Wizarding Guild?"

"I," McGough said firmly, "am a magical forensic investigator. I know as much magic as ten average wizards, but every week I find some perp abusing magic in a new way. I don't have time to learn how to do card tricks with pixie dust—I have a job to do."

"You go, Detective McGough," I said. "So . . . what's up with this?"

"The Guild has 'requested,'" McGough said, "that you accept a representative onto your magical oversight committee until a body with legitimate authority is established."

"Huh," I said. "Have they. Well, tell the Guild that I will consider their request."

"It's not really a request," McGough said.

"It wasn't really a request when they put it to you," I said, "but it is a request when they put it to *me*. Right now *I* determine the makeup of the Council, and even then every appointment also has to be approved by the vampires and the werewolves."

McGough put his hand to his brow. "Damnit. Damn those stupid, touchy, *violent* fangs and claws. All right, I think you'll like who they've chosen, but I'll tell the Guild we need to be sensitive about our request. The last thing we want is a vamp-werekin war."

"Good, you do that," I said. My mouth quirked up in a smile. "Seriously, you old toad . . . it will be good to work with you, officially this time."

"Oh, it won't be me," McGough said. "My relationship with the Guild is strictly incognito—has to be, or I couldn't help prosecute crimes. The Guild picked someone you already know, a friend with good relations with the Guild here and in San Francisco . . . "

At first I was completely baffled. Then I slowly realized there was only one person he could have meant, although I couldn't for the life of me figure out why they'd picked him. "*Alex?*" I said. "Alex Nicholson? Valentine's former assistant? The fire magician?"

McGough smiled. "Right first time, you tattooed witch."

"Oh, blow me, you old toad," I said, grinning back at him. "Hey, can we go get some coffee? I've been up since seven yesterday, and we can fill each other in on the walk."

We talked on the way to Starbucks, me filling him in on all that had happened and him filling me in on what stake the Wizard's Guild wanted with the Council. After I had a full cup of coffee in me, felt a bit more energized, I steeled myself and asked the question.

"One more thing, you old toad," I said. "Can you give me a ride?"

"Where to, you tattooed witch?" McGough asked.

"City Hall East," I said, holding out my hands. "I need to turn myself in."

McGough scowled, then pulled out his handcuffs. "All right," he said. "It *is* time."

At Homicide, I was questioned. Oh, was I questioned: first by McGough, then by Rand, then by Philip, and then by more detectives and agents, for hours and hours and hours. Helen Yao had to practically *sit* on Damien Lee whenever I mentioned anything even *vaguely* nefarious. But something . . . *different* . . . was in the air, and eventually it was Assistant District Attorney Paulina Ross who came in and spilled the beans on why I hadn't been charged.

"I received a package in the mail," Ross said. "New evidence in the case against you."

"What kind of evidence are we talking about here?" Lee said. "The U.S. Postal Service is not a typical link in the chain of evidence."

"Not for the prosecution," Ross said, with a slight smile, "but for the defense . . . gold."

Lee's jaw dropped. "Do you have a present for me, Miss Ross?"

"Oh, yes," she said. "A box of videotapes. The security cameras from the Masquerade."

Now *my* jaw dropped.

"I'm having them checked out, but I think they're genuine," Ross said. "And they show, from multiple angles, virtually the whole assault on you, Miss Frost. What you did was *clearly* self-defense. I could never in good conscience push this forward. We're dropping all charges."

I was stunned. "Thank you ... but ... *how?*" I said. "The person who took the tapes ... I can't see why he would have kept them ... "

"There was a note attached," Ross said, somewhat uncomfortable. "It said, 'Lay off Frost. Valentine had it coming,' and it was signed, 'T.'"

"Transomnia," I said, rubbing my tongue over the implants in my right jaw where he'd knocked out two of my molars. "Now isn't *he* the gift that keeps on giving?"

"This has come up more than once," Ross said, "and I hate to even raise it—but I have to. Do you have some kind of agreement with the vampire Transomnia?"

"Now, now," Lee said smoothly. "My client isn't admitting—"

"Hush, Damien," I said. "Ross, you saw the tape. If Transomnia hadn't turned on Valentine, I'd be dead, and my skin would be the new lid on his damn box—but Transomnia didn't do it for my health. He basically used me to free himself from Valentine."

"And?" Ross said.

"Well, there's a reason he used me. Dumb old me screwed up his attempt to escape Valentine by getting him fired from the Oakdale clan. He was under a control charm. Outside the influence of a more powerful vampire, he had no choice but to go back to Valentine."

"So he ... convinced Valentine to make you his next victim," she said slowly, "knowing that you had the skills to free him from bondage?"

"Or, more likely, hoping to watch me die on the table, and to then lick the scraps," I said. She looked away. "But at some point, I think he decided I was powerful enough to free him, and took a gamble. Afterward, our agreement was to leave each other the hell alone."

Ross looked back at me, then nodded. "I can't blame you," she said. "And not just for defending yourself. The security cameras were running through the whole Masquerade. They showed not just what was happening to you ... but who you were doing it for."

"For Cinnamon," I said. "They had Cinnamon ... "

"I know," Ross said. "And I've shown these tapes to Janet McCarthy of DFACS. She's calling for a special meeting. Almost certainly, they're going to drop their case."

"Which means ... " I stood up. "I'm going to get Cinnamon back!"

And so, on Wednesday, the first of March, over two months after I'd first dropped her off at the Academy, I turned up the drive to see Cinnamon standing there at the curb waiting for me between Fremont and Palmotti. She was wearing a brand new school uniform, new shoes, and had a sharp little denim bag bulging with schoolbooks.

And perched on her tiny nose were cute, owlish glasses, hooked into earrings at the base of her cat ears. "Don't say anything," Cinnamon said, adjusting them. "Not one word."

"Not even cuuuute?" I said, stepping off my bike and tousling her hair.

"*Faahh!*" she said, twitching. "Mom! They are not cute. They're . . . necessary."

"Exactly right," Palmotti said. "A lot of werecats, including weretigers, are nearsighted. They get that from the cat DNA in their Niivan organelles."

"You had to have paid for those," I said quietly. *And* he'd researched it. "Thank you."

Palmotti smiled, sadly, and a bit tired; then he gestured towards Cinnamon. "She's a handful, but also a treasure. Godspeed to you and your daughter, Miss Frost. I'm sorry she was taken from you. I just hope that in the time I had her, I did her a little good."

And then, without saying goodbye, he turned and limped off.

We watched him go. Cinnamon stepped in front of me. I let my hand fall on her shoulder, and sighed. All was right in the world again. But . . . her breath caught as he walked away.

"Go give him a hug and thank him," I said. "You probably won't see him again."

Cinnamon snapped her head, but before something awful popped out, she reached up and bit down on her knuckle. After a moment, she released herself.

"No," she said, sniffling. "He knows how I feels."

He got into his car and drove away, and Cinnamon took a big deep sigh. Then she turned into me, burying her head into my chest. "Mom," she said. "Let's go home."

"Where's that?" I said, patting her head. "We got kicked out, and can't move in yet—"

"Your house, your hotel, a cardboard box by the Chattahoochee," Cinnamon said. "Wherever you are, Mom, that's where home is."

"All right, Cinnamon," I said, holding her close. "Let's go home."

69.   PAYOFF

The adoption went through. Cinnamon and I are mother and daughter for real now. I think it actually scares her. She was so glad to have someone who cared for her, I don't think she realized she was also getting someone who was responsible for her, both in good times and bad.

We moved into our new house the same week the adoption went through—thanks to the Valentine Foundation. I had to swallow my pride and settle with them, but the truth was, they *couldn't* pay up, any more than I could buy a house out of pocket. Valentine never expected to lose his Challenge, so coughing up a million bucks would have bankrupted his Foundation.

But, just like a house payment, the Foundation could pay up over time. So, in exchange for letting the payments stretch out over the next ten years (and for not suing them), I got the Valentine Foundation to pony up the closing costs on the house (and my legal fees).

Once Cinnamon and I really were home, and everything was settled, we had a long walk, and a long talk. She looked crushed. She didn't hear me say how glad I was she was home and alive; all she seemed to hear was how disappointed I was in her, how irresponsible she had been, how upset I was to find she'd been running out with Tully almost every night.

I didn't take her iPod, which would have interfered with her studies. She's the math whiz at school now, and I'm trying to encourage that as much as I can. I didn't forbid her to see Tully again, which would have been pointless. They're childhood sweethearts, and I'm not going to discourage that, because I know I can't.

But I did ground her. No running at night, only jogging at the school. No solo dates with Tully, only with me chaperoning. And next full moon, she stays in the safety cage. I know, that last bit sounds cruel. But I find myself thinking that's a parent's job, sometimes: being cruel to your child, so she learns not to do things that will destroy her.

It takes a real effort of will to leave it at that, to not blame Cinnamon for the death of Calaphase, or to give her a walk and shift the blame onto Tully. They really didn't know what they were helping unleash; the blame rests upon the Streetscribe. Thanks to him, no one knows how much Calaphase came to mean to me—and I'll never know what we could have had.

That last bit burns me. I miss Calaphase. I really do. But everything happened so fast. I hadn't lied. I *had* planned to take him home, but that was it; literally, to take him home. I never expected our relationship to progress that quickly, and seemingly moments later it was over. I still couldn't process it. I just felt a void. So I've been throwing myself into my new work.

Doug has been working with Tully to find and destroy all the remaining copycat marks, and he says it's a wonder Cinnamon and Tully weren't killed just spraying the damn things. McGough's been revisiting the arson sites with a magical disenchantment squad, making sure nothing pops up out of the soot. And I've been bouncing back and forth between Arcturus and a dermatologist, treating the damage to my skin when my vines were ripped off.

All in all, we were lucky. The tags were all over the city, as were copycat taggers. Tully spread the word about the dangers of the marks, and the copycats stopped; but from them he found enough photocopies to reassemble the blackbook. After Doug had looked at it, he went around for a whole week muttering things damnably Lovecraftian.

Doug wrote up a report on the blackbook, first thinking to publish it, then thinking to suppress it, and finally passing it around, with ample warnings, to all his most trusted contacts. After enough people had read it . . . the Magical Security Council turned into a real thing, and not just a Hail Mary play to get the lich and his lieutenants to back off.

Delancaster's announcement of my appointment came just in time for *Magnolia* magazine to slap together a full story on me, the graffiti, and the Council, running with a spectacular cover of me and my vines looming over

Keif and Drive in a shot that looks pretty damn prescient now, even though it was totally unplanned. *Magnolia* called me an "unexpectedly cantankerous tattoo wizard," and I was oddly pleased—Arcturus apparently trained me too well.

Between all the publicity and the very real threat, everyone is playing along. Even the Wizarding Guild: they won't show in person, but have been speaking effectively through Alex (and unofficially, through McGough), analyzing the blackbook and passing on strategies that will help us eliminate the tagger's marks safely.

I know, I know, councils like this are more about which group is in control of what than about solving the problems we all have, and I keep on expecting one of the old-school vampire or werekin groups to stab us in the back. But it hasn't happened yet, I think mostly because anyone who takes the time to read Doug's dossier ends up scared shitless.

So far the arrangement has worked well. We've got the misuse of graffiti magic under control, have put procedures in place to keep it from happening again, and are starting to draft rules to guide us in the future. Everyone appears to be pulling their weight, and more importantly, everyone seems to be talking.

Except Nyissa. Scara's crossbow bolt left her mute. The doctors think that they may eventually restore her voice, but until then, it serves a purpose. She comes as my escort, glares ominously, twirls her metal poker anytime anyone says anything threatening—and, when it comes up, gives Iadimus an excuse to tell Scara to leave. This happens all too often.

Everyone on the council, me included, is looking for my replacement. No one wants me heading this board permanently. But they're all helping me find people they think can do the job. Unfortunately, while there are plenty of good candidates on paper, it's hard finding anyone who is competent in practice, willing to take on the problem, and acceptable to everyone.

I've even talked to Philip about replacements, but our relationship is strained. Personally, he still resents me dumping him for Calaphase. Professionally, neither he nor Namura are happy about this new concentration of power. But we're civil, and so, as Alex has taken on speaking for the Council of Wizards, I've taken on responsibility of speaking for the DEI.

Hopefully, soon, better hands will take this over. I'm not trained in law enforcement, or law, or even management. Heck, I'm only half-trained in magic or science; I'm a dropout. I'm supposed to be a *tattoo artist*, for goodness sake. I know I can't keep doing this forever.

But I'm not going to go through life in the dark anymore. I'm not going to *hope* that if shit sweeps up on me I can clean up the mess. I have a daughter, friends, and colleagues that count on me, people that have my back, and I'm not going to let them down.

I know I can't fix everything—the world is darker, deeper, stranger than I ever imagined. I know I can't make my little corner of the world into heaven—but God gave me the skills to keep it from going to hell, and by God, I'm going to keep it that way.

I'm Dakota Frost, skindancer—and Atlanta is *my* city. *Nobody* trashes it on my watch.

ACKNOWLEDGEMENTS

First off, thanks to Chris Baty for founding National Novel Writing Month, during which I wrote the single largest chunk of BLOOD ROCK: if you're interested in writing, you should try this annual challenge to write 50,000 words in November.

Thanks also to the Write to the End group (formerly the Writing Group at Barnes and Noble at Steven's Creek) at which most of BLOOD ROCK was written. We meet every Tuesday (except the first Tuesday) of every month at Mission City Coffee; join us.

And thanks most of all to my beta readers: my wife Sandi, my in-laws Wally and Barb, and my friends in the Edge: Fred, Diane, Gordon, and Dave. The betas also included Keiko, Gayle, Liza and Betsy from Write to the End.

BLOOD ROCK was the first Nanowrimo I read on Ann Arbor's Unbedtime Stories at KFJC; since then I've appeared on her show nearly ten times, including the first few chapters of FROST MOON and BLOOD ROCK over the last two summers. Thanks!

I am also indebted to my research staff: to Vandybeth, who inspired the Gentry, to William, who inspired their hideout, to Keiko, who helped refine werespeech, and my wife Sandi for inspiring the 'Candlesticks'.

I can't begin to cite all the books I've read while researching BLOOD ROCK; that would need a separate bibliography. GRAFFITI WORLD by Nicholas Ganz and GRAFFITI KINGS by Jack Stewart stick out in my mind.

BLOOD ROCK is set in a world next door, so thanks to the city of Atlanta, especially the very real restaurants I loved and made a part of the story: Manuel's Tavern, the Flying Biscuit, R Thomas, of course Cafe Intermezzo, and many more.

BLOOD ROCK was the longest novel I've written to date, and it was a long hard slog to get this sprawling story under control while preserving its distinctive voice. Thanks again to my beta readers, and especially to my editor at Bell Bridge, Debra Dixon, who spent hours at Dragon*Con discussing the story and then months hammering away at it with me until we were both satisfied.

In fact, BLOOD ROCK would not be in your hands if it wasn't for Bell Bridge Books. Thanks again to Nancy for recommending them to me, for Debra for taking a chance on me, and to Debs and the rest of the crew with putting up with me.

Finally, I want to thank you, my readers, for making FROST MOON a success. I hope you enjoy the continuing adventures of Dakota Frost in BLOOD ROCK.

-the Centaur, July 12, 2011

P.S. Thanks, Big G. You know who you are.

ABOUT ANTHONY FRANCIS

By day Dr. Anthony G. Francis, Jr. builds intelligent machines and emotional robots; by night he writes science fiction and draws comic books. He received his PhD from Georgia Tech in 2000 for a thesis applying human memory principles to information retrieval; since then he's worked on search engines, robot pets, military software, police software, and software for the CDC. Robot pets have been the most fun and currently occupy his 20% time on the Cloud Robotics team at Google.

Anthony loves exploring the collision of reality with fantasy, starting with throwing vampires and werewolves into the firmly grounded setting of the Skindancer series: Atlanta, Georgia. Anthony spent almost two decades in Atlanta before he and his wife were lured out to the San Francisco Bay Area by the Search Engine That Starts With A G. Like Dakota, Anthony dropped out of college chemistry and is a brown belt in Taido, but unlike Dakota, he doesn't have a single tattoo.

BLOOD ROCK is the second in the Skindancer urban fantasy series, following FROST MOON and preceding LIQUID FIRE, and Anthony has plans for many more. He's also started a YA spin-off featuring Dakota's adopted daughter, Cinnamon. You can visit him and learn more about the world of Dakota Frost at www.dakotafrost.com.

CPSIA information can be obtained at www.ICGtesting.com
Printed in the USA
LVOW041839100612

285468LV00001B/200/P

9 781611 940138